CONTRACTED AS THE ITALIAN'S BRIDE

JULIA JAMES

HIS ASSISTANT'S NEW YORK AWAKENING

EMMY GRAYSON

MILLS & BOON

First published in Great Britain 2023
by Mills & Boon, an imprint of HarperCollins*Publishers* Ltd,
1 London Bridge Street, London, SE1 9GF

www.harpercollins.co.uk

HarperCollins*Publishers*, Macken House, 39/40 Mayor Street Upper,
Dublin 1, D01 C9W8, Ireland

Contracted as the Italian's Bride © 2023 Julia James

His Assistant's New York Awakening © 2023 Emmy Grayson

ISBN: 978-0-263-30697-2

10/23

This book is produced from independently certified FSC™ paper
to ensure responsible forest management.
For more information visit: www.harpercollins.co.uk/green.

Printed and Bound in the UK using 100% Renewable Electricity
at CPI Group (UK) Ltd, Croydon, CR0 4YY

Julia James lives in England and adores the peaceful verdant countryside and the wild shores of Cornwall. She also loves the Mediterranean—so rich in myth and history, with its sunbaked landscapes and olive groves, ancient ruins and azure seas. 'The perfect setting for romance!' she says. 'Rivalled only by the lush tropical heat of the Caribbean—palms swaying by a silver sand beach lapped by turquoise water… What more could lovers want?'

Emmy Grayson wrote her first book at the age of seven, about a spooky ghost. Her passion for romance novels began a few years later, with the discovery of a worn copy of Kathleen E. Woodiwiss's *A Rose in Winter* buried on her mother's bookshelf. She lives in the US Midwest countryside with her husband—who's also her ex-husband!—their baby boy, and enough animals to start their own zoo.

Also by Julia James

Cinderella in the Boss's Palazzo
Cinderella's Baby Confession
Destitute Until the Italian's Diamond
The Cost of Cinderella's Confession
Reclaimed by His Billion-Dollar Ring

Also by Emmy Grayson

Cinderella Hired for His Revenge

The Van Ambrose Royals miniseries

A Cinderella for the Prince's Revenge
The Prince's Pregnant Secretary

Discover more at millsandboon.co.uk.

CONTRACTED AS THE ITALIAN'S BRIDE

JULIA JAMES

MILLS & BOON

For Family Carers everywhere—
you know the good you do.

PROLOGUE

DANTE CAVELLI SAT on a bar stool in the cocktail lounge of one of London's fanciest West End hotels, long fingers curved around the stem of his martini glass. He glanced at his watch—a slim, gold, ultra-expensive item—to check the time. She was running late.

He threw his glance out across the plush cocktail lounge. It was low-lit, with tables spaced out across its wide expanse, and in the corner was a white grand piano on which a female pianist was playing soft blues music. Dante's gaze rested on her for a moment. Blonde, very attractive, long hair curled appealingly around one shoulder. His thoughts flickered, then became rueful. No—out of the question.

He moved his gaze on, towards the entrance to the lounge, arched brows frowning over dark, long-lashed eyes. Lifting his glass, he took a mouthful of his drink, then put it down, his gaze still focussed on the entrance, fingertips lightly drumming a staccato beat on the bar's shiny surface.

Then they stilled. A woman was standing on the threshold, and if the blonde pianist had caught his passing interest a moment ago then the woman in his eyeline right now did so completely. The change in lighting from the bright hotel foyer beyond to the more dimly lit cocktail lounge gave her a chiaroscuro effect as she stood there, framed in the entrance.

And what an effect…

Dante felt every Y chromosome in his body come alive.

It was her figure first of all—tightly sheathed in a cocktail dress of dark peacock-blue-green that moulded every centimetre of her oh-so-lush body, knee-length, skimming her shapely legs, which her high-heeled shoes extended in an enticing fashion. The fingers of one hand were folded around a clutch bag that matched the colour of her dress, and her other hand was lifted to just above her full, exquisitely moulded breasts as if—Dante's Y chromosomes gave another jolt—as if she was drawing breath. As if she was slightly nervous…

But what she had to be nervous about he had no notion. Not with a body like that.

As to her face…

Another slight frown formed between his brows. Poised as she was in the doorway, she was half in shadow, half not, which made it hard to see her features. He caught an impression of sculpted cheekbones, deep eyes, lush mouth. Her hair, glinting mahogany in the light, was swept into an updo that revealed her long, graceful neck, accentuated her delicate jawline. Quite enough to make him want to see more of her—all of her.

Then, just as he was mentally urging her to step forward, someone else entered the lounge, and perforce the woman had to move slightly to let him by. It allowed the full light from the overhead spot to fall on her, illuminating her clearly.

As it did, the breath froze in Dante's lungs.

And total shock detonated through him…

It can't be!
Because it couldn't be. It was just…impossible.
Non credo…
The words echoed numbly in his disbelieving brain.

CHAPTER ONE

Twelve months earlier

DANTE WAS DRIVING way too fast, especially for these country roads, his face set. His mood was vicious, just as it had been ever since the bombshell in his grandfather's will had exploded. His hands tightened over the wheel of the hire car, anger coursing through him.

Didn't I do everything he wanted me to? At his beck and call twenty-four hours a day. I gave him my total loyalty—met every demand he ever made of me.

And now his grandfather had done to him what he had—made that outrageous, pernicious demand in his will.

Fury seething, Dante glanced at his satnav. It showed he was nearing his destination.

A wedding.

The irony of it was without a scrap of humour. But it was where he would find the one man he needed now. His lawyer.

His old friend Rafaello Ranieri might be as smooth as burnished silk, but he knew his stuff. He damn well should, Dante thought grimly, given that Rafaello's law firm handled the affairs of half of Italy's richest families.

Dante, despite being in that elite company, had never needed Rafaello's professional services.

Until now.

He felt his black mood improve marginally. OK, so it had been a complete pain to chase Raf down to this back-of-nowhere country house wedding venue in the UK's West Country, where his friend was a guest of the Italian groom, but if anyone could find a way out of the trap he was in, surely Raf could.

But less than half an hour later Dante was staring—no, *glaring*—at his old friend, his face stark, his expression as furious, as disbelieving, as it had been when he'd read his grandfather's will.

'Raf, come on! There *has* to be an escape clause!'

Rafaello shrugged elegant shoulders in his expensive dinner jacket.

'He's made it crystal-clear. And watertight,' he repeated to Dante. A smile almost of amusement crossed the lawyer's saturnine face. 'So, tell me,' he asked, handing back the copy of Dante's grandfather's will, with a tinge of humour in his voice, 'who is going to be the lucky woman snapping up one of Italy's most eligible bachelors? So far you've only ever indulged in oh-so-fleeting affairs.'

Dante's eyes flashed darkly. 'Don't hang that one on me. I've never damn well had time for anything else, and you know it! No time for any kind of meaningful relationship.'

His friend lifted the glass of champagne he'd placed on a nearby pier table in the empty lounge they'd been shown into, well away from the wedding guests, so he could peruse the will.

'Well,' he mused, 'isn't that what your grandfather is seeking to rectify? To ensure you now form a permanent relationship. Or, of course,' he said, 'you could forego your inheritance.'

Something showed in Dante's face that was not just fury.

'I worked for that inheritance, Raf. I damn well *worked*! I gave my grandfather everything he ever wanted of me!'

There was frustration in his voice, but more than that. Hurt, bewilderment…

His grandfather had raised him from a boy—a boy whose own father had never worked a day in his life. Who had ended up crashing his car, killing himself and his wife in it. As for his mother—well, her idea of work had been to paint her nails and stress over which gown to wear to whatever party she was going to.

That was why, Dante knew, not without a stab of bitterness, his grandfather had insisted that a boy with such idle, self-entitled parents should understand that money did not grow on trees—it had to be made, by putting in hard work and long hours.

And that was just what Dante had done for the last dozen years, since leaving university with his first-class degree in economics and finance. Worked non-stop as his grandfather's deputy—and his eventual heir. That had been understood. Promised.

And now, instead, he'd been cheated of it.

'Dante, don't take it to heart so.' Raf's voice was not amused any longer, only sympathetic. 'Look, while the will is watertight, it may not be perpetually binding. He stipulates marriage as a condition for your inheritance, but…' he looked meaningfully at his grim-faced friend '…it doesn't stipulate a lifelong marriage.'

Dante's eyes narrowed. He understood immediately what his friend was saying.

'What's the minimum term?' he asked bluntly.

Rafaello took a considering sip of champagne. 'Well, you must avoid any risk that the marriage might appear…artificial. That might well void the terms of the will. So I'd say, off the top of my head, it would probably be safe to consider a term of around two years.'

'*Two years? Dio*, I'll be nearly thirty-five by then. Looking at forty!'

Rafaello shrugged again, but sympathetically. 'Well, let's say eighteen months at the minimum, then. Could you stomach a marriage that brief?'

Dante glowered. 'Marrying,' he said bleakly, 'for any length of time at all, is the very last thing I want to do.' He looked at his friend. 'Raf, you knew my grandfather. He controlled my life while he was alive, telling me it was both my responsibility and my privilege to be the man to keep the company he founded going, given that my father was such a waste of space. And now,' he went on, the bitterness blatant, 'he's still trying to control me from the grave. Keep me chained...tied down. Allowing me no freedom even over my own damn personal life!'

Rafaello was frowning again, consideringly. 'Well, what if you found a woman who would make no demands on you? Who only wanted a marriage of convenience herself? An outward formality, nothing more, and for a limited period of time?'

'As if that's likely,' Dante growled.

Whether or not Raf's cynicism about Dante being one of Italy's most eligible bachelors was justified, he knew from his own necessarily fleeting affairs, snatched out of his punishing work schedule, that many females would snap at the chance of marrying him. But it wouldn't be some form of in-name-only marriage they would be after. They'd want the full cosying-up-for-ever-with-a-lavish-dress-allowance-and-a-baby-or-two-to-tie-him-down-with kind. Permanently.

The very thought was anathema to Dante. To be constrained—*imprisoned*, damn it—in marriage to a demanding wife every bit as much he had been by his grandfather's iron control…

But his friend was undeterred by Dante's rejection of his idea.

'I don't see why not. She might have reasons of her own for wanting marriage for a very limited period of time, and in name only—for having, in fact, very little to do with you. There would still have to be good reasons for it, though, so it didn't arouse suspicion and potentially breach the conditions of the will.'

Rafaello's ruminations did not impress Dante.

He gave a dismissive snort. 'And how do I find such an ultra-convenient bride?' he asked sarcastically.

'Who knows?' Rafaello said genially, placing an arm around Dante's tense shoulders and starting to guide him towards the hall, which was empty now as the wedding guests took their places for dinner. 'You might find her here tonight. So I think it would be a good idea for you to crash my friend's wedding…'

Another derisive snort from Dante was his only answer.

Connie was harassed. She always was at these events. Ideally, she wouldn't be here at all—she'd be at home with her grandmother. But apart from cleaning the two holiday cottages next to her grandmother's, the only work she could take on was in the evenings, when Mrs Bowen from across the way was happy to come over and sit with her grandmother.

And evening work meant either putting in a stint at the local pub in the village or, as tonight, up at the Big House— Clayton Hall—where another fancy wedding was taking place. Wedding work was always stressful, but it paid better than the pub, and she was in no position to turn money down. Especially now.

Connie's stomach pooled with cold dread. What on earth were they going to do, she and her grandmother? The cottage they'd rented for decades had recently been sold, and the new owner wanted to make it a holiday let, like the two next door, which would bring in far more money than a permanent tenant.

But where can we go?

The question circled in Connie's head, finding no answer. More and more landlords were turning their properties into lucrative holiday lets here in the West Country. She'd applied to the council, but had been told that local authority accommodation would mean a pokey flat in town. Even worse, they had suggested her grandmother going into a care home.

Now the cold in Connie's stomach felt like ice. Her heart squeezed painfully. No, she wouldn't put her grandmother in a home—and nor would she move her into an upstairs flat with no garden, in unfamiliar surroundings. People with dementia—the dread disease tightening its grip on her grandmother with every passing day—needed familiarity, or their distress only mounted.

Oh, please can she see out her days in the cottage that has been her home for all her adult life?

That was the heartfelt prayer Connie made every day—but it looked as if it was not going to be answered.

Because how could it be?

How could it possibly be?

She pushed through the service door into the now deserted hall, scooping up the used glasses left on side tables. Tray full, she hurried past the door leading off the hall just as it was yanked open and someone exited, careering right into her. She gave a shocked cry, the jolt unbalancing her level hold on the heavy tray, and half a dozen of the stacked empty glasses slid to the edge and plunged off, smashing on the tiled floor.

Another cry broke from her—dismay.

Simultaneously a voice exclaimed behind her. *'Accidenti!'* It sounded angry.

She dropped down, placing the tray on the floor and frantically gathering up as much of the broken glass as she could see.

Suddenly there was another pair of hands doing likewise. *'Mi dispiace*—my apologies.'

It was the voice again, but not angry this time, merely impatient.

Connie glanced sideways. A pair of powerful thighs hit her eyeline, trouser material stretched taut, and she blinked and lifted her gaze slightly to take in the rest of him.

Her eyes widened. The man hunkering down beside her was, quite simply, out of this world. Dark hair, dark eyes and a face… Oh, a face that looked as if it should be on a movie screen! For one timeless moment she could only gaze, aware that her mouth was falling open and she had turned completely gormless. Then, with a mental start, she resumed gathering up the broken shards.

Another voice spoke—not impatiently, but rather with a drawling quality. Though it was hard to tell as Connie realised he was speaking Italian, so she had no idea what he was saying. The man with the movie star looks straightened, then said something back in Italian to the other man.

Connie grabbed the final shard of glass and got to her feet, lifting the tray somewhat precariously as she did so.

'I'm so sorry,' she said automatically, her gaze anxious.

'It was not your fault,' the Italian movie star said. He

glanced down at the floor at her feet. 'There is a fair amount of liquid from the glasses—you will need a mop, I think.'

Connie swallowed. 'Oh, yes—yes, of course. Um…'

She didn't know what to say, standing there flustered and nervous, knowing that her brain was in meltdown because a stunning man was speaking to her. The other one, whose looks were saturnine rather than drop-dead fabulous, was saying something—in English this time.

'A mop?' he prompted.

His tone was dismissive, like the look he gave her. She felt herself flush, shoulders hunching self-defensively, and fled towards the service door. She was used to dismissive looks and comments. Particularly from men.

And a man who looked like that would be even more likely to make them!

She frowned slightly. Except that it had been the other Italian who'd given her the usual kind of glance, not the one with the incredible movie star looks—the drop-dead gorgeous one who'd been so nice to her about the dropped tray and smashed glasses.

She gave a faint sigh and didn't know why. Then, with a mental shake, she walked through the service door and went off to find a mop.

Dante glanced unenthusiastically around him at the other wedding guests as everyone tucked into the lavish wedding breakfast. Rafaello had had a quiet word with his friend the groom, and his English bride, and Dante was now included in their number to replace a no-show. Although he couldn't help thinking rather cynically that being young, wealthy and not exactly ugly meant his presence here was probably quite welcome.

'You can… What is that English expression…? *Case the*

joint,' Rafaello said in his languid manner. 'See if any unattached females here meet your urgent requirements. I can already see that you are being eyed up as an object of new interest...' he added, with the same wry amusement.

His answer was an unamused scowl from Dante. Raf might be finding his predicament hilarious—damn him—but it wasn't him facing it!

How would he like having to lose his freedom—just when he thought he'd gained it?

Living his life under his grandfather's control had become increasingly chafing as the years had gone by, and, love him though he had—he'd been grateful for the stability of his upbringing when it would otherwise, courtesy of his feckless parents, have been chaotic and haphazard, spent mostly packed off out of his neglectful parents' way in boarding schools—Dante knew that his grandfather's unexpected and sudden death from a heart attack three months ago had also been a kind of release for him, harsh though it was to acknowledge it.

I felt I had finally got my life to myself—free to do whatever I wanted. No responsibilities. No answering to anyone else! Making my own decisions about my own life.

Of course he would still have the responsibility for taking on the running of Cavelli Finance—that was understood and accepted. Welcomed, even. He already had plans to develop his grandfather's business and take advantage of new opportunities for investment—especially in the field of green finance, which his highly conservative grandfather had obdurately blocked, despite all Dante's persuasive arguments.

But when it came to his personal life... Well, he'd thought he would finally be free to do whatever he wanted with it. Which was, he'd decided not settling down into marriage, or starting a family, but also not being anything like his own self-indulgent, party-loving parents had been either. There had to be a happy medium.

And now his grandfather had reached from beyond the grave to get his own way...

Frustration and anger roiled in him again, darkening his mood even more. He couldn't even drown it in alcohol—he was booked into a hotel in the local town, and the wedding venue was packed solid, so he needed to drive tonight. Besides, he wasn't in a mood to drown his frustrations. Only to let them feed upon themselves. Dark and brooding—and totally unsolvable.

Connie was hurrying down the long drive from the Hall towards the electronically controlled gates, head bowed, for it was starting to rain. The wedding party was still ongoing, but she'd made it clear to the catering manager she had to leave at eleven. She could not ask Mrs Bowen to stay any longer with her grandmother, and besides, Gran would need to be put to bed, not just doze in her armchair. Even though these days she hardly noticed what time it was.

A sigh escaped her. Oh, what were they going to do now that their home was going to be taken away from them? The problem went round and round in her head. Totally unsolvable.

Her tired feet stumbled slightly on the gravelled drive. She still had half a mile to walk down country lanes to reach the village, and she would need a torch once she was beyond these gates.

She'd just passed through the gates, which had opened to the exit code she'd been given, and was standing on the other side, fumbling for her torch in her handbag, when she heard a noisy car, accelerating fast. She saw the gates were starting to close, then was blinded by headlights approaching at speed. Presumably the driver wanted to make it through the gates while they were still wide enough, rather than slow down and wait to reopen them.

With a final roar the car made it through the narrowing gap, throwing up a slew of gravel, a little of which hit Connie in the legs as she lurched back instinctively to get away from the car. She gave a cry of shock, mixed with pain from the stinging gravel, and dropped her torch. Immediately she crouched down to find it, not registering that the speeding car had slowed to a halt and the driver's door was opening.

'Are you all right?'

The voice that spoke out of the darkness was sharp. And accented. And familiar.

Her head flew up. 'I dropped my torch,' she said.

He hunkered down beside her—the Italian wedding guest with the face of a movie star.

'Here,' he said, picking it up from the place it had rolled away to, holding it out to her.

'Er...thank you,' Connie said, clambering to her feet.

The drop-dead gorgeous man did the same. Light from the security lamps fell on his face, making his features even more arresting, and the rain created diamond drops in his dark hair and on his ridiculously long eyelashes.

The light also showed her he was frowning.

He said something in Italian, then in English. 'You're the waitress who dropped the glasses.'

'Yes,' said Connie. There wasn't much else to say.

His frown deepened. 'You have no umbrella,' he observed.

'Er...no,' said Connie.

She made to shuffle away. She was getting wetter and wetter and she needed to get home.

Suddenly she felt her arm taken.

'Get in the car,' he said. 'No, don't object—I'm getting wet too.'

He said something in Italian, which sounded condemning of English summertime weather, but he was simultaneously leading her towards his car, its headlights now cutting through the more heavily falling rain. He yanked open the passenger door, propelling her forward with his hand at the small of her back.

'No, really…please, it's quite all right.'

An expressive look came her way.

'It clearly is not "quite all right" at all,' he said stiffly. 'I will drive you home—it cannot be far if you were intending to walk.'

'Just into the village,' said Connie, collapsing into the car seat because it was easier than arguing.

It was a very plush seat, and a very plush car—the most expensive she'd ever been in, in her life. She sat back, hurriedly pulling at the seat belt as he got into the driving seat beside her, gunning the engine with a powerful roar.

She glanced sideways at him surreptitiously, feeling awkward and horrendously self-conscious about what was happening. In profile, the impact of his stunning good looks was just as jaw-dropping, bone-melting as full-face, and she jerked her head away lest he catch her looking at him. Gawping at him, in truth.

'Er…it's very kind of you to give me a lift,' she said, addressing him while staring rigidly out through the windscreen as the wipers slashed furiously to and fro.

'Do you start all your utterances with "er"?' came the pithy reply.

'Do I…?' she answered, flustered. 'Um… I suppose I'm just—well, a bit nervous.'

He expertly rounded a tight bend at a speed she was not

comfortable with, but with which, she allowed, he seemed to cope very well.

'Nervous?' His voice changed and she almost heard the frown in it. 'I assure you, *signorina*, you are perfectly safe with me.'

Connie felt herself colour, was thankful that he could not see it. Of course she was perfectly safe with him. The very idea of anything otherwise...

His sort of females are like those ones at the wedding— designer frocks and killer heels and real jewellery, all groomed and coiffed and with long nails and perfect make-up. The total opposite of me...

Her rueful but resigned thoughts were interrupted. 'We are approaching the village. Where do you wish to be dropped off?'

'It's just past the church. A little row of cottages. Gran's is the last one.'

'Gran?'

'Yes, I live there with my grandmother. At least for now.' She could not stop something entering her voice that had no business being there in these bizarre circumstances. 'We have to move out soon,' she said bleakly.

The car was coming up to the church, with its ancient graveyard and the small terrace of cottages beside it.

'That's a shame,' came the voice of the fabulous fantasy Italian. 'It looks very attractive—this whole little row.'

Even in the rain and the light from a solitary streetlight some way away the cottages were chocolate box pretty, with roses round the door and little front gardens with picket fences.

'Yes, the other two are holiday lets. The new owner wants Gran's to be one too. So we have to leave.'

Connie fumbled for the door, glancing back at him, ready

to thank him for the lift and hoping her colour would not rise as she did so. That would be too embarrassing.

'That will be hard for her at her time of life. The elderly like familiarity,' she heard him say.

It seemed an odd thing to hear from someone like him, but she could not disagree.

'Especially when they have dementia,' she said. 'Anything new is horribly confusing for her. And besides...' she knew she sounded bleak '...nowhere else will be as nice as here. There's nothing available to rent privately that we can afford—everything is becoming holiday lets now. We've been offered an upper floor council flat in town, with no outside space, or Gran will have to go into a care home. I'm dreading it, but it has to be faced—there's just no way for us to stay here.'

She heard her voice tremble. What on earth was she thinking about? Saying something so personal to a man who was a complete stranger and had only offered her a lift out of pity?

She closed her hand over the handle, pushing the door open now, swinging her legs round heavily. The rain had lessened, so that was good at least.

'Thank you very much for the lift. It was very kind of you,' she said politely, getting out.

'You're welcome,' he replied, almost absently.

She allowed herself a glance back at him. After all, it would be the last time in her life she would ever set eyes on him. Although a man like that—from another world!—might well crop up in her dreams, or her silly mooning fantasies as she did the housework.

He was looking at her, a frown between his dark arched brows, eyes narrowed in thought, mouth set.

Just looking at her.

Looking her over.

Although she deplored it, she felt her cheeks flush, and hoped desperately he could not see. There was no reason for the flush, because his looking over was doing nothing except imprinting upon him all her unloveliness. Frumpy, dumpy, and undeniably carrying too much weight for her height these days.

She gave an inner sigh and shut the passenger door with a slam, pausing only to raise her hand in a tentative wave of thanks as the car moved off down the lane leading out of the village. She gave another sigh, deeper this time, as she opened the garden gate. She had just seen the last of the most incredible-looking man she had ever seen in all her life.

Quite obviously, she would never see him again.

Except in that she was to be quite wrong...

Dante was driving again the following day, but this time far more slowly—as if he doubted whether he should be heading to this destination at all. He felt his thoughts pierce like arrows, As if he was, in fact, being entirely insane in heading there at all. Entirely insane to have in mind what he had been thinking about all night long.

But he was heading there, all the same.

When he arrived it was already late morning, and the little row of three chocolate box cottages looked ridiculously pretty in the bright early-summer sunshine, with their white picket fences and front gardens full of flowers. His eyes went to the one where he had dropped off his unintended passenger last night.

No wonder she does not wish to leave it.

He felt his thoughts churn again and silenced them. This was no time for emotion—only for cold, rational practicality. Needs must, and there would be an end to it. Rafaello had confirmed as much. Even though Raf would think Dante totally insane right now.

Dante's expression tightened even more and his mouth twisted. Well, he *was* insane—of course he was. But there was no help for it. Time, he thought as his face darkened, was of the essence. There was none to waste. He had to get this sorted—and fast.

He drew the hire car up outside the end cottage. He could see an olde-worlde pub nearby, some more pretty cottages, the medieval church and a small village shop—all very pretty, all very quaint, all very quintessentially rural England. He could see how attractive it would be to holiday-makers—and how attractive letting their cottages to them would be to their owners. There was good money to be made in high season.

Trouble was, that left no room for permanent residents...

There was no one about as he got out of the car. Deliberately, he took a deep breath, impelling himself forward lest he bottle it and cut and run instead. He swung open the garden gate and in two short strides was standing in front of a pale green door around which a climbing rose was trailing.

Lifting his hand, his face grimly set, he rapped sharply with the knocker.

Time to put his fortune to the test.

However insanely he was behaving.

CHAPTER TWO

CONNIE WAS SETTLING her grandmother in a chair in the garden. Moving her from one place to another was a slow business. Gran could not be hurried these days. She wanted things just so, and queried them several times. Connie was learning patience, showing no sign that what Gran had just asked she had already asked twice before.

That was dementia for you. Cruel, progressive, and—her heart squeezed painfully—eventually lethal.

Gran's GP had been sympathetic, but honest as well.

'Unless something else carries her off first, you must be prepared for the long haul. It could well take years—are you prepared for that?'

Yes, she was prepared. Nothing else was even to be considered. She would never willingly put Gran into a home—never!

She felt the familiar mingling of fear and dread twist in her now, as she went back indoors. The bright, cheerful smile she'd put on for Gran, who had no idea what the future was about to inflict upon her, disappeared, to be replaced by her customary expression of worry and stress.

In the little kitchen, she flicked on the kettle to make tea for them both. Then gave a start.

Someone was knocking on the door. She frowned, wondering who it could be. The rap came again, sounding impatient, and she walked warily out to the little front hall, opened the door.

As she did so, she stepped back—and saw who was standing there. Her jaw dropped and she froze on the spot.

Dante's expression did not change. But it took a degree of effort not to let it do so. *Por Dio*, he was definitely insane. He could not possibly be thinking of going through with what he'd intended.

All his angry, frustrated cogitation during the previous sleepless night had brought him to this point—but now, dear God, it was impossible...just impossible.

With an effort, he steeled himself. He was here now—no point bolting.

He nodded at the figure standing there in the doorway, staring at him open-mouthed. 'I hope you will excuse this intrusion,' he began, making his voice smooth, however rough he felt inside, 'but there is something I would like to discuss with you...if you will permit?'

For a moment her expression did not change either. It looked totally blank. Then, with a little shake, she spoke.

'What on earth is it?'

There was complete bewilderment in her voice—and something more than that, Dante detected, wondering at it.

Disbelief.

Yes, well, he thought savagely, *you and me both.*

'That, I will explain,' he answered her now, 'But not,' he added pointedly, 'on the doorstep.'

She stood back, as if yielding to his will without realising she was doing so. Maybe, he thought morosely, that was a good sign.

'Er...yes,' she said, and he saw her swallow. 'You had better come in.'

She stood aside and he walked into the tiny entrance hall, his height dominating it. A narrow staircase led upstairs, and to the right he could see a front sitting room, and to the left a kitchen. Past the stairs a corridor led to a door that stood ajar, open to the rear garden beyond. He cast a querying look at her, to indicate she should show him the way.

She did—into the kitchen.

'I just have to make a cup of tea for my grandmother. She's sitting in the garden.'

She turned away, busying herself at the kettle and with the tea caddy.

Dante took the opportunity to let his eyes rest on her. Protest rose in him. Yes, he was insane. Completely insane. Of course he could not do what he'd thought he could. He should leave—immediately.

He steeled himself again. No, he'd tough this out. He had to.

He watched as she made a mug of tea, putting in milk and a heaped teaspoon of sugar, then she cast him an apologetic glance and muttered, 'I'll just take this out to Gran.'

She walked off down the corridor to the garden door. Dante followed her. He wanted to see her grandmother. After all, this entire mad scheme rested on the elderly woman and what he'd been told last night.

As he stepped through the door he found himself on a small paved patio beyond which was a lawn, neatly mowed, bordered by flowerbeds and terminating in an area which, he could see, was a dedicated vegetable garden. A few ornamental trees marched down the edges, under one of which an ironwork bench was positioned. Like the front of the cottage, it was all ridiculously pretty.

Again, the thought came to his mind—*no wonder she does not wish to leave here.*

Then his eyes went to the occupant of a comfortable-looking wicker garden chair, old-fashioned, padded with cushions.

'Good morning,' he said pleasantly.

Blue eyes were turned slowly upon him, and in them he saw—and recognised—a vacancy that betokened the nature of her affliction. Her granddaughter was setting down the cup of tea on a table beside her, from the centre of which a parasol cast shade over the old lady's face.

'We've got a visitor, Gran. Isn't that nice?'

The voice was bright and pleasant, and designed to be cheering and reassuring.

The elderly lady said nothing, only turned her head, carefully picking up the mug of tea and taking a sip. Her gaze went back out over the garden and she seemed to relax a little. She looked calm, and peaceful too—contented, even. For a moment Dante just looked at her, a veiled expression on his face.

'You had better come inside.'

The woman he had come to see had spoken and was gesturing back into the cottage. Dante strode through the door, back to the entrance hall.

'The sitting room's probably the best place,' she suggested quietly.

He walked in and glanced around. Like the whole cottage it was small, but cosy-looking, with a chintz-covered sofa and armchair, a small open fireplace, a TV in the corner and a worn carpet on the floor.

He sat himself down on the sofa. The armchair was obviously the grandmother's, so he avoided it. The granddaughter was standing, hovering, clearly still bewildered.

Dante sat back, crossed one long leg over the other, and began. He would take charge of this affair from the start.

'You will no doubt be wondering what I have to say to you,' he opened. 'It is this. I have a proposition to put to you—a business proposition, shall we say? It will be of mutual benefit to us both. And…' He paused, then said significantly, 'And most of all to your grandmother.'

'My grandmother?'

The waitress from last night stared at him.

'Yes,' he said. 'Hear me out.'

He saw her swallow again, her hand clutching at the open door as if for reassurance. Dante's gaze took her in. She was in a pair of dark leggings, bagging at the knees, over which she wore a large, loose and completely shapeless top which did nothing for her. Its short sleeves were tight around her upper arms. Her dark hair was screwed up into a flattened knot, unflattering to her face.

A flicker of pity went through him. There were many reasons, he knew, why females neglected their appearance or turned to food for comfort, and surely, he allowed, a young woman—in her mid-twenties, he estimated—whose days were spent looking after an elderly woman with deepening dementia, had reason to find comfort where she could.

Especially if she is facing losing her home....

He saw something change in her face as he glanced at her, and immediately shuttered his gaze. It was obvious what her expression had indicated. She did not like being looked at that way and she was all too used to it.

He felt a swell of pity go through him again. Then he put the emotion aside.

Time to get down to business.

And quite definitely time to steel himself.

Connie stood there, half hanging on to the door, while the man who might as well have landed from another planet—

the planet of beautiful people, she thought, bemused—or, indeed, stepped through from a movie screen, proceeded to set out for her what it seemed he had come to tell her.

And as he did so she felt herself wonder if there was something wrong with her ears. Because what he was saying to her was just....

Impossible.

Insane.

Absurd.

Ludicrous.

Unbelievable.

Unreal.

He fell silent finally. She stared at him, unable to speak. Unable to credit what she had heard him say. Yet say it he had.

'Well?' he prompted.

His face was without expression, and she couldn't understand why.

'You can't *possibly* be serious,' she said faintly.

Something shifted in his eyes—eyes that were quite impossible for her to look at, so she kept shearing her own gaze away. It told her that he, too, was of that opinion. And yet he had said it quite seriously. She felt an unpleasant lump form in her insides.

'It makes sense,' came the answer.

The accented voice, just as much to die for as the entire man, was cool. Impersonal.

Connie opened her mouth, then closed it. No, it did not make sense. At all.

But he was speaking again. in a calm, even tone—as if, she realised, he was forcing himself to speak.

Well, of course he is! She felt hysteria start to gather in her throat and knew why. *Of course he's forcing himself!*

He'd be forcing himself if he said what he's just said to any woman on earth—let alone to a woman like you.

As she so often did, she felt colour start to rush into her face and had to fight it back. How she hated the way she looked these days—just *hated* it.

And in the presence of a man like this...

She steered her mind away. It was pointless thinking it, feeling it, giving it the slightest mental time at all. And pointless giving *him* the slightest mental time, let alone what he'd just said to her.

He was getting to his feet. He was tall—easily six feet— and the low beams which ran throughout the cottage were perilously close to the top of his head.

'I will leave you to consider what I have said,' he was saying now, and his glance at her was equally as cool and impersonal as his voice.

He was reaching into his jacket pocket and Connie could see the pale grey silk lining. The beautifully styled jacket perfectly fitted his lean, elegant form, just as his dinner jacket the night before had. He flicked out a business card, held it out to her between two fingers.

'I advise you to check out my details—that would only be prudent in the circumstances. And then please give what I have said your due consideration.'

Connie took, perforce, the business card he was still holding out.

'But I cannot give you much time. I will need a decision by the end of the week.'

She opened her mouth to speak. She could give him her decision right now—probably already had, with her stupefied reaction to his suggestion. But he did not let her.

'No.' There was the very faintest hint of a smile at the

corners of his sculpted mouth. 'You must think it over. Especially as I have had more time to do so,' he pointed out.

She stared at him. 'You only met me last night—if you can even call it a meeting!' she protested.

He gave a shrug. 'I have told you. Time is of the essence. If we're going to make a deal, it needs to happen soon.'

He walked towards her, clearly intent on leaving. She stumbled backwards into the tiny hallway. He opened the front door for himself, then turned.

'It does sound insane,' he said, and now she could hear something in his voice that was almost conspiratorial, 'but there is a great deal of sanity in it.'

There was nothing she could say. Just…nothing.

Then, a moment later, there was no opportunity anyway. He had walked through the door, pulled it shut behind him, and was gone.

Connie stared. Then, turning very, very slowly, as if with no breath in her body at all, she went back into the sitting room. She stared at the sofa where he'd sat a moment ago, putting to her the most ludicrous proposal she'd ever heard in her life.

To marry a man who was a total stranger and to stay married to him for at least eighteen months…so that he could claim his inheritance and she could ensure her grandmother saw out her days in their cottage…

'I'm dreaming,' she said to herself.

It was the only explanation that made sense.

Because absolutely nothing else did…

'Raf? Answer the phone! I don't care if you're asleep, or who you're with, or if you're hung over! I need to speak to you.'

There was a pause—a long one—and Dante drummed his fingers with severe impatience on the dashboard of his car, parked outside the hotel he'd just checked out of.

He needed to get going—back to Milan. See his grandfather's lawyers, the will's executors. Tell them he was meeting his grandfather's outrageous, high-handed, damnable condition and would, therefore, be claiming his inheritance. Without further delay.

'Dante—what the hell? Where are you?'

'About to leave for London. Then Milan,' Dante's grip on his phone tightened. 'I've found her,' he said. 'The woman I can marry.'

Silence—complete silence.

Then: 'Who?' The single question came in Rafaello's best lawyer voice.

Dante took a breath. 'That waitress. The one who dropped the glasses.'

A silence even longer than the last one travelled across the ether.

Then: 'Are…you…mad?'

Three words that summed up the situation completely. Dante knew it and did not care. Could not afford to care.

'Listen,' he said. 'I'll explain.'

When he'd finished, Rafaello said frostily, 'I wash my hands of you, old friend. Until you get your sanity back.'

The line went dead.

Dante tossed his phone on to the empty passenger seat. He didn't care. He just did not care.

Face set, he gunned the engine and drove off in a roar.

A stray line from Shakespeare sounded in his head: *He must needs go that the devil drives…*

Well, the devil was driving him, all right. And he had his grandfather's face…

Connie lay staring at the low, beamed ceiling of her little bedroom. It had been her bedroom since she was eight years old, when the safe, happy world of her childhood, with parents who'd adored her and each other, had ended in a hideous car crash which had killed them both and put her in hospital for weeks.

It had been her grandmother who'd remade the world for her, bringing her to live here at the cottage, to recuperate slowly, physically and emotionally. She had stood by Connie ever since—and no way was Connie not going to stand by her grandmother now, when she needed her the most.

Getting the diagnosis of dementia nearly two years ago—when it had already been taking its toll—had been bad. Receiving the eviction notice was even worse.

Outside she could hear an owl hooting, a familiar sound, and the soft rustle of leaves, the church clock tolling the quarter hours and then the hours.

Her head was full—how could it not be? Full with so much going round and round in her head.

While her grandmother had dozed in the garden Connie had fetched her laptop, then stared at the business card of the man who had, without doubt, offered her the most bizarre proposition that could ever be imagined.

Dante Cavelli. That was his name. He'd told her that, and it was there on the stiff, expensive-looking card. *Dante Cavelli, Cavelli Finance*—that was what it said. And in Italian on the reverse side.

Carefully, she'd typed 'Cavelli Finance' into a search engine. A lot had come back, mostly in Italian, and she'd hit 'translate'. As she'd read, she'd had to admit it all seemed real—not made up, nor a scam or whatever.

Some of the links had been to articles in Italian newspapers, the economics section. And some, though far fewer, had been links to social pages. Those had come with photos.

She'd stared, taking in just how incredible-looking Dante Cavelli was. She had swallowed.

Impossible...just impossible...

A few of the photos had showed him with a grim-faced elderly man—Arturo Cavelli, founder of Cavelli Finance. More of the photos, though—and Connie had only been able to stare at them hopelessly—had been of Dante Cavelli with a beautiful female draped over him...a wide variety of beautiful females...

As she'd stared, what he'd said to her had just made no sense. If he really wanted to do what he'd so unbelievably said that he did—make some kind of *pro forma* marriage in order to secure his inheritance—then why on *earth* did he not just take his pick from all those women hanging on him in these photos? Chic, elegant, fashionable, beautiful...

She felt the colour run up her cheeks, mortifying and humiliating. She might almost think that what he'd said to her had been some kind of sick joke. But to what purpose?

No, he'd been serious, all right. His voice, as he'd explained, had been taut and grim. For obvious reasons, given what he was saying to her.

'I don't care to marry someone of my acquaintance—she would be unlikely to understand or appreciate the specific limitations I am setting upon the marriage I intend to make.'

Connie had stared at the photos of all those slender, eager beauties clinging to Dante Cavelli's tall, lean, drop-dead gorgeous form, their varnished nails curving possessively around his sleeve. No, no woman in her right mind would want *any* limitations on her marrying him...

Which was why...

Which is why there is a kind of weird logic in his thinking that a female like me is preferable. Because I would never, ever get any ideas whatsoever that he might want more than he'd stated.

And what Dante Cavelli stated was very straightforward. He wanted a wife in name only, who had absolutely nothing to do with his life other than the barest minimum, ideally living in another country. They would stay married for at least eighteen months, after which a clean break divorce with a pre-agreed settlement—he'd named a sum which had made her eyes widen—would terminate their association.

But it had not been that sum which had made her breath catch; it had been something far more immediate. Far more precious to her.

'On the day of our marriage you will receive the deeds to this cottage—I will ensure its purchase...you may leave that to me—and for the duration of the marriage you will receive the monthly sum of six thousand pounds. In the event of your grandmother requiring medical treatment, or end-of-life care, this will be paid for privately, by me. I will provide a car for you, and travelling expenses, and I will also pay for a professional carer or nurse for those times when you will be required to be in my company for short periods, in order to comply with the legalities of the marriage.'

He'd gone on, and there had been a twist in his voice as he'd spoken.

'In exchange I, simply by being married, will inherit all that my grandfather has conditionally left me. I suggest that you ascertain for yourself, via the financial press, just what that entails,' he had added, his voice dry.

Well, she had checked out the financial press, and it had spelt out in black and white how very large an enterprise Cavelli Finance was, and just how very profitable it was. And how excruciatingly rich Dante Cavelli would become.

Just by getting married.

Married—as he had said that morning, sitting on her grandmother's sofa, in her grandmother's home, his tone impersonal, his expression impassive, his voice brisk and businesslike—to *her*...

She stared up at the ceiling. She could feel her heart starting to pound.

Could I do it? Could I really do it?

Oh, she might be the most unlikely woman on earth that a man like Dante Cavelli would ever marry, but so what? All that mattered were those magic words he'd said to her.

'You will receive the deeds to this cottage...'

She felt emotion strike through her—the most wonderful emotion in the world. Relief...sheer relief.

She felt tears prick her eyes. Tears of abject gratitude. Yes, of course what Dante Cavelli had proposed was bonkers—but she didn't care. Not when it would give her what she had longed for with all her being: security for her grandmother in her fading final years. That was worth anything—anything at all! Even a marriage so bizarre that no one could ever have believed it.

I'm doing it for you, Gran—all for you.

And for the first time since she had heard that a new owner had acquired the little row of cottages, and what that change of ownership would portend for her, she slept a sound and peaceful sleep. All anxiety, worry and fear vanished.

Dante stood in the waiting room at the county register office, his tension mounting. He'd sent a car to collect the woman he was about to enter into legal marriage with and it should have delivered her here by now. He'd allowed plenty of time, and yet she still wasn't here.

A dark thought possessed him. Was she going to cry off?

It was unlikely.

He glanced at the briefcase on the chair beside him. As well as the documents necessary for him to marry in the UK, it contained the deeds to the cottage—he'd bought it simply by offering the new owner a ludicrous sum for it. His hand had been all but bitten off. Just as his bride-to-be had all but bitten his hand off at his proposal.

His expression changed. But of course she had—had he expected anything else?

If you offer people what they want, they say yes.

There was the sound of someone arriving and he turned his head to the door. His bride-to-be—arriving to get what she wanted.

Just as I am getting what I want.

His rightful inheritance.

Resentment spiked in him again. To have to go to such lengths as he was doing now in order to get that rightful inheritance was galling indeed. Marrying a complete stranger...

His eyes rested on her, studiedly impassive, as she hurriedly walked in. He should be used to her by now. They'd met, of necessity, a few times now, though each time only briefly. Once for him to receive her highly predictable answer on his return from Milan the week after he'd first put his proposition to her, and thereafter so he could brief her more fully as to how their marriage was going to play out. Then there had been the question of the pre-wedding paperwork, from birth certificates and passports to her signing the essential prenup which set out what she would get financially in their divorce.

He'd been generous, given that she was key to claiming his inheritance, but obviously he'd had to carefully limit what she could claim, given the extent of his wealth. As to his actually claiming that inheritance—immediately after the wedding they were flying to Italy, to meet with his grandfather's lawyers, to prove his married status and present his bride to them.

What they would make of her he couldn't care less—so long as they accepted that he'd met the terms of his grandfather's pernicious and damnable will, and at last released his grandfather's funds to him, so he could finally take control of all his business affairs.

'I'm sorry I'm late!' she announced breathlessly.

It was obvious she'd run up the stairs, as her colour was high, her breathing laboured. She was wearing a dress, though it was as tentlike as all her clothes—designed, it was obvious, to conceal her figure, not reveal it.

A passing thought struck Dante that of all the women he knew she was alone in not constantly demanding his admiration of her looks. Connie was the complete opposite. If anything, he'd sensed she didn't like him looking at her, so he tried not to make her self-conscious, always ignoring her less than chic appearance. Even so, he found himself noticing how the blue of her dress was bringing out the blue of her eyes. A surprisingly deep blue...

He frowned slightly.

How might she look with a little make-up, a better hairstyle, and more fashionable clothes?

He shook the thought from him. It was not relevant to the marriage he was about to make. Or the one she was about to make. As her grandmother's carer she had more on her mind than the way she looked and he respected her for that, for her dedication to her grandmother's needs, making her grandmother her priority.

She was still addressing him with apology in her voice. 'Gran was restless. She'd picked up that I was going away and was upset. The nurse you helped me engage is very nice, but Gran doesn't like change, I'm afraid.' She swallowed and looked away. 'I got a bit upset too. In the end the nurse told me to go, as me being upset was just upsetting Gran more. I'm… I'm sorry.'

Dante felt a pang of pity for her. 'Please, there is no need to apologise,' he said. 'I am sure your grandmother will settle in a day or two,' he went on, making his tone reassuring. 'And you will be home, I promise you, within a week. Now, shall we…?'

There was, after all, no point in delaying matters. They had to go through with this, each of them for their own compelling reasons.

So let's just do it.

He felt his breath tighten in his chest, his jaw set like steel. This had to be done—he had no choice.

He nodded at the door leading through to the register office itself. He saw his bride take another breath—a deeper one. Suddenly he realised she lookcd terrified. His own tension dropped away and he moved to her, took her hand in his. It felt clammy, but he gave it a comforting squeeze, looking down at her reassuringly. He didn't want her to feel terrified at the prospect of marrying him—she didn't deserve that.

'It will be all right. I promise you,' he said calmly. 'This is good for both of us—for you and for me. You are doing it for your grandmother. Remember that.'

He gave another brief, reassuring smile, then dropped her hand, opening the register office door and ushering her through. Inside, the registrar and several officials, two of whom would serve as their necessary witnesses, were waiting for him.

'Ah, Mr Cavelli and Miss Weston—there you are,' the

registrar greeted them warmly. 'Are you both ready to proceed?'

Dante heard his bride give a gulp, but he gave the smooth, expected answer and they took their places.

The ceremony was brief, and legally binding. His bride's voice was faint, but she made the required responses in a clear and businesslike manner. As did he.

It did not take long.

And then it was done.

He was a married man.

His inheritance was finally his.

And his bride, the new Signora Cavelli, stood at his side.

It felt completely unreal.

'Do we fly to London and then to Milan?' Connie asked in the car, as they headed for the local airport.

'No, we go direct,' Dante answered her.

She frowned. 'Oh? I didn't know you could fly from here straight to Milan.'

'You can if you fly by private jet,' came the answer.

'Oh,' she said again. And then she didn't know what else to say.

Perhaps there wasn't any reason to say anything at all. Dante had got out his phone and was busy texting, completely absorbed.

With a start, she realised she should do likewise. She texted the nurse looking after her grandmother, asking after her. A reply came shortly, telling her that her grandmother was having lunch, and seemed a little less agitated. Connie was half reassured, half not.

But I have to be reassured because this has to happen—that's all.

She put the phone away in her handbag, staring out of

the window with a troubled expression on her face. An air of complete and absolute unreality possessed her. But then, it had ever since Dante Cavelli had returned, as he had said he would, a week after he had walked into the cottage with his incredible offer and she had given him her reply.

Since then, everything had felt dreamlike. Including the brief civil ceremony that had just taken place.

Had the registrar wondered at how bizarre it was…marrying two people who could not have been more unalike?

If she did it's something I'm going to have to get used to—that kind of reaction from people.

She felt her heart grow heavy. How was she going to get through this coming week, being paraded as the wife of the man sitting beside her—a man who might as well be from another planet to the one she lived on?

At least it will all be in Italian… All the comments, the disbelief, the murmurings, the shock and astonishment.

Not just that Dante Cavelli had returned to Italy with a wife. But with such a wife… So completely and utterly not like the kind of beautiful, svelte, chic, elegant wife a man like him would be expected to have.

I'm nothing like that! Nothing at all—in fact I'm the very opposite.

She felt the colour start to mount in her face again and forced it back. She had no reason to feel so abashed. So what if she wasn't the kind of woman a man like Dante Cavelli was likely to marry? It was no one else's business what she and the man beside her chose to do.

She was aware that Dante was putting away his phone and turning to her. As ever, Connie gave a silent sigh. He was looking as breathtakingly drop-dead gorgeous as ever. His grey silk-lined suit had obviously been tailor-made for him, designer-styled, and he wore it with the flair that only Italian males seemed to possess. His movie star looks, those fabulously expressive dark eyes fringed with impossible lashes and his sculpted cheekbones and chiselled jawline—all just compounded to make her want to gaze and gaze and gaze.

But that was something she must not do. Or at least must not be caught doing. That would just be too embarrassing—mortifying, in fact.

Though he must be totally used to females gazing at him, swooning over him...

Even women who looked as unappealing as she did.

She gave another silent sigh. She'd made an effort today, dragging on a dress for the occasion, but she had known, grimly, that trying to make herself look good by styling her hair or putting on make-up would hardly turn her into a suitable bride for a man like Dante Cavelli. So she'd left well alone, contenting herself with looking neat and tidy. It was the best she could do—and a poor best at that, as she knew all too well.

But he didn't marry me for my looks. He married me because I'll stay out of his hair—not make any demands on him!

Nor would she, of course. All she wanted was security for her grandmother and herself—and that was what she had. The deeds to Gran's cottage were now in her own handbag, and the feeling of relief at their possession was worth anything—anything at all.

'So, how do you feel?' he asked.

His voice was friendly, and she was grateful. Friendliness was really all she could cope with from him. All she would get, obviously. She knew that perfectly well. And was glad of it.

It was the way she would treat him in return. It was the only way she would be able to deal with this whole situation.

As if their vastly different looks—him so gorgeous, her so totally the opposite—were simply non-existent.

It's the only way I can manage—by ignoring it.

They were, after all, simply two people solving their own respective predicaments in a way that had absolutely nothing to do with anything personal between them.

We'll just have to get on with it—deal with it, and deal with each other, in whatever way it's easiest to do so. Honest and upfront and not making a fuss....

It was therefore in a robust fashion that she answered him now. 'Weird,' Connie said bluntly. 'You must too, surely?'

He nodded. 'We'll get used to it.' He paused. 'We won't be seeing many people in Milan. Just my grandfather's lawyers—his executors.'

She frowned, a thought striking her. 'Didn't he make you one, if you're his only grandchild?'

'No,' Dante said tersely. He paused again, then spoke. 'I suspect he thought I would try and use being an executor to evade the terms of his will.'

'You said that was impossible,' Connie said.

'Precisely,' came the tight-lipped reply.

The car was turning into the airport precinct, moving towards a security gate further along from Arrivals and Departures. The gate opened and they drove slowly through. Connie could see on the Tarmac, well away from the commercial flight area, a small jet parked up. Her sense of being in a dream increased.

It did so even more as she sat herself down in a capacious leather seat—one of only a handful on board the plane. A smiling stewardess paid her some brief attention, but the bulk of it was targeted at Dante. Connie was hardly surprised. She was the kind of person people didn't notice. Dante was exactly the opposite.

He took the seat just across the aisle from her.

'Forgive me, but I will need to work during the flight,' he said to her, fastening his seat belt, and opening his brief-case. 'With our marriage I finally have clearance to make the executive decisions about Cavelli Finance that have become pressing since my grandfather died. I will be at full stretch these coming months, and I must make a start now.'

He gave her a brief smile, and soon became immersed in his work.

The stewardess was closing the plane's door, and Connie could hear the engine starting up. She sat back, a sudden feeling of excitement filling her. To be flying at all, let alone in a private jet, was a thrill.

I haven't been abroad for ages and ages...

A student jaunt—that must have been the last time. To Corfu, to celebrate her finals being over. Her face shadowed. Holidays, travel—any kind of life for herself, really—had disappeared as her grandmother's needs had increased. She'd put her life on hold.

Well, for now—just for now—she would enjoy this adventure...

The plane was taxiing, its engine note increasing, and the pilot's voice came over the intercom, informing them that they were joining the main runway. Connie peered out of her porthole, eager for take-off. It would be so exciting to feel the powerful engine lifting them skywards.

As they got their clearance, and the jet started to accelerate, she clutched the arms of her chair.

'Are you nervous?' Dante's voice was concerned as he glanced at her.

She shook head. 'No, it's brilliant!' Her eyes were shining, expression animated.

For a second—just a second—she seemed to feel Dante's

gaze still on her, as if something had surprised him, but then the whoosh that came as the plane parted company with the earth was echoed in her gasp.

'Wow, you really feel it in a small plane like this!' she exclaimed.

'You do indeed,' Dante said dryly.

He seemed unaffected by the experience, and Connie realised this was probably his usual way of travelling. It brought home to her with a jolt that, except for the chauffeured car collecting her that morning, this was the first experience she'd got of just how very wealthy he was.

Thanks to me marrying him.

It was a thought she knew she needed to stay conscious of. She might be the very last female on earth that a man like Dante Cavelli would *ever* have actually chosen to marry out of personal preference, but for all that she was doing him just as big a favour as he was doing her.

I need to remember that whenever I start to feel overwhelmed by this whole thing!

Her eyes went to him. His laptop was open and his focus was on the screen. For all her determination to ignore the disparity between them, she felt something break through that dogged resolve. Something that welled up from the depths. That swept through her like a warm, liquid tide of emotion, taking her over...

How gorgeous he is! How incredibly handsome! I could never be tired of looking at him...

She felt the little plane levelling off, reaching its cruising altitude. The stewardess was walking towards them from her jump seat near the cockpit.

She smiled, but only at Dante. 'Do please let me know when you would like me to serve lunch, Signor Cavelli. Would you like an aperitif first?'

Dante looked up, and then immediately glanced across at Connie. 'Aperitif?' he asked.

'Um…' said Connie, feeling awkward suddenly…deflated.

That strange, elated emotion drained away abruptly. In its place, another one came. A sudden and instant dislike of the stewardess, who so obviously considered her plain and frumpy and unlovely, and therefore utterly unqualified to be travelling as a passenger with the divine Signor Cavelli.

Her chin lifted, eyes sparking defiantly. 'Champagne,' she announced. 'To celebrate.'

And there was a lot to celebrate.

Dante Cavelli was going to be very, very rich, thanks to her. And she, thanks to him, was going to keep her grandmother safe for the rest of her life.

However weird their marriage was, and however bizarre, however unreal it would seem—not just to her, but to everyone else who heard about it—it was indeed, undeniably, something to celebrate.

He gave a laugh, glancing up at the hovering stewardess. 'Champagne it is,' he said warmly.

With a murmur of assent, the stewardess glided away.

'You're right,' Dante said, looking directly at Connie. 'It is something to celebrate. We've both got what we wanted. That's certainly worth toasting.'

The soft pop of a champagne cork came from the galley area, and then the stewardess was walking back with a tray on which stood two gently fizzing glasses of champagne. She offered one to Connie, with a perfunctory smile, and then, with a much warmer smile, gave the other to Dante. She glided away again.

Dante held his glass out across the aisle. 'To getting what we want,' he said to Connie.

He clinked his glass against hers, and took a mouthful of the beading liquid, as if assessing its mousse.

Connie took a sip of hers, feeling it effervesce in her mouth. Her eyes slid across to the man she had just married and she felt again that strange, irrelevant, impossible emotion well up within her—utterly and totally out of place as it was.

To getting what we want.

Dante's words echoed in her head, and in their wake came a sudden sweeping desolation.

That would never be true for her.

Never *could* be true…

CHAPTER THREE

Eleven months later...

DANTE FROWNED. The email from Connie was brief, and all the more poignant for it.

Gran is fading—it is only a matter of time, the doctor says. It's impossible to say how long, but she is now in end-of-life care.

He phoned her immediately. He could hear the tears in her voice as she spoke. He let her talk, knowing that that was what she needed to do.

He knew her better now. Even though their marriage was as minimalist as it was, some familiarity was inevitable. Though she had not come to Italy again after that first time, he'd occasionally visited her for the weekend. He'd stayed not at the cottage, which only had two bedrooms, but at one of the holiday cottages next door. The trips had been for appearances' sake, to validate their marriage for his grandfather's lawyers, but he'd found it refreshing—relaxing, even—to be out in the countryside, away from the high-pressure demands of city life and high finance.

Connie wasn't high pressure at all—she was the complete opposite, gentle and sweet-natured—and that was refreshing too in its own way. She was so easy to be with. Familiar and undemanding.

In the time he'd spent with her they'd got more used to each other, become easier in each other's company. They might come from different countries—different worlds— yet there were similarities that resonated. Like her, he had lost his parents when he was young, and been raised by a grandparent—in that respect they were alike, and they understood each other.

He'd fallen into the habit of phoning her on Sunday evenings, listening to her talk about her grandmother, knowing it helped her to do so—to have someone to express her concerns to—and in turn he had told her about how his week had been, about the work he was doing, his clients and their interests, the destinations he was going to on business.

Sometimes those included London, and twice she'd come to stay with him there overnight, sharing a suite with him at his favourite hotel. Again, it had been to help their marriage appear real, though she had never felt easy about being away from her grandmother, even with a nurse staying in her place. It was a devotion he had respected and admired and sympathised with as dementia had taken an increasing toll on her grandmother's life.

And now, it seemed, as she told him what the doctor had said, her dementia had been compounded by a series of mini strokes, each one more incapacitating, each one weakening her grandmother further.

It was a sad business, to be sure, and he was as comforting as he could be on the phone to Connie.

'Her life is drawing peacefully to a close—her long ordeal is nearing its end,' he said sympathetically.

As was Connie's long ordeal—though he did not say that. But in their most recent meeting, when he'd gone down to the West Country to visit her, he'd been taken aback by how exhausted she was looking.

Worn out—that was the phrase that came to mind. Though he'd provided funds for external carers and nurses, Connie had insisted that she wanted to do all the care she had the strength to do herself—and if that meant interrupted nights and endless coaxing to get her grandmother to take easily digestible food, to keep her hydrated, not to mention all the difficulties of personal physical care, she had doggedly got on with it.

Though he would not dream of saying so, Dante hoped that this final stage would not last too long. It was draining all of Connie's strength—testing her to the limit.

'I'll fly over tomorrow morning,' he promised her now.

Her answer surprised him, but he knew it made sense.

'No—Dante, please. I know it sounds ungrateful, but… but this is the last time I shall ever have Gran to myself, and I want… I want…'

She could not finish. Her voice was choked.

Immediately Dante backed off. 'If you change your mind, just say. And if there is anything else I can do—'

'No—truly, thank you. 'Connie's voice sounded disjointed. 'Dante, I have to go—that's the district nurse arriving.'

She rang off and Dante disconnected, staring at the phone for a moment. A frown furrowed his brow.

After Connie's grandmother died—what then?

What will happen to this strange marriage I've made?

He put down the phone, staring blankly at the wall, not coming up with any answer at all.

Connie sat quietly on the bench in the churchyard—the churchyard that would soon contain her poor grandmother's remains. The plot was ready—next to the husband her grandmother had lost so many years ago, long before Connie's own parents had been so tragically killed and she'd come to live with her still-stricken widowed grandmother.

The gaping earth was like a wound, raw and agonising, echoing the pain in her heart. Oh, she might know with her mind that her grandmother's death had been the kindest way out of the cruel clutches of dementia, but for all that she missed her with all her heart. That ache could not be eased.

Dante was coming over for the funeral. He had been adamant. 'It is my place to be at your side,' he'd said to her, his tone quiet but firm.

And she was so very grateful to him. Not just for the financial support he'd given her as part of their deal, but for the kindness he'd shown her. The sympathy and support. It had made her feel less...alone.

Oh, her neighbours and the vicar, all the hired carers, had been sympathetic to her plight, and helpful in practical terms, but at the end of the day they all went back to their own homes. As for her friends from school and uni... well, they were all pursuing their own lives, most of them geographically far away. Being the sole carer of an elderly grandmother with dementia was very isolating, physically and emotionally, and had cut her off from the rest of life.

With Dante, for all the strangeness of their unusual marriage, which was not really a marriage at all in any normal sense, it was different. There was a link between them—a bond. A reason for them being in each other's lives, however limited, that was in a strange way comforting and reassuring. Private and personal to them.

As the months since their wedding had passed she had become far more at ease with him when they'd met out of necessity for the validity of their marriage. She had lost much of her awkwardness with him and had found him easy to talk to about her grandmother, her fears for her, and her other daily concerns. And listening to him quietly telling her about his life in Italy had been something of an escape for her too, opening a window on a world far beyond the confines of caring for Gran. He'd become familiar…reassuring.

No one here even knew she was married. She wore no wedding ring and had not changed her name. She had explained Dante's visits, and his involvement in her life, such as it was, by saying he was a cousin of her late father, who had got in touch with her and been kind enough to offer his help and support. It was plausible enough. After all, no one would believe a man like Dante Cavelli could ever think of her in any kind of romantic light.

But what was he to her now?

She swallowed, her throat tight, and her eyes went to the empty grave again. Pain tore at her, tears welling and spilling with a raw, terrible grief. Awkwardly, she got to her feet. Dusk was gathering and the rooks in the trees around the graveyard were cawing, the sound mournful and desolate. Tomorrow was the funeral service, and now she must go back to the empty cottage, have a shower, wash her hair, make herself presentable for the next day, force herself to eat something…

Her appetite had disappeared weeks ago as her grandmother had weakened so inexorably. Instead of the comfort eating that she had resorted to previously while looking after Gran, she had gone in the opposite direction, picking at her food, pushing away her still-full plates. The pounds had dropped off her, but she couldn't care less. Her appearance had never mattered—not since she'd dedicated herself to her grandmother's care. And it certainly did not matter to Dante…

Into her head flitted what Dante had said as they had flown off after their wedding.

'To getting what we want.'

Well, that was just what they *had* got. He'd got his inheritance, and she had got security for her grandmother for the rest of her days. And now those days were over...

Tears of loss choked her again. The funeral tomorrow would be unbearable.

But I will have Dante at my side, to help me through it.

It was her only comforting thought, and she clung to it with surprising strength.

Dante stood beside Connie by the waiting grave as the pall-bearers slowly lowered their burden into it and the vicar intoned the solemn words of the Committal. At his side, shoulders hunched in the concealing black coat she was wearing, Connie wept silently.

His memories went back to the funeral of his grandfather. His grief had been infused with shock—the suddenness of the fatal heart attack, unexpected, despite his grandfather's age. He had seemed so indomitable. As if he would go on for ever. Instead, he had died, leaving his grandson completely alone in the world.

As Connie is now too.

It was a strange thought...that both of them had no one else at all.

Except each other.

The thought was fleeting—disturbing. He put it aside. The Committal was ending, the vicar was intoning the final words, and a sob was audibly breaking now from Connie.

Instinctively, he put his arm around her shoulder, in an urge to give her the kind of natural human comfort she so obviously needed. He could feel the shaking of her body as she wept. It was strange to feel her so close to him—but it felt right, too. At his grandfather's funeral he had stood completely alone…no one at his side. No one with any claim on him—or he on them.

The funeral was complete. Dante's thoughts came away from his own memories to the present moment. It was time to leave the graveside, and he and the vicar guided Connie down the path across the churchyard. There would be no wake, as Connie had said she could not face it, and he understood.

They took their leave of the vicar at the lychgate and he walked her back to her cottage. Connie's head was still bowed, tears undried on her cheeks, shoulders hunched. She looked, thought Dante with concern, shrunken and lost…

Inside the cottage he guided her into the little sitting room, helped her off with her coat. The black material of her mourning dress seemed to hang on her, too loose for any semblance of elegance. But what did appearance matter at a time like this? Her expression was haunted, eyes too large in her face.

A memory pierced him out of nowhere. Of how he'd first noticed, so incongruously, the vivid blue of her eyes on their wedding day all those long months ago. And then how they'd shone so brilliantly with excitement as the jet winging them to Milan had taken off, animating her face, lifting her features. Now they were smeared with tears, red-rimmed with weeping.

'I will make you a cup of tea,' he informed her.

It was the English remedy for all ills. Even grief…

When he came back, mug of tea in hand, and one of instant coffee for himself, she had not moved. She was sitting inertly on the sofa, gazing blindly at the armchair, empty now. Empty for ever. Memory hit him again—a different scene this time.

He lowered the mug of tea to the small table by the sofa. 'When I went into my grandfather's study the day of his funeral,' he heard his own voice say, 'I could not bear to see his chair behind his desk. To know he would never sit there again—'

He broke off. Swallowed. Death was hard. However it happened.

He sat down abruptly at the far end of the small sofa, curving his hands around his own mug. Connie turned her head, as if it weighed too much, and looked at him through her tears.

'I see her there… Gran. In her chair. Though she has not sat there for weeks…'

Her voice was low, thready, exhausted.

Dante's, as he answered her, was low as well.

'It will ease in time. I promise you,' he said. He frowned, looking away, down into his coffee. 'In the end, there will only be good memories left.'

Even as he spoke he knew that was not completely true. He had many good memories, yes—but not all were good. His sense of hurt—betrayal—at the conditions in his grandfather's will still remained like a canker. A jab of emotion came—bitter and harsh. His eyes lifted to the woman sitting there beside him. A woman he'd had to marry…who'd been a complete stranger to him.

But she was no longer a stranger…

She was once again shifting her gaze to the empty chair where her grandmother would never sit again, bleakness in her expression.

'I miss her so *much*,' she said haltingly. 'I cannot bear it that she's gone. That I will never see her again—never…'

He saw tears filling her eyes again, misting the deep blue that he'd so seldom noticed, making them grey with grief.

Pity filled him.

She was a woman who, without the machinations of his grandfather's malign will, he would never have known at all. Yet now she sat beside him, haunted in her grief, the most extreme of all emotions, calling echoes in himself.

We both lost our parents. Each only had a grandparent for so much of our lives. And now we don't have even that.

Without realising it, he slipped one hand from cupping his coffee, moved it sideways, picked up one of the hands, lying so inertly in her lap. He took it into his. Her hand felt warm and soft. The sofa was small, and she was only a short distance from him. He'd only have to draw her against him, take her into his arms, to give her the human comfort that grief allowed.

Only grief?

Was that all it was?

His gaze went to her. Her face, so tear-stained, seemed gaunt and strained, and yet there was something about it—a haunted quality that accentuated her cheekbones, sculpted her mouth, deepened those eyes brimming with more as yet unshed tears, like diamonds on her eyelashes.

For a moment he felt something within him that had never been there before…a sense of closeness he'd never experienced.

Because I am remembering my grandfather just as she is remembering her grandmother? Is that why?

He did not know. Knew only that he kept her small hand in his. He went on sitting there quietly, saying nothing. Silence all around them. Between them. Only broken by the ticking clock on the mantelpiece.

He felt her fingers tighten over his. And it seemed to him, in that moment, that it was right that they should do so.

He did not stay much longer. Though of course he had offered to stay, Connie had said she wanted to be alone, and he respected her wishes.

But as he took his leave, he turned to her by the cottage front door. 'Connie…' He paused. Then, 'If there is anything you need—anything at all—you must phone me at once and I'll be here. Do you understand? I know this is hard for you…so very hard.'

Her voice was strangled as she answered, half lifting her head to look at him. 'Thank you—it's kind—but…'

He nodded again. She was at the end of what little strength had remained to her.

He reached for her hand, squeezed it lightly, then let it go. 'You can be proud of what you did,' he said, his voice intent. 'You saw her through the last of her life to her passing beyond it. You were a loving, loyal granddaughter, and you gave her your love and loyalty to the very end.' Something changed in his voice as suddenly he knew there was something he urgently wanted her to hear. 'And now, Connie, now she is free—do you understand?'

She didn't answer him. She could not speak, he could see. And her head had bowed again, tears flowing once more. She didn't look at him—could not, he could see that too—but turned away, shoulders shaking, completely breaking down. She all but stumbled back indoors, pulling the door shut, disappearing inside.

For a moment Dante just stood there, disquieted and concerned. Then, knowing she truly did not wish him to be there, he took a breath and walked away, lowering himself into his car, and driving off.

Heading back to his own, quite separate life. The way he wanted it to be.

Connie lay on her bed, all alone in the cottage.

I'm on my own now…completely on my own.

Except for—

No, that was not something to be thought. She must not think of Dante in that way. She had no claim on him. No real claim…

I mustn't think anything otherwise. I just mustn't—however kind he is, and however much he supported me over Gran's death and funeral.

Thoughts moved in her head, difficult and painful. The sense of loss still overwhelmed her, but with part of her mind she was also aware that with her grandmother's death her life had changed for ever.

Or had it?

Dante had made it clear that he wanted their marriage to last at least eighteen months—which was still seven months ahead. So, were they supposed to continue as they had been doing while her grandmother was alive? She didn't know, and right now she could not focus on it. Dante was back in Milan and she was here, in the cottage she called home, filled still with the presence of the grandmother she had loved so much.

For now, it was all she could cope with. All she could cling to with her grieving heart.

Dante opened the email from Connie, reading what he'd expected to read. Her grandmother's probate had gone through as smoothly as he'd assured her it would—he'd asked Rafaello to glance over the brief will, but Connie's grandmother had had little to leave her granddaughter after the cost of her care.

His expression shadowed. It had been Rafaello who'd put to him the question that Dante felt take shape again in his mind now, as he read Connie's email.

'What's going to happen now, Dante?' he'd asked. 'You made this marriage on the assumption that Connie would

likely be looking after her grandmother for the duration. Would therefore always need to be based in England. But now...?'

Dante had batted his friend's concern away.

'Let the poor girl be, Raf! She's only just buried her grandmother. Time enough for future plans. I don't want her hassled or upset even more.'

Had he sounded defensive? Protective, even? Well, if he had, he wasn't sorry for it.

Raf had stared at him, a quizzical look in his eye. Dante hadn't liked it. Raf had had that damn perceptive lawyer's expression on his face, as if he was all too eager to probe beneath the surface of Dante's response.

Well, there was nothing *to* probe! Though Raf had made his objections to his impulsive and desperate marriage clear enough, once it had been done, he'd kept quiet about it. He'd met Connie briefly, when she'd come to Italy to be presented to Dante's grandfather's lawyers, and been perfectly civil to her, if somewhat guarded. As for himself, whenever he'd met up with Raf, or chatted with him online, he'd never *not* mentioned Connie, or the contact he had with her. He'd been completely open about her. Why shouldn't he be?

'Will she come out to Milan now?'

Raf had followed the quizzical look with that direct question. A question Dante hadn't wanted to hear, let alone answer.

'Why should she?' he'd countered.

The quizzical look had changed into something different, less easy to interpret. It had annoyed Dante even more.

'Raf, apart from my grandfather's lawyers, you're the only person who knows about Connie...knows that I'm married. And I want to keep it that way. There's no reason not to. Connie's a lovely girl and I've got used to her...to the

fact she's in my life for the reasons she is. I'm fond of her, even. She's been through a lot, and I'm glad I've been of help to her, that she had me to turn to. But—'

He'd broken off, still not liking Raf's expression. Anyway, Connie and his relationship with her, such as it was, was none of Raf's business! It wasn't anyone's business but his and Connie's.

He'd drawn a sharp breath and said, *'Our marriage still has more than six months to run—Raf, you told me yourself that was the minimum length to fulfil the terms of that benighted will! As to how those months are going to pan out now... Well, I'll work something out with Connie.'*

Yes, but what? He hadn't come up with an answer for Raf, and he hadn't come up with an answer for himself either. But something had to be done—that was the thing.

His brows drew together in a frown. So what would Connie do now? What *should* she do? They'd been able to live almost completely separate lives from each other, just as he'd intended from the off, because her circumstances had been such that she'd had good reason to live in a different country from him. But now that reason was gone.

Raf's question rang in his ears again.

'What's going to happen now?'

He was still not getting an answer.

Connie stared at herself in the mirror set into the old-fashioned wardrobe in her grandmother's bedroom, hating the way she looked.

It was a familiar feeling. Had been for a long time.

When she'd been a student she'd thought she looked OK, even though she'd always had the kind of figure that could end up a little plump if she wasn't careful, but when she'd had to start looking after Gran her social life had disappeared, and she'd had neither the time, nor the inclination, nor any purpose in caring what she looked like. It just hadn't seemed important.

And also, she thought depressingly, the more she'd let herself go, the worse it had got. Once she'd piled on the pounds with her comfort eating, it had seemed pointless to pay any attention to her hair, or her complexion, let alone to what she wore. It had all gone swiftly downhill from there.

She gave a defeated sigh. The irony now was that in the stress of the final weeks of her grandmother's life she'd totally lost her appetite, and she'd shed most of those extra pounds. But she was still untoned and unfit...

She turned away, not wanting to look at herself a moment longer, reaching for a baggy tee shirt to pull over her bra and pants and hoisting herself into a pair of loose cotton trousers. Camouflage clothing. She had a lot to camouflage.

That sense of depression washed over her. Looking after her grandmother had been her life—but now Gran was gone. So what came now? She knew she must make an effort, must not let herself sink any deeper, but it was so hard to find any sense of purpose right now. She tried to think back to what her hopes and dreams had been before she'd set them aside to devote herself to Gran. She'd been undecided, she remembered, torn between continuing her studies, getting her Master's, or starting a career—maybe in publishing... something like that? Or perhaps she'd just take off...go travelling for a while before settling down?

The trouble was it all seemed so daunting now—and it was impossible to focus her mind on anything at all, as fuzzy as it was. Everything seemed like a major effort... just getting all the paperwork after a death completed had been hard for her.

She stomped downstairs, closing in on herself. What

would Gran want for her? She paused as she went into the living room, ready to pass the time dully watching TV programmes she paid no attention to. She caught a glimpse of herself in the mirror over the fireplace. Her hair was pulled back off her face, as it always was, plain and unlovely.

You should get your hair done, Connie, dear.

She stilled. It was almost as if she could hear her Gran's familiar voice from long ago, before dementia had gripped her so tightly.

You've let yourself go—and that's such a shame. It's time you spoilt yourself a little!

It came again—and though she knew she was imagining it Connie felt a trickle of warmth go through her. Had dementia not clouded Gran's mind she would have deplored the way Connie had given up on herself. She felt herself take a breath—a deep one.

Maybe that was what she should do. Not try to think too far ahead but focus instead on something more immediate. Something to make her feel better both in herself and for herself. Stop letting herself go—start getting herself back again.

It could be done...

But I don't want it to take for ever. I don't want to do it little by little, or I'll slip back into bad old ways. It would be all too easy to go back to comfort eating—especially here, with so much pulling me down, missing Gran so much. I want something to stop me backsliding...to make me keep at it intensively, productively. Something like a boot camp or a health spa, maybe?

Almost without realising it, she picked up her laptop, plonking herself down on the sofa. Could she really do this? Places where they licked you into shape did not come cheap...

But I've spent almost nothing of all that money Dante kept paying into my account—there's pots and pots of it, just sitting there!

She clicked on to the Internet, keying in her search terms. For the first time in a long time the blanketing fog of grief and depression seemed to lift as she searched for what she needed...

Dante was reading another email from Connie—a surprising one this time. It was telling him she was heading to the Lake District, of all places. She'd booked herself into a wellness resort. For a month.

He read it again, as if to convince himself it was actually what she'd said. The very idea was totally unlike the Connie he knew. She was a home girl...unhappy if she was away from her beloved cottage.

But that was when she was looking after her grandmother.

Now that was no longer a necessity.

Yet the thought of Connie at a health spa, let alone one hundreds of miles from where she lived, was still a startling one.

On the other hand, he mused, maybe it would do her good. She could do with some pampering, thinking about herself for a change, not her grandmother's needs. Yet he was conscious of having mixed feelings. He would not need to worry about her while she was there. Nor spend any time thinking about her for a while...thinking about what she was going to do with her life now that her grandmother was no more.

With a slight feeling of discomfort he realised that, if he were to be completely honest, he would have preferred it if Connie's grandmother had *not* died when she had. Not just for Connie's sake—but for his own. While Connie had been nursing her grandmother, he'd known where he was with her. But now...?

Now it was much more complicated.

Selfishly, he acknowledged ruefully, his preference would be for Connie simply to go on living as she had, in her cottage, until it was OK for them to get divorced. But that, he knew, was a completely self-centred preference. What if Connie didn't want to go on living as she had? Wanted something new in her life?

But what could that be?

And, whatever it was that she wanted, how would it impact him?

He just did not know—and he didn't like that feeling.

Connie felt the treadmill slow into cool-down mode and satisfaction filled her. Ten kilometres at a modest but definite incline. And though her heart rate was elevated, she wasn't puffing and breathless. A distinct change from when she'd first arrived at the spa.

And it wasn't just her physical fitness either.

The complete change of scene and daily activity had transformed her. Opened the lid of the box of grief and bereavement she'd been closing herself into. Up here in the Lake District, with the lakes and the peaks, the dramatic beauty of the stark, wild landscape, she'd felt her spirits lift imperceptibly day by day. And as for the wellness resort...

She gave a wry smile now as she stepped off the treadmill and headed towards the fixed weights section of the superbly equipped workout area. She would never, *ever* have thought she'd actually enjoy the vigorous facilities it offered, and yet it was filling her with satisfaction and a wonderful sense of achievement that she had put herself in the hands of the skilled personal trainer who oversaw her exercise regime. He had drawn up a programme that put her long-neglected body through its paces, toning and trimming, stretching and sleeking, day by day turning flab into fit...

Nor had she confined herself to the gym, either. The resort came with an indoor training pool, there was aquarobics, yoga and Pilates sessions, as well as all the sybaritic pampering treatments she'd so self-indulgently splashed out on—because, after all, she might as well, while she was here, and daily massages felt well deserved after all her exertions in the gym. But most restoring of all to her spirits, she knew, was access to plentiful mountain and lakeside walks that let her get out into the fresh air, breathe deeply, and achieve, little by little, day by day, a new perspective on life.

It was impossible not to feel the fog of grief lifting, as, her workout completed, a light but nutritious and healthy lunch consumed, she headed off outdoors each day into the bright, bracing air, to gaze at the grandeur all around her as she strode up the fell towering over the deep, dark lake.

Impossible not to start to want to re-join the world she had withdrawn from for far too long.

Impossible not to accept that embracing life again was what her grandmother would want for her.

In her head she could hear Gran's voice, warm and loving.

Go out and live, my dearest, dearest girl, for my sake—and for yours.

She felt Gran's blessing on her every day—including this one.

Felt, too, more unwelcome thoughts plucking at her. And although this was harder, she knew she would have to face up to it when the time came, as soon it must.

Face up to letting Dante leave my life. Going our separate ways.

She knew it must be so—and yet a pang of grief of a different sort pierced her. From the very start their marriage had been only a means to an end, for both of them, but as the weeks and months had passed, even with the limited contact they'd had with each other, she knew that Dante had become…

Important to me.

She paused by her usual viewpoint on the fell as she gained elevation, her expression troubled suddenly. Forbidden thoughts came to her as words returned once again to her mind. The toast Dante had made on the plane that day so many months ago.

'To getting what we want.'

Something clutched at her insides. She had known then that what she wanted was so much more than he did.

Because what she wanted—dreamt of—yearned for—was impossible.

Surely it was.

Wasn't it?

Dante closed down his laptop and slid it into his monogrammed leather briefcase, then checked his seat belt as the plane started its descent into Heathrow. He was fitting in a trip to the UK because Connie had finished her stay at the wellness resort she'd taken herself off to, and he really did need to talk to her about what was uppermost in his mind. And hers too, no doubt.

With her caring duties ended sooner than either he or Connie had anticipated, what did she plan to do with her life?

Until it's possible for us to get on with our divorce.

The divorce that would finally set him free from his grandfather's control.

Why did he do it to me? I did everything he ever wanted of me and still he betrayed me...

The old painful question rose again in his head, and he pushed it away. There was no point letting it in. He'd found a way to cope with the hurt, and he had to try and move on. His expression changed, became rueful. The conditions of his inheritance might have been malign, but that had never been a term to apply to the woman who had made it possible for him to fulfil them!

A half-smile played around his mouth and he felt his tension ease. He'd lucked out with Connie, that was for sure. Oh, it was not just that she was the perfect wife for his highly imperfect circumstances, needing to live a thousand miles away from him to look after her ailing grandmother, but because...

He paused mentally. Because what, precisely?

Because she's a sweet, kind person, and in my own way I've grown fond of her.

Of course he didn't actually see her as a wife—not a real one. He didn't see any female as a wife and settling down with anyone wasn't on his agenda. He wanted freedom, untrammelled by anyone making claims on him, whether that was his grandfather, or any woman his grandfather wanted to saddle him with.

Or Connie.

His thoughts returned full circle. How were they going to see out the remaining few months of their marriage? His thoughts went back to casual conversations, snippets and bits and pieces they'd chanced to have in the times they'd met up or chatted on the phone, or things said in emails. She'd mentioned, hadn't she, that after graduating she'd been torn between staying on to get her Master's, or getting stuck into building a career, maybe in publishing, or something in that sort of world? Then, of course, all that had been derailed by her grandmother's worsening health, and Connie had put all her plans and ambitions on hold.

But now Connie was free to take them up again. To do something with her life that was her own.

Whatever it is she wants to do I'll support her—of course I will.

And of course she'd want to stay in England, wouldn't she? Whether it was to continue with academic life or get a job. That would suit him perfectly.

I can rent an apartment for her, wherever she wants to be based. And I can go on dropping in on her, or we can meet up in London—whatever is necessary to make our marriage still look genuine.

Besides, he mused, if she was working in the UK, or continuing her studies, that would be reason enough why she was not living with him in Italy. His grandfather's lawyers surely couldn't kick up about that, could they? Since she'd had to put her own life on hold to nurse her grandmother, it would be natural that she'd want to pick up her career or her studies now she was free to do so.

He settled back into his airline seat as the plane came into land, his mood definitely improved. He'd have tonight in London, then head to the West Country tomorrow. From Connie's texts and emails, it seemed she'd enjoyed herself at the resort. It was nice to think of her pampering herself for once. Starting a new life after what she'd been through.

Just as I will—finally—once I'm free of a marriage I never wanted.

It was a cheering thought.

Wasn't it?

He shook his head impatiently. Of course he wanted to be free of his marriage. Free of its fetters and constraints.

A frown formed on his brow as the plane taxied to its stand. Free of marriage—yes, definitely. But free of Connie...? His frown deepened, then cleared. Just because they'd be divorced it didn't mean he'd cut her out of his life completely—why should it? They could go on seeing each other, meeting up from time to time, just as they did now, and having the same relaxing, easy-going relationship. Well, friendship, really, as that was what it had become. After all, why not?

He was used to her, liked her and respected her. He enjoyed her company, was even fond of her. That was enough—more than enough.

In good humour, he prepared to disembark.

Connie stepped into the taxi carefully, settling herself with care in the capacious seat.

'Where to?' the London cabbie enquired over his shoulder.

She gave the name of Dante's hotel, conscious of butterflies in her stomach. She was not surprised at their presence—not least because Dante had assumed she was going to be at home at the cottage, not here in London.

She fished out her phone, tapping out a message. His flight had landed, and she knew he always stayed at the same hotel on Piccadilly when he was in London.

Dante, hi—I've ended up coming south via London. Can I come to your hotel? Is half-six OK?

As she sent it, she wondered whether it would suit him for her to be in London tonight. Maybe he had made other plans for the evening? Well, too late now. And if she didn't go through with this tonight, she'd lose her nerve completely.

She felt the butterflies swoop inside her again, staring

at the blank phone screen as the taxi made its slow way through the busy London traffic from Knightsbridge.

Was she mad to be doing what she was?

The butterflies swooped again. And then again as Dante's reply flashed up.

It conveyed surprise that she wasn't at the cottage, but made no objection to her coming to his hotel.

I'll be in the cocktail bar.

She texted back a quick thumbs-up and then sat back, letting the butterflies swoop again.

And go on swooping...

CHAPTER FOUR

DANTE GLANCED AT his watch. Nearly ten to seven. They'd agreed half-past six. Ah, well, she probably wasn't used to London traffic at this hour, slowing down the taxis. He still wasn't sure why she'd come via London at all—it was hardly en route to the West Country from the Lake District. Still, it would save him driving down to the cottage. And a couple of days in London would do Connie good, he thought.

He'd booked them in for dinner at the hotel's excellent restaurant, and changed his room to a suite. Maybe tomorrow night she'd like to go to a show, or a play? London's West End provided a rich choice. He'd ask her tonight. As well, of course, as starting the necessary conversation about what she wanted to do with her life going forward.

Another pleasing thought struck him. Now that she'd spent time pampering herself at the wellness resort, while she was in town he could encourage her to indulge herself some more—go shopping, buy some new clothes, have her hair done...that sort of thing. He'd always felt sorry for her, even though he'd understood why the last thing she'd cared about was the way she looked. But now, surely, she could focus on herself for a change.

Memory sifted through him—how he'd noticed all those months ago that, despite her baggy clothes and scraped-back hair, she had incredibly lovely eyes. Blue, deep-set, long lashed… In fact, the most beautiful he could remember seeing on a woman.

The barman placed the second martini he'd ordered in front of him, and Dante took an appreciative sip. The bar was filling up and he glanced at his watch again—more impatiently this time. Nearly seven and still no sign of her.

The pianist settled at the white baby grand in the corner really was very attractive, he thought.

He flicked his eyes away. No, not appropriate…

He moved his gaze on, resting it on the entrance to the lounge, as he took a mouthful of his martini. Then, just as he started to lower it back to the surface of the bar, he stilled. A woman had just walked into the lounge and paused, standing in the entranceway. Framed in the light.

And this time it was totally impossible for Dante to move his gaze away…

Connie paused, the butterflies inside her now starting to flap manically. It had taken more nerve than she'd thought it would just to walk into the hotel lobby. Now, though, she was going to need every bit of courage she possessed. For an abjectly cowardly moment she wished she was back at her cottage, hundreds of miles away. Not here, and about to do what she was going to do.

Her thoughts skittered. She did not want to think about why she was doing it. It had been an impulse on leaving the resort, feeling so good about herself for the first time in a long time. She'd wanted to keep that going—build on it. To head for London and meet up with Dante there, not at the cottage.

At the cottage in the country she'd just be the same old

Connie. But here, meeting him at his elegant five-star hotel, where she'd always felt overly conscious of the frumpy, dumpy way she looked…

Surely that justified what she'd done today? That was why she'd done it, wasn't it? Gone shopping for the outfit she was wearing. To look more the part for a swanky hotel. Not for any other reason. None she would admit to, anyway.

Or dare admit to…

A sudden fear struck her as she walked to the entrance of the cocktail lounge. She was about to come face to face with Dante. She hadn't seen him since the funeral, weeks and weeks ago. And now, after her time at the resort, after what she'd done today in London…

Will he think me ridiculous?

Fear darted in her. Then subsided. If he did think her ridiculous…well, he would not show it. She knew him well enough to be certain of that. He'd always been courteous, tactful—*kind*, in fact, about how utterly different she was from the type of women a man like him would normally be seen with. Her self-consciousness, she knew, came from herself—not from Dante making her feel it tactlessly or cruelly.

She swallowed, still nervous, pausing in the entrance to the dimly lit cocktail lounge, unaware that she was silhouetted against the brighter light of the lobby behind her. She let her eyes adjust, heard low blues music coming from a grand piano nearby, wondering where Dante was.

Then, with relief, she saw him, and her breath caught as it always did. He was sitting on one of the tall bar stools, looking as effortlessly fabulous as usual.

He was in a business suit. The dark silk of his tie contrasted with the pristine whiteness of his shirt, and she could see the glint of his gold watch strap around the wrist of the hand holding his martini glass. His sable hair, immaculately cut, feathered over his brow and the nape of his neck. His features, as ever, looked as if he were gracing a movie screen.

She gave a familiar inner sigh.

It was exactly the same breath-stilling impact he'd made on her the very first time she'd set eyes on him at that wedding reception, unable to tear her gaze away from him.

For a second—an instant only—she felt emotion flare through her, pain and longing. Familiar and, oh, always so hopeless…

But she couldn't just stand there like a dummy, gazing upon the physical perfection that was Dante. She gave a slightly jerky lift of her hand, to indicate that she'd seen him, but he did not return it. He seemed to be quite motionless. She started forward, burningly self-conscious, heading towards him.

It was only a short distance to where Dante was sitting, still unmoving, his martini glass suspended in his hand. His face was utterly expressionless, and she felt her heart start to thud uncomfortably, nerves plucking at her, breath tight in her lungs.

She stopped dead in front of Dante, stuttering a little as she said, 'Um…sorry I'm late. The traffic was awful.'

Dante still hadn't moved. Hadn't said a word. His face frozen in that blank expression. Then…

'Connie?'

The disbelief in his voice was searing. She felt colour flush up her cheeks, and for one hideous moment she felt like the biggest fool in the world. Humiliation rushed like a furious tide in her veins.

Oh, God, he thinks me completely ridiculous!

Her face worked. She swallowed painfully. Then something broke from him in rapid Italian, which she couldn't make out.

He swapped to English, his expression still incredulous. 'You look absolutely *amazing*!'

The warmth in his voice was like a balm to her. And the expression in his eyes...

She felt heat rise in her, and a sense of wonder so deep that it made her feel faint. Her legs were suddenly weak. Everything in her was trembling. She was made weak by the way he was looking at her, the way his gold-flecked dark, expressive, long-lashed eyes were fixed on her. Warm. Appreciative. Admiring.

She grabbed at the empty bar stool next to his and hoisted herself up onto it, needing its support. Her heart rate was hectic, and there was still a strange, utterly novel and incredible feeling coursing through her.

Because Dante Cavelli is looking at me....

And looking at her as he had never looked at her before.

As I have always longed for him to look at me...

'I've had a makeover,' she said. Probably unnecessarily. She took a breath. 'It started at the resort, getting myself fit again, getting back into shape, eating sensibly, taking exercise and long walks. Then today... Well, I've spent the afternoon in Knightsbridge, having my hair done, professional make-up, all that stuff—and buying this dress.' She looked abashed for a moment. 'It was hideously expensive, Dante, but for once I just wanted to splash out!'

As she spoke she was blissfully conscious of the way his intent gaze was resting on her. She knew it was the exquisitely beautiful dress that had grabbed his attention. Slub silk, peacock-blue, it hugged her newly svelte, tautly toned body so lovingly, accentuating her enticing curves, moulding her breasts, skimming her sheer-stockinged legs. Not only that, but her newly cut, coloured and chicly styled hair, and her complexion-flattering, eye-deepening, cheekbone-enhancing make-up, including the most luscious lipstick, was all creating exactly the impression she'd hoped for, and Dante's response made her head spin.

Elation coursed through her, and she was only dimly aware that the barman had approached them, asking her what she might like to drink. She blinked for a moment, and a sudden memory came to her of that snooty stewardess on the private jet winging them to Milan on her wedding day...of how she'd all but ignored the frumpy, dumpy, badly dressed female presuming to travel with so divine a male as Dante Cavelli.

'Champagne,' she heard herself say, just as she had said so defiantly to that disdainful stewardess. 'A champagne cocktail, please.'

As the barman nodded and glided away, she turned to Dante. There was still a look of incredulity in his expression, and it warmed her just as much as the open admiration in his eyes.

She gave a little laugh. 'I can hardly believe it myself,' she admitted. 'A posh frock and all the trimmings works wonders!'

He gave an answering laugh, warm and appreciative. 'Ah, it was there all along, Connie. But you had other, more important things to focus on.' He nodded. 'Now you can start to live your own life.'

A shaft of sadness shadowed her face. 'I wouldn't have had it any other way, Dante, truly not.' Her voice lifted,

'But all the same I know Gran would want only good things for me.'

The barman was placing her champagne cocktail in front of her, and she lifted the glass. Dante did likewise with his martini glass.

'To all the good things for you, Connie,' Dante toasted, his voice as warm as his eyes.

Into her head, yet again, came the toast he had given on the private jet on their wedding day.

'To getting what we want...'

The words hung in her mind, mingling with those he'd spoken just now. Teasing her. Tempting her...

She took a mouthful of her cocktail.

And promptly choked.

Grabbing a nearby paper napkin, she clutched it to her lips. 'Oh, my God! What's *in* that?' she exclaimed hoarsely.

A laugh broke from Dante. 'You mean apart from the maraschino cherry and the slice of orange, and the added sugar? Well, Angostura bitters for bite, and a hefty slug of cognac for punch. It's the cognac that gives it its kick,' he said kindly.

'Oh, my God,' she said again. 'I thought it would be just champagne diluted with juice. You know...orange or peach or something.'

'That's a Buck's Fizz or a Bellini,' Dante informed her. His eyes met hers, and once again the high-voltage charge of terror mixed with excitement went right through her. 'But this moment definitely calls for something with a kick.'

Something changed in his expression...something she could not read this time.

'Just as you have given me a kick I never thought was possible, Connie.'

He reached his hand out to her just lightly, touching the fall of her hair, then dropping back. Then he tapped the rim of his glass against hers again.

'Drink up.' He smiled. 'But this time just sip, OK?'

Bravely, Connie did just that. She was ready for the kick this time.

Ready for so much more…

And those butterflies soared again, iridescence in their wings.

Dante was still in something of a disbelieving daze. His incredulous eyes kept going to Connie across the table in the hotel restaurant, where they had repaired once she had cautiously finished her champagne cocktail, and he—much less cautiously, for he'd felt strongly that he needed something to deal with what was coursing through his veins—had demolished the rest of his martini.

His gaze went to Connie yet again, as though magnetised. He'd guessed that with some pampering and new clothes she might look different from the way he'd become used to, but this…

Her upswept hair, tinted a rich mahogany, was styled so that delicate tendrils whispered around her face, and her eyes, already deep and blue, with the aid of subtle make-up were now so much deeper and so much bluer that he blinked. Her mouth was accentuated with rich lipstick and her delicate cheekbones sculpted with blusher. And, of course, there was that stunning cocktail dress in shimmering shades of peacock-blue and green which skimmed lovingly over her svelte curves and was utterly perfect on her.

Oh, the whole impact was just as he had exclaimed—

amazing. Somewhere deep inside, at the very centre of him, he felt a low, dark purr start up.

But he didn't want to over-focus on the physical impact she was having on him. He knew very well that there was more to her than that. Oh, she was still Connie as he had come to know her—natural and unpretentious and open and sweet-natured—but now... He tried to give words to his thoughts. Now he could see a glow about her—a new confidence, a sense of vitality that she'd been missing. It was as if she were rediscovering, reclaiming, something of her own. Something that had been put aside in her years of caring for her grandmother.

She can look forward to the future now—with new confidence in herself, new assurance, new hopes and prospects.

He was glad for her—and he said as much now.

'I feel this is the beginning of something new and exciting for you, Connie,' he said. 'And you deserve it—you truly do.'

He lifted his wine glass, took an appreciative sip of the expensive vintage. He wanted Connie to have a wonderful evening, to celebrate this fresh start to her life.

'Tell me, have you any thoughts...ideas...about what might come next for you?'

For a moment he thought he saw something in her eyes—but it was gone before he could identify it.

'Well, I feel a lot fitter—thanks to all those weeks at the resort—and with more energy too.'

Her voice changed, and again Dante felt there was something in it that he could not quite place.

'I know that with Gran gone I have to look forward now. Pick up the reins of my life again.' She frowned a little. 'I'm just not really sure quite yet what I want, or how to go about it.'

He took a forkful of his melt-in-the-mouth lamb.

'You used to tell me that you'd once considered doing a Master's degree,' he reminded her. 'Is that still a possibility? An ambition?'

'I'm not sure. Maybe I should job-hunt instead. Although...' She bit her lip. 'To be honest, lovely as the cottage is, there aren't a lot of jobs around there that require any knowledge of English literature!'

'Move here—to London,' he said promptly. 'Loads more options.'

She made a face. 'Accommodation here is fiendishly expensive. On the other hand,' she mused, 'that incredibly generous allowance you made me is mostly sitting in the bank still. I used a wodge of it for my month at the resort, but it would fund me for a good while here in London, until I get settled with a job and a salary.'

'I'd be happy to rent a flat for you,' Dante replied. 'After all, you are my wife!'

She shook her head decisively. 'I couldn't possibly let you do that,' she said. 'That was never part of the arrangement between us. Besides...' something elusive flickered in her expression, her voice '...there's the very generous settlement you offered for when...well, when our marriage ends.'

He watched her reach for her wine glass, noting the way her fingers—now with their beautifully manicured and painted nails—tightened around the stem.

'Well, there's a while till then,' he said evenly. 'But London would certainly be the best place when it comes to jobs. Are you still keen on finding something in publishing?'

'That would be lovely,' she said reflectively. 'But it's highly competitive, and I'm older than most new starters. And do I really want to be in London? It's fine occasionally—like now—but would I want to live here all the time?'

She gave a faint sigh, and Dante picked up on it.

'There's no rush to make your mind up. In fact,' he said slowly, 'what might be best for you right now is to take a complete break. Your time at the resort obviously did you good—so why not continue to broaden your horizons?'

He let his eyes rest on her. Deep inside, he could feel that low, dark purr start again. It was even lower now, and deeper. More disturbing to his peace of mind. He knew he should be helping Connie make her mind up about what to do next with her life, helping her move forward. Knew, too, that the makeover she'd indulged in was primarily for her own benefit.

Not mine.

And yet…

Instinctively his eyes went to her, rested on her. Taking in the extraordinary change in her appearance. He didn't want to be shallow…didn't want to be predictable. He knew perfectly well that there was a lot more to Connie than just the way she looked. He'd known it since he'd met her. He knew that he already liked her for who she was—not what she looked like.

And yet…

The pause came again—more potent this time. He'd been stunned by the difference her makeover had made, and had been open in his appreciation of the difference in her—not just physically, but emotionally—and totally honest in his compliments. He wanted her to bask in the moment after all she'd been through.

And yet…

There it was again. Pushing itself into his consciousness, despite his best endeavours not to give it house room. Not to claim it for himself, greedily and selfishly. But now, as he noticed how very lovely Connie looked sitting there, he knew with a certainty that was coming from deep inside him that the way he was responding to her was very, very personal.

And he knew the name of it. Knew the name of what had never been between them—what had nothing at all to do with their marriage or their relationship, their friendship, up to this point.

But it was there now. Rich and potent and growing more powerful with every moment that he let his gaze rest on the long-lashed cerulean depths of her eyes, on the delicate curve of her cheek softened by the wisping tendrils from her upswept hair, on the sweet contours of her mouth…

He felt it quicken within him and knew it for what it was, and what he could not deny. Could only acknowledge and accept.

Desire…

'That was a truly superb meal,' Connie was saying with a smiling sigh. 'Worth every last calorie!'

Dante turned from sliding his key card down the lock on the door to their suite. 'I'm glad you enjoyed it,' he said. 'But Connie, I don't want you worrying about calories. You look fantastic, and I'm so pleased for you, but don't for a moment stint yourself over food—promise me?'

He ushered her inside the suite. He was still in something of a daze, trying to process what he was feeling for Connie. It had happened so suddenly. In one sense Connie was still exactly the person he'd come to know in the months since they'd married each other. In another…

She is completely new—a revelation to me!

He tamped it down—which was the only safe thing to do right now. For his own sake and, more importantly, for Connie's.

Is she reacting to me the way I am to her?

He didn't know—couldn't tell. Knew only that he must tread very carefully.

'Coffee,' he said cheerfully. 'I ordered it from the restaurant. It should be waiting for us.'

It was—sitting on a tray on the low table in front of the sofa in the reception area of the suite. Connie went and sat down, giving a sigh of relief. Making a face, she bent to take her high heels off as Dante took his place on the sofa, ensuring he was not sitting too close to her. That would be risky.

'Oh, gosh, that feels so much better!' Connie exclaimed with a groan, flexing her stockinged feet.

They were narrow and elegant, Dante noted absently. Something else he'd never noticed about her yet was now burningly conscious of.

Like the way she's relaxing back against the cushions, her beautiful dress moulding her figure, rounding her breasts...

He dragged his gaze to the coffee tray, pouring for them both. Behind his smile as he handed her a cup his thoughts were teeming. The low pulse in his body was tangible. He needed to get a grip on his libido—not indulge it.

This is happening too suddenly.

He told himself to speak, find an innocuous subject, avert his eyes from the way her curves were on display, the way she was lazily, almost sensuously, flexing her feet and rotating her ankles while taking sips of her own coffee.

Does she have any idea of the impact she's having on me?

She was unconscious of it, he was sure. And that only made it all the more potent.

'So, did you buy any other fabulous outfits this afternoon?' he asked conversationally, hoping it would divert him.

'No, just this one,' she answered.

'Well, why not buy some more?' he suggested. 'London may not be Milan, but it's got plenty to offer fashion-wise. Let's go shopping tomorrow.'

She stirred her coffee, dropping her eyes. 'I ought to go home tomorrow,' she said quietly.

'Why?' said Dante. It was a blunt question, but it was asked instinctively. He didn't want her leaving him. Not now.

Not now that my eyes are opened to her. Now that things are changing between us. Now that I've realised I want them to change—and want her to want it too...

She went on drinking her coffee. Dante got the impression she was doing it to avoid looking at him.

'Well, I've been away for a long time,' she said at last. 'I ought to check on the cottage.'

'It can wait another day, can't it?' he replied. 'How about if we go shopping tomorrow,' he went on, 'then I drive us down to the cottage the day after?'

Her glance went to him then. 'Oh, you don't have to do that, Dante. I can take the train, no problem.'

'I'd like to,' he insisted. 'And anyway—'

He broke off and she looked at him, a puzzled expression on her face.

He set down his coffee cup. 'Connie, I mentioned earlier about you broadening your horizons. I've had an idea. While you're thinking about what you might want to do next, how about having a break away completely?'

He took a breath, held her eyes. The sense that she was hiding something came to him again, though she was looking at him straight on.

'Why not come back to Italy with me?'

He made it sound like a casual suggestion, though there was nothing casual at all in what he was asking her. He knew perfectly well what the reason was.

'You saw nothing of it when you came after our wedding, but now—well, I can show you Milan, and Lombardy—show you all of Italy, if you'd like that?'

He was conscious of a growing enthusiasm in himself. Taking her back to Italy with him was exactly what he wanted to do!

He pressed his argument. 'You've been largely confined to the West Country, but now you can spread your wings if you want to.'

'Do…do you mean it, Dante?' Connie's voice sounded hesitant.

He met her gaze—it was questioning and uncertain. Met it full-on.

'Yes,' he said. And then it was his turn to sound questioning. 'Doesn't the idea appeal?'

He wanted it to appeal to her—he wanted it very badly. All evening the feeling had been growing, becoming insistent, demanding he recognise what was happening between them. That what he had with Connie was changing, becoming something new. Something he could not resist. Did not want to resist.

Did not want her to resist either…

He was looking straight at her, into her eyes, her beautiful, deep-set blue eyes, with their delicately arched brows and their incredibly long, thick lashes. Almost he reached out his hand to stroke the silky peach of her cheek…

He felt his wishes coalesce into one. That she should want what he wanted…that they should share all that was changing between them—all that he had realised about her.

Desire me, Connie—desire me as much I now know I desire you.

He saw her eyes change, become less shadowed. And suddenly they blazed.

'Oh, yes…' she breathed. 'Oh, Dante, yes—*yes*!'

Her eyes were shining now, widening, pouring into his like sapphire jewels. His breath caught. She was so beautiful, so incredibly, stunningly beautiful. So perfectly irresistible…

With a strength of will he had not known he possessed, he got to his feet. With another surge of iron willpower he kept his voice light, his smile only warm and friendly.

'Good,' he announced. He drained the rest of his coffee, set down the cup. 'So that's settled. Tomorrow we'll extend your wardrobe, and then we can head for Italy. Does that sound good?'

She hadn't moved, was still staring at him with those beautiful widened cerulean eyes. He felt desire stir within him.

No! He had to shut it down. Now. Right now.

'OK, finish your coffee, then it's time for bed. We've a full day ahead of us tomorrow. All that shopping… And we'll need to get your passport couriered here as well.'

She gave a shake of her head, and instantly Dante saw how it feathered the fall of her hair, bringing tendrils around her face so attractively…

'I've got it with me,' she said. 'It's a useful form of ID.'

She was getting to her feet, scooping up her high heels as she did so, holding them loosely in her hand. Her eyes were wide and shimmering, lips slightly parted, and her beautiful shapely body, sheathed by the silk of her dress, was so close to his that he could catch the scent of her perfume.

Did she seem to sway for a moment, gazing up at him with what he thought was desire in her eyes? It was making every muscle in his body tighten in anticipation… But

Dante kept himself rooted to the spot, as if he were mentally driving spikes through his feet to keep himself there.

Don't look at me like that, Connie. Just don't! Because if you do...if you do...then...

His self-control held—just.

'*Buona notte,*' he said, keeping his voice firm and keeping an even firmer hold on his self-control.

To his abject relief she turned away, eyes dropping suddenly, heading towards her bedroom.

'*Buona notte, Dante,*' she echoed, and he would have had to be deaf not to hear what was in her voice.

Exactly the same emotion as had been in her shimmering gaze.

He drove those spikes through his feet deeper yet. He had to—just *had* to—hold on.

I can't rush her—not like this—however much I long to do so.

He watched her gain entrance to her room, and only then did he dare breathe. His gaze rested on the bedroom door she'd closed behind her. Closed against him.

I should go to my own room. Take a cold shower—as cold as I can bear.

Yes, that was what he should do. And he would do it. He must. He'd lift one foot off the ground, and then the other, and head to his own bedroom.

He didn't know how he did it, but he started to walk—purposefully, determinedly—towards the one place he should go. Right now...

Connie sat at the vanity unit in her bedroom, gazing at her reflection in the soft light above the mirror—the only light she'd put on in the bedroom. She'd slipped out of her dress—that beautiful, extravagant dress that had made her into someone completely different, someone she'd never known she could be—and hung it on one of the padded hangers in the wardrobe, lovingly smoothing her hand down the lustrous material.

Now she sat in her new, luxuriously silky lingerie, knowing she should head for the bathroom, get into her pyjamas and go to bed. But not just yet...

She was still reliving, moment by moment, how she'd walked into the cocktail bar and seen Dante catching sight of her. He was the most gorgeous man in all the world. He had been for her from the very first time she'd seen him. And in his eyes...in his frozen stillness...she'd seen what she had so longed to see in her secret dreams and fantasies. What she had crushed down, never admitted to, but what was somehow now wonderfully real.

What it might portend for her and Dante she set aside. She would think about that later. For now, she would just give herself to the moment...to the wonder and delight swirling within her.

That sense of wonderful, bemused delight had gone on all evening. All through drinks at the swish, swanky bar, and all through dinner in the swish, swanky restaurant, with its celebrity chef and hushed exclusivity and its no-prices-on-the-menu expensiveness.

That look in his eyes...in those dark, drowning, long-lashed eyes that did such delicious things to her...that look had never left him.

And she knew it for what it was—knew how glorious it was to see it in his gaze.

To be desired by Dante.

Her secret, impossible dream.

Which was seemingly no longer impossible…

Yearning filled her, and longing, and a soft, seductive quickening in her blood.

She could see it in her own reflection.

And she could see one thing more in the vanity mirror.

She could see that her bedroom door was opening, and Dante was standing there, framed against the light.

He could hear his heart thudding in his chest, feel the tightness in his lungs, in his whole body. Could hear his own protests inside his head that this was not what he should be doing, not where he should be. Yet he knew with an overriding certainty that it was the only place he wanted to be.

He felt his breath catch as his eyes went to her, sitting at the vanity unit, pooled in golden light. And then, with a surging in his blood, he saw that she had taken off that incredible dress which did such fabulous things to her body and was seated in nothing more than a silky camisole and lacy panties.

His blood surged again, coursing through him, rampant and arousing.

He stepped forward blindly, instinctively.

She did not move. But her reflected gaze in the mirror met his full-on, clashed and melded and fused with it. He walked towards her, saying not a word. No words were necessary. He stood behind her, looking down at her, and slowly…infinitely slowly…placed his hands on her almost bare shoulders.

Then, and only then, he said her name.

And she said his.

The touch of his hands on her shoulders, then grazing the delicate nape of her neck with his fingertips, sent sheets of exquisite sensation through her. She gave a shiver, a quiet moan emanating from deep in the throat his fingers were now brushing. He was standing so close behind her that she could catch his heat, his scent, his eyes holding hers in the reflection of the glass.

Faintness drummed through her. Melting her. Dissolving her.

He said her name again, his voice husky. She felt herself rise to her feet, lift her face to him. Her breath caught. In his eyes was a blaze that set her aflame.

His mouth descended, caressing hers with the lightest, sweetest touch. Instinctively her arms wound around his neck, pulling him close against her. The hard wall of his chest pressed the cresting peaks of her breasts, engendering in her such an arousal of her senses that it was as if she'd been drinking strong, heady wine.

His kiss deepened, and he crushed her to him. With a little shiver of shock—of newly rising eagerness—she felt the evidence of his desire for her. A rush went through her…a sensual excitement that was like a forest fire within her.

His fingers were sliding down the narrow straps of her chemise and the bra beneath, sliding them from her body, freeing her swollen, sensitive breasts. Holding her shoulders, he dipped his head, and with a catch in her throat, her head tilting back, she felt his mouth close over their rounded orbs. Sensation after sensation speared her. Her own desire was quickening, answering his. She wanted more—oh, so much more.

As if answering her unspoken plea, he slipped the rest of her skimpy underwear from her body, discarding it on the floor. Then he started on his own unwanted clothes. She could hear his heavy breathing. His eyes never left her, the hunger in them blatant as she stood there in the low light.

Naked for him.

Waiting for him.

Waiting for him to make her his.

It was the most glorious feeling in the world...

Her eyes feasted on him—on the smooth, strong expanse of his muscular chest, on the narrowness of his lithe hips. On the proof of his desire for her.

He saw the direction of her gaze. Gave an amused chuckle, soft and sensual, that sent another dart of excitement through her.

Then he was taking her hand, leading her to the bed. And the sheet was cool on her back against her heated skin. Restlessly, filled with an urgency that was shooting through her veins, she reached for him as he slipped into bed beside her. She wanted him so much, so desperately...

She said his name, and in her voice was all her plea, all her desire. He gave another wicked little laugh, deep in his throat, his eyes pouring into hers.

'I wanted to give you time,' he said hoarsely. 'Time to realise what you were doing to me.'

She wound her arms around his neck, glorying in it. '*This* is the time,' she said. And drew his mouth down to hers.

He came over her, and the weight of his hard, naked body was all that she'd ever wanted to feel. She had longed for the strength of his arousal, his desire for her, for so long, and here it was now. *Now* was the time for his desire for her. *Now*, as his hands shaped her breasts, her waist, her flanks, slid down between her thighs, which parted with an instinct old as time to let him reach where she ached most for his touch.

She gave a helpless moan as he drew from her the wonder of what her aching body was capable of feeling. It was exquisite, ecstatic, sensual, and it was giving her a hunger for him, a desperation, an urgency for more, and more, and more…

Restlessly, she widened her legs further, tightening her arms around him. She wanted…and craved…and longed for everything he could give her. She said his name again—a helpless plea, a yearning, an invitation—with desire in her voice…

She felt him lift his body away from hers and gave a cry of desolation. But then he was coming down on her again and now… Oh… Her neck arched back, her hips instinctively lifted, and she was receiving him, taking him into her, fusing her body with his, making them one, melding herself with him, and he with her.

She cried out as sensation exploded within her. Wave after wave after wave…convulsing her body around his. And in the tsunami of pleasure overwhelming her she heard him cry out too, hoarse and triumphant, and then the wave was possessing them both…endlessly, eternally.

Suddenly she knew that she was his, and he was hers, and that giving herself to him with all her being, all her heart, was everything she could ever want.

Dante.

Her Dante.

Hers…

Connie woke and curved her body into Dante's, revelling in the closeness of their embrace. His arm was still thrown over her, enfolding her, her back to his front, and her head was nestled against his strong chest. Their legs were tangled together, heavy and inert. The rest of the world did not exist. Only her and Dante. Dante and her…

She felt him stir slightly as she moved, then subside again,

as she did, sleep calling to her once more, heavy and som-
nolent, warm and embracing. She gave a sigh of sweetest
contentment and drifted off again…dreaming of Dante as
she had dreamt so hopelessly for so long.

Now—magically, wondrously, ecstatically—it was a
hopeless dream no longer.

But one filled instead with the sweetest bliss…

CHAPTER FIVE

DANTE STOOD THERE, looking down at the woman so peacefully asleep, her breathing quiet and even, her dusky eyelashes brushing her cheeks, one lock of hair curved around her shoulder.

For a while he just went on looking and wondering.

Had last night really happened? The most unexpected thing in all the world?

This time yesterday I had no idea—none!—that I'd be standing here this morning, gazing down at Connie like this.

For a moment—just a moment—doubt washed through him. Not doubt that last night really had happened, regardless of what he'd just thought—because it was impossible to doubt that with the evidence in front of his eyes—but doubt as to whether it should have happened at all.

I rushed it! I told myself I mustn't—but in the end I just could not resist her.

Compunction smote him—but only for a moment. Connie was stirring, as if aware of his gaze upon her, and she opened her eyes, blinking in the morning light, her gaze going straight to him.

Radiance suffused her face, telling him, with the blazing delight and wonder in her eyes, that what had happened last night had been as impossible for her to resist as for him. Gladness filled him, banishing all doubt, sweeping all feel-

ings of compunction—so obviously and thankfully unnecessary—into oblivion.

He lowered himself to sit down on the bed, leaning forward to kiss Connie softly on her parted lips. 'Good morning,' he murmured, lifting his head away, and holding her
gaze. 'Are you ready for breakfast?'

She didn't answer immediately, only went on gazing up
at him—as though she doubted he were really there…as
though he was all she ever wanted to look at. Her eyes
glowed sapphire, luminous and revealing. Too revealing?

Dante got to his feet, tugging his dressing gown more
tightly around him.

'Don't look at me like that,' he said, with wry humour
in his voice, knowing she had no idea just how powerfully
that candid gaze of hers worked on him. 'Or breakfast might
have to wait a bit longer.'

He headed for the ensuite bathroom of her bedroom,
knowing how close he'd come to showing her just why
breakfast would have to wait. He lifted down the towelling
bathrobe and brought it across to her.

'Your robe, milady,' he said lightly, and draped it on the
bed. Then he crossed to the door. 'See you shortly—breakfast is on its way.'

He didn't want to see her put the towelling robe on, covering all her beautiful silky skin—that, too, might delay
breakfast for quite a while.

He made it out of the room, moving to the large window
overlooking the rooftops of London. He was trying to understand what his feelings were, to make sense of all that
was going through him, but all he knew was that taking
Connie into his arms, into his intimate embrace, had been
like nothing and no one he had ever known before. She was
like no other woman in his life.

Because I know her. I have spent time with her, getting to know her, our lives are linked together. We already have something between us—warmth, familiarity, friendship, companionship—and that makes everything feel...

Different.

Just why or how exactly, he didn't know. It was new to him—quite new.

And special.

That was the word that came to him, even though he could not define it, or explain it, or understand it, as he turned at hearing her come into the room. His face broke into a smile, encompassing her totally, and the blazing radiance of her answering smile sent him reeling.

His gaze feasted on her. In the morning light she looked as lovely as she had last night, but in a totally different way. She was not the stunningly glamorous creature she had appeared to be last night, done up to the nines, but she had a kind of soft sensuality about her, with her tousled hair, her sleepy gaze, her bee-stung mouth and the way the lapels of her towelling robe were quite insufficient in concealing the generosity of her cleavage...

The doorbell pinged and he was relieved: breakfast was arriving. The business of the suite's butler, the laden trolley, getting themselves seated and all the dishes set out or set to keep warm on chafing trays, seemed to take for ever, but at last they were on their own again. His eyes were on her the whole time as they got stuck in to the lavish breakfast in front of them. And her gaze on him was constant, glowing, filling him with warmth.

A warmth which, when they were finally replete, Dante took ruthless advantage of.

'There's no rush to hit the shops,' he told her, taking her

hand, knowing his voice was huskily suggestive and his eyelids were drooping with quickening desire.

She meshed her fingers with his, saying nothing, letting him lead her to where he wanted her to be.

Her bed. With him. Making love to her again. And then again…

In Italy, they didn't intend to spend very much time in Milan. Just long enough for Dante to touch base with his office, clear his diary—to the obvious surprise of his staff—and whisk Connie off to the fabled Quadrilatero area of the city, where the most famous fashion houses were based.

Though it was with wide-eyed wonder that she tried on the gorgeous creations, Connie was resistant to allowing Dante to buy too much for her, on top of what he'd bought her in London.

'I feel bad accepting what you've already bought for me,' she told him ruefully.

He looked taken aback. Then kissed her forehead indulgently. 'It is my pleasure,' he said.

But she still shook her head. Of course she wanted to look as stunning as possible for Dante, now that she finally felt so good about her body—but not at his expense. They bickered about it good-naturedly, and Connie compromised by agreeing that when they returned to Milan she might go shopping again.

But first they were going on holiday.

Again, Connie had initially demurred. 'Dante, I don't want to drag you away from your work. I know how important it is to you,' she'd said anxiously.

Again, he'd dropped an indulgent kiss on her forehead.

'It is my pleasure,' he had said to this objection too.

Now he drew her closer to him on the massive sofa that

was the centrepiece of the living area of his apartment in Milan. It was a ferociously modern apartment, and it was so very strange to Connie for her to be here again.

The only time she'd been there before had been immediately after their wedding, and they'd spent only two nights there. She'd been anxious about leaving her grandmother for too long, and Dante had been anxious about his grandfather's lawyers, whom they'd had to call upon, vital marriage certificate in hand, to demonstrate his new eligibility for his inheritance.

Dante had been tense and preoccupied, and Connie had kept as quiet as possible, stayed as unobtrusive as she could. It had been an awkward visit, ramming home to her the sheer weirdness of what she had done—marrying a complete stranger for the reasons she had.

'To getting what we want...'

That toast Dante had given on the private jet was in her head again. And, oh, how different it was to hear it now!

She snuggled into him, feeling his strong shoulder under her head, and gave a happy sigh. On that brief, awkward former visit she had, of course, slept in the guest bedroom. Now, as she lifted her face to Dante, who met her ardent gaze with one of his own, it was entirely, utterly different.

Happiness surged through her. Back then, Dante had been as far beyond her as if he were on the moon. She might have looked, and gazed, and yearned...but that was all.

But now she was here with him because he wanted her to be here, and no longer as the stranger he'd had to marry and wished he hadn't.

Now he desires me passionately...irresistibly... He wants me in his life. Wants to be with me and wants me to be with him.

She saw his expression change as she gazed up at him,

her body moulded against his. She felt his arm around her shoulder tighten, his eyelids start to droop. Saw his mouth start to lower to hers...felt the first feathering velvet touch of his lips. She answered it with hers, her fingers splayed deliciously against the hard, muscled wall of his chest.

In moments the rest of the world had faded away and there was only her and Dante, Dante and her, and their bodies craving each other, their desire like a flame. Then he was scooping her up, carrying her to his bedroom—*their* bedroom—to his bed—*their* bed.

And time, as well as the world, vanished.

Dante parked the car at the ferry dock and glanced across at Connie. 'Nearly there now,' he said.

'Nearly *where*?' Connie asked with humorous demand.

'You'll see.'

That was all Dante would offer her. It was only once they were aboard the waiting ferry that he relented.

'We're heading for one of the islands that make-up the Tuscan Archipelago.'

Connie's eyebrows rose. 'I've never heard of the Tuscan Archipelago,' she exclaimed.

'The most famous island is Elba,' Dante elucidated. 'We can visit while we're on holiday if you're interested. It was where Napoleon was first exiled. But the island we're going to is much smaller. Cars are very restricted—only allowed for deliveries and local essentials, not for tourists.' He paused. 'I hope you'll like it. It's very quiet and sleepy and old-fashioned, but that, I think, is its appeal.'

'It sounds idyllic. I'm sure I'll love it,' Connie assured him.

It was the answer Dante wanted. He'd chosen their destination specifically because he'd thought it might best suit Connie's obvious love of 'old' in general. She was polite about his apartment in Milan, but it was clear that her tastes had been moulded by her grandmother's little Victorian cottage, and he was happy to indulge her when on holiday.

Besides, the island had one other salient virtue. It wasn't fashionable in the least—which meant he was highly unlikely to run into anyone he knew. And that meant he could have Connie entirely to himself.

Just the way he wanted her.

Thoughts flickered in his head, trying to be heard, but he dismissed them. He didn't want them there, disturbing what he had with Connie.

What I never in a million years thought I would ever have!

In the middle of the night he would still wake sometimes, with Connie naked in his arms, embracing her lovely body—trimmer now, and more toned because of her healthier diet and her exertions in the gym, but still soft and rounded and deliciously curvy—and find himself stunned at what had happened.

But it had happened, and he was simply going with it. It wasn't in the least what he'd imagined was even a possibility, but here it was—and he was giving himself to it completely. Right now, it was all he wanted.

His gaze went to her now, drawing away from the azure sea. Watching the little island get closer, Connie leant on the ferry's railings, the breeze winnowing her hair. She was a knockout, as ever, in stylish navy blue trousers and a loose-knit jersey top, looking relaxed and happy.

He draped an arm around her back and she turned her face to his, smiling at his touch.

'Do you know the island we're going to?' she asked. 'Have you been before?'

He shook his head. 'No, it's not somewhere I'd think of doing business.' His expression changed. 'Most of what I've seen of my own country—let alone any others—has generally been for business reasons.'

It sounded rather depressing, said out loud like that, and he gave a shrug to dispel the feeling. 'So this will be a real change for me,' he added, his voice lightening.

Connie smiled up at him again, then went back to gazing at the horizon. 'It's so gorgeous being out at sea like this,' she said. 'The sun on the water...the breeze in my hair.'

'If you like,' he said, 'we can hire a motorboat and take off around the island. There are little bays and remote rocky coves...we can go snorkelling.' His eyes glinted. 'Even skinny dipping, perhaps?'

She gave a laugh. 'They'd have to be *very* remote coves for that!' she warned. She looked at him again. 'Where are we going to be staying, by the way? Or is that a secret too?'

Dante shook his head. 'No, not at all. I've rented a beach villa a little way out of the main town—the only town. It's not luxurious, but it looked good online, so I hope it won't disappoint. There's a decent hotel in town, if you'd prefer.'

'A beach villa sounds perfect,' Connie said enthusiastically. 'Can we do barbies on the beach?'

'I'm sure we can. And if we get bored we'll stroll into town and eat at some of the restaurants—there are a good few. Many of the people who come to the island do so on day trips, either from the larger islands or from the mainland, so the place caters for visitors.'

'It all sounds absolutely lovely!' Connie exclaimed.

Dante's arm tightened around her and he went back to gazing out over the water at the approaching island, pointing out the harbour they could already see at the far end of the little town that curved around the sweep of the bay.

It was not long before the ferry docked and they were disembarking. A few taxis waited, but Dante had a different means of transport in mind, as he told Connie.

'Bicycles?' she guessed.

He gave a laugh. 'Not right now—but we can hire them if you like, to explore the island. No, our transport is just there.'

He pointed to the edge of the quay and Connie gave a squeal of delight. 'A pony and trap!'

'Trap?' echoed Dante, nonplussed.

'A small horse-drawn carriage,' Connie explained. 'I've no idea why it's called a trap.'

They walked across to it. Dante pulled their suitcases, which he hefted up into the trap. The driver—an ancient individual with an even more ancient straw hat—said something to him in a strong dialect, raising his whip in greeting.

Meanwhile Connie had gone to meet and greet the steed who would be doing all the work. Not a pony, but a placid-looking working horse, also wearing a straw hat to protect him against the sun, his long ears poking through. Dante saw her speak affectionately to him and stroke his velvet nose, at which he whickered softly.

'All aboard,' said Dante cheerfully.

His mood was excellent. Connie was on board with his choice for their holiday, the sun was shining but a sea breeze freshened the heat, and now they were about to head for their private beach villa—very private!

He helped Connie up and they moved off at a sedate walking pace. Dante didn't mind the slowness. It gave him time to look about with Connie as they made their way along what was, effectively, the main road of the little town, along the seafront.

The houses and restaurants and café-bars along the way

were old-fashioned-looking, with wooden shutters and faded pastel-painted fronts and walls. The whole place had an unhurried, sleepy feel to it. The ancient driver greeted various acquaintances in almost unintelligible tones as they progressed, and Connie gave a laugh.

'I feel I ought to wave at them. You know—like the Queen? All very gracious. And maybe nod my head as well!'

'Go ahead.' Dante gave an answering laugh. 'Who knows? They may take us for royalty.'

He stretched out his legs, relaxing completely, feeling his good mood increasing. This was going to be an excellent holiday...

And so it proved. The beach villa was simple, yes, but with all that was needed—including a brick-built barbecue, just as Connie had wished for. It was ideal, and only a few steps from a small and secluded beach. There was no pool—but who needed a pool when the clear, calm azure waters awaited them?

Dante found himself wondering whether any female he'd ever run around with before would have condescended to stay in so quiet and rustic a destination. But Connie was like no other woman he knew—and she clearly loved it here.

So did he.

The days passed in easy succession—undemanding, totally relaxing—and Dante gave himself over to them. Work seemed a million miles away, and he was glad of it. Internet connection was not great, and he was glad of that too. It gave him a good reason not to let himself be plagued by his office.

And why should he be? He had competent staff, and in the time since his grandfather had died he'd overseen the smooth transfer to his own executive control, adding in some of his key people, letting some of his grandfather's retire, but without any acrimony. The company was making even more money than when his grandfather had been in charge, and all the years of dogged apprenticeship he'd put in as his grandfather's heir had trained him completely to do what was necessary.

His thoughts sheared away. He wasn't here to think about work. He was here to have what he had very seldom had before—a holiday. A solid two weeks—not just a few days snatched out of a hectic work schedule and invariably including some business meetings, even if he had managed to bring one of his fleeting *inamoratas* with him for the duration.

Both holidays and *inamoratas* were not something his grandfather had approved of.

Well, he thought defiantly, he was enjoying both right now.

Then a frown creased his brow, his eyes shifting to Connie, lying basking in the heat on her sun lounger beside him, face-down, the sculpted line of her back bared courtesy of her undone bikini top. How very lovely she looked…

And she was no *inamorata*, was she?

His gaze flickered. Connie was the woman he'd undergone a brief, hurried wedding ceremony with—the woman who had made it possible for him to claim his inheritance.

'*Inamorata*' was not the correct term to apply to her. She was far more than that.

His former flings had never lasted long. But why? He remembered telling Raf that because his grandfather had worked him so hard he'd never damn well had time to build a relationship with anyone. Was that why any affair he'd started had never lasted?

Or was it because I never wanted them to last?

And if that was so, then why?

His expression tightened. A shrink might say it was because of his parents...the fact that they'd been killed when he was only a boy. But how did that tie in—if it even did? Or was it because he had bought into his grandfather's obsession with work? Leaving no time for anything else? Or was it because it had been bad enough that his grandfather had controlled his life, and letting a woman do that too would have been intolerable?

There was a shadow in his eyes now, and a memory plucked at him of how fiercely he'd rejected the idea of picking one of his exes to marry to meet the terms of the will, on the grounds that no female he knew would be prepared to make so temporary a marriage. They'd have wanted to tie him down...curb the freedom he'd never even had the chance to enjoy...

That, after all, was what had made Connie so ideal as his wife. She had no interest in a permanent marriage. Not then, when he'd married her, and not now either.

He felt a sense of relief go through him. This was exactly why he and Connie got on so well. And what was happening between them now—amazing as it was—didn't change any of that.

We're just enjoying ourselves...having a wonderful time. Friends who have quite unexpectedly become lovers—for now.

Yes, that was the way to look at it—that made sense. And now that it did his expression changed, became lighter. He could put his concerns aside and just get on with enjoying this time with Connie while it lasted. There were several months ahead still to enjoy. That was good—very good.

A feeling of intense satisfaction filled him. He reached his hand across to her as he put all complicated thoughts out of his head. He didn't want complications. He wanted what he was having now.

A holiday. Relaxation. An easy time.

And Connie.

Oh, he most definitely wanted Connie...

In bed and out. By day and by night.

And right now, too.

He gave a wry smile. Though they wouldn't be up for anything too passionate in this heat...

He let his fingers run lazily down the length of her spine. She stirred at his touch, stretching languorously.

'Time for a cool-down swim,' Dante said. 'Then lunch.'

'Sounds good,' she said, retying her bikini top.

'You could always try going topless,' Dante remarked. His eyes glinted hopefully.

He got an old-fashioned look as his reward, and laughed, contenting himself with helping her lever herself up from the lounger and head down to the water's edge.

The swim have them an appetite, and they ate *al fresco* on the villa's shady terrace, tucking into fresh bread, ham, cheese, tomatoes and peaches. Simple, but delicious. Tonight they were going to stroll into town and try out another of the restaurants along the seafront...

Over dinner, washed down with a local wine, tasty and robust, listening to the lapping of the sea against the harbour wall, they discussed the next day's delights.

'How about crossing over to Elba tomorrow?' Dante ventured, glancing at Connie. 'Giving ourselves a dose of Napoleonic history?'

Connie's face lit up. 'Oh, yes, let's! Is there a ferry, or shall we take the motorboat across? Can you manage that distance?'

'Let's get ourselves taken over, shall we? I'm sure we can find a pilot. That way we can make a day of it.'

'Sounds good,' Connie said. 'So, tell me about Elba? I know Napoleon was first exiled there, and then managed to escape and get back to France in time for Waterloo, but that's about all...'

Dante had sounded forth with what he himself knew, but it was all amplified hugely by their visit.

'It's really too much to absorb in only one day's visit,' Connie said sadly. 'I hadn't realised Boney had *two* residences here—and we haven't time to see both.'

'Well, we'll just have to come back another time—have a holiday here, on Elba, and do it at our leisure,' Dante said easily, and the notion sounded attractive.

'That would be lovely,' Connie said.

But there was a quality to her voice that Dante could not interpret. He wondered at it for a moment, then dismissed it.

'Let's get a coffee,' he said. 'History always makes me thirsty.'

She laughed. 'Considering that Italy is absolutely *full* of history—from the Etruscans onwards—you must be perpetually thirsty!'

He gave an answering laugh, putting his arm around her waist as they strolled towards a likely-looking café not far from Napoleon's town villa—now a museum, which they'd just visited.

It was good to put his arm around Connie, to have her close to him, to stroll along with her, amiably and leisurely, in an easy-going way. It was very relaxing to be with her, he mused. Probably because she lived life at a slower pace than he customarily did in his work-focused existence.

She gives me more time to appreciate things.

And he appreciated the present—this relaxing, getting-away-from-it-all holiday, this time with Connie, who had become what he had never before envisaged having at his side or in his life. Yes, it was good—definitely, unquestionably good.

They settled themselves down at a pavement table, under the café's striped awning, and ordered coffee. Dante, feeling peckish as well as in need of a caffeine shot after so much Napoleonic history, ordered a pastry as well.

Connie looked at it enviously.

Dante lazily pushed the plate towards her. 'Indulge,' he said genially.

She shook her head, reluctantly. 'Tempting—but not as tempting as you, Dante,' she said. 'I don't want to put all that weight I shifted straight back on and find you don't fancy me any longer!'

She spoke lightly—humorously, even—but Dante didn't want her thinking such thoughts even for a moment. They were totally unnecessary.

He retrieved the pastry, deliberately cut off the end and, forking it up, presented it to Connie.

'Let's test that theory out, shall we? You eat this, and I'll tell you if I still want to take you to bed. Then I'll eat the rest, and you can tell me if *you* still want to take *me* to bed. Fair enough?'

She gave a laugh. 'OK, you win,' she said, and helped herself to the cream-filled sliver of flaky pastry. 'Mmm… Oh, yes, that is good.' She sighed happily.

Dante's eyes rested on her. 'I can confirm,' he said with mock solemnity, 'that, yes, I definitely, definitely still want to take you to bed. In fact…' a husky note entered his voice '…if you like, we could spend the night here on Elba. Book into a hotel right away…'

She threw him a wicked glance. 'But my toothbrush is at the beach villa,' she teased.

'Another can be purchased in this very town, I believe,' he riposted dryly. 'Together with toothpaste, so I am told.'

In the end they didn't spend the night on Elba, but took the motorboat back to their own island, piloted by an individual as ancient as the driver of the pony and trap, who knew the currents and the sea lanes expertly.

The sun was setting, bathing the sea with gold and fiery red, as Dante relaxed back with Connie, his arm around her shoulder, her head resting on his, the breeze tossing their hair and cooling their faces as they cruised over the darkening waters of the Tyrrhenian Sea.

'Can anything be more perfect than this?' Connie murmured.

Dante could hear the happiness in her voice. Feel it echoing inside him.

His arm around her shoulder tightened, holding her even closer to him.

It felt amazing...

CHAPTER SIX

Connie was chopping vegetables for dinner, carefully following the Italian recipe displayed on the laptop propped up on the gleaming work surface of the kitchen in Dante's high-tech kitchen in Milan. She'd bought the ingredients that afternoon, and wanted to surprise Dante. It would be the first time she'd cooked for him.

They'd come back from their island idyll a few days ago. Dante had headed back into the office, and she was spending her days happily exploring Milan. So far Dante had always ordered food in for the evening meal. Not pizza or curry—something far more gourmet than that! But now she wanted to prove that she could produce an edible meal for him by herself. It seemed a wifely thing to do.

A memory drifted through her head from long ago. Watching, as a little girl, while her mother chopped vegetables for dinner. Her father would come in from work, kissing her mother affectionately, saying how hungry he was, how good a cook she was, and her mother would beam with pleasure, telling him about the recipe she was preparing.

Connie had watched them, feeling safe, secure, and her father had come across to her, scooping her up into a protective hug, telling her with a grin that he hoped she'd grow up to become as good a cook as her mum and then her husband would always love her, like he loved her mother...

She felt her mind flicker between the long-ago past and the vivid present.

As if on cue, she heard Dante letting himself into his apartment and she called out. 'I'm in the kitchen!'

He strolled in, looking gorgeous as he always did, whether he was wearing casual holiday clothing or, like now, a business suit. He came over and kissed her lightly on the cheek, then surveyed her culinary preparations ruefully.

'I hate to say this, but would this keep till tomorrow? We've been invited out to dinner,' he announced.

Had he looked somewhat taken aback to see her so domestically employed? she wondered. But she was happy to cook for him—more than happy.

The echo of her father's words so long ago sounded again...

'It's Raf,' Dante went on. 'He's in Milan tonight. Flown up from Rome on business. Says he's looking forward to seeing you again.'

'Oh,' said Connie.

She had wondered if she was going to be introduced to some of Dante's friends here in Milan. And she had no objection to seeing Rafaello. He was a close friend of Dante's, even if he did live in Rome.

When they arrived at the restaurant where they were meeting him, Connie was aware that she felt self-conscious. Though Dante often mentioned him, she hadn't seen Rafaello since being in Milan after the wedding. It hadn't been hard to pick up the fact that he'd thought Dante mad to marry her, though he'd been nothing but polite. Would he think differently now?

She gave a mental shrug. Even though he was Dante's friend, Rafaello's opinion was immaterial. Even so, it would be nice, for Dante's sake, to see appreciation in his friend's eyes at her new appearance—so very different from when they'd first met. Maybe he might finally consider her worthy of his friend, she thought a touch tartly.

Rafaello greeted her courteously—smoothly, even—but made no comment about her changed appearance.

The outfit she was wearing now could not have been more different from the tent-like blue dress she'd worn for her wedding. It was a cream two-piece, with a narrow skirt and a bolero-style bodice with delicate, self-coloured embroidery around the neckline and cuffs. Her hair was in a low chignon, with ornamental combs, and she'd applied her make-up with care.

Glancing around the upmarket restaurant at the other fashionable Milanese gathered there, she knew she passed muster and was glad of it.

They went straight to their table, Dante's arm coming protectively around her back. He was being very attentive, but there was an air of slight tension about him all the same. Maybe he, too, was conscious of the vast gulf in appearance between old Connie and new Connie…

Well, she was new Connie now, and she had no reason to feel anything but confidently assured in a place like this, knowing she looked like every other designer-clad female here.

Her expression softened. But she was infinitely more privileged than they were.

Because I have Dante.

'A little different from the trattorias we've been used to on holiday,' Dante remarked dryly, as they took their places at the table. 'Raf likes to dine in style,' he added with a wink.

'Trattorias aren't exactly your usual style either, my friend,' was Rafaello's cool reply. 'But perhaps things have changed since we last met...' His glance went between them. Veiled. Assessing. 'So where did you go on holiday?' he went on, his voice less cool, more simply enquiring.

Dante named the island in the Tuscan Archipelago and Rafaello raised his arched eyebrows. 'Definitely off the beaten track,' he murmured. 'But it's done you good—you're looking very relaxed, old friend.' His tone was warmer now as he continued, 'And that's good to see.'

He turned his attention to Connie, and when he spoke again his voice was sympathetic.

'I was sorry to hear about the death of your grand-mother—please accept my condolences.'

It was sincerely said, and Connie felt her throat tighten, tears threaten. Immediately Dante took her hand, squeezing it comfortingly.

'Thank you,' she managed to say to Rafaello. His un-readable gaze had taken in Dante's protective gesture, she could see.

'I hope this move to Italy will help you adjust,' Rafaello went on. 'Tell me...have you seen much of Milan yet?'

'I've been exploring,' she said, her voice firmer now, 'while Dante's busy at the office. I've found the nearest food market, for a start. And I'm going to try out some recipes on Dante,' she added lightly.

'Very domestic,' Rafaello remarked, as if amused.

His glance went to his friend. He murmured something in Italian to him that Connie did not catch—only two words 'treasure' and 'wife'.

Dante did not answer, but Connie had the impression that he resented what Rafaello had said.

Rafaello seemed unperturbed, though, and simply went on smoothly, 'Once Connie has settled in you should do some entertaining,' he said. 'Your friends will want to meet her. They'll be glad to see something of you, too.' He turned to Connie. 'Dante has become a complete workaholic since he took over the reins from his late grandfather.' He nodded. 'That's why I was glad to hear he'd taken off with you on holiday. It's definitely done him good.'

The warmth was back in his voice, and Connie liked him for it.

'And it's good that you can now be here with him,' he added.

He sounded approving, and Connie liked him for that too.

She smiled widely. 'It's wonderful to be here,' she said, casting an affectionate glance at Dante. He seemed to be tense, though, and she wondered why.

But the waiter was approaching, and the sommelier, and they all paid attention to their menus for a while, making their choices.

Rafaello shut his with a decisive click. 'Champagne,' he announced, 'is definitely in order!'

When a bottle was promptly presented, and flutes filled, he raised his foaming glass to his dinner guests.

'To Signor and Signora Cavelli, so very full of surprises.' That sardonic light was in his dark eyes again. 'Welcome ones, of course,' he added. 'In fact…' Connie saw his glance go between them '…very welcome…'

Connie smiled a little uncertainly and took a sip of the beading liquid. At her side Dante also took a mouthful, but said nothing. There was a tightness around his mouth, and again she wondered why.

Then Rafaello was setting down his glass, addressing Dante directly. 'I mean it, my friend—I am glad to see what I am seeing.'

Abruptly Connie felt Dante relax. Relieved, she felt herself relax as well. Their first courses soon arrived, and as they all got stuck in Rafaello asked some questions about their holiday. She and Dante answered readily, enthusiastically reminiscing, capping each other's recollections.

She was aware of Rafaello's shrewd gaze, but it no longer seemed to be assessing. If anything, it was amusedly approving. Presumably, she thought absently, because he'd originally been wary of Dante's choice of wife and now he could see just how happy they were.

Because Dante *was* happy. She knew it with absolute certainty. And she was so glad of it. A wash of that very same emotion went through her, and her eyes grew misty. Did she feel Rafaello looking at her? Well, he was welcome—more than welcome—to see how happy she was… how happy Dante was.

How happy we both are together.

The evening wore on and became increasingly convivial. Connie relaxed, enjoying the occasion. The gourmet food was beyond superb, and even if she could not appreciate the vintage wines as they should be appreciated, she certainly enjoyed them. Conversation was easy. Rafaello regaled her with tales of Rome, and she and Dante told him of their plans to tour the north of Italy, taking in new places every weekend.

'Well, don't wear Connie out,' Rafaello said, and smiled at Dante. 'And make some time for socialising in Milan too. Like I said, your friends haven't seen you out and about for a long time.'

'Connie prefers sightseeing,' Dante replied.

Was his voice tighter? Connie wondered. Perhaps he didn't like the suggestion that he was forcing her to go jaunting about, when the very opposite was true. It was she who didn't want Dante feeling he had to show her the sights.

But he seemed as keen on it as she was, and that was both reassuring and delightful. Just being with Dante was all she wanted. Her dream come true...

Her eyes went to Dante and softened as they always did. She felt her heart rate quicken. Emotion filled her with a rich, sweet warmth, setting her aglow.

A burst of Italian sounded behind her. Excited and voluble. She didn't understand a word of it.

Except one.

'Dante!'

She saw Rafaello look up sharply, and felt Dante stiffen beside her. She turned her head, as more Italian sounded.

'Dante! Mi caro! Che bello verderti! E passato cosi tanto!'

The speaker was gushing—there was no other word for it. And she looked exactly the kind of woman to gush.

Connie stared. Blonde, incredibly slender, tall like a model, she was wearing, Connie could instantly see, an outfit that had come from a top Milan fashion house. The woman stooped on her six-inch heels and swooped an air kiss down on Dante's cheek. Rafaello and Connie she completely ignored.

Connie's eyes went to Dante. His face had become expressionless, although he'd got to his feet politely.

'Bianca,' he greeted her, and took his seat again.

In front of Connie's eyes, the woman—Bianca—helped herself to the fourth chair at their table, and gushed again, targeting Dante with more Italian that Connie did not understand.

Then, as if belatedly aware of her and Rafaello's presence, she turned towards them, bestowing a dazzling smile upon them.

'E Rafaello Ranieri, vero? Ci siamo conosciuti, ma credo in Roma—'

The smile widened to encompass Connie now.

'E tu sei l'ultima fidanzata di Rafaello? Che bello!'

Then, dismissing them again, she returned her lavish attentions to Dante, blatantly touching his cheek as if in reproach, her voice becoming sorrowful. Connie guessed that Bianca was lamenting the fact that Dante had been depriving himself of her affection. She could see Dante's expression freezing, his eyes darkening, but it was Rafaello who interjected.

He spoke in English. 'There's a slight misunderstanding here, I'm afraid. Connie is not with me—she is with Dante.' His voice was cool.

Immediately the blonde's expression changed. An openly hostile look was flashed towards Connie.

'Since when?' she demanded bluntly, eyes narrowing. She too, spoke in English now.

'Since they were married,' Rafaello answered, his voice icy now.

'Sposato?'

Another volley of Italian broke from the blonde, and then she pushed back the chair she'd commandeered and bolted to her feet. The look she threw at Connie was pure poison.

As for Dante, he'd gone completely rigid, his expression steeled. But not because of Bianca, Connie realised with an awareness that came to her at a level she could not explain.

Because of Rafaello.

The blonde threw one last angry word at Dante, then stalked off. Connie stared at Dante—then at Rafaello. Not understanding. Not wanting to understand. Something was passing between the two men—something that was registering in Dante as a rigid tension and in Rafaello as a studied coolness.

Dimly, something occurred to her.

He said that deliberately—about Dante being married to me.

But why was Dante reacting like this? They *were* married. So why—?

'Thanks, Raf,' Dante said bitingly, casting daggers at his friend. 'Bianca Delamondi is the very last damn person I would have wanted to know that!'

He glared furiously at Rafaello, but his friend, Connie could see, was sublimely unconcerned.

'It seemed the quickest way of getting rid of her,' he said, calmly reaching for his coffee cup and draining it. Then he glanced at his watch. 'I'd better call it a night,' he said, in the same unruffled manner. 'I'm on a morning flight to Palermo. An elderly client is being sued for divorce by his much younger second wife, and is objecting to her financial claims,' he said lightly, but with a discernible touch of cynicism. 'I must see what I can do to protect his money from her.'

'You do that,' Dante said shortly. 'It's what you're best at.' His voice was tight. 'That and shooting your mouth off!'

The only response he got was a laugh from Rafaello as he summoned the bill for their dinner.

Connie felt awkward. Currents were running, and she did not fully understand them.

As if conscious of her disquiet, Rafaello threw her a half-amused look. 'Do not be alarmed—Dante and I have been sparring with each other since we were teenagers. He runs hot and I run cold—it's why we're such good friends.'

Connie eyed him doubtfully. Dante still had that tense, closed-off look on his face.

The waiter approached, proffering *l'addizione* discreetly in a leather folder. Rafaello signed it off with a careless hand. Then he turned to smile at his guests, encompassing them both.

'I'm so glad to have met you again, Connie—it has been such a delight.'

He helped himself to Connie's hand, and before she'd quite realised what he was intending he lifted it to his lips, kissing it with a Latin flourish before releasing it.

'And I very much hope that my old friend appreciates just what a gem he has in you.' His voice was drier now, and she saw him throw a challenging glance at Dante. 'I own I was concerned for him at first, having to make such a marriage, but no longer. You are doing him a great deal of good—more than he realises, I suspect.'

She could see Dante was glowering, but whether it was because of the hand-kiss or what his friend had just said, she didn't know. In either case there was no need for him to look so dark, surely?

Then Rafaello was getting to his feet, taking his leave of them with a graceful *buono notte*.

When he had gone, Dante turned to Connie, taking her hand. His grip was enfolding.

'Raf can push my buttons sometimes,' he said tightly. 'He likes to think he knows me better than I know myself. As if!' His voice changed, and there was an apology in his eyes now. 'I'm sorry about Bianca,' he said frankly, with a rueful twist to his mouth.

Immediately Connie softened, felt the unease that Dante's tension had engendered in her dissipating. 'No need,' she assured him. 'I didn't understand what she was saying anyway.'

Dante gave a wry laugh. 'Just as well—she was referring to times past.'

Connie made herself give him an understanding look, to show she was not in the least embarrassed by this collision of Dante's past and his present. The blonde, ballistic Bianca would not be his only ex in Milan…

'But I could have done without Raf damn well shooting his mouth off.' Dante's voice had formed an edge again.

'Does…does it matter? Him saying that you're married to me?' Connie asked.

Uncertainty was filling her. Confusion. She wanted him to say something reassuring, but his expression flickered, then became veiled.

'It's no one's business,' he said shortly. 'I've never worn a wedding band and nor have you. Our marriage and our reasons for marrying are private—our concern only, not anyone else's.'

Questions stabbed in Connie's head. Questions that were hardly formed, barely shaped, that could only articulate themselves into one single thought.

But everything's changed now—hasn't it?

Dante was getting to his feet and she did likewise, a sense of unease still plucking at her though she couldn't really say why. Surely there was no need for it?

He guided her out on to the pavement, where the restaurant's doorman was pulling a taxi over for them. As they got in, Dante took Connie's hand again, pressing it warmly, his thumb smoothing across her palm in a seductive manner.

His mood was clearly lifting, so Connie's did too.

'I can't wait to get home,' he said, turning to her, his voice low, with a rasp to it that Connie had learnt to recognise.

She gave a delicious shiver of anticipation and her sense of disquiet dissolved. Even in the intermittent streetlight she could see the way his lashes were sweeping down over his eyes, and the equally tell-tale glint of gold in their depths.

All her questions—unformed, unshaped, unspoken—vanished from her head. All there was in her consciousness was the knowledge that she was as eager as he was to get back to his apartment, be swept into his arms and into his bed. To experience the ecstasy that awaited her there.

The most blissful place in the world to be...

Connie was chopping vegetables again, and this time she was not interrupted by Dante. Instead, he was overseeing her progress through the latest recipe she was happily trying out, reading the instructions to her in instant translation.

Happiness filled her. This undemanding, unglamorous domestic scene was dearer to her than all the indulgent luxury of shopping for designer clothes, even though that came with her still incredulous delight at seeing admiration for her transformed appearance in Dante's eyes. It was dearer to her than all the pleasurable excitement of him taking her sightseeing, speeding them away in his scarily fast supercar, which he obviously got a boyish kick out of driving, to while away the hours exploring the lushly scenic countryside, soaking up the atmosphere of the historic towns and medieval cities with which Italy was so richly endowed.

Just doing something as simple, as easy-going, as chopping vegetables, with Dante reading her a recipe, made her feel supremely satisfied.

It's all I want—just to be with him. I don't need anything more. I don't need designer clothes, or lavish sightseeing, wonderful though all that is. All I want is... Dante.

At some point she must go back to thinking about a career of some sort—or she might be able to do a Master's out here in Italy, for all she knew, or perhaps even teach English Literature to Italian students? It was all to find out... all to discover. But there was no rush, no urgency. For now she was content—oh, *so* content—simply to be here with Dante like this.

Her eyes went to him now, absorbed in flicking lazily through some other enticing recipes on the website, leaning against the breakfast bar, his free hand casually curved around a beer glass from which he drank from time to time. A lock of stray hair had fallen over his brow, and his sculpted cheekbones caught the light from one of the kitchen's ceiling spots. He'd changed out of his business suit, and the soft cashmere of his sweater lovingly moulded his torso...casual chinos emphasised the length of his legs.

Her breath caught—how fabulous he looked, and how wonderful it was just to stand here and look at him and know that she was with him.

That wave of emotion came again...sweeter and more powerful. She knew it for what it was. Knew it and gloried in it. Gave herself over to it completely.

It was the most precious emotion of all...

Dante glanced up from the screen. 'OK, so now add the chopped tomatoes to the mix. Then you need to slice and salt the aubergines to draw off the excess liquid and add them too. Because they'll be salty you don't need to add any more salt, the recipe says.'

'Yes, Chef,' said Connie dutifully, with a nod and a smile.

His answering smile was a slash of white. 'Tomorrow night I'll be cooking and you can be the one giving orders,' he said, and laughed.

They ate at the apartment every night—sometimes cooking themselves, sometimes ordering in. At weekends they went touring, staying in boutique hotels full of charm and character, though always very upmarket. They ate out then, of course—both lunch and dinner.

But they hadn't been out to dine in Milan since that evening with Rafaello, some weeks ago now. Connie had no objections—she loved these domesticated evenings with Dante, just her and him in his apartment. There would be plenty of time to meet his friends here in Milan, go out in public with him as she had when they saw Raf. For now, she was happy—more than happy—to devote herself to him. Just the two of them, together.

Like an old married couple...

It was another happy thought.

A contented smile hovered at her lips as she reached for the salt to sprinkle it on the sliced aubergine on the chopping board. The herby aroma of the already cooking vegetables was enticing, and she was looking forward to the meal. Dante had poured her a glass of white wine, fresh and crisp, as an *aperitivo*, and she reached for it now, taking a sip of its chilled fruitiness.

'OK, I've found a recipe for my turn tomorrow,' Dante announced, and described it to her. 'I'll bookmark it, so if you like maybe you can pick the ingredients up tomorrow?'

'Happy to.' Connie smiled. She was getting used to shopping for groceries, trying out her halting phrasebook Italian.

I need to knuckle down and really learn the language properly, she thought in passing, crossing to the sink to rinse the excess salt off the aubergines.

Her vocabulary was improving every day, but her grammar was very shaky, she knew. And to settle fully into a new country one really did need to crack the language.

Adding the final ingredient to the pot, and turning down the heat to let it simmer till it was ready, she picked up her wine glass and went to join Dante at the bar, perched on a high stools. A memory came to her of how she'd done just that at the swish cocktail bar in London, when Dante had seen her for the very first time since her makeover. How his stunned gaze had devoured her.

It had changed everything he'd ever thought about her.

Changed everything between them from that night onwards to this moment now.

That same wave of emotion went through her, just as before, and as before she gave herself over to it, so dearly precious it was to her.

'Saluti,' Dante said casually, clicking his beer glass against her wine glass and sliding his tablet aside. 'So,' he asked, 'where do you fancy going this weekend?'

'What about the mountains?' Connie suggested. 'The Italian Alps? Or are they too far away?'

'Not at all,' Dante assured her, and ran through some of the options.

They went on discussing an itinerary for the weekend and then, dinner ready, repaired to the dining area of the spacious apartment. It was a long and lazy meal, followed by a long and lazy lounge on the sofa, where Connie happily indulged Dante's desire to watch a football match on the huge wall-mounted screen. She was content to curl up against him, reading a woman's magazine in Italian—or attempting to read it—interrupting him from time to time to ask for translations of words she didn't yet know.

'You're getting pretty good.' Dante dropped an admiring kiss on her head.

'Well, I need to study the language properly,' Connie said. 'I'd love to get really fluent.'

'Is that necessary?' Dante asked. 'Considering—'

He broke off, his attention suddenly snapping back to the screen as the commentator's voice rose in excitement and the crowd became even noisier. A goal was scored, and Dante enthusiastically punched the air with a happy exclamation.

The match ended soon after, with the team Dante supported winning, much to his satisfaction. He reached for his coffee, draining it down.

'By the way, I've got some business coming up that will take me down to Rome—at the end of next week, most likely. We could add the weekend and see the Eternal City in all its glory, if you like?'

Connie smiled. 'Oh, that would be brilliant!' she said. A thought struck her. 'Would you want to meet up with Rafaello?' She frowned a moment. 'Is he partnered, by the way? I mean, I know he's not married—he doesn't wear a ring. Not that that necessarily means anything, of course,' she said, conscious that Dante did not either. Nor did she.

Maybe now we should?

The thought was in her head before she could stop it. But Dante was speaking, banishing it as swiftly as it came.

'Raf,' he said, his voice dry, 'is what I believe in English is called "a smooth operator". Getting him to the altar, or anywhere close, will take a very clever female indeed...'

Connie frowned. 'Maybe he'll just find he's fallen in love one day, with the woman he wants to spend the rest of his life with.'

Dante didn't answer, and she twisted her head slightly to glance up at him. The veiled look was back in his eyes. Then he gave a shrug.

'That's a very romantic view of life,' he said.

There was a definite edge in his voice. Connie could hear it.

'Raf's far too cynical to believe in love. He's a born lawyer.'

Then his expression changed, with the veiled look disappearing and a far more open one taking its place—one Connie was all too familiar with.

He dropped a soft, sensual kiss on her upturned lips. 'Why the hell are we discussing Raf?' he said in mock indignation, kissing her again.

His kiss deepened, and Connie felt herself melting into it, as she always did when he kissed her like this. In moments all thoughts of Rafaello, all thoughts of anything at all, were lost—and so was Connie, drowning in the sweet sensuality of Dante's kisses...

CHAPTER SEVEN

DANTE DEPRESSED THE ACCELERATOR, speeding up along the autostrada. They were closing in on Rome and would be there in time for dinner. Beside him, Connie was gazing with interest at the passing landscape, as she had all the way from Milan.

'There's *so* much to learn about Italy!' she exclaimed. 'I just want to gulp it all down now that I'm living here.'

Dante made no answer, focusing on overtaking a lorry irritatingly in the way of his powerful, fast, low-slung car. But Connie's words echoed in his mind. Hung there a moment.

Then she was asking him another question, about a town the exit to which they had just passed, and he gave her the best answer he could, glad of the distraction. He was not entirely comfortable about why he'd been glad of it, but he put it out of his mind. He was looking forward to Rome. Looking forward to squeezing a few days away from the business clients he was seeing while he was there and showing the city off to Connie. They'd meet up with Rafaello one evening, but that was all.

And if Raf damn well tries any of his tricks—oh-so-amusing to him but to no one else, like he did with Bianca in Milan—he can take a hike!

He glanced at Connie, his expression softening as it always did when he looked at her. She'd enjoy Rome, he'd make sure of that, for he always wanted to please her. And in turn she was so appreciative—as sweet-natured as she had always been.

He knew and rejoiced in the fact that she was finally without the cares and worries that had assailed her while she was looking after her grandmother, even though their marriage had eased the financial pressure on her. Now there were no pressures on her at all, and he could ensure that she was enjoying herself as she so richly deserved.

And he could share in that enjoyment. He was enjoying all they did together, whether it was sightseeing or having quiet evenings in Milan, cooking dinner together, vegging on the sofa, watching undemanding TV and then heading off to bed, with her as eager as he was to reach their final destination of the day.

Has it ever been like this for me before?

It was an unnecessary question. He knew it hadn't been. And it was all thanks to Connie.

She's so easy to be with—happy, good-tempered, sweet-natured... And as passionate in making love with me as any man could dream of. She gives herself completely...

And he, in return, did all he could to show her how much he desired her in return.

His thoughts turned to how quickly she could arouse and inflame and then satiate him...

'Where are we going to be staying in Rome? Remind me again?'

Connie's question interrupted thoughts that were getting too heated for a long car journey, and he was a little relieved.

'The Falcone,' he answered, overtaking another lorry that was going as slowly as a slug, relishing the acceleration of his powerful car at his command. 'It's a little out of the *centro storico*, but quieter for that reason. Just a taxi ride from all the sights in Rome. Speaking of which—what's top of your agenda to visit once I'm clear of my business appointments?'

'Ooh, there's so much to choose from!' she answered.

They ran through some of the major attractions, drawing up a flexible list, and continued to discuss them that evening over dinner at their hotel.

The Falcone, converted from a grand nineteenth-century villa, was set on the slope of one of Rome's fabled hills, surrounded by extensive gardens and with a view over the city. There was a pool in the grounds, and Connie had assured Dante that she would be more than happy to spend her first day enjoying it and the hotel's amenities in the still-warm weather of early autumn, while he went off to his business meetings.

He would be glad when he was done with his appointments, though, he thought again. And was looking forward to spending a leisurely few days here with Connie.

It was a quite different pace of life from the one he'd had to keep when his grandfather had been alive. He'd been at his beck and call, always focused on business, snatching brief, shallow affairs when he could fit one into his nonstop schedule. Now his time was his own, and if he wanted to cut back on his working hours—well, he was free to do so. And not constrained to brief affairs any longer, either.

He shied his thoughts away. He didn't want to dwell on the restrictions of his past. He just wanted to enjoy the present—the entirely pleasurable present. It was enough. More than enough.

Bidding Connie farewell as she packed a bag for the pool, he headed off. A hotel car would take him into the city for the first of his appointments, and then he was taking a client to lunch, followed by another two meetings in the afternoon. He was cramming them all into one day, so as to devote himself to Connie's entertainment thereafter.

He was looking forward not just to being with her—that was always good—but to seeing the sights again himself. His visits to Rome, as to any other city, had always been work-focused. Now, with Connie, he could take a more relaxed approach.

He'd just bade farewell to his lunchtime companion, after a mutually satisfactory discussion, when he was hailed by a familiar if unexpected voice.

'Raf? What are you doing here?' Dante glanced up from checking the bill for the meal—a hefty sum, but worth it for the valuable client he had just impressed with his financial recommendations.

'Same as you—I've been lunching with a client.' He sat himself down at Dante's table. 'So, what evening would be good for us to meet up? Given the Falcone's renowned gourmet chef, I'd be happy to come to you.' He paused, glancing at Dante. Then, 'How's Connie?' he asked.

'Fine,' said Dante. 'I'm showing her Rome. The Forum tomorrow, and the Hippodrome too, and then St Peter's and the Vatican the day after.'

Rafaello leant back in his chair. 'I'm giving a party at the weekend—it's my birthday, in case you'd forgotten. Why not come along?'

Dante shook his head. 'No, I don't think so—thanks all the same.'

Rafaello raised his eyebrows. 'Why not? You'll know enough people there through me, and Connie would enjoy it, I think.' He let his eyes rest on Dante in a way Dante did not care for. 'And I'm sure people would like to meet your wife.'

Dante felt his face set. 'Connie would find it overwhelming,' he said tersely. 'I wouldn't expose her to all that!'

'Expose her—or you?'

Dante's expression hardened, and he spoke bluntly, knowing he needed to make himself clear. 'Raf, back off. I know you find it amusing—hilarious, even—that I had to marry to get hold of my inheritance, but it's been a sore point with me ever since. Both your amusement *and* the fact that my hand was forced from beyond the grave!'

His friend held up his hand, as if to acknowledge Dante's objection. But the look in his eye continued to be speculative.

'What?' Dante demanded. His irritation was rising, and he didn't want Raf needling him.

But Rafaello only looked at him inscrutably.

His damn lawyer's face, Dante thought, irritation spiking again.

'Nothing at all,' Rafaello said smoothly. He rose to his feet, with the same unreadable expression on his face. 'OK, forget my party—but why don't I come over to the Falcone for dinner? Say tomorrow night? How would that be?'

Dante agreed with a rather terse, 'Fine, yes.'

But as Rafaello strolled off he was still conscious of that feeling of irritation. Annoyance. It was none of Raf's damn business, him and Connie. They were fine as they were—just fine.

Just leave us alone—that's what we want.

As if on cue, his phone pinged—it was a text from her.

Hope your business lunch went OK. I'm lounging by the pool. Dead lazy!

On impulse, he texted back.

If you want a change of scene, how about meeting me for cocktails later, when my afternoon appointments are done? We could do the Spanish Steps and the Trevi Fountain if that appeals?

Her reply was enthusiastic, and he was pleased. He felt his irritation at Raf dissipating. Raf just didn't get what he and Connie were about, that was all.

In a much better mood, he headed off for his next appointment, checking out a good venue for cocktails as he did so. There were plenty to choose from…

When Connie met him later, near the foot of the famous Spanish Steps, he guided her to a bar where they could sit outside and watch the Romans—and the tourists—making their evening *passeggiata*. Then, having made the ritual ascent and descent of the steps themselves, he took her for dinner.

Afterwards they ended up at the Trevi Fountain, floodlit for the evening, its water luminescent. It was still jammed with tourists.

'Ready to throw your coin in the fountain?' Dante smiled down at Connie as they edged their way forward.

'Do I need to?' she asked.

'Only if you want to be sure of coming back to Rome again,' Dante teased.

'What? Even if it's only coming from Milan? I thought the legend was just for those living in other countries? Oh, well, I'd better be on the safe side, I guess!'

She dug out a coin, turned her back on the glories of Bernini's masterpiece waterworks, and threw it over her shoulder in time-honoured fashion. She looked round to see where it had landed, but it was impossible to tell amongst all the coins under the water.

'They get collected daily and given to charity,' Dante assured her. 'Come on—we'd better get out of here before we get pushed into the fountain by the crowd. Let's get a *gelato*.' He indicated the famous *gelataria* to one side of the fountain. 'And then a coffee before heading back to the hotel.'

He put his arm around her shoulders as they strolled away from the fountain. As ever, it felt good to have her at his side.

Choosing a *gelato* from the huge selection on offer took some time, and then, choices made, they wandered off into the still-mild night. It was relaxed and companionable, walking with her arm in arm, consuming their ice-creams, eying up likely cafés for their late-night coffee.

He told her that he'd run into Raf that day, agreed to dinner at their hotel the following night, and then he trailed another suggestion, putting it to her as they sat down at a pavement café and ordered their coffee.

'Once you've seen enough of Rome, how about we keep heading south and take in Amalfi as well?' he asked.

She raised her eyebrows. 'That's quite a distance. Can you afford to take so much time off work? I'm more than happy, truly, to head back to Milan.'

Her expression changed, and he saw there was a tinge of anxiety in it.

'Dante, honestly…you don't have to show me all of Italy in one go. There's loads of time for me to see it, little by little.'

She took his hand, squeezed it as if reassuring him.

'I'm perfectly happy in Milan, I promise.'

He cocked an eyebrow 'You're not that keen on my apartment, though, are you?' he said perceptively. 'It's too modern for you.' He smiled knowingly.

'Well, it's ideal for city living,' she allowed. 'But with the countryside of Lombardy being so beautiful, it's a shame for you not to have at least a weekend place there to get away to, out of the city.' She frowned a moment. 'Where were you brought up, Dante? Where did your grandfather live?'

He answered her, but unwillingly, not wanting to dwell on the past. The present was what he was enjoying—and he liked it that way.

'He had a massive mansion on the outskirts of the city. I sold it when I inherited. It cost a fortune to run. It wasn't ancestral, or anything like that—he bought it when he first made serious money. I never liked it much,' he admitted. 'One of the few things I had in common with my father,' he heard himself adding.

Connie was silent for a moment. 'That's a shame,' she said quietly. 'Were...were you and he not close before he was killed so tragically?'

'No,' said Dante.

He reached for his coffee. He didn't want to spell out his life story for Connie. There was no point.

He looked across at her, his face shuttered. 'I've told you, Connie. I was brought up by my grandfather. My parents were off, gadding about, social butterflies the pair of them. My grandfather worked me hard, but I grew up with a sense of responsibility and the expectation of being the one to run Cavelli Finance after my grandfather died. He was fond of me, in his own way, but he was a tough cookie—he'd made his fortune from scratch, and that requires a certain level of ruthlessness. As he aged, he got keen on my taking over more and more, being trained up for the job, but always under his close supervision—supervision that extended to way beyond work.'

As he went on he heard his voice change and tighten.

'He wanted to supervise my whole life. Make sure I lived it the way he thought best.' His gaze slipped away. 'Maybe as he got older it made him think of posterity…the next generation…that sort of thing. And maybe,' he said, still not looking at her, 'that's why he tried to manipulate me with his will. Forcing me to marry. Presumably he thought to kickstart the next generation after me.'

His gaze snapped back to her. Sharp now with remembered anger.

'I was furious at being manipulated from beyond the grave. Determined to find a way to outwit him—outmanoeuvre him.' His expression lightened finally. 'And I did. I found *you*, Connie. And together—well, together we've found a solution to our own problems, and it's worked out well. I think we'd both agree on that…' His expression changed again, his eyes glinting, voice softening. 'And we've both got a bonus payoff neither of us dreamt of at the start of all this.'

He reached for her hand, lying inert beside her coffee cup, and raised it to his lips, kissing her knuckles softly, sensuously.

'An incredible bonus…' he said huskily.

Abruptly, he let her hand go, bolting down the rest of his coffee, finding his wallet and tossing the requisite notes on the table.

Holding out his hand to Connie, he got to his feet. 'Shall we get back to the hotel?' he suggested.

Desire was unhidden in his voice.

Connie gave a sigh of deep contentment, looking around the small, cobbled *piazza* lined with ancient-looking higgledy-piggledy houses, some draped with ivy, some with peeling paint. The whole place had, to her mind, a charming, boho feel to it.

After taking in the splendours of St Peter's, she'd asked to see the Trastevere area across the Tiber, and Dante had obliged, after warning her that it had become very touristy, and could be down at heel in places. But Connie liked it, despite his warning, and said as much now, as they settled down to have a late lunch at a very ordinary-looking *trattoria* whose simple, pasta-dominated menu was a far cry from the gourmet delicacies conjured up by the Falcone's celebrity chef.

Her spaghetti, when it arrived, was delicious, and even Dante conceded his was as well, and washed it down with one of the many craft beers for which, he told her, Trastevere was famous.

He glanced around him. 'God knows when I was last here,' he remarked. 'Probably when I was a student, with a bunch of mates, enjoying the bars…sampling all the beers! It gets very lively in the evenings, and that would have suited me at the time. Not that I ever got much time to gallivant about,' he added, forking up his pasta, his voice changing. 'My grandfather kept me on a tight rein.'

Connie looked at him with sympathy. From this and what he'd mentioned to her over coffee the night before, it sounded as if his grandfather hadn't been easy to live with.

'Were you at university here in Rome?' she asked.

He shook his head. 'No, Milan—and I had to live at home for the duration. I managed to go AWOL sometimes, though…heading down here to Rome, where Raf was studying, and I experienced a bit of nightlife then.'

Connie's expression was troubled. 'That seems pretty harsh of your grandfather,' she said. Her voice softened. 'My gran urged me to choose a uni far from the West Country. She wanted me to be independent. Quite the opposite from your grandfather's attitude,' she said, with sympathy in her voice.

Dante shrugged. 'He didn't want me getting a taste for self-indulgence, like my father had.'

She shook her head. 'Everyone needs to enjoy their student years, as well as studying hard.'

He reached for his beer, took a slug. 'Well, like I said, I was kept on a tight leash. Which is why I was so determined to break it after his death. And to keep it broken.'

He set his glass down with a decided click and she could see the tension in him. Her gaze was troubled. Dante might have been raised without any money worries at all, but that didn't mean he'd had an easy time of it.

But that's all over now. Now he's free from his grandfather's controlling nature. Free to make his own choices in life.

Wasn't he?

The answer was instant.

Yes—yes, he is. And he's chosen me.

After all, why else would she be here with him now?

And he's happy now. I know he is! Anyone can see that—anyone at all.

She felt her spirits lift and that precious emotion that she hugged so close welling through her, washing towards him, embracing him.

He'll be happy from now on, too. I'll make sure of it.

His eyes met hers across the table and she saw them soften.

'So, what shall we do after lunch?' he asked, his voice holding the cheerful warmth it usually had.

She was glad of it. Glad to respond in kind.

Getting stuck into her spaghetti again, as he was too,

she ran over some of the attractions she'd read about in Trastevere.

'There's the old ghetto area, and the Basilica di Santa Maria, which my guidebook says has mosaics by Cavallini—of whom, I admit freely, I have never previously heard, but which look beautiful in the photos. Or we could go to the Galleria Corsini,' she ran on enthusiastically. 'Which is, apparently, a baroque palace with paintings by Titian and Caravaggio, of whom I definitely *have* heard!' She looked at Dante a little anxiously. 'But if you're bored we don't have to,' she assured him.

'Let's see everything while we're here,' he answered cheerfully.

The shuttered look, and the long shadows cast by the past, had all gone from his face, reassuring Connie.

'Then we can get back to the hotel in time for a late dip in the pool, before we primp ourselves for Mr Uber-Smooth Rafaello,' he said sardonically.

Connie had laughed, but all the same, by the time she was ready to head down to the hotel's bar to meet up with Rafaello that evening, she knew she had indeed primped herself for the occasion.

The old-gold-coloured dress she'd chosen came with a matching hip-length jacket, loose-fitting and elegant, with a beautiful soft sheen to it, and she wore her hair up, painstakingly pinned to give her a little height and a touch of what she hoped was sophistication.

The overall effect certainly drew Dante's praise and admiration, and she basked in its warmth.

As they went into the elegant bar area adjoining the restaurant she saw Rafaello had already arrived, and he got to his feet, paying her an extravagant compliment and smiling down at her.

It was set to be a convivial evening. The gourmet menu on offer was superb, the vintage wines equally so, and Rafaello was on form—and openly amused by Connie saying they'd spent the day in Trastevere.

'Trastevere?' A musing look came into Rafaello's face. 'I seem to recall Dante and I and some fellow *raggazzi* spent a pretty wild night there once in our misspent youth!'

He spoke lightly, but Connie replied with a troubled look in her eyes. 'Dante told me—but he didn't really have a chance to have much of a misspent youth, did he? Thanks to his grandfather.'

'Oh, he fitted in some misspending for all that—as the likes of the fiery Bianca can testify,' Rafaello observed, with that sardonic note in his voice again. 'Mind you...' He took a reflective mouthful of wine, his eyes resting on both Connie and Dante for a moment. 'It looks like all that's changed now.'

Connie saw Dante's face alter. Close down. Like it had briefly when they'd had lunch and he'd talked about his grandfather's strictures. Clearly he didn't like Rafaello talking about all the exes Dante had in his past. She was glad of it.

'So, what are your plans after Rome?' Rafaello asked, changing the subject briskly. 'Are you heading back to Milan? And what about after that? Are you happy with Dante's bachelor pad apartment, Connie, or do you want to go house-hunting with him? Somewhere more settled for you, perhaps? More suitable for connubial domestic bliss?'

He'd spoken lightly, in nothing more than pleasant enquiry, but Dante set down his knife and fork and looked straight across at his friend. Connie could see that the shuttered look was still on his face, and his eyes were glinting—not in a good way.

'Raf, I have told you before,' he spelt out. 'Back off. I am aware of your deep amusement over my having to marry as I did, but that joke has been played out! Now…' his voice took on a warning note, became admonitory and deadly serious '…just lay off.'

Connie felt a stab or alarm, but his expression changed again and he threw a glance at her and she could see concern in it—and reassurance.

'Please do not involve Connie in your amusement. She has been an absolute Trojan in all of this. I can't thank her enough for what she's done for me, coming to my rescue the way she did. Yes, I hope I have made things a great deal easier for her, too, financially, but now…' he reached out, brushed Connie's arm, his voice softening '…after all she did for her grandmother she deserves this break—and I'm glad she is having it. A good, long, luxurious holiday, as much time as I can give her and a whole lot of pampering. That is what she totally deserves!'

Dante cast a warm look at her—yet for some reason this time it did not warm her.

His gaze snapped back to Rafaello. 'I won't have Connie upset or embarrassed. *Por Dio!* She's coped really well with a difficult and insanely awkward situation and she can do without your unfunny jibes. And so,' he said pointedly, 'can I. Not to mention that I can *definitely* do without your trying to make trouble with—'

He broke off, switched to Italian, speaking rapidly. It was too fast for Connie to follow, but she caught words here and there—and a name. She dropped her eyes away—not wanting to be the cause, however unintentionally, of any discord between the two friends.

As Dante finished Rafaello said something, short and to the point, it seemed. She glanced up, seeing Dante scowl, his mouth compressed. Then, in a deliberate gesture, he reached for his wine. Reverted to English.

'OK—let's drop the subject.'

His tone of voice had relaxed, and Connie could hear him trying to inject good humour into it.

'You asked what our plans were after Rome?' he said, addressing Rafaello. 'I'm thinking of taking Connie down the Amalfi coast. I know it's getting late in the year, but this run of fine weather is tempting me to risk it. What do you think, Connie?' Dante turned his head to her, an enquiring look in his eyes.

'Well, it would be lovely, but…' She let her voice trail off. Emotions were rising in her and words were failing her. Her Italian was rudimentary, still, and highly imperfect. Had she really heard Dante say what she thought he had? Why would he say it? She must have misunderstood…

Mustn't she?

Rafaello took over smoothly. Although Connie was aware that he was observing her from beneath lowered eyebrows.

'But she's terrified of the thought of your driving along those hairpin bends,' he said lightly.

Connie gave a flickering smile. 'Dante does like to drive fast,' she conceded. 'But I'm getting used to it,' she added quietly.

'I won't crash, and that's a promise,' Dante said, patting her arm reassuringly.

As reassuringly as when he'd praised her for agreeing to marry him so he could inherit his grandfather's fortune and for putting up with their bizarre marriage…

She used her uncertain smile again—all she could manage right now. She was aware that something seemed to be making a lump in her throat...or maybe it was in her stomach. She wasn't sure. She only knew she had to go on conversing as convivially as Dante and Rafaello were now doing again. Because for some reason it was essential she did so.

Their gourmet meal continued, but though she knew she was eating the most delicious and terrifyingly expensive dishes, she knew she was not doing them justice. And not because of all the calories she'd cut down on, but for a reason she did not want to think about.

Must not think about.

Not now.

Not yet.

But she did feel, for all that, as if she were a balloon which had just been punctured with a tiny pinprick, deflating very slowly...

Worse, she was aware that Rafaello, despite his bonhomie, seemed to be keeping her under surveillance through those lidded eyes of his. As if he were in lawyer mode, assessing a witness...or a defendant...

A defendant with something to hide...

It made her overreact, to hide her feelings, and she became more outwardly cheerful, more vocal, trying to participate in the lively conversation, focusing on Dante's proposed expedition to Amalfi and what awaited her there.

'I'm not sure I can face Pompeii, though,' Connie heard herself saying. 'So unbearably sad. All those lives destroyed...'

There was a melancholy note in her voice, and yet she knew it was not just because of the hideous tragedy of two millennia ago, sweeping over the unsuspecting Pompeiians. It was about something much closer...far more personal.

Something that she did not want to give voice to. Could not bear to contemplate right now.

'Then we shan't go,' Dante said decisively. 'I'm not having you upset. But how about a trip across to Capri instead? If the weather is good enough?'

'Oh, that sounds much nicer,' she said gratefully.

Dante gave her another warm smile, personal and intimate—and, again, it should have reassured her. But something was happening to her...something she couldn't explain and wasn't sure about. Despite her chattiness she felt distracted—and disquieted by the feeling that Rafaello was watching her, speculating about her...

Does he think I'm bad for Dante? Clingy...? Possessive, maybe?

It was an unpleasant thought. He'd never approved of Dante's marriage from the first—she knew that.

She became anxious for the meal to finish, for reasons she couldn't articulate, but when it finally did, in leisurely fashion, and Rafaello took his leave, lightly kissing Connie on the cheek and slapping Dante equally lightly on his shoulder as he thanked him for his hospitality, adjuring both of them to enjoy the rest of their stay in Rome and then Amalfi, Connie found she still wasn't relaxing.

Dante took her hand as they made their way towards the lifts, having waved off Rafaello in the hotel lobby.

'Let's have another coffee and a nightcap upstairs,' he said genially.

Connie smiled and nodded, conscious of feeling constricted. Up in their room, with its view over the city of Rome, and the vast dome of St Peter's lit up, Dante flicked on the in-room coffee machine and poured them both a liqueur—sweet for her, strong for him—carrying them over to the sofa positioned by the window.

'Too cold for the balcony,' he said, and Connie agreed.

He sat down beside her, stretching out his legs and putting his arm companionably around her shoulder. Then he kicked off his shoes and flexed his ankles, loosening his tie with his free hand.

Connie glanced at him. There was something about a loosened tie that made her insides melt, and combined with the incipient signs of darkening along Dante's jaw she felt the melting accelerate. Oh, sweet heaven, he was just so irresistible…

For the first time since Dante had silenced Rafaello she felt her feelings of disquiet subside. She nestled into Dante's encircling arm, reaching for her liqueur and taking a tiny sip of its sweet but fiery contents. She could hear the coffee machine beginning to perk as Dante reached for his own glass.

'Good old Raf,' he remarked, and his voice was much more relaxed, Connie was glad to hear. 'Always knows how to push my buttons… But I don't want him doing the same to you.' He took a taste of his liqueur. 'I can take it—and I give back as good as he hands out—but I don't want you dragged into it. He doesn't mean anything by it, but all the same…'

His expression darkened, and annoyance was now visible in it.

'His warped sense humour did enough damage that night in Milan. I told him straight off that I'd had to go into damage limitation mode with Bianca Delamondi, and phone her the next day to tell her he was just fooling around.'

Connie swallowed. She'd hoped she hadn't understood the gist of what Dante had said to Rafaello in Italian over dinner earlier. But now…

'Dante, is that what you said to Rafaello tonight? I… I caught some words, but I wasn't sure I was understanding. Did you say you'd told Bianca that of course we weren't married…'

Dante pulled back from her a fraction, to look at her up-turned face. 'It was the easiest way to get her off my case,' he said warily.

Connie stared. 'But…but we *are* married,' she said.

Dante lifted a hand, then dropped it. 'That's our business—and no one else's. I'm not going to tell the world what I was forced into doing. The only person who knows other than my grandfather's lawyers is Raf. And I want to keep it that way,' he said tightly.

There was irritation in his voice, in his face. More than that—a taut sense of frustration. Resistance. Resentment.

Rejection of what he's been forced into.

A word formed in her brain. Brutal and stark.

Denial.

She felt cold to the bone, but Dante was still speaking.

'That's why I've kept you to myself,' he said. 'I don't want any talk or speculation—let alone having to make explanations. Like I've said, it's no one else's business!'

His expression softened, but the cold was still running in her veins. He dropped a light kiss on her upswept hair, then relaxed back again. He was cradling his brandy glass in his cupped free hand. The other was warm on her shoulder as she sat nestled against him. But the warmth of his hand did not penetrate the coldness filling her.

Nor did the words he spoke now, his voice becoming ruminative.

'The thing is, you and I have had to cope with a situation that neither of us would have given the time of day even to consider in normal circumstances. But we were forced into it. If I could have got my inheritance any other way, I would have. And if you could have protected your grandmother any other way, you would have. Neither of us *wanted* this marriage, and the consequences have been a challenge for us both in different ways.'

His voice softened, warmed. Yet there was no trace of warmth in her.

'You've been a godsend to me, Connie. You know that. And I hope you know just how much I appreciate what you did for me, agreeing to my proposition. I meant what I said—that after everything you've been through, caring for your grandmother, you deserve to have a wonderful time now.'

He dropped another light kiss on her hair, and then crooked his head forward to reach her cheek, brushing it with gentle affection. His eyes met hers, and in them she could see what had always before set her melting.

But now—now everything seemed frozen. As if a glaze of ice had formed over him—and her. Chilling her to the core.

'And you don't need me to tell you how fantastic this time with you has been,' he said gruffly.

He took another slow mouthful of his brandy, drawing a little away from her so he could see her more clearly.

His eyes held hers. 'I want you to know that, despite Raf's idiotic remarks, I completely respect that you have your own life to lead and that you want to make a career for yourself—whether in publishing or academia or anything else you choose. We still have another good few months of our marriage to run before I can safely avoid any legal challenge by my grandfather's lawyers, but you absolutely must not feel under any obligation whatsoever to stay in Italy with me till then. Whenever you want to head back to the UK, just say the word.'

He brushed her lips with his, and Connie could taste the heat of the brandy on them—a heat that was in his eyes as well. Which was strange, because her lips felt frozen, just like the rest of her.

'Of course I'm self-indulgent enough to hope that won't be too soon. Let's definitely pack Amalfi in!' A thought clearly struck him. 'And with winter heading our way, how would you feel about checking out the Dolomites? Have you ever been skiing?'

Connie swallowed. 'No...never...' she said. She managed to get the words out through stiff lips, but she didn't know how.

Dante smiled in satisfaction. 'Then why not give it a go? The Dolomites are spectacular in their own right. We could have Christmas there, maybe. What do you say to that?'

She didn't answer. Couldn't. Could only give the briefest of flickering smiles and clutch her liqueur glass in fingers that were suddenly numb.

Like her insides...

Dante was still talking. 'The best snow is after the New Year, mind you. And maybe after Christmas we'd like a taste of heat again—to head for warmer climes. The Seychelles, Mauritius, the Maldives... Loads to choose from. And plenty of time in the next four months or so to do it before we need to think about our divorce.'

She heard him speaking, but his voice seemed to be coming from very far away, across a gulf that had without warning opened up like a chasm between them. A gaping, jagged chasm into which she was falling, falling, falling...

And she could do nothing at all to stop it.

CHAPTER EIGHT

THE PALMS OF Connie's hands were moving slowly, sensuously, across the planed smooth torso of Dante's chest, the tips of her fingers tracing every contour of his perfect, honed musculature. Her head dipped to let her lips follow the path of her fingers. She heard Dante groan dimly from the pleasure she was giving him.

She was making love to him. Making love to him with all the dedication and all the devotion that filled her.

As if it might be the very last time she would ever make love to him...

Slowly, she moved her naked body over his, her lips caressing the strong column of his throat, to seek and find what she yearned for. The answering softness of his mouth as it yielded, with another low groan in his throat, to her kisses.

She felt his hands come around her waist, guiding her over him as her breasts made contact with his chest, pressing her down on him as her thighs slid across his. Another groan broke from him and she could feel his arousal strengthen. It called to her own arousal, and she felt her breath quicken, her pulse quicken, her longing for him overwhelming her.

Their kisses deepened, their mouths opening to each other as his hands tightened around her waist. She moved her hips slowly, sensually, knowing she was increasing his arousal, loving how strong he was, how fully engorged.

She felt her own body answer in kind, the delicate tissues of her femininity moistening. Instinctively, she parted her thighs, slackening them, positioning herself over him, lifting just a little to catch him and guide him into her waiting, aching body.

His moan matched hers and her hands splayed either side of his head, her back arching to take him, oh, so fully into her. Her need for him was absolute, and only with him was her completion possible.

She moved over him rhythmically and his thighs, so taut and hard beneath hers, strained as he thrust himself up into her. His hands were like a vice around her waist now, splayed out over the roundness of her hips, holding her to him exactly where he wanted her to be, needed her to be—where she needed to be, ached to be. The only place in all the world.

Her body fused with his, taking him as she gave herself, as her arousal intensified, matching him movement for movement, knowing that the release that would soon come for him and for her would be...

Glorious.

A radiance of sensation that was so intense it was unbearable blossomed inside her and she cried out, her head falling back, her hair streaming down her back as her body surged with his, melting, dissolving into ecstasy.

She was his!

Oh, she was his he was hers.

They were one—one flesh, one union, one body, one pulsing, beating heart...

She dropped to him, a sob breaking from her, hands clutching him, holding him closer and yet closer still. She could still feel him throbbing inside her as the waves of her own body continued to pulse gently, holding him tightly inside her.

Slowly, so very, very slowly, the passion ebbed from them both, slackening their bodies, leaving them fulfilled and completed. Their closeness now was the closeness of limbs suddenly heavy and torpid, exhaustion fusing them one to the other. Her hands slipped to his arms, curving around his biceps, and her cheek rested on his shoulder.

She felt his hands slide down to rest on her flanks. His mouth grazed her lowered brow so lightly, his voice, low and drowsy, murmured her name. And then, her eyelids heavy...so heavy...sweet, embracing sleep drew her down into its consoling peace.

Dante heard his phone bleep and reached for it. Who the hell was calling him at this time of night, when all he wanted to do, in his sated post-coital state, was sleep through till morning?

When he saw the caller ID he groaned, but accepted the call, levering himself out of bed and padding across to the far side of the room so as not to disturb Connie. The conversation was blessedly brief, but the outcome far from welcome.

Swiftly, and deeply reluctantly, he set a low-volume alarm on his phone and headed back to bed, enfolding Connie in his arms. It was the place he liked her to be, with her soft body embraced by his.

Sleep swept over him again until, still at an ungodly early hour, his alarm went off. It didn't wake Connie, and he was glad as he levered himself totally unwillingly from their bed and went into the en suite bathroom for as swift a shower and shave as he could manage.

Quickly dressed, he crossed back to the bed and Connie's sleeping form. For a few precious seconds he gazed down at her in the soft light thrown from the bathroom.

How truly beautiful she was! Every time he looked at her he wondered at how she'd concealed such loveliness from him for so long. He loved everything about her—from the way her hair curled over her rounded shoulder to the way her eyelashes dusted her soft cheeks…the way her lips, slightly parted as she breathed steadily in slumber, were tempting him even now to brush a kiss upon their velvet contours.

But, damn it, just when she looked so alluring—so embraceable—just when he'd been looking forward to another lotus-eating day with her, relaxed and leisurely, wandering around Rome, now he was going to have to do without her. *Accidenti.*

He let his mouth touch hers, just for the briefest moment, and then he lifted away, gently rocking her shoulder as he did.

Her eyes fluttered open, fastening to his. For a second he saw something flare in their depths and then retreat into shadow. Alarm, probably, at him waking her like this, fully clothed, at such an early hour.

His tone apologetic, he broke the bad news to her. 'I have to fly to Geneva to see a client. It's a total pain, but I can't get out of it. I'm taking the earliest flight out.' He made a face. 'I'll be back in time for dinner, so… Look, have an easy day, OK? Lounge around the hotel or get the concierge to put a limo at your disposal. I'll see you this evening.'

He dropped another, even swifter kiss on her mouth, burningly conscious that he was cutting it very fine to make it to Fiumicino for his flight.

'Mi dispiace molto—'

And he was gone, striding out of the room, heading for the lift banks, wanting the flight over, the day over, and the evening to come, so he could get back to where he wanted to be.

Here.

With Connie.

* * *

For a long while Connie just lay there. Scarcely moving. Scarcely breathing. The room was deathly quiet, with not even the hum of the air-con to disturb the silence—for the temperature was dropping and it was no longer needed. But not heating yet, either.

It was poised between hot and cold.

Scalding hot and killing cold...

Like me.

She was poised between two overpowering impulses, completely contrary, that were tearing her in two.

Random thoughts were going through her head, almost like the wisps of a dream—not that she could remember dreaming last night.

But was that so surprising, given that her dreams had been completely shattered...obliterated...with a few simple words from Dante.

She heard them again now, in this 'in between' place where she seemed to be, with the room dim from the early hour and the drawn curtains, the air so quiet. Only the sound of her shallow breaths penetrated.

'Plenty of time...before we need to think about our divorce...'

They were repeating themselves on a loop. A loop she couldn't stop, or change, or get out of her head.

Such simple words. Such devastating consequences. Circling around and around in her head.

Round and round they went—like millstones, crushing her to pieces between them. Crushing her stupid, *stupid* dreams and all her hopes and secret longings. Grinding them all to dust...

She must have slept again, somehow, with the millstones grinding still, because when she surfaced again it was to the sound of the hotel phone beside her. She fumbled for the handset, barely awake. It was the reception desk, telling her she had a visitor.

She glanced at the time display—it was gone ten in the morning, and bright sunlight was pressing behind the curtain drapes.

'Signor Ranieri is here, *signora*.'

She started. *Rafaello* was here?

Still hazy with heavy, comfortless sleep, she struggled to sit up.

'I'll… I'll be down shortly.'

She dropped the handset, staring blankly. What on earth was Rafaello doing here?

Her mobile phone pinged with a text, and she stared at it.

Connie, hi—I hope I'm not disturbing you. Dante asked me to look in on you since he had to abandon you at short notice. I'm at your disposal for the day if you like. Ciao. R

She swallowed. Part of her wanted to text back and tell him to go away. She could not cope with him. Could not cope with anything at all.

But I have to!

She stared bleakly into the luxurious bedroom, so handsomely appointed, from the velvet window drapes to the huge carved wooden bed and the ornate carpets. It seemed alien, so entirely alien.

She threw back the bedclothes, stumbled up, her mind in pieces, her thoughts in pieces…ground down to dust.

Dante's plane was touching down in Geneva—the last place he wanted to be. Because the only place he wanted to be was back in Rome. With Connie.

Maybe I should have brought her with me. She could have had the day in Geneva while I got my business meeting over and done with and then—who knows?—we could have spent the night here, and flown back to Rome tomorrow?

That way she'd have been with him on the flight there and back, and he wouldn't be missing her the way he was right now.

It had seemed so wrong to leave her like that. OK, so he'd left her during the day in Milan, when he went into the office, but that wasn't the same thing as flying off to a different country without her—even if he was going to be back in time for dinner.

As he waited for the plane to draw to a standstill so they could disembark, he quickly texted her.

Missing you already. I've asked Raf to come and keep you company. See you tonight. I will text when I know what flight I can make. The earliest I can!

He ended it with a line of smiley faces, which would make her smile too, he knew, and then slid his phone away, seized up his briefcase and levered himself from his seat to get off the plane as soon as he could.

The sooner he was in Geneva, the sooner he could see his client, and the sooner he could turn right around and get back to the airport again.

Back with Connie.

The only place he wanted to be.

'Connie…'

Rafaello's greeting was friendly as he came towards her in the hotel's opulent lobby. But when he reached her, he stopped. Scrutinised her.

Concern filled his face. 'You look as white as a sheet,' he said.

He took her elbow, guided her into the nearby lounge. It was possible to have breakfast there, seated in comfortable armchairs with low tables between, overlooking the glorious gardens. But it wasn't busy, and he headed for a pair of armchairs away from the other occupants.

She sat down, as limp as a rag doll.

'What's happened?' Rafaello asked quietly as he took his seat opposite her.

She looked at him. Her face wasn't working properly, she knew.

'I don't know what to do,' she said finally. The words fell from her like stones.

Rafaello's level gaze rested on her. 'In what respect?' he pressed when she went silent again.

'Dante,' she said. And his name, too, fell like a stone.

Rafaello crossed one leg over the other. 'Ah...' he said.

A waiter was hovering, and Rafaello turned to Connie. 'Have you had breakfast?'

She shook her head numbly.

'Then you should,' he said.

He ordered food for her, and coffee for himself, and the waiter disappeared.

Connie swallowed. There was a huge stone in her throat and needles in her lungs. She became aware that Rafaello was speaking and looked at him. He had that lawyer look about him and his eyes were resting on her, their expression guarded.

'It was what he said at dinner last night, wasn't it?' he said.

Her eyes widened, stared, then dropped away.

She heard Rafaello's voice continuing. 'You understood what he told Bianca?'

She could only nod numbly. What use to deny it? None.

'He…he confirmed it when I asked him about it later… in our room. He said he'd told her we weren't married. At first I didn't understand why he'd said that to her…'

She lifted her heavy gaze to Rafaello—his face was impassive, unreadable.

'And then…then he…he explained. Oh, not in relation to Bianca. But what he said about us. About him. About…' she swallowed, and it hurt to swallow over the stone in her throat '…me.'

'And what did Dante say about you?' he asked.

She shouldn't tell him. It was private, wasn't it? And Rafaello had never approved of his friend's marriage in the first place, so he would agree with Dante anyway. He'd be glad to hear it.

But she couldn't *not* say it.

Because it filled her head and her lungs and her consciousness.

'He said…he said that he respected that I had my own life to lead, and that although he'd prefer to keep our marriage going for another few months, to be on the safe side, I must not feel any…any obligation to stay in Italy with him for all that time…that I could head back to the UK whenever I wanted.'

The stone in her throat was harder and larger than ever. It was suffocating her now.

'And then…then he said there was plenty of time before we had to think about our…our divorce…'

She fell silent. Her mouth was as dry as dust. Her eyes sank again, too heavy to keep looking at Rafaello. She didn't want to. She didn't want to see what expression might be on the face of Dante's friend, who had never wanted him to marry her at all—for any length of time or for any purpose.

For a moment there was silence. Then she heard Rafaello speak, calmly and dispassionately.

'Well, he has spoken his mind, and now you know where you stand. Ah…here is your breakfast. While you eat, you must tell me what you plan to do now.'

Connie drew a breath. It was painful. Her throat was tight and she felt weak as a kitten, with incoherent thoughts whirring in her head like a swarm of flies.

The waiter was setting out her breakfast—orange juice, hot fragrant coffee, freshly baked *cornetti* and delicate pats of butter and pots of apricot jam. She didn't want to eat, but knew she must. She had no strength in her. None at all.

Rafaello poured coffee for them both and sat back, his cup in his hand, crossing his legs in a relaxed fashion. As she ate, forcing herself to swallow slowly but steadily, he kept silent, but he was still looking at her, she knew.

She finished her *cornetti*, then looked back at him… Dante's friend. 'You never wanted him to marry me, did you?' she said tiredly.

He paused before answering. Then: 'I thought it very… risky. You were strangers to each other—complete strangers. And he was running on anger at the time, and that's never a good aid to wise decisions. But since then…' He paused again, and now he was frowning slightly. 'Since then you seem to have worked things out between you. I'd hoped—'

He broke off, taking a breath.

His voice was gentle when he said, 'Connie, what do you intend to do now?'

She forced herself to speak. To say what she dreaded having to say. She had tried to deny the need to say anything, but no longer could. She had to face saying the words.

'I have to leave him,' she said.

The words fell into a heavy silence.

'I think,' Rafaello said eventually, 'that is the right decision. For both of you.'

His eyes rested on her but she could read nothing in them. They were as inscrutable as any lawyer's.

'But I also think you should do one more thing,' he added.

She stared at him dully. She was breaking up inside and it was agony.

'What...what thing?' she asked, her lips numb.

And Rafaello told her.

Dante stared at the text on his phone, frowning as the taxi edged through the traffic in Geneva, en route to his client's hotel.

Dante, ciao. Connie wasn't at the Falcone—looks like she's headed into the city on her own.

Immediately, he texted Connie.

Sorry to hear you missed Raf. Have fun in Rome. What are you going to be seeing?

He didn't get an answer before the taxi pulled up and he had to go into his meeting. But when he emerged a couple of hours later there was still no reply from Connie. He frowned again.

Hi—how are you doing? My meeting's finished and I'm in with a chance of making an earlier flight back to Rome. I can meet you in town, or back at the Falcone. You choose.

He didn't get a reply to that either.

He texted Raf. Not wanting to, but feeling an edge of anxiety. Rome was safe enough, but maybe Connie had been mugged for her phone? These things happened.

Raf knew nothing, and told him so. He said he would text Connie as well, to let her know Dante was trying to get in touch.

Next Dante phoned the Falcone, to see if Connie had got back there safely. But she hadn't.

His frown deepened. So did his level of anxiety.

Repeated texts to Connie got no response. Fear bit at him, warring with reason.

She was OK—of course she was OK! Maybe her phone was dead. Maybe she just wasn't checking it. Maybe...

He was on board his flight, waiting for take-off, when a text finally arrived from her.

Dante, I'm so sorry—I'm back in England. I've heard there's a chance of getting on a Master's course at very short notice, so I thought I should go for it! I'm sorry to cut short our fabulous holiday, but perhaps it's for the best. Time to get on with our own lives—they've been on hold long enough.

The text ended with kisses—four of them. That was all.

A flight attendant was coming by, checking seat belts. Dante stopped her progress.

'I need to get off this flight immediately.' His voice was urgent, imperative.

'I am so sorry, but that isn't possible now.' The flight attendant was polite, but adamant.

He sat back, closing his eyes in frustration.

But also in so much more than that.

* * *

Connie let herself into her cottage. It was dark already. The coach from Heathrow had only taken her to Taunton. She'd had to change to a local bus to the village, and then get a taxi here. Exhaustion filled her—but it was not of the body.

The cottage was cold and bleak and it smelt fusty, having been empty for so long. Slowly, numbly, she went around putting on the lights, picking up the pile of post that had accumulated since Mrs Bowen, who had keys, had last done so on her behalf, and dumping it on the table, where the rest of it was neatly stacked.

She went into the kitchen, flicked the heating on. She wouldn't light a fire—she had no energy for it. She had no energy for anything. No will for anything. Except to crawl up to her room, get under her duvet, and sob her stupid heart out.

But what was the point of doing that? None.

Bleakly, she stared into the little living room. This was where Dante had proposed to her. Proposed a bizarre marriage of mutual convenience. He would get something he wanted. She would get something she wanted. It had been equal. Fair. A perfectly balanced contract. Win-win for both of them.

And it had worked. Worked while Gran was alive... worked while Connie was the way she'd been when they had tied the knot: lumpy, frumpy and dumpy.

But then...

Then I went off contract.

And that had changed everything between them.

She shut her eyes in misery.

Because I just could not resist taking the chance of making my wildest fantasy come true.

The fantasy of having the most fabulous man in the

world look at her with an expression in his eyes that was not friendliness, or pleasantness, or even, after her grandmother's death, sympathy and concern.

She had wanted what she had never thought she would ever see in his eyes.

Desire.

And when that magical moment had come, and Dante had indeed looked at her with desire in his dark, gold-flecked eyes, and taken her into his arms to make her his, it had been so much more blissful than she had imagined.

And there had been more—so much more to her fantasy. And it had only grown stronger and stronger with every day she'd spent with Dante in Italy. Those days in Milan…him going off to his office, she to the market, to buy ingredients for their dinner, preparing things, cooking with him…

Like a proper married couple—a real married couple…

Because that, in the end, had been her ultimate fantasy, hadn't it? To settle down with Dante in married domestic bliss.

It was what her parents had had. She knew that from her own memories and from what her grandmother had told her. For her parents it had been cut tragically short, but for herself and for Dante she had hoped—oh, how she had hoped—that they would be given what her parents had not had. What Dante's own parents—however they'd lived their lives—had not had either.

But instead…

Dante never wanted that! Never wanted it at all! Not with me.

She gave a smothered cry and turned away, unable to bear looking at where Dante had sat, offering her the means to keep Gran at home, lifting her crushing money worries from her.

And all she'd had to do was sign her name on a marriage certificate…

For a limited time only.

That stone in her throat was back again, and she could not breathe.

A truth so harsh, so cruel, so brutal, was slamming into her, taking the air from her lungs.

I thought his desire for me would change that—would make him want our marriage to be real for the rest of our lives…

Bitterness filled her mouth.

It was not his fault. It was hers and hers alone.

Mine only.

And she would have to live with it for the rest of her life.

A life without Dante.

CHAPTER NINE

DANTE WAS IN the office, working. He was poring over the complex investment plan which one of his financial analysts had prepared for a particularly demanding client. He needed to give it his full attention, but that seemed impossible right now. His brain wouldn't focus. Not on pages of figures and graphs and lists of potential shareholdings and loans.

There was only one thing his brain could focus on.

Connie.

And she was not with him any longer.

Why?

That was the question burning a hole in his brain. OK, so she'd said she wanted to apply for a Master's. But couldn't she have done that from Italy? Everything was online these days; she could easily have applied remotely. And if she'd been offered an interview she could have flown back to the UK for a few days—hell, he'd have gone with her. They could have looked in on the cottage, caught a few days in London...

But no, she'd upped sticks and gone. Just like that.

When we still had months left to be together.

His face tensed. But if she got on this damned course they wouldn't have months to be together, would they?

Her time here, with me, will be over.

It was like a punch to his guts.

But it was absolutely nothing like the punch that came

when his PA came through his door and carefully, knowing how black his mood was, placed in front of him a sealed package that had just arrived by air courier from London.

Numbly, he tore it open and yanked out the documents within. And then, as if all the breath had been forced from him by a paralysing blow, he stared in shock at what they told him.

Connie sat on the train, staring out of the window at the sodden countryside, the leafless trees. Autumn was fast turning into winter, and the weather was miserable. She pulled her coat around her, wriggled her feet in her boots. It wasn't her old winter coat, nor were they her old winter boots, but when she'd gone to stock up on winter clothes she'd been modest in her purchasing.

Memory plucked at her, of Dante taking her shopping in the fabled Quadrilatero in Milan. Of wandering blissfully, wonderingly, in and out of the famous fashion houses. Dante had spent a fortune on her...

Well, she would have no use for those fabulous clothes now. She'd left them all behind—even the ones she'd taken to Rome. She hoped he'd be able to sell them...they must be worth a huge amount, even second hand.

Her mind skittered away. She did not want to think about it—did not want to think about Dante. Because there was no point. Not any longer.

She felt misery clutch at her, bleak and desolate. She missed him so much.

How could she face the rest of her life—decades and decades and decades—without him?

You have to—that's all there is to it.

And if she'd yielded to temptation that terrible morning—to stay with Dante even after what he'd revealed to her, to stay with him every single day she could until he decided it was safe to divorce her—when that time had come it would have been an even greater agony to leave him!

No, nightmare though it had been, she'd had to do what she had done. Leave him that very morning.

She felt her throat constrict even more as she remembered what Rafaello had said to her in his calm, lawyerlike way on that hideous morning when she had decided she must leave Dante. Even if she could not yet divorce him.

Rafaello had argued otherwise.

'You should not believe, Connie, that you must prolong your marriage any further. Divorcing Dante immediately, on the grounds of irretrievable breakdown, would not invalidate the terms of his grandfather's will because it is, after all, quite true...is it not?'

A stifled sob broke from her.

Irretrievable breakdown—

Those words were like weights, crushing her—crushing all those hopes and dreams that she had once so stupidly believed in.

I believed that what I wanted was what Dante wanted too! That he would want what we had together to last for ever. But he never did want it to last—never intended it to last. For him, it was always going to end—always!

She gave another smothered cry, thankful that the train was not crowded, that she had a no one near her to witness her misery. There was only the sodden landscape passing her by outside, as bleak and bare as the landscape of her mind and her heart.

She hadn't wanted to come to London today, but Rafaello had said it was necessary. This next stage of the divorce was not something that could be done virtually, he'd told her. It had to be face to face.

She'd wanted to use a local West Country lawyer, but Rafaello had said that, given Dante was Italian, and she had signed a prenup, and his financial resources were so vast compared with hers, only a London lawyer of sufficient calibre would do. Fortunately Rafaello was personally acquainted with just such a suitable lawyer, and she had gone along with his recommendation.

In a remote way she was grateful to Rafaello for taking charge…guiding her through the whole hideous process with his legal expertise. It was kind of him—he must be feeling sorry for her.

But maybe he's only doing it for Dante—to free him from me as quickly as he can.

And now the tears she had been trying not to shed spilled from her. Tears from the agonising pain of knowing that Dante—the man she had married as a stranger, who had become her friend, kind and compassionate, and then her lover, desiring and passionate, the man she had woven her stupid, delusional dreams over—had never wanted her to be the wife she had come to long to be with all her heart.

Never.

Dante sat on the plane, his expression closed. But thoughts were crowding into his head. He was keeping them all crammed down under a heavy weight. It was essential he do so.

Memory pierced him of how he'd driven down to the West Country, fury in his heart, to seek out Rafaello at that damn wedding and demand he find a way to get him out of the trap his grandfather had sprung on him.

His anger had been paramount, all-consuming. Was it anger in him now, storming beneath that heavy weight he was crushing his thoughts with? He didn't know. Wasn't going to look. He was simply going to go on staring at the document in his hand, taken out of the briefcase beside him.

The petition for divorce.

And the letter that had arrived since from Connie's London lawyer, requesting a meeting.

'Connie—how are you?'

Rafaello's greeting was courteous as he came forward to meet her. She'd arrived by taxi from Paddington Station to an elegant eighteenth-century townhouse in the Inns of Court, the premises of the law firm Rafaello had recommended, and he had been waiting for her in the narrow lobby.

She swallowed as he shook her hand. It was hard to see him again, even though she was grateful for his support through this whole agonising business. He helped her off with her coat, and came with her as she was shown upstairs to a wood-panelled office, where she was introduced to the senior partner to whom she had only spoken virtually so far.

He got to his feet behind an old-fashioned mahogany desk. 'Ah, Mrs Cavelli—how good to finally meet you in person.'

Numbly, she returned his handshake, took the chair Rafaello drew up for her. She felt frozen all over, inside and out.

'What…what happens next?' she asked.

The man resumed his seat and looked at her in a kindly fashion over the rim of his spectacles.

'Well, as you know, your husband has been served with your petition. You were married in the United Kingdom, so that is good—it keeps things simpler. However, your husband being an Italian citizen adds a degree of complication…as I believe you already appreciate.'

He nodded at Rafaello who, sitting beside her, said, 'But not to a great degree, as I have explained to you.'

She looked bleakly at him, and then the senior partner.

'I just want it done as quickly as possible with the mini-mum fuss.' Her voice was low and strained, as her fingers knotted in her lap over her handbag.

'Of course. Very understandable...' said the lawyer, nod-ding in agreement. 'Very well, let us continue—'

The phone on his desk suddenly rang, and with a mur-mured apology to Connie he picked it up.

He listened a moment. Then: 'Thank you. Yes, right away, if you please.'

He replaced the handset and looked across at Connie. His expression was unreadable.

And so, she realised with a sudden stab of alarm in her breast, was Rafaello's.

Through the oak door of the office she heard rapid foot-steps, and then the door was unceremoniously pushed open.

Dante strode in.

He stopped dead. A man, middle-aged, bespectacled, was getting to his feet, politely greeting him. Dante ignored him. He had eyes for one person in the room, and one only.

His wife.

His wife, upon whose shoulder Rafaello Ranieri's hand was pressing.

All the emotions that had been hammered down so ruth-lessly on his journey here smashed through.

Rage ignited.

Explosively.

'Get your hands off my wife!'

A shocked sound came from the man behind the desk.

'Mr Cavelli! If you please!'

Dante ignored him. Ignored everything but the sight of Rafaello touching Connie.

Rage came again.

'It's you, isn't it? You're the one who's stirred all this up! Well, damn you! Do you hear me? Damn you to hell!'

He was speaking Italian now, and anger was boiling from him. He saw Rafaello getting to his feet, holding up a hand, his other hand still pressing down on Connie's shoulder.

'Dante—cool it.'

His words were perfectly calm—which enraged Dante all the more.

He started forward. He wanted to knock Raf's hand off Connie's shoulder, and then he wanted to knock him out cold.

A cry stopped him in his tracks. Connie had jolted to her feet, dislodging Rafaello's hand with the movement.

Dante's rage turned. Turned on her.

'Just what the *hell* is all this about?'

He'd gone into English now, but his anger was just as searing in that language as in his own.

'You walk out on me without a word—without a single damn word you just walk out and disappear, high-tail it back to the UK on some totally spurious pretext—and next thing I get petitioned for *divorce*? What the *hell*?'

Rafaello spoke again. In English. 'Why the surprise, Dante? You were always going to get divorced, weren't you? Connie's just accelerated the procedure, that's all.'

His voice was still cool and calm. And it still enraged Dante.

'Shut your damn mouth, Raf! This is your doing! You've put Connie up to this! Though God knows why—or how!'

His eyes flashed back to Connie. With the small part of his brain that wasn't in total meltdown he saw that she was as white as a sheet.

He opened his mouth to speak, his anger even blacker. Because of course it was anger—what else could this all-consuming, overpowering emotion be?

But her pale, drawn face was twisting, her hand was flying to her mouth, stifling another cry torn from her, and then she was stumbling past him, pulling open the door, hurtling from the room.

Running from him.

She was gasping, no air in her lungs, as she pounded down the stairs. Only one thought possessed her. To get away...

The shock of Dante's arrival—the horror of his rage at her... She couldn't bear it. She couldn't bear it a moment longer, not for a second...

Her coat was hanging on a hook in the lobby and she grabbed at it, pushing her arms into the sleeves, fumbling with her handbag as she did so, yanking open the front door.

Behind her she could hear voices full of consternation, footsteps running down the stairs behind her. She could hear her name being called—urgent, angry. In a flurry of desperation she started blindly down the short flight of stone steps leading to the pavement, still trying to thrust her right hand into her coat sleeve.

She felt her heel catch on the lowest step, tried to grab the railing. But her hand was not free. She felt herself being impelled forward, knowing in a moment of utter panic that she was falling...could not stop herself. Could not stop the pavement slamming up towards her, the lamppost smashing into her head as she fell, with a sickening thud, on the rock-hard, merciless paving stones.

'Connie!'

Dante's voice was hoarse with horror and he was there in an instant, crouched down beside her. He cried her name again, but she did not move.

In terror, he lifted his shaking hand to her throat. His

eyes closed in abject relief and he breathed again. There was a pulse.

But blood was seeping through her hair, trickling onto her forehead.

'Get an ambulance!' he demanded.

Then Raf was there, crouched down too, his phone in his hand, jabbing out the emergency number, demanding an ambulance immediately.

Dante grabbed the phone from him. *'Now!'* he yelled into it.

And then he was trying to lift Connie, attempting to get his arm under her shoulder.

Rafaello's hand clamped down on him with all its weight, restraining him.

'*No!* It's a head injury—and maybe her neck, too. You are not to move her—not even a centimetre!'

Dante still wanted to punch Rafaello, but he lifted his arm away. Other people were there now. Connie's lawyer, the woman who had shown him in. All were expressing their concern. Connie herself was not stirring.

Numbly, Dante kept his fingers at her throat, on the thin, frail pulse still beating there.

And as her blood trickled slowly over her chalk-white cheek onto his hand, as he knelt on the pavement beside her, words formed in his head, carving into him, one by one.

Her blood is on my hands...

The ambulance came. Scooped Connie up and drove off with her, blue lighting through the traffic.

Rafaello hailed a taxi, piling Dante into it, but by the time they reached the hospital Connie had been rushed away.

Dante strode up to the reception desk in A&E, numb with dread.

'My wife,' he said curtly. 'She's just been brought in. Unconscious. Head wound. Where is she?

His questions were staccato, demanding. His face looked like stone.

The receptionist checked, conferred with a colleague, then looked at him.

'She's in X-Ray,' she said. 'She needs a CT scan. They'll know more soon. Could you please fill out this form with her personal details?'

Dante ignored the form and headed for the seating area closest to the door that said *X-Ray and Imaging*.

It opened, and a man in a white coat with a stethoscope around his neck walked through.

Dante stepped in front of him.

'My wife,' he said urgently. 'She fell. Unconscious. Head injury. Bleeding—'

The doctor glanced at him for a moment, then nodded, gave a tired smile. He didn't always get to give good news, but this was one time he could.

'She'll be OK,' he said.

Dante's eyes closed, and emotion drenched through every fibre of his being.

CHAPTER TEN

THERE WAS A mist in the room. Connie could see it. Feel it. It was all around her. Inside her. Blurring her vision. Blurring everything.

She tried to blink, to clear it, but it would not go. The mist was covering up her thoughts, her feelings, and she could not get through it to find them, even though she had a feeling it was very important that she do so. The effort was hideous, and with a low moan in her throat she gave in…giving herself up to the mist.

When she next surfaced the mist had gone—not completely, but it was only around the edges of the room now, blurring the walls and the edges of her brain, blurring the edges of her thoughts, her feelings.

Those thoughts and feelings had come into sharp, agonising focus. Each one edged with a knife blade like a razor.

Dante. Dante in front of her like an avenging god of old, denouncing her.

Misery filled her, piercing the edges of the mist. Misery and so much more.

The door was opening and a nurse came in. 'How are you feeling?' she asked brightly.

'Groggy,' said Connie.

The nurse nodded. 'That's to be expected. But you'll be glad to know you're doing very well. We'll keep you in for observation, but all the signs are looking good, so you should be OK to go home before too long.'

She went on with her checks and Connie just lay there inertly. When the nurse had finished, she looked down at Connie.

'Your husband's *very* keen to come in and see you—do you think you're up to it?'

Connie's stomach hollowed.

'No,' she said.

She shut her eyes, the lids suddenly as heavy as lead, and sleep took her. A blessed relief.

Dante was pacing. Pacing up and down the wide, carpeted corridor outside Connie's room. He'd had her moved to the private wing of the hospital, into a room of her own.

Further down the corridor, in a wide area that was provided with comfortable chairs, Rafaello was seated, reading one of the newspapers provided. He was still as calm as Dante was agitatedly restless.

'The doctors say she is fine, Dante,' he said, and not for the first time. 'She was concussed, but the scans are clear. She needs rest, and observation, and some pain meds.'

Dante ignored him. He went back to pacing. Up, and then down. Up and then down.

Connie, so close, just the other side of a door, might as well have been on the far side of the moon.

Connie was sitting up. She felt frail, but that was all. She was on painkillers, still wired up so the medics could check her blood oxygen and whatever else they wanted to keep an eye on, but other than that she was OK.

Or so they kept telling her.

It was a lie, of course.

How could she be OK?

How can I be OK ever again?

The nurse finished her latest round of checks and readings, then smiled brightly at Connie.

'If I don't let that husband of yours in soon,' she said, 'he's likely to tear the door off its hinges! Can I let him in, finally?'

Connie shut her eyes, the way she had last time, but this time blessed sleep did not come to her rescue.

'I'll take that as a yes,' said the nurse. And there was more than a touch of humour in her voice as she said, heading towards the door, 'I can tell you now: if I had a husband who looked like that I'd have him right in here holding my hand!'

She gave an extravagant sigh and went out.

Connie heard her saying, 'You can go in now, Mr Cavelli. But not for very long. Your wife is still very tired.'

Connie heard the deep sound of Dante's voice answering the nurse, and then he was thrusting open the door and striding in. But she was busy—very busy—keeping her eyes tight shut.

She felt his shadow fall over her, felt his presence. Heard him speak her name. His voice was low, strained, hesitant. Not the harsh anger that she had been expecting.

'How…how are you feeling?'

She wanted to keep her eyes closed. Wanted sleep to claim her, or oblivion in any form, but knew she could not avoid him for ever.

She opened her eyes and he was there, in her vision instantly. Standing by her bed, so tall and so dark against the light.

'We…we have to talk,' she heard him say.

His voice was still quiet and a little hoarse. His face

worked, and she saw emotion flashing across it. Incomprehension.

'Connie—*why* did you leave me? Leave me when you did?'

Her eyes slid away from him. It was impossible to tell him the truth.

'It…it was just as Rafaello said. We were always going to get divorced. I just…like he said…accelerated it…'

It was all she could get out.

'But *why*? Connie—why then? What happened? I don't understand! We were so *good* together, and we were having such a wonderful time. It was like a non-stop holiday. So *why*—?'

He broke off. She'd heard the total incomprehension in his voice. It matched the look on his face. Like a knife in her heart, it told her everything that she already knew. Had known since he'd clearly spelt it out to her on that last unbearable night in Rome. Spelt out just why all her stupid dreams had been just that.

Something was changing in his face. Something hard, and edged like a blade.

'Is this to do with Raf?' He stood there, looking down at her. Eyes like knives. 'Egging you on. Resting his hand on your shoulder like he has a right to touch you.'

She was staring at him. Staring at him with an incomprehension in her face that outdid even his.

'Raf…?' she breathed. 'You think *Raf*—?'

She broke off, not even capable of putting into words what Dante was implying.

'Maybe that's why he's so keen on you getting divorced ASAP! So *he* can move in on you!'

Her face worked. She tried to speak, but couldn't. What could she say? What could she possibly say to that?

She saw emotion flash again across Dante's face. A different one this time. Vehement and possessive.

'Well, he can take a hike! I won't let him near you! Because you're mine, Connie! *Mine!* My wife!'

She felt her face start to crumple.

'Don't say that, Dante. Don't say it. It doesn't mean anything!' She took a breath…a rasping one. 'We both know why we married—it got us what we wanted. You got your inheritance and I got security for my grandmother.' She shut her eyes. 'That was all we wanted…'

'To getting what we want.'

The words of his toast as they'd drunk champagne to celebrate their wedding on the private jet stabbed in her head again.

True for him. But, oh, not for me—not for me! Because I have come to want so much more! Something that he cannot give me—can never give me…

Anguish filled her…possessed her utterly.

There was silence. Silence all around her.

Then she heard Dante speak. Slowly. Heavily.

'That isn't actually true.'

She heard him breathe in, then go on.

'It stopped being true that night in London. When you walked into that cocktail bar and knocked the breath from my lungs.'

She shook her head, eyes still shut. 'No,' she said.

She opened her eyes, looked right at him before she spelt out the truth that it had cost her so dearly to discover…to face up to.

'What has been between us since that night,' she said, speaking slowly, carefully, every word a blade on her skin, 'has nothing to do with marriage. It was simply…simply an affair.'

She had known that since that last dreadful night in Rome. An affair was all that Dante had wanted from her. That was the truth that had made a mockery of her hopes and dreams. She'd wanted to make their marriage a real one—had thought that was what was happening between them. But it wasn't. Because all Dante had wanted from the moment she'd walked into that cocktail bar and seen desire flare in his eyes—desire for *her,* the woman he'd made himself marry to get his inheritance—was an affair.

An affair to while away the time until he could safely divorce her, as he'd always intended. Until he could part company with her. Get his life back.

'It was all you ever wanted,' she said now. 'An affair. And now I've called time on it.'

Dante heard her words. They hung in the air between them as she looked at him, so pale, propped up on the hospital pillows. There was a dressing on her head where she'd smashed into the lamppost. A drip in her arm. She was wired up to a monitor. An oxygen meter on her finger.

I could have lost her today.

The words rang in his head. Just as they had when he'd seen her fall, seen her lying on the payment. Unconscious. Bleeding.

Her blood is on my hands.

He felt emotions rise in him like a river, a tide, an ocean. Flowing together, coming together, surging in his veins.

Slowly, he began to speak. Feeling for each word, placing one after another so carefully. And all the while that great tide of emotion was sweeping around his body, forcing out those words that rose to his lips.

It was impossible not to speak. It was essential that he

speak. As essential as air to breathe and water to drink and food to eat... Essential to his very existence.

Each word was distinct, coming, it seemed, from very far away—from a place that no longer existed nor ever could again.

'You know that when I married you, Connie, I bitterly resented having to do so. Having to marry at all! Having my hand forced by my grandfather. Being controlled by him from beyond the grave the way he'd controlled me in life. I wanted only two things from my marriage to you—to get my inheritance and then to end that marriage.'

He frowned.

'What I said to you, Connie, that last evening in Rome, was completely true. For all that I never wanted to marry, you had proved to be an absolute Trojan. I appreciated you so much. You'd accepted everything on the terms I wanted. Everything.'

He stopped, tried to look at her, but wasn't seeing her.

'Even after you came back from that health resort looking so incredible...even after that you still accepted everything on my terms. And I realised I could have it all. I could have you, so warm and lovely and irresistible. I could have you and I could still, when the time was right, have my freedom back. Courtesy of our divorce.'

His expression changed. Became troubled.

'That was why I was so adamant that no one knew of our marriage. I didn't want wedding rings, or you changing your name, or even for you to meet any of my friends—except Raf, who knew all about you anyway. I didn't want you to be my wife in more than name only—because I didn't want a wife at all.'

His frown deepened. Suddenly it felt as if a stiletto were

being slipped into his ribs—intangible on impact, but deadly in effect...

'But when you left me the day I flew to Geneva...when it was *you* filing for divorce...it was then I realised how completely and totally meaningless it had been to want my life back.'

He felt emotion soar from some deep place inside himself he had never known existed. A place that was suddenly blazing with light. With clarity. With truth.

'Because you *were* my life, Connie. And I knew that without you I had no life. There would be no life worth living without you in it.'

He saw her face work...her beautiful deep blue eyes fill with diamond tears. But she did not speak or move.

So he did. Lowering himself to sit on her bed, he took her hand—the hand that had never had his ring upon its finger, nor put one on his, anticipating the day when he'd get his own life back and be free again.

But I shall never be free—for freedom would only be loss. The loss of all that is most precious to me.

He felt her fingers press into his, heard her try to speak, and then he was lifting her hand to his mouth, bringing it to his lips, holding it fast. He lowered it, closing his other hand around it so that both her hands were held tightly, so very tightly, between his.

It was as if his very life depended on it. The life he wanted—the only life would ever want now that he could see, could know, the truth of it...

'No life worth living,' he said again.

And he was seeing her now—who she was and what she was and what she would *always* be to him.

'No life worth living without the woman I love.'

A cry came from her as if torn from deep inside her. The diamond tears in her eyes spilled over.

'I'd begun to hope that you had started to feel for me what I was feeling for you,' she said. 'I wanted so badly to believe that you had come to think of me as a real wife— a wife for ever...'

Her tears were coursing down her cheeks. Tears he had caused. Tears he would never let her shed over him again. Emotion was pouring through him, rich and warm and golden. Filling every cell in his body.

He bent forward, kissing her tear-wet eyes, and then, in tender homage, grazed her soft, trembling lips with his.

It was, without doubt, the sweetest, most precious moment in all the world.

How could I have not known? How could I have not seen? Not realised what was happening day after day? Night after night? Not known how precious she is to me?

It seemed extraordinary to him now. Extraordinary and unbelievable. That he had gone on thinking for so long that the original reasons why they had married still had anything at all to do with what was between them now...

He lifted his mouth away from hers, his eyes pouring golden love into the beautiful blue ones that were lifted to his with an expression of wonder in them that made his heart turn over until he felt breathless.

He gave a smile. A crooked smile. Pressed her hands fast between his. Holding them against his heart, which from this moment on would beat for her and her alone.

Then a regretful expression appeared in his eyes. He shook his head in rueful self-castigation. 'You know,' he said, and there was sincere remorse in his voice as eyes poured gold into hers, '*la mia amata moglie*—my most beloved—you're going to have to face having a husband who, for all his financial savvy, is absolutely, shamefully and extraordinarily stupid.'

A voice spoke from the doorway. 'I will second that,' said Rafaello.

Dante's head whipped round. Rafaello was lounging against the doorjamb, perusing the scene. Dante was about to speak, but Rafaello's attention was on Connie now.

'He's an idiot,' he said, with a smile in his voice, 'and I've had to go to quite ridiculous lengths to get him to finally realise it—shocking him into it with the threat of the divorce I urged you to pursue, Connie.'

His smile deepened.

'But for all his idiocy and blindness in not realising that you were the one he must keep and cherish all his life, he's still my friend.' He levered himself away from the doorjamb. 'And if he hasn't told you yet that he loves you just as much as it is obvious to me that you love him—well, then, he's an even bigger idiot than I think him already!'

Dante threw him a dagger glance, but this time it had no real blade in it. 'Raf, get out!' he said warningly, but in a friendly fashion.

Rafaello threw up a hand. 'I only looked in to tell you the nurse says five minutes longer and no more.'

He retreated, closing the door behind him. Dante turned his attention back to Connie. The only place he wanted it to be—would only ever want it to be.

He pressed her hands. 'Five minutes, hmm…? Well, I think I can do it in that time.'

He bent forward, dropping down on to one knee but never for an instant letting go of Connie's hand. He thought he would never let it go again, for all his days.

He lowered his mouth to Connie's knuckles, which

seemed to tremble at his touch. And as he lifted his mouth away his eyes pinned hers, blazing with golden light.

'You stole into my heart, Connie, and I didn't even know you were doing it. Your sweetness of nature, your devotion to your grandmother, the way I could talk to you, relax with you, be myself with you… You were becoming important to me, but I never realised just how much. And then, when you came to London and I saw just how beautiful you are, I wanted to sweep you away with me, into my arms, and keep you there. All those wonderful days and nights in Italy were so incredibly precious to me. The happiest time of my life—'

He broke off, emotion choking him.

Then: 'I want that happiness to be for ever. For you and for me. I want our marriage to be a real one.'

His grip on her hand tightened.

He took a breath and said what was in his heart. 'I proposed to you once, sitting in your grandmother's parlour, and you stared at me as if I were mad.' He gave a rueful twist of his mouth. 'Would you stare at me that way again if I proposed now?'

He saw the tears well in her eyes again, felt her hand tremble in his again.

He took it as a good sign.

And proposed to her all over again.

She heard his words. Heard his voice. Heard in both all that she'd longed to hear.

'I initially gave you many reasons for our marriage,' she heard him say, 'but now I give you only one.'

She saw his expression change, felt his clasp on her hand tighten. Emotion welled within her, and her fingers tightened on his in return.

Dante's eyes clung to hers. 'The reason I'm asking you to

make your life with me, for ever and for always, is purely one abiding, eternal reason. For love.'

She leaned forward, kissed him on the mouth. His name broke from her, and it was apparently all he needed to hear, for his hand loosed hers and snaked around the nape of her neck, returning her kiss.

It was bliss, it was wonder, it was glory and it was happiness.

And above all it was love.

All that she had ever longed for.

And now possessed.

EPILOGUE

'THIS REALLY IS the most beautiful garden...' breathed Connie. 'The scent of the lavender is heavenly.' Her expression grew poignant. 'Like the lavender in Gran's cottage garden...'

She leant back into Dante's sheltering arms. The West Country cottage would always be there for them, but Connie had given the use of it to a charity that provided respite care for family carers in need of a break— and she knew her grandmother would have approved of that.

Their main home—hers and Dante's—was a spacious villa surrounded by gardens in the lush Lombardy countryside, within commuting distance of Milan for Dante.

Dante had kept his modern apartment for when they wanted to be in the city. Although... He smiled to himself. He was finding that country life was suiting him fine. Just fine.

And how should it not?

His arms wound around Connie—his adored, most precious Connie, the light of his life and the wonder of his heart. He stood with her there on the sunlit terrace, bathed in the warm Italian sun, with the heady scent of lavender all about them.

'She would be so very happy for me,' she said quietly.

Dante gave a wry laugh. 'And so, I know, would my

grandfather for me. Everything he plotted and schemed for has come about.' His voice changed, became sad, regretful. 'I wish I had realised just why it was he put that clause in his will. I thought it was because he wanted to control me... the way he had controlled me all my life. But...' he took a difficult but necessary breath '...but now I know it was for a different reason. He wanted to protect me.'

He was silent for a moment, then spoke again.

'He wanted to protect me from having no one in my life. With my feckless parents gone, and with him gone too, he wanted me to have someone who was important to me. Someone who mattered. And for me to matter to someone in turn.'

Connie felt his arms tighten around her, and she pressed her own hands over his encircling ones.

'He gave me a gift I'd never realised I wanted,' he said, and now his mouth kissed her throat, soft and sensuous and blissfully possessive. 'A gift that is beyond price.'

She craned her head back, turning so that she could catch his lips with hers.

'As you are to me,' she said, her eyes aglow with all the love she felt for him, the love she would always feel. Her heart was overflowing with it.

For a while they stood there in total, absolute contentment, drinking in the scent of lavender, basking in the sunshine, Dante holding Connie close against him.

'When did Raf say he would be here?' she asked.

'Late afternoon,' Dante answered. He gave another wry laugh. 'I still resent that he could see so damnably clearly what was happening to me. That I was falling in love with you and didn't even know it myself!'

It was Connie's turn to laugh. 'Just as he could see that I was utterly in love with you.'

Dante made a face. 'All that needling—all that interference of his. For one purpose only. To get me to realise what you meant to me. He was baiting me about domestic bliss just to wake me up to the fact that that was exactly what I wanted!'

Connie turned in Dante's arms, winding her own around his neck and gazing up at him adoringly. 'And that is what we have, haven't we?' she said, love lighting up her eyes.

The same loving expression was in his own eyes as he looked down at her. 'Can you doubt it, Signora Cavelli, for one single, solitary second?'

She shook her head.

No, there were no doubts, and no possibility of doubts.

She felt her heart catch.

No possibility of anything except endless happiness.

All that she, and he, could ever want.

* * * * *

HIS ASSISTANT'S NEW YORK AWAKENING

EMMY GRAYSON

MILLS & BOON

For Chad, Emma and Gene.

October souls gone too soon.

CHAPTER ONE

THE MUSIC SLID over Damon Bradford's skin like a lover's caress. He sipped his cocktail, the smooth taste of gin lingering
on his tongue. Better to focus on that then the slow, languid
heat spreading through his veins as he watched her.

The cellist.

Music had never been an important part of his life. He knew
the difference between classical and rock, paid hefty sums
for bands and singers to perform at the various functions he
hosted throughout the year. But the actual music had always
been background noise.

Whereas this…the rich somber notes of her solo rising and
falling with perfect precision, the languid tempo encouraging listeners to slow down, to forget the demands of life for
a moment…

It was unlike anything he'd ever heard before.

Just like the woman behind the cello was unlike anyone he
had ever encountered before.

He would have dismissed her at first glance if she hadn't
been playing. Blond hair wound into a tight bun at the base of
her neck. Black dress loose about the torso, sleeves down to
her elbows, a full skirt draped over her knees as she cradled
the cello between her legs.

Nondescript. Plain. Boring.

It had been her fingers that had first caught his eye. Pale, slender and elegant as one hand moved the bow with exactitude, the other sliding up and down the strings with graceful mastery that made his muscles tighten.

Turned on by a damn cello.

He sipped his cocktail, savoring the flavors of gin and lavender as he waited for the cool drink to calm his errant libido.

No such luck. The music had penetrated his body, piercing through his custom-tailored tuxedo and the calm, collected exterior he usually portrayed to the world. His gaze was drawn back up to her face.

Wide lips set into a heart-shaped face, the sharp cut of her chin at odds with her rounded cheeks. *Striking* was the first word that came to mind. Yet she downplayed her appearance with simple clothes and a severe hairstyle. A woman, he decided as he listened to her coax emotion out of every note, who was trying to keep the focus on her music and off herself.

The rest of the orchestra joined in, the harmony of the four dozen or so instruments filling the ballroom. A volunteer symphony made up of musicians still working toward their big breaks. He'd been hesitant when his event manager, Kimberly, had submitted the entertainment schedule and it included the opening-hour music being performed by the New York City Apprentice Symphony. When he'd questioned her, she had presented it as an opportunity to engage with a community organization.

With one more glance at the woman who had captured his attention, he was suddenly very glad he'd let Kimberly have her way.

Damon tore his gaze away from the cellist and gazed out over the modern ballroom, filled with the richest people in New York City.

The majority of the guests at the annual Bradford Global Gala Fundraiser were there to be seen in their most expensive clothes, enjoy exclusive cocktails, perhaps pick up a new

lover or cement a business deal over caviar. A couple were
there because they genuinely wanted to see a new wing added
to the children's hospital, the selected recipient of this year's
fundraiser.

But none were there because of the music.

A pity, Damon thought as he watched the crowd of people talking, laughing. Unfortunately, he was more like them
than he cared to admit. Not noticing the simple joys around
him. Always focused on something else, the next to-do on his
never-ending list. He moved from one goal to another with
thoroughness and a speed that impressed his employees and
clients, irritated his competitors and, most importantly, kept
him moving forward.

Never back.

Yet he had found himself at that place he'd heard others
mumble and complain about but never thought he himself
would end up at—a crossroads. Bradford Global was one of the
top manufacturers of a variety of products and was in the final
running for a major contract with a luxury European airline.
He owned homes on four continents, spoke three languages
fluently and was a frequent feature on the covers of maga-
zines like *Fortune*. Edward Charles Damon Bradford had it all.

So why did he feel so damn empty?

It was a notable lack of pleasure, joy, even a hint of contentment that had driven him to the edge of the ballroom tonight. Restlessness had carried his feet past the people trying
to get his attention, past his personal assistant and the event
coordinator wanting his input on the décor to the secluded
alcove. Boredom had driven him to sit down in one of the
two wingback chairs hidden from view of most of the people milling about, his primary view the musicians on the elevated stage. He had wanted different, craved a change, no
matter how small.

And he'd found that change sitting toward the back wall of

the ballroom with a cello between her thighs, sadness flickering across her face as she tilted her head up, eyes still closed, her body bound to the music she created.

He should stand up, rejoin the crowd. Yes, he'd wanted different, new, exciting. But the lust simmering below the surface for a woman he'd just seen was a little too heated, like a fire about to break free and burst into a raging inferno. Yes, he wanted change.

He also wanted—needed—to stay in control.

He started to stand up, to resume visiting with politicians, billionaires and movie stars. To walk away from the temptation that had unexpectedly wrapped around him and sunk talons deep into his skin.

Then the music stopped. Noises still filled the ballroom—glasses clinking, a man laughing a little too loudly, heels clicking on the marble floor. People continued on as if nothing had changed.

The musician opened her eyes. From this distance, he couldn't discern the color. He watched as she leaned over, acknowledged something another musician said with a small smile. Damon's event planner took to the stage to announce a fifteen-minute break between the symphony and the next band that would play.

The cellist propped her instrument on a stand and stood. Slight of figure, a little shorter than he'd anticipated but strength evident in the set of her shoulders, the confident tilt of her chin.

Then she looked up. Their gazes collided, held as something electric sizzled between them.

Oh, yes. He should definitely walk away, back into the safety of the crowds and the people who wanted nothing more than a minute of his time or a few millions of his fortune.

But, he thought with a sudden wild abandon, where was the fun in that?

* * *

Evolet Grey walked back into the ballroom and, despite her best intentions, found her eyes drifting to the small alcove at the edge of the space. Awareness filled her body as her eyes connected once more with that of the handsome behemoth of a man lounging in a wingback chair. Others might've perceived his posture as relaxed, but he reminded her of a predator lying in wait, deceptively calm as he waited for his prey to come closer. A shiver danced down her spine, but God help her, she couldn't look away.

Her gaze traveled down over his black tuxedo, stark against the white of the chair, and then back up to his face. Notes danced in her head, landing on the imaginary staff lines she'd conjured and creating a brooding, sensual melody for the mystery man in the alcove.

Classically handsome. Dark brown hair worn thick on top and short on the sides. The aloof expression on his square face, coupled with the slight hollows beneath his cheekbones, made him seem cold, distant.

Except for his eyes. A hint of something wild lurked beneath the tightly buttoned-up surface.

That hint of wild did funny things to her insides. Like quicken her heartbeat and make heat pool low in her belly.

Stop.

She looked away, cutting off the naughty direction of her errant thoughts. She made her way over to the bar closest to the stage. It wasn't every day she got to have a drink in a hotel like the Winchester. The ballroom was a little more modern than she'd prefer, with soaring pillars and floor-to-ceiling windows that overlooked Central Park just across the street. But still, she had to acknowledge, elegantly done up for tonight's gala. Whoever had planned tonight's event had money with a capital *M*. A dance floor of wood so dark it was almost black dominated the center of the room. White chairs and couches had been clustered around the edges, creating intimate spaces for one to escape to if they needed a breather or a quiet place to conduct business. The walls glowed with blue-and-violet lighting. A minor detail, but it managed to make the space feel intimate even though there were close to five hundred people milling about dressed in their most glamorous clothes.

A woman passed by in a backless red dress with several feet of silk trailing after her. A man walked by with an actual monocle trimmed in what she guessed were real diamonds.

Evolet's stomach did a nervous roll. This wasn't her world. Far from it. She hadn't felt it onstage. There she had been in control, in her element. But out here, among the jewelry and the haute couture clothes and the scent of money thick in the air, she felt like a nobody.

¡Para!

A smile curved her lips as she heard her adoptive mother Constanza's husky voice in her head. She was every bit loving and supportive but had zero tolerance for self-pity and no patience for those who placed value on money rather than family.

If Constanza were here, she would have arched her razor-thin brow at the silk trailing on the floor, tsked at the waste of good material and then said something like, *You've earned your place here,* mija. *Now stop moping and enjoy yourself.*

With the much-needed boost to her self-confidence, Evolet continued across the floor. She would have a drink, enjoy a few minutes in the most elegant room she'd ever been in and then go home for a soak in the tub.

And, she thought as her smile spread, perhaps entertain a fantasy or two about the mysterious man who had made her pulse race. She'd learned from the few dates she'd been on since graduating that fantasies—at least when it came to romance—were usually more enjoyable than the actual experience.

She was almost to the bar when a hand gripped her elbow.

"Aren't you a sight for sore eyes?"

The stench of too much alcohol stung her nose. She started to turn just before an arm slid about her waist and pulled her closer to the offending smell.

"What's your name? Haven't seen you at one of these galas before."

She found herself face-to-face with a bleary-eyed blond man. His leering smile didn't quite stretch all the way, as if his lips were just as intoxicated as he was and couldn't hold themselves up.

"I'm with the symphony," she said in as polite a voice as she could muster. She grabbed his hand and pulled it off her waist while taking a deliberate step back.

"I've heard great things about musicians. Very talented hands." The suggestive lift of his eyebrows made her cringe. "Perhaps after the gala we could find out if they're true."

She barely stopped herself from gagging. Wealth obviously didn't equal class or charm. Her eyes dropped to his hands, one clutched around a martini glass, the other sporting a fancy silver watch and an ornate wedding ring.

She forced a smile onto her face even as disgust rolled in her belly. "I'm fortunate to play alongside some very gifted musicians," she replied coolly. "Unfortunately, we only perform as a group. I'm not available for private performances."

He blinked at her, a frown breaking through his intoxication. "I'm not asking for a musical," he sputtered. "I'm asking for—"

"Is that your wife?"

A look akin to fear crossed the man's face as his head whipped around. Evolet took the opportunity to lean forward, place a finger under the martini glass and lift up. A flick was all it took for the peachy-pink drink to spill onto the man's white shirt. The glass tumbled from his fingers and crashed onto the floor. The music playing from the speakers and the chattering of the guests muffled some of the commotion, but a number of people turned to see who had dropped the glass.

The man's face reddened as he looked from his shirt down to the offending pile of broken glass at his feet.

"Did you…" He looked up at her and then back down again. She almost felt bad for him as he blinked and struggled to make sense of what just happened. "Did I do that?"

"You did, Harry."

Evolet froze. The deep velvet-timbred tone came from behind and slid over her skin, sparking little fires as it wound around her and made her suck in a breath even as panic fluttered in her chest. Had the owner of the seductive voice seen her maneuver?

Harry's face paled at an astonishingly fast speed.

"Oh…um, I think I just had a little too much—"

"Harry!"

Evolet almost felt sorry for Harry when the remaining color in his face disappeared, replaced with stark white fear as a slender woman with jet-black hair piled high in an elegant arrangement of curls walked up to him, her eyes hard.

Almost.

"Darling, there you are." The woman slid her arm through Harry's, her manicured fingernails digging into the sleeve of his jacket like claws. "The Joneses have been asking after you." She aimed a brittle smile at Evolet and whoever stood behind her before dragging off a very unhappy-looking Harry.

Evolet steeled herself for whatever was behind her and turned.

You.

CHAPTER TWO

HER MYSTERY MAN stood before her, tall and dark and brooding. She tilted her chin up and met his gaze head-on. And
what a gaze it was. Emerald shot through with flecks of gold,
framed by thick brows that were currently drawn together as
he studied her. The amused twist of his full lips told her he
had seen her little maneuver.

"Thank you," she said.

One of those brows shot up.

"For what? Seems like you had everything in hand."

Heat rose in her cheeks. "It was just—"

"A clever way of dealing with an insufferable ass who
drinks too much and hits on anyone who is not his wife."

Evolet bit down on her bottom lip to stop her grin.

"Well…thank you." She cast a quick glance around. Thankfully people had returned to their private conversations, and
a fast-acting server had already swept up the glass. No permanent damage seemed to have been done. "I appreciate your
discretion."

His lips tilted up another notch. "You're welcome." He nodded toward the bar. "Anthony is a magician when it comes
to drinks. After your run-in with Harry, you could probably
use one."

She focused on the menu, written in an elegant script, and
not on the distracting man standing a breath away from her.
"The Lavender Spy, please."

She felt the man start next to her. But when she glanced up, his face was impassive as he looked out over the crowds with a bored expression. Anthony handed her a glass filled with a pale purple drink topped off with a sprig of lavender. She thanked him and raised the glass to her lips.

"Oh, wow," she breathed as the mixture of gin, lavender and lime hit her tongue. "That's delicious."

"Do you enjoy gin often?"

"This is my first time," she replied as she took another sip. "I don't do much drinking. None at all, actually. I'm usually practicing or performing." Or working as a floating executive assistant, but she kept that part out. It was just a stop on the way to her ultimate goal of playing professionally for an orchestra. "Leaves little time for happy hour."

"How did you decide on the cello?"

The rumble of his voice rolled through her once more, deep and delicious. Her fingers tightened on her glass as butterflies fluttered in her stomach.

Down, girl.

"The first time I heard one was in the subway. I was walking and heard music. It was incredible."

The memory of it washed over her. She'd only been with Constanza a few weeks and had been pushing her then foster mother away with biting insults or cold silences. That Constanza had replied with a table heaped with traditional Haitian foods, freshly laundered clothes and a gentle smile had made her feel guilty, which had made her angrier. The walls she'd built over the years had trembled with every kind gesture, and damn it, she hadn't wanted that. She hadn't wanted to get attached when she could've been yanked away at any moment.

Which had made the deep tug in her chest as she'd heard the first haunting strains of the cello in the tunnels more powerful, as if someone was calling to her who finally understood all of her pain, her heartache and loss.

She'd followed the music through the people crowding the tunnels at rush hour. Everything else had faded: the rumble of the trains, the cacophony of voices, the incessant beeping and ringing of phones.

There had only been the music.

"Like angels singing?"

She blinked and refocused on the man with a frown.

"No, the opposite. He was…" Her hand came up, her fingers moving in the air as she mimicked the movements she'd seen the day her world had changed. The day she'd stopped surviving and started living. "He was making the cello weep."

"Weep?"

She took another drink to cover her wince. Not the most PR-friendly way of describing the beginning of her music career. These people wanted glitz and glamour, not sad and depressing.

But something in the way he looked at her, with an intensity that made her feel as if he could see beneath all the years of practice, made her want to tell him. To share what had led her from a tiny two-bedroom apartment in East Harlem to performing in a string orchestra in one of the ritziest hotels in New York City.

Don't do it.

Hadn't she learned her lesson over the years? Trusting and confiding in someone opened the door to getting one's hopes up. To getting hurt. Constanza had been a miracle, a gift she'd never expected to receive, but also a rarity. No one before or since had been there for her.

The reminder helped her rein in her memories. She let out a light laugh.

"Musicians can be a bit dramatic. I enjoyed the music. The cellist was kind enough to answer my questions after he played. I started taking lessons, and here I am," she finished with a gesture to one of the nearby glass cocktail tables topped off with white blooms and flickering candles.

The man's frown deepened. "That's not what you were going to say."

Now it was her turn to frown, partially at his firm tone and partially at his bold words. Had she misread him?

"Excuse me?"

He leaned in, but unlike with Harry, his closeness didn't inspire disgust. It made her breath catch in her chest and that damned heat burn hotter, intoxicating even as she silently cursed it. She did not want to be attracted to anyone, let alone a rich playboy who probably dated models and actresses and politicians.

Someone who would never look twice at someone like her.

The urge to flee descended on her rapidly. Her pulse started to flutter, and she cast about for a reason to leave as the lead singer of the band called everyone to join him on the dance floor. Her lips parted, some inane excuse drifting up. She nearly dropped her own drink when his fingers closed firmly about her hand. Her head jerked up, and she read in his eyes that he knew she'd been about to walk away.

"Dance with me."

Evolet had always thought nothing could be more seductive than the sounds of her cello. More than one man had accused her of being a cold fish, a criticism she'd taken in stride because no man had ever enticed her beyond a second date or an unsatisfying kiss good-night. Ever since she'd wandered down a subway tunnel at fifteen in search of a song that had called to her, only two things had mattered to her in the world: Constanza and her cello.

But now, as his invitation penetrated her shock, she had the unsettling feeling of her world shifting. If she said yes, it would shift even further. She wouldn't see this man beyond this night. Yet she would always carry the memory of his touch, the remembrance of his hand wrapped possessively around hers.

And the lingering memory of what a dance with him would have been like.

"All right."

Before she questioned her own judgment, before she could even blink, he plucked her drink from her hand, set it back down on the bar and, with a light touch of fingers on the small of her back that burned through the material of her dress, whisked her onto the dance floor.

"You've done that before."

He gave her a wolfish smile. "Done what?"

His fingers firmed against her back, the palm of his hand pressing her body closer to his. His other hand captured one of hers in a gentle grasp, as if he knew if he squeezed too tightly she would leave. The contact of skin against skin made her dizzier than any embrace or kiss she'd ever experienced.

"Seduced a woman to dance with you," she said breathlessly.

Fire flashed in his eyes. "Do you feel like I'm seducing you…?" His voice trailed off as he arched a brow. "I don't know your name."

"Likewise," she retorted. She was rewarded with a deep rumble of laughter that seemed to surprise both of them.

"Let's trade, shall we?"

Her eyes drifted down to his mouth. His smile stole some of the shadows from his eyes. What would it be like to kiss him? To taste his lips against hers, open her mouth to his and—

"Trade?" she whispered.

His smile widened, and her chest tightened.

"You tell me your name. I'll tell you mine."

Oh, no, she was *enjoying* this. Enjoying the banter with a handsome, wealthy man who, for whatever reason, was interested in talking to her. For someone who wasn't used to being wanted in any capacity, to have a man want to dance with her, to spend time with her, was exhilarating.

The tempo of the music picked up. Uncertainty made her stumble. The man's hand tightened on hers, steadying her.

"Relax."

"It's hard when I don't know what I'm doing."

"Trust me."

He said it with humor in his voice. But his gaze was intense, piercing through the armor she kept wrapped around herself. Torn between vulnerability and defiance, she paused.

Until one corner of his mouth quirked up in that sexy half smile. Daring her.

She raised her chin as she forced herself to ease into his embrace. As he spun her into a turn, she leaned into him. The first moment was terrifying. When was the last time she had surrendered control, trusted someone else?

But he didn't give her time to be afraid. He took advantage of her submission and spun her into another turn with a bold confidence that brought an entranced smile to her lips. He replied with a smile of his own that transformed his brooding attractiveness into one of devastating handsomeness.

He led her through the rest of the dance with strength and skill. Most of the other dancers swayed back and forth. A few attempted similar moves as her mystery man, but none replicated his talent.

As the music wound down, Evolet arched a brow. "Are you a professional ballroom dancer?"

He chuckled. "Far from it. That is the one dance I know how to do well."

"Very well."

"My mother was a good teacher."

The humor in his eyes dimmed, replaced by an emotion Evolet knew all too well.

Anguish.

"What happened to her?" she asked softly.

His gaze slid back to her. In the span of a breath, Evolet saw it all: heartbreak, agony, despair.

Then his stare hardened, freezing out the emotions displayed so nakedly just a moment ago. This time his smile was practiced, one she'd spied on the faces of the other richly attired men in the ballroom.

"I'll get you a fresh drink."

She felt the rejection like a slap. She stepped back, frowning when he took his time releasing her from his hold. Their interlude had been wonderful, a fairy tale come true for a drink and a dance.

And now it was over. She'd learned her lesson and stopped reaching for the stars when it came to relationships and people. Some stars would always be too far out of reach. That she had wanted their time together to last longer than the song they'd danced to made it even more imperative that she leave now. When it came to people, wanting and hoping were fatal flaws. People died, like her father. People left, like her mother. Constanza had left her in the end, even if it hadn't been her choice.

People were unpredictable. Uncontrollable. They could inflict pain, even if they didn't mean to.

Evolet's eyes drifted back to the stage. The memory of the gleaming wood of her cello calmed the tumultuous emotions tangling and fighting for dominance in her chest. She could depend on her cello, her talents and her own hard work.

Yes, she'd been able to depend on her dark-haired stranger for a dance. She hadn't even realized that she had entertained a brief fantasy that their time together would extend beyond the music. But he had reminded her with his swift rejection of her inquiry that there was nothing between them but the novelty of a few minutes spent together in a luxurious surrounding. He'd find her interesting tonight, perhaps a little longer. Then his curiosity would pass, along with the uniqueness of the company of a struggling cellist. He would return to his world, and she'd return to hers.

She had no desire to experience that emotional roller coaster. Especially, she acknowledged reluctantly, because this man had the potential to leave her with some deep scars on her already battered heart.

"It's late," she said in answer to his frown.

He glanced down at his watch. The stainless steel band glinted under the lights of the chandelier. Probably cost more than her cello.

"It's just past eight o'clock."

"And it'll take me an hour to get home." She held out her hand. "Thank you for the dance."

She knew she'd made a mistake the moment his fingers enveloped hers in a firm grip. The sensation of his skin sliding against hers made her gasp. Her heart pounded so fiercely she wondered if he could hear it above the music.

Yet when her eyes darted up to his face, it was to meet an impenetrable emerald gaze that doused the lingering sparks of her attraction.

"Enjoy the rest of your evening," he said coolly.

She nodded and turned away, then wove her way among the dancers as she tried to keep her pace steady so it didn't look like she was running. She breathed in deeply and summoned her mental checklist. The music, clinks of glasses and murmurs of conversation faded as she ran down her tasks: collect her cello, grab her coat, walk to the Fifty-Ninth Street subway station.

She'd almost made it to the edge of the ballroom when temptation reared its evil little head. With a resigned sigh, she looked over her shoulder for one last glance at the opulence she'd enjoyed and, perhaps, the man who had briefly whisked her into a fantasy.

Another mistake, she realized belatedly. He stood on the

opposite side of the ballroom, a fresh drink in hand, leaning against the bar with a casual, aloof stance as two women in stunning evening gowns talked to him. The redhead laid her hand on the sleeve of his jacket in a gesture Evolet recognized as the move of a woman who had found something she wanted.

Her stomach sank. Ridiculous to experience jealousy over a man she had just met—and would never meet again. Even more foolish to be disappointed that her suspicion that she was nothing more than a blip in his wealthy existence had been proven accurate.

He looked up, and she bit back a gasp as he stared right at her. Desire flared low in her belly before burning a trail through her veins. Images filled her mind, of bodies tangled together in a carnal dance far more intimate than the one they had just shared.

The erotic vividness of her fantasy shocked her. Her lips parted, and despite the distance between them, she saw his gaze darken. Was it her imagination, or did the air around her grow heavy, pressing on her skin with the promise of what could be between them?

Between you and a man you barely know?

She grabbed on to the thin thread of sanity that broke through. A man who, in less than ten minutes, she'd shared one of the most defining moments of her life with.

No matter what existed between them for a night, a man like that would walk away with a woman's heart and never look back.

Evolet turned and fled.

CHAPTER THREE

DAMON HIT END on the call and let out a slow, satisfied breath. His lips quirked up at the corners as his blood hummed with pride. Bradford Global was in the final three for the manufacturing of Royal Air's upcoming fleet of jets.

Based out of Sweden, Royal Air had taken the travel world by storm ten years ago. They'd released a line of luxury planes that offered amenities on their transatlantic flights no longer found elsewhere unless someone had the good fortune, literally, to afford a first-class ticket. Three-course meals served on china plates, a complimentary cocktail and enough space for passengers over five feet tall—all at the same rates as their competitors—had catapulted them to superstardom.

Now they were building ten new planes, to be completed in two years or less as Royal Air's contract stipulated. With each plane worth close to $130 million dollars, it was a contract that had ignited fierce competition.

Winning the contract would be the ultimate achievement of his tenure as head of Bradford Global.

He glanced back at the hotel, at the glittering people wandering in and out of the bank of glass doors that lined the main entrance facing West Fifty-Ninth Street and the southern end of Central Park. There were some people inside he genuinely liked, some he even considered friends.

None of them would understand the value of the Royal Air

contract beyond the dollar signs attached to it. In moments like this, the faint pain that lingered just out of sight swelled into an ache that wrapped around his heart and squeezed so hard he had to force himself to breathe deeply.

Fourteen years. Fourteen years he had led Bradford Global. Fourteen years' worth of holidays and other important milestones he'd spent alone. Most of the time, he could keep the pain at bay. But tonight, more than anything, he wanted his parents by his side, to share the news and revel in how far Bradford Global had come, from a small plant in Illinois to being considered for Royal Air's luxury airplane contract, one of the most coveted projects in the manufacturing world.

Brown eyes ringed in gold appeared in his mind, with humor glimmering in their tawny depths. Damon's fingers tightened around his phone. He'd let down his guard tonight with the mysterious cellist. She'd intrigued him the moment those first haunting notes of her solo had carried across the ballroom and grabbed hold of something deep inside him. His interest had been furthered by her amusing way of handling Harry Dumont's drunken attempts at seduction.

Although his own flirtation had surprised him. He had no interest in long-term relationships, in marriage. Losing his parents had severed most of his interest in loving another person. He'd found salvation from his pain, his nightmares of the hell of his parents' final moments, in work, in things he could control.

If there had been any lingering desire for something like what his parents had enjoyed, it had been torpedoed by the kind of women he'd dated or associated with professionally. His last lover, Natalie Robinson, was the daughter of a senator. Refined, driven in her work as a marketer for a prominent hospital. Yet her true colors had shown as soon as he'd shown an ounce of leeway and allowed her to keep some things at his Park Avenue penthouse. On Valentine's Day less than two months later, she'd pounced like a predator and told him she had decided they were getting married.

Damon still thought about her sometimes when he walked past Cartier on Fifth Avenue and the $1.2 million ring they had tried to charge him for the next day. He'd sent her the bill and a professional mover with her things neatly packed in cardboard boxes. She'd accused him in a series of text messages and one nasty voice mail of being cold, of never opening up and forcing her to take action. He hadn't corrected her. He was cold. He had no interest in opening up, of being emotionally vulnerable to anyone.

Emotions couldn't be controlled. Emotions were chaos.

But he was more than capable of conducting a discreet, enjoyable affair without letting himself succumb to feelings.

He glanced back at the hotel once more. He'd been rude when she'd asked about his mother. He hadn't intended to be. His initial reaction had been one of surprised pleasure that someone would ask about her. That was by his choice, he reminded himself. He had made it clear to everyone, from his uncle and distant family to employees and lovers, that his parents were not to be a topic of conversation.

The realization that he'd done both himself and his parents a disservice by burying their memory had unnerved him. As had the sudden desire to tell a woman he'd just met what had happened the night a college student had drunk one too many, gotten behind the wheel and taken his family from him.

It was that want to share with her that had made him step back. He'd seen the hurt in her eyes, felt an uncomfortable prick of guilt that she had shared a moment that was obviously personal to her while he'd kept his walls firmly in place.

Irritated, he shoved his phone into his pocket and looked back out over the sea of taxis, limos and other vehicles inching their way along the road. He had no reason to feel guilty. She was, after all, just a woman he'd shared a drink and a dance with. She'd made the choice to share her past. He'd made the choice not to.

His logic failed to dislodge the discomfort that lingered on the edges of his satisfaction with Bradford Global's latest accomplishment.

With a softly muttered oath, he turned around to go back inside and do his due diligence as CEO. Make the rounds, shake some hands, keep Tracy Montebach's manicured talons off him and...

His checklist faded as the cellist walked out of the hotel. Incredible what the simple act of letting one's hair down could do. He'd already been intrigued by the mix of elfish softness and sharp angles in her face, displayed prominently when her hair was pulled back into the tight bun.

Now her hair fell in golden waves just past her shoulders as she stopped at the edge of the sidewalk. The casual disarray of soft curls sent a bolt of heat straight to his groin.

She looked up and down the street, probably searching for a cab, one hand wrapped around the strap of her purse, the other carrying her cello case. He was close enough to the building that he'd escaped her notice so far. He took advantage and let his eyes rake over the confident set of her shoulders, the flattering cling of a black trench coat belted at her narrow waist, her elegant legs clad in black tights, which were a far more sensual sight than Tracy's plunging neckline.

What would she look like, he mused as her head turned toward Central Park, *in red*? *Or gold, to match her eyes*?

Black suited her, added a layer of mystique. But it also made her seem aloof, distant, like an exquisite painting or sculpture one might gaze on in a museum.

Untouchable.

Which was for the best, he reminded himself as she crossed the street and started down the sidewalk. She intrigued him too much to be worth the risk of getting to know her better.

His resolution dissolved like a puff of smoke as she turned onto Center Drive, walked past the collection of horse-drawn carriages lingering on the street and disappeared into Central Park.

He stared for a moment. She'd struck him as an intelligent woman. Surely she wouldn't be so foolish as to walk in Central Park alone at night.

But she didn't reappear.

Before he could question himself, his feet carried him across the street, down the sidewalk and into the park. Her meandering pace and the giant cello case in hand made it easy to reach her side.

"Where are you going?"

She glanced over her shoulder, surprise passing over her face before her features settled into a wary frown.

"Walking through the park. What are you doing out here? Did you follow me?"

"I was outside taking a call when I saw you leave. You're walking in Central Park at night?"

"Yes."

"Why not catch a cab?"

Her frown deepened. "Cabs are expensive."

"Then I'll get you one."

The frown morphed into an expression of thunderous indignation. If he hadn't been so irritated at her lack of critical thinking, he would have taken a moment to enjoy the vivid play of emotions across her face.

"Don't you dare. I'm not paying you back for a cab when I have two perfectly good feet for walking."

"It's dangerous."

She sighed as if he had annoyed her. He fought to keep his own annoyance under control. She had no idea who he was, that he could easily buy her a hundred cellos or a damned limo to ferry her around the city. How many people back at the gala would snort with laughter if they knew a musician had offered to pay back the CEO of Bradford Global for a cab ride?

"I wouldn't have pegged you for one of those," she said, her disappointed tone rubbing against his skin like sandpaper.

"One what?"

"A worrywart."

"I am not a worrywart," he replied, trying—and failing—to keep his own indignation out of his voice.

"Yes, you are." She gestured to the lantern-lined road that ran through the southern end of the park. "I'm talking about walking down Center Drive surrounded by people, not dashing through the trees on some unlit path."

A valid point, he inwardly conceded as people strode by. Couples walking hand in hand, a few families, cyclists and some tourists with cameras. A police car drove slowly down the lane.

But as she stood there, backlit by the lanterns and holding her ridiculously oversized cello case in her small hands, he didn't want to let her out of his sight.

"Are you walking all the way home?"

"No." She said the word slowly, as if she couldn't believe his stupidity. "That would take me hours. I'm walking to Sixty-Eighth Street station. I decided I wanted to walk through Central Park because it's nice outside, the park looked beautiful and, oh, yeah, because I wanted to." One hand stayed clenched around the handle of her case, the other landing on her hip as her eyes narrowed. "Why a man I just met and shared one dance with needs to know all that, I have no idea. But now that you do, are you satisfied?"

Her last word rippled across his skin, rekindled the arousal she had stirred in the ballroom, then again on the sidewalk. How holding her in his arms, feeling her body lean into his with complete trust, had made him want to peel away that bulky black dress and trace his fingers over her naked skin. He had always left his previous lovers satisfied.

But with this woman, it wasn't just courtesy mixed with male pride that had him wanting to see her lips parted on a moan of pleasure, her eyes glazed as he stroked and kissed and savored. No, it was something more primal. Not just a want, but a need.

No, he thought, *I am nowhere near satisfied.*

"I don't like you walking through the park alone at night."

"You don't have to. Good night."

And then she turned and walked away.

Damon stared after her, barely keeping his mouth from dropping open in surprise. No one walked away from him. Ever.

Part of him wanted to let her go. She didn't want his help—fine. She was obviously used to doing things on her own without help from anyone.

The perfect opportunity to let her walk away, out of his life, and take temptation with her.

Except he couldn't. He told himself it was because he couldn't allow a woman to walk in Central Park alone, no matter how many strides the city had taken toward security and public safety. Told himself escorting her to the station was the polite thing to do.

He steadfastly ignored the rush of heat through his veins that told him there was something much more dangerous pushing him on and followed his cellist into Central Park.

Evolet cursed under her breath as her heartbeat sped up at the sound of his footsteps on the path behind her. She didn't know which she had hoped for more—that he would follow her or that he wouldn't. Judging by the slight hitch in her breath as he fell into step beside her and that sensual, rich scent of sage and wood, her body had hoped for the former.

Embarrassment at his questioning had made her irritation with her self-appointed protector more poignant, her tone sharper than she had intended. And even though she certainly didn't need looking after, he was just trying to help. The women he associated with were probably waited on hand and foot by servants, chauffeurs and the like. He wouldn't be used to a woman who had moved from house to house every year or so, her meager belongings shoved into a threadbare pillowcase as she said goodbye over and over again until she hadn't been able to say goodbye anymore. Instead, she'd withdrawn into herself, become sullen and angry, ignoring the overtures of her well-meaning foster parents until they gave up and counted down the days until she was moved again.

No, her mysterious escort wouldn't have experience with women like her at all.

Walking five minutes to the station nearest the hotel would have been the practical thing to do. But tonight, she didn't want to be practical. She'd been practical for so long, shelving her fantasies for more pragmatic endeavors. Even her dream of becoming a professional cellist had evolved into something sensible, a goal to be achieved instead of a wish to be fulfilled. A subtle difference, but one that had left her a hollow shell of herself.

The artist in her had been stifled, the dreamer left adrift in a sea of rationality.

Just for tonight, she wanted to indulge the romantic side she hid behind walls constructed of black clothing and old wounds. The same desire that had made her say yes to a dance with a stranger had guided her feet into the park as her heart cried out for the magic of a walk among the budding trees and lantern-lit walkways.

But the brooding man at her side wouldn't see the magic. No, he struck her as the kind of man who would be more comfortable with facts, numbers and reports.

What did he do for a living, she mused, as he stalked alongside her. Dressed in a tailored suit and a guest at one of the most prominent fundraisers of the year, he was most likely a somebody with a capital *S*. He was an intriguing mix of contradictions: proper in his expensive tux, yet rakish with those top buttons undone. Arrogant in his overall demeanor, but kind enough to walk a virtual stranger through Central Park at night instead of enjoying cocktails and hors d'oeuvres at a fancy gala.

Don't get too involved, Grey.

Except he made it very hard to keep her mind from wandering to what-ifs when he insisted on doing nice, if misguided, things like walking her to the subway.

His dark, brooding handsomeness, coupled with that slow-burning smile he'd tossed her way a couple times, didn't help, either.

"Can I at least know the name of my knight in shining armor?"

Several seconds passed before he finally said, "Damon."

The name conjured up a smoky ballad, one simmering with repressed power and raw strength.

"Reminds me of the little boy from that horror movie."

Damon's chuckle rippled across her skin. "Are you calling me the son of the devil?"

"I don't know you well enough to know that."

Although with the way he tempted her, she could easily picture him in such a role.

"And you?" When she looked up at him, he arched one brow. "Who am I escorting?"

"Evie."

She went with the name Constanza had called her for years. Something kept her from divulging her full name, from sharing even more of herself with this man who tied her up in knots.

"Where do you live, Evie?"

She rolled her eyes at his persistence. "I never answer that question on a first date."

She winced. *Not a date.*

"Do you go on many first dates?"

"Not really."

"Why not?"

"I'm usually practicing, auditioning or performing." She lifted her cello case up. "Constance is my only love." She looked over to see Damon's lips quirk up.

"Constance?"

Words rested on the tip of her tongue, words to honor the woman who had become her mother. How Constanza had grown and sold geraniums on the fire escape to help pay for Evolet's first cello. The husky, delighted laugh when Evolet had played her first piece. The hands crinkled like paper as they'd wiped away Evolet's tears after her first failed audition.

But she stopped herself. It wasn't just that she'd already shared so much with a man who had made it clear he was sharing nothing. Thinking of Constanza trapped in the nursing home, succumbing to the illness of her own mind as disease slowly leeched away what little she had left, made Evolet want to scream and rage at the world. It had given her the one thing she had wanted more than anything—a family—and was now cruelly snatching it away.

"My adoptive mother. Her name is Constanza."

"It looks heavy."

"It is, but I'm the only one who carries it." She hurried on before he could press her for details. "What about you? Any lonely hearts waiting for you back at the gala? Perhaps two," she added impishly, even though she didn't like the image of the redheaded woman's hand on Damon's arm nor the jealousy that curled low in her stomach.

"Tracy Montebach and a friend whose name escapes me. Probably latched on to her newest prey."

The knot in her chest loosened at his casual dismissal. "So it's not true love?"

His deep laugh rippled over her skin once more and slid into her senses. The rich sound transformed his expression of cool elegance to devastatingly handsome as his teeth flashed white in the darkness and his eyes crinkled at the corners.

"I don't think Tracy would know love if it bit her. And," he added, "love isn't a part of my future."

"Ever?"

"Ever."

The finality in his voice made her look up. His face had smoothed into a blank mask, his eyes cold once more.

"There's a story there," she observed.

"Yes."

She wanted to push, to ask who or what had turned him away from love. But she had no desire to relive the rejection she'd experienced in the ballroom. She let his final word hang in the air between them as they continued on through the park.

As they crossed a bridge above one of the numerous paths that crisscrossed through the park, Evolet's feet slowed. She stopped and leaned over the railing, looking down at the carousel below. Golden lights glowed within the redbrick structure that housed the ride. Calliope music sang through the trees as horses soared up and down. At this hour there were only a handful of people on the carousel: two men with a little girl and a couple who seemed more interested in each other than the horses.

Damon joined her at the railing, silent and contemplative. His presence unsettled her, as did the comfort she found in standing beside him. So often she was alone. Over time, she had come to prefer it.

But right now, gazing down at one of her favorite places in the city with a complete stranger who had slid past her usual defenses, she understood at least some of the allure of sharing one's secrets with another.

"I haven't been here in years."

"Did you ever ride it?" she asked.

"Yes. Once, when I was little. For my fifth birthday, I think."

"No big party?"

"No." He paused. "My parents were down-to-earth despite their wealth. They never forgot where they came from."

She sensed that the words cost him somehow, as if he never spoke of his parents. She also heard the unspoken apology for his earlier dismissal in the ballroom and accepted it. How could she judge him for wanting to keep what was obviously a great source of pain close when she did the same every day?

He nodded toward the carousel as it slowed. "Did your parents ever bring you here?"

"No," she managed to whisper past the thickness in her throat. She watched as the fathers helped their daughter dismount from a chestnut horse with a violet saddle, her gleeful laughter rising up as the music wound down. The man with his girlfriend placed his hands on her waist and helped her down, then kissed her forehead as her feet hit the floor.

Oddly, the day she'd first laid eyes on the carousel had been the day the social worker had bought her ice cream on their way to her first foster home. A consolation prize to help her deal with her mother's abandonment. The ice cream cart had been parked just off the drive that meandered through the southern end of the park. She'd wandered over to the railing on the bridge, almost to this very spot, and looked down to see kids giggling as the carousel had spun round and round. Parents had laughed, snapped photos and hugged their children.

Love. Security. Family. Things she had craved for years.

She turned away and continued down the sidewalk, suddenly feeling foolish and shy that she'd almost shared her story with him. Damon caught up to her, his inquisitive gaze hot on her face. He knew there was more lurking beneath the surface, something deeper than just pausing to watch a carousel spin around.

"Thanks for indulging me," she said lightly.

He nodded, and she released a relieved breath that he didn't press.

They walked along in silence for a moment, crossing the road and continuing on another path that wound through trees full of unfurling green leaves and down steps framed by tall grasses.

"There's a story there."

She nearly stumbled on the last step as he repeated her words. He caught her with one hand, his fingers strong and firm on her elbow.

"What?" she whispered.

"The carousel." He cocked his head, his handsome features dusted with gold light from the lanterns. "It means something to you."

"Or maybe it just looked pretty."

Before he could respond to her retort, a single raindrop fell. She held out her hand and smiled up at the dark sky, grateful for the reprieve.

"It wasn't supposed to rain tonight," he grumbled with a glower aimed skyward.

"It's just water."

He cast a glance at the case clutched in her hand. "Aren't you worried about your cello?"

"If this were a downpour, yes. But it's just a light spring rain. I don't spend money on a lot of things, but I spent a small fortune to make sure this case was waterproof."

Lightning flickered above, followed by a soft growl of thunder. Evolet looked up to the sky. She had behaved herself for so long, forcing her dreams and longings deep down where they were safe, untouchable by the capricious and too often cruel nature of the world.

But not tonight. Tonight was about fairy tales and fantasies, dances with handsome strangers and elegant ballrooms.

The rain started to fall in earnest, a gentle whisper that kissed her skin. For the third time that night, she followed impulse and tilted her head back to the sky to embrace the storm.

Rain fell onto Evie's face, a dozen glistening drops that glimmered like diamonds. Her lips curved into a carefree, happy smile as a laugh bubbled up like champagne.

She was beautiful. Captivating. In this moment, he knew he was seeing the real Evie. And by God, she was dazzling.

When he slid an arm around her waist, her laughter faded. Her eyes met his. A lifetime passed in the span of a heartbeat as he waited for an answer to his unspoken question, gave her the opportunity to pull away. Her answer, her body softly pressing against his, ignited a firestorm in his veins that couldn't be stopped. He lowered his lips and claimed hers.

The first brush of lips was teasing, testing. She moaned softly, and his control quivered. He swept a wet curl off her cheek before his fingers tangled in her hair. Her mouth firmed beneath his, her body pressing closer. If the feeling of wet cloth could inspire such a deep need to touch, to taste, what would feeling her naked skin against his do?

His tongue teased the seam of her mouth. When her lips parted on a sigh, he tasted her, taking them both deeper. The kiss changed, grew more intense as her hands slid up his neck. Who knew the stroke of a woman's fingertips, the tug as her fingers tightened in his hair, could drive him to the edge?

The spring air grew colder as the rain fell. But here, in the middle of a park in a city of millions, passion blazed hotter than anything he'd ever experienced. The coolness of the rain only made him more aware of the heat between him and this woman he'd just met. This woman who seemed to look past his defenses and straight into his heart.

A dangerous woman.

Her hips rocked against his in a rhythm he dimly recognized as instinct over finesse. The knowledge that she wanted him so much urged him on. He growled against her mouth, savored her cry as his hands moved down to cup her rear and haul her closer. She gasped as his hard length pressed against her most intimate flesh.

Dimly, he realized she was trembling. It nearly killed him to loosen his grip.

"Don't stop, Damon."

Her whispered plea stripped him bare. He crushed her lips beneath his again as he bound her against him in an iron hold. His hands and mouth touched her with a possessiveness he'd never experienced with anyone. They spiraled upward, wrapped in the feel of each other's bodies, the taste of each other's desire. A dream he never wanted to wake from.

A dream interrupted by shrill laughter from the rain-slicked path behind them.

"Come on, it's this cute little—oh."

Damon raised his head and saw two teenage girls standing behind them. The dim light from a nearby lantern did little to hide the embarrassed look of fascination on the face of one or the delighted smirk on the other.

"Sorry," the smug one said, not looking sorry at all. "Have fun."

Another burst of laughter and they were gone.

Slowly, Damon turned to look down into gold eyes wide with shock. Her lips were swollen, her breathing ragged as she clung to his arms like she might collapse without his support.

"Evie, I…"

The whisper of her name on his lips seemed to shock her back to life. She wrenched herself from him, gathered up her cello case and lurched down the steps carved into the hillside.

"Wait!"

His command whipped out, one that some of the wealthiest men in the world would have heeded. But it had no effect on her as she dashed away into the night. Damon stared at the empty path as the storm pounded harder, flattening the tall stalks of grasses and wildflowers edging the walkway. The part of him she had bewitched with her gold eyes and bold, if not foolish, bravado as she'd traipsed through Central Park demanded he follow. His rational side, the part that had ruled for over a decade, ordered him to let her go. She was an adult. She'd made her choice to leave.

By the time he gave in to desire and stalked down the steps and back onto a paved path, she was gone.

Swallowed up by the darkness and the rain.

CHAPTER FOUR

EVOLET'S FINGERS TIGHTENED around her coffee as the subway car swayed. The train curved around a corner, wheels screeching in protest. Commuters leaned with the turn, eyes fixed on phones or books or companions. An out-of-town family chattered away about the lengthy list of tourist spots on their itinerary.

Another Monday on the subway, Evolet thought with a small smile as she inhaled the dark, delicious scent wafting up from her cup. Her second coffee of the morning.

Normally she pinched pennies and made her own coffee. But the rich aroma of roasted beans and coffee grounds had lured her to the open-air market beneath the Park Avenue train tracks. That and the exhaustion no amount of sleep seemed to defeat.

It didn't help that every time she had closed her eyes she'd been plagued with memories of Damon's lips moving over hers, arms like steel pressing her closer to his warmth.

Or, worst of all, the echo of his groan slipping into her veins, drugging her with the knowledge that he had wanted her. She'd woken more than once hot and tangled in her sheets.

The subway gave another lurch. Coffee splashed onto her hand. With a muffled curse, she reached into her pocket for one of the napkins the perky barista had insisted she take. She looked up to see a young girl watching her with wide eyes.

Feeling guilty over her verbal slipup, she gave the girl a wink and was rewarded with a gap-toothed smile.

The subway, Evolet had long ago decided, got a bad rap. Not only had the tunnels winding beneath the legion of skyscrapers led her to her passion, but they were fun.

Judging by the disapproving scowl on Damon's face when she had mentioned the subway, he had not experienced its underrated pleasures.

The man, and his incredible mouth, wouldn't stay out of her thoughts.

But, she acknowledged with a smile as an electronic voice announced her station, it had had unexpected benefits. She'd visited Constanza at the nursing home Saturday morning, then spent Saturday afternoon and most of Sunday in the park practicing. For the first time, she hadn't poured pain and mourning and loss into her music. It had been passion that had ruled her bow, desire that had coaxed sultry notes from her cello. Playing had been an almost erotic experience, one that had left her warm and flushed by the time she was done.

It had been her best practice session in years. She hoped dearly that the next time she got an audition, they would allow independent showcases in addition to the music often chosen by the orchestras.

Until then, however, she also needed to make some rent money. Which was why, she thought with a resigned sigh as she moved with the crush of bodies toward the doorway and stepped onto the concrete platform, she had accepted the last-minute request for an executive assistant from the temp agency she worked for. Her talents for organizing, concise communication and getting things done quickly had come in handy when she'd started working for NYC Executives Inc., a temporary employment agency that specialized in executive assistants, secretaries and receptionists. She'd worked for airlines, shipping companies, hotels, restaurants, even a theater. Certainly not her passion, but the temporary nature of her work kept things interesting. Most importantly, it paid well.

The call had come in at six a.m. that morning from Miranda, one of the heads at the agency. The executive assistant for a high-ranking executive at Bradford Global had gone into labor overnight and welcomed her bundle of joy four weeks early. With a potentially lucrative contract from a European airline company on the line, the officer, a Ms. Laura Roberts, needed all the help she could get preparing for the final round of bidding.

When Miranda had said the name of the company, Damon's handsome face had flashed through Evolet's mind, along with a jolt of panic. He hadn't said he worked for the company, and there had been plenty of people there affiliated with other organizations. But what if he did? What if she ran into him in the halls or had to work with him?

Typing *Damon* into Bradford Global's website had netted a zero. She hadn't known whether to be relieved or disappointed.

Focus. She would be working with Ms. Roberts for at least two months. Entertaining thoughts of an incredibly sexy, brooding guest from Bradford Global's gala was the opposite of professional. Being an executive assistant wasn't her dream job, but it was a job and one she did well.

With her resolution of banishing thoughts of Damon from her mind, she marched up the stairs into the weak light of early morning sunshine. The Financial District of Lower Manhattan vibrated with activity. Buildings of various heights lined the road, from limestone behemoths nearly a hundred years old to brand-new creations of steel and glass.

Bradford Global occupied the top floor of the Pomme Building, a newly constructed high-rise that dominated the city's skyline. An elevator whisked her up to the seventieth floor. The doors whooshed open to a lobby with dark wood floors, wrought iron chandeliers that looked as if they'd been fashioned out of black piping and brown leather chairs that encouraged one to sink into their buttery-soft depths with a good book. The floor-to-ceiling windows overlooking Midtown offset the darkness of the decor and offered a view that nearly made her jaw drop.

Not, Evolet mused, what she had expected. Based on the lavish wealth on display at Friday night's event, she'd anticipated lots of sterile white and modern, hard-edged furnishings. Not the cozy and welcoming atmosphere of a library.

A massive desk stood off to one side with the company's logo emblazoned on the front. The woman sitting behind the desk was more Evolet's idea of what the guard to a multibillion-dollar company looked like. Late fifties to early sixties, but, oh, Evolet hoped she looked that good as she aged. With a sleekly cut blond bob that framed elegant cheekbones, diamond studs glinting at her ears and a slender form clad in a navy sheath dress, the woman was the definition of class.

Before Evolet could tug nervously at ties on her blouse, the woman stood and shot Evolet a bright smile that lit up her face, the crinkling around her eyes softening her expression.

"Welcome to Bradford Global. I'm Julie, the front secretary. You must be Evolet Grey." At Evolet's raised eyebrows, Julie chuckled. "Security notified me you were on your way up."

Julie's bubbly voice and the soft twang of an accent Evolet couldn't quite place loosened the tension that usually accompanied her on the first day of a new assignment.

"Thank you," she said with an answering smile. "I'm excited to be with you all for the next couple of months. Although I hope the woman I'm replacing and her baby are all right?"

Julie beamed with approval as she pulled her phone out of her pocket.

"Aren't you sweet to ask. They're doing wonderfully." She showed Evolet a picture of an exhausted but very happy looking woman in a hospital gown with a tiny baby cradled in her arms. "Gave us a bit of a fright with how early she came, but Louise did beautifully." Her grin broadened. "Your contract might even get extended. Louise swore she wanted to come back in two months, but I'd bet my retirement she decides to take her full leave."

Before Evolet could comment, the phone on Julie's desk rang. Julie bustled back around and picked it up.

"Yes?... Yes, she just arrived. I'll show her back."

She hung up, grabbed a leather folio off her desk and turned to Evolet with another big smile. "Mr. Bradford is in the conference room with representatives from another company. He'd like you to join them there."

Evolet frowned. "I was told I'd be working for Ms. Roberts."

"Oh, there must have been a misunderstanding." Julie gestured for Evolet to follow her down the hall. "Ms. Roberts put the call in to the agency for a temporary executive assistant, but it was for Mr. Bradford. She's worked with them before, so Mr. Bradford asked her to reach out personally and find someone who had your experience."

Momentarily unsettled, Evolet glanced out the window. She preferred to be prepared going into a new job. An online search of her new employer was a must and, if she had time, a quick check-in with the group chat the temp agency maintained to see if anyone else had worked for the company before.

Couldn't be helped. But who, she wondered, was Mr. Bradford? Some intimidating billionaire who would bark out orders? Or someone spoiled with a lack of focus, someone who would expect her to do most of the heavy lifting?

"Is everything all right, dear?"

Evolet turned and smiled reassuringly at Julie. "Yes. I thought I was working for Ms. Roberts," she confided to ease some of the concern in Julie's eyes, "so I did some snooping on her online profile this morning. I like to know a little about who I'm working for and their interests." She smiled again in reassurance. "I don't like going in unprepared, but I'll manage."

"Well, I can tell you all you need to know about Edward Bradford," Julie said as her heels clicked against the wood floor. "He likes to portray himself as stodgy and unreachable, but we're very fortunate to have him leading us. Very intelligent, just like his father, and doesn't mind getting his hands dirty. I've seen him work the assembly line at his manufacturing plants to understand what his workers are going through. You don't get many *Fortune* 500 CEOs doing that," Julie added proudly as they neared a wide doorway.

Reassured by Julie's staunch defense of her boss, Evolet relaxed. It was just eight weeks. She'd worked for a variety of bosses—some friendly and engaging, some distant and even downright rude. Just because this was the most profitable and esteemed company she'd worked for didn't mean anything in the long run for her ultimate career goals.

Just a means to an end, she reminded herself.

Her eyes widened as she spied the last door at the end of the hall just past a flight of stairs that hugged the wall. Covered in tufted burgundy leather with gleaming brass buttons, the door stretched nearly to the ceiling.

"A beauty, isn't it?" Julie said with pride. She paused and gestured toward the door. "Edward's father had it in his office. When we moved here, Edward had the door installed." Her smile turned sad. "David would have appreciated that. We don't talk much about him, but Edward loved him very much."

"You worked for Edward's father, then?" Evolet asked gently.

"And David's father."

"His father?" she repeated. "But...you..." At the humorous gleam in Julie's eyes, she plowed ahead. "You don't look old enough to have worked that long."

Julie's laughter echoed down the hall. She reminded Evolet of Constanza, happiness and contentment radiating off her small frame in palpable waves that couldn't help but make one smile.

"That is a wonderful way to start off a Monday. I think you're going to do just fine here at Bradford Global, Evolet Grey."

She resumed walking and turned into an open office space. People lounged on leather couches, sat around low-slung coffee tables scribbling on tablets and typed away at state-of-the-art computers at one of the many desks artfully arranged in the giant room. More of the black iron chandeliers hung from a soaring ceiling. The black-and-white photographs on the navy brick walls made Evolet feel like she'd been shoved back in time to the industrial era. A blend of past and present.

Her esteem for Edward Bradford rose. She'd seen enough bland office settings with cubicles that encouraged solitary work and little to no social interaction. Bradford seemed to have gone in the opposite direction, with a coffee bar in the corner and a balcony just beyond filled with sumptuous outdoor couches and chairs.

Julie called out a few greetings as she led Evolet toward a staircase that hugged the bricks and led up to a glass-enclosed room. Evolet responded to the curious glances with a smile. She liked getting to know the people she worked with on her assignments, chatting with them in the break room and making small talk. But the benefit of being a temp was just that—she was temporary. It was easy to brush off overtures of friendship because in a matter of days, weeks or even occasionally months, she would be gone. No need to get her hopes up or to have the threat of losing someone she started to care about looming over her head.

The interior of the glass room came into view. The glass was broken up by thick black beams, beyond which sat several men and women around a large conference table having what appeared to be a heated discussion.

"What was that?" Evolet asked as Julie murmured something under her breath.

"Titan Manufacturing," the older woman responded. Perhaps Evolet was reading too much into Julie's tone, but she didn't sound like she was a fan. "They didn't move past the first round of bidding for the Royal Air contract, and now they're trying to...encourage us to partner up for the final round." She turned and handed Evolet the leather folio. "There's a tablet in there for taking notes. Please note any details about any proposals so Mr. Bradford can review it later. There's a chair and a small table at the back where you can sit. Mr. Bradford will meet with you in his office afterward to go over the details for the next few weeks." Her sunny smile returned as she laid her hand on the door handle. "Welcome to Bradford Global, Miss Grey."

Just like before she went onstage, butterflies rushed through Evolet's stomach. And then they were gone, replaced by determination and an iron will to succeed.

"Thank you."

The door opened. An angry voice rolled out, vibrating with desperation. "You undermined us in the first round of bidding, Bradford! The least you can do is bring us on."

"You undermined yourself, Thad. Don't blame us for your company's shortcomings."

The familiar deep voice rolled over Evolet's skin like a lover's caress. The air grew heavy as her breathing quickened. Her head jerked to the right.

And there he was. Larger-than-life as he sat at the end of the conference table, his broad shoulders clad in a charcoal-gray suit that simultaneously seemed tailor-made for him and yet barely contained the muscles that rippled beneath the wool.

He leaned back in his chair, one hand on the table, the other hanging casually at his side.

But she knew better. Her heartbeat quickened until it was pounding so wildly in her chest she couldn't believe the sound didn't rise above the near shouting. She saw the sharp edge in his gaze, the restrained temper in the cords of muscle in his neck.

Her eyes flicked to the still-arguing man with thick black hair and artificially golden skin. A man, she decided, who didn't notice details, like when he was in the crosshairs of a much more powerful predator.

Damon's gaze slid to hers. Did she imagine the flare of surprise, the slip of control? She blinked, and all she saw was the calm mask he'd worn when he'd dismissed her on the dance floor. Cool, competent and unapproachable.

The initial stab of hurt at seeing how unaffected he was disappeared, replaced by questions like why he had given a false name. Was it something as simple as a nickname? Or something more scheming?

Resolution and determination took hold. It didn't matter. He'd had his reasons, and they were none of her concern. She turned her back on him and walked to the chair. She couldn't work for the man she'd so shamelessly kissed in Central Park. But she was still a professional. She would finish the meeting, take notes and then speak with him afterward to formally resign. Her nose wrinkled at the thought of calling her agency. She'd worked for them long enough, and certainly earned them enough money, that they would be kind. But she'd never walked away from a job before. She would owe them an explanation.

Because I wrapped myself around the CEO of Bradford Global like a python as he kissed me senseless?

She bit back a snort of laughter. The humor wiped away the last traces of shock and cemented her control over the moment.

She removed her coat with quick, methodical movements, took the tablet out of the folio and sat.

Damon's attention was still focused on the man with the artificial tan. She took one last look, allowed herself one more indulgence of remembering the way his fingers had grazed her cheek, the way he'd held her as if he couldn't get enough of her…and then slipped into her role as Evolet Grey, temporary executive assistant to the CEO of Bradford Global, as she banished her feelings for the man she'd kissed in the rain.

CHAPTER FIVE

IT HAD, Damon decided as he walked down the hall toward his office with Evie or Evolet or whatever she called herself walking behind him, been the longest meeting of his life. Given the number of meetings he'd sat through, that was saying something. The more Thad Williams from Titan Manufacturing had argued, the more Damon had entertained fantasies of having security summoned to haul the man out by his designer paisley tie.

Better to indulge in that fantasy than ones centering on the woman who'd sat calmly in the back of the conference room throughout the entire circus.

Evolet Grey, his temporary executive assistant for the next two months.

He had barely survived one meeting. How could he survive eight weeks with her in his building, his meetings, *his office*?

When he had looked up to see her standing in the doorway, staring at him as if she'd seen a ghost, he'd pressed his feet into the floor to mentally anchor himself so he didn't go to her. Never had the sight of a woman with her hair bound at the base of her neck and a billowing trench coat aroused him so much.

Never, either, had the sight of a woman distracted him from a meeting. That thought had been enough to pull him back from his memories of Friday night to focus on the people seated around the table. It was also enough for him to know that, once they reached his office, he would need to dismiss her.

He pushed the door open, the feel of the cool leather a sharp contrast to how hot he felt. Good God, he had *kissed* the woman. A simple kiss that had slid like a drug through his veins and left him wanting as he'd never wanted before.

"Come in," he said over his shoulder when he didn't hear her follow him in. "And shut the door." His eyebrows rose as he heard her mumble something. He circled around his desk. "What was that?"

She looked at him then. How had he thought her cool and reserved at the fundraiser? He must have been blind because now that he saw the banked temper simmering in her eyes, he couldn't see her as anything but fire and passion seething beneath the surface.

"I said, 'Are you sure that's a good idea, sir?'"

A shudder passed through him at her proper tone, the primness failing to cover the underlying sass.

"Why wouldn't it be? We're both professionals. Unless," he added with a mocking smile, "you're concerned you won't be able to control yourself."

A flush crept up her neck and over her cheeks. Her eyes glittered as her lips thinned. He returned her stare, keeping his face smooth even as his eyes devoured the sight of her. Her bun was still perfect, every hair smoothed into place. It didn't erase the memory of the golden strands wound between his fingers as he had claimed everything she had offered with a ruthless need that had only grown after she'd fled into the storm.

Now, with her standing before him, dressed in a billowing white blouse with a prim tie at her throat and black pants, the perfect professional, his need was almost ferocious.

All the more reason to dismiss her. She would be a distraction, one he couldn't afford right now. That and he didn't care for the strength of his fascination. He had no doubt that sex with Evolet Grey would be one of the most pleasurable experiences of his life. But he also suspected that it would involve giving more than he had ever given before to another woman. Giving meant surrendering control.

No infatuation would ever take precedent over staying in control.

He gestured for her to take a seat, waiting until she sat before he sat behind his desk. "I'm glad to see you made it home safe."

"Thank you," she replied stiffly. She glanced around the office. "Not bad for Edward Bradford, the CEO of Bradford Global. Or is it Damon? I wasn't aware CEOs used aliases these days."

Irritated, he leaned forward and steepled his fingers. "Thank you, *Evie*."

She had the good grace to flush. "It is my name," she said defiantly, and damned if that pert tone didn't make him hard.

"Just as Damon is mine." When she frowned at him, he shrugged. "Edward Charles Damon Bradford."

"Middle name," she grumbled. "Why didn't you tell me who you were?"

"I enjoyed being anonymous. It's rare to find someone who doesn't know who I am, what I do and the estimated number of zeroes in my bank account."

"Rather presumptuous to think I'd be dazzled by four names and a fancy office."

He couldn't help himself. He grinned. "Most people are impressed when they learn who I am and what I do."

"I'm not most people, am I?"

"No," he said, suddenly serious. "You're not."

She blinked, some of her bravado slipping as she looked at him with an almost confused expression on her face. Her gaze slid away from his. Silence descended, along with the pressing weight of what he had to do next.

But before they dealt with the uncomfortable business of

having her reassigned, he held out his hand. "The tablet, please, and your notes."

She handed over the leather folio. He opened the folder and leaned back, his eyes scanning the screen. The more he read, the more a headache started to pound at his temples. It was easy to see why the temp agency Laura had contacted had recommended Evolet.

She was good. She was very, very good. Not only had she taken detailed notes, she'd also kept a separate column where she'd transcribed some of the conversations taking place around the table while Thad had monologued at Damon.

"Brigid LaRue is considering quitting Titan Manufacturing?"

"She is." Evolet's lips twitched. "Mr. Williams has little interest, or respect, for her ideas."

His mind conjured up an image of Titan's head of marketing, a svelte woman whose olive green suit had complemented her brown skin and black hair braided into a thick bun. She'd been polite yet assertive, managing to slide in a couple pitches between Thad's rants that, even though Damon had no interest in a partnership with Titan, had been impressive.

"How did you hear all this?"

She shrugged. "Many people don't think of executive assistants. And when they do, it's because they need a cup of coffee or a new pen. They talk around us like we're not even there."

Damon frowned. "Then you've been working for the wrong people."

Her eyes narrowed. "This isn't my career, Mr. Bradford. It pays the bills until I join a professional orchestra."

"You're very good at it."

"And you're good at dancing, but I assume you're not pursuing professional ballroom dancing anytime soon." Her smile took the sting out of her words. "I like what I do for NYC Executives. I like the details, the organization, the dependability." She hesitated on the last word, as if she'd revealed more than she had wanted, but continued. "I'm fortunate that I have something I like while I pursue what I love."

He regarded her for a moment with a thoughtful stare before glancing down at the document Julie had printed for him that morning—Evolet's résumé from the agency, which included relevant positions she'd held. He'd been both relieved and energized by her experience given that he had been depending on Louise still being here through the submission of the final proposal to Royal Air. He'd reviewed the résumé before the meeting with Titan, before he'd known Evolet Grey was the same woman whose lips he had plundered and body he had claimed without a single article of clothing shed.

His gaze slid back up to her. He steeled his body against the initial rush of desire, battled it back with reason and the knowledge that it would be very hard to find someone of Evolet's capabilities and knowledge. Not in time for the next stage of the Royal Air contract.

She was beautiful. She was intriguing. But she was a temporary existence in his life. Nothing mattered more than Bradford Global and seeing the company succeed. He could contain his libido for the duration of Evolet's contract. His fascination with her would fade with time and doing what he did best— throwing himself into work. It had been the cure for more than one emotional ailment in the past. It would work again.

The white of her blouse made her blush all the more noticeable as it crept up her neck.

"Well…" She cleared her throat. "On that note, I will notify the agency that this won't work and I—"

"Why won't it?"

Her eyes widened to an almost comical size, large and gold, emotions flashing through them without concealment or artifice.

"Did your agency brief you on the project Bradford Global is bidding on?"

Suspicion lingered on her face, but she nodded. "Royal Air. They're adding to their fleet and need a reputable manufacturer who can produce planes under a tight deadline."

Damon nodded, pleased. "Bradford Global is one of the three companies in the final running for the contract."

Interest sparked in Evolet's eyes. "Congratulations."

The sincerity in her voice warmed him. He inclined his head. "Thank you." He gestured to the résumé on his desk. "You worked five months as an executive assistant for a CFO for a major US airline and four months for the head of marketing for another. You have over six years of experience in this type of work. Past employers have remarked on your diligence, talent for details and 'pleasant manner,'" he added with a coy look in her direction. "When Laura called the temp agency, you were their first recommendation."

"And I appreciate that, but..." Her voice trailed off as her blush deepened. "What about...well, the...thing?" she finished weakly.

"Thing?" he repeated casually.

She rolled her eyes. "You kissing me in Central Park."

"As I recall, you kissed me back. Yet so far, we've managed to exist for—" he glanced at his watch "—eight minutes in the privacy of my office without a repeat performance." He arched a brow, ready to deal his final card. "Unless you think you can't keep your hands off me."

Bull's-eye.

Her eyes hardened as she sat up straight. "Of course I can. It was just a kiss."

It was exactly the attitude he needed her to have to make this working relationship successful. The little stab of irritation that she could deem what had happened between them as "just a kiss" was inconsequential.

"Good. In that case, Miss Grey," he said with a sharp smile, "let's get to work."

CHAPTER SIX

EVOLET'S FINGERS DRUMMED a steady beat on the handle of her cello case as the elevator soared upward. Hauling the instrument on the subway was less than fun in the early morning rush, but it was worth it to have the extra practice time. The first couple of days, rushing home on the subway, getting her cello and making the walk to Central Park, had left her with precious little time to practice. By Wednesday, she'd taken to bringing her cello with her and hopping off at the Fifty-Ninth Street station and practicing in the park. With her audition for the East Coast Chamber Orchestra later in the week, she needed all the practice she could get.

Excitement hummed inside her. It was her first audition in over a month. Not her dream position, but a respected and growing orchestra that would be a good first step into the world of playing professionally.

But that was later, Evolet reminded herself as she exited the elevator. Right now, Bradford Global commanded her focus. It had been two weeks since she'd joined the company. Two weeks that had dragged on and flown by in equal measure. No matter how early she arrived, she had not yet beaten Damon to the office. They started off with an overview of what the day would look like, from touring the existing manufacturing facilities to reviewing pieces of the reports filtering in from various departments that would be submitted to Royal

Air. Dizzying amounts of information, hours spent poring over documents.

And the man who starred in what was turning into nightly erotic fantasies often just a few feet away from where she worked.

She had an office, a beautiful room with a large window that overlooked the Brooklyn Bridge and the blue waters of the East River. At first, she had resisted adding any homey touches. She was a temporary worker, not an employee. She'd spent months at other companies and never once felt the inclination to personalize whatever space she was assigned.

But there was something different about Bradford Global. Amazing, she thought as she stepped off the elevator and waved to Julie, what working for a company that invested in their employees could do. It wasn't just the perks, like the coffee bar in the cavernous workroom she'd passed on her first day or the catered luncheons. It was the genuine friendliness Julie greeted every employee with, how Damon knew the names of everyone who came into his office and remembered to ask about their children, their college studies, their dog. His other executives, like Laura Roberts, mirrored his attitude of respect.

The first time she had been invited out for after-hours drinks with a group of engineers and assistants, she'd been so startled she'd said yes. She'd silently cursed herself all the way to the bar, only to stay two hours and find herself relaxing, enjoying conversation with people who were quickly turning from strangers to casual acquaintances.

A thought that would have made her uneasy just a short time ago. Instead, it had made her look forward to her days at the office.

Another red flag. She had fallen into her job with NYC Executives when she'd been attending college. It had offered flexibility and, best of all, temporary placements. No time to get attached to people, a job, if she moved every few weeks to months. She preferred no attachments.

Then why, she groused at herself as she walked down the hallway to her office, *am I getting involved?*

She'd turned down the second invitation for another night out with an excuse of needing to practice. But the third invite—a group dinner at an Italian restaurant that served savory pastas and bruschetta topped with tomatoes and fat slices of mozzarella—had resulted in her staying for three hours, sipping on wine and laughing as her coworkers had debated current events and swapped stories.

They'd even asked about her music—questions that had both surprised and touched her.

She was getting involved. She needed to stop.

A text lit up her phone as she walked into her office and set her bag on her desk next to the photo she'd put up of her, Constanza and Constanza's son, Samuel. She laid her cello case down in the corner.

"Hey, did you get my text?"

Evolet looked up with a smile to see Audrey Clark, one of Bradford's marketing pros, standing in the doorway. She reminded Evolet of Julie, her thousand-watt smile a flash of white against smooth dark skin. The two had connected over drinks that first night, chatting about everything from Audrey's father's playing for a jazz band in his retirement to their mutual interest in murder mysteries.

"My phone just dinged," Evolet replied with a laugh.

"We're all going to a dance club Saturday night in the West Village. Want to join?"

Yes. Evolet stomped down her initial reply.

"Um…can I let you know? I'm not sure what all I have to do for work, and I've got an audition coming up for the East Coast Chamber Orchestra. I really need to practice."

"Whoa. I heard them perform at Bryant Park last summer. You must be excited!"

Guilt spurted through her. She knew the material for her audition backward and forward. As much as the extra practice boosted her confidence, one night out wouldn't doom her audition. But she couldn't get used to this camaraderie, didn't want to want the connections she was reluctantly but steadily forming with others.

"Don't congratulate me too soon. I haven't had a successful audition since I made it on to the Apprentice Symphony."

"Hey," Audrey said as she came forward and enveloped Evolet in a hug, "don't sell yourself short. How many people apply and don't even get an audition?"

Evolet stood frozen for a moment before she indulged in hugging Audrey back. Constanza had hugged her all the time. But other than that, physical touch had been in short supply during her life.

"Thank you, Audrey," she whispered.

"You're welcome. And I get it. Maybe next weekend."

"Everything okay?"

Evolet stiffened as Damon's voice washed over her. He stood framed in her doorway, devastatingly handsome in a three-piece charcoal suit and black tie. She'd never thought about waistcoats, much less how sexy they would look molded perfectly to a muscular chest and tapered waist, but she certainly did now.

She wrenched her gaze away before Audrey picked up on the sudden tension humming in the air.

"Yes. Audrey was just congratulating me on securing an audition."

"That is cause for congratulations."

"Thank you."

Damon glanced down at his watch. "Evolet, if you could report to my office in fifteen minutes, we've had some updates from our public relations department."

"Yes, sir."

He leveled an enigmatic gaze at her before disappearing down the hall.

"Sir?" Audrey said with a laugh. "I don't think anyone has called him 'sir' in years."

Evolet tried to shrug off the sensual energy clinging to her like a second skin. "He's my boss."

"Technically your agency is your boss. But regardless, it is okay to call him Damon. It takes a little getting used to, but once you do, he seems more accessible, less scary."

But she couldn't. The last time she had called Damon by his name, it had been moaning it, begging him not to stop seducing her with kisses in the middle of a spring storm.

"I don't know if anything could make him less scary."

Audrey frowned. "Has he done something to make you uncomfortable?"

Her guilt doubled. Damon had been nothing but a gentleman since she'd started working. That was probably part of what set her on edge. He tempted her with his very presence, whereas he continued to type away at his computer, field numerous phone calls or host meetings without a single glance in her direction.

"No. He's been great." She shrugged, trying to appear nonchalant. "It's me. He just seems…larger-than-life, I guess. The bachelor billionaire in the fancy office."

Audrey's laugh echoed down the hall as she headed out. "I would pay to see you say that to his face directly."

Evolet managed to answer a few emails, grab cups of coffee for both her and Damon, and make it into his office one minute before the deadline.

He didn't look up as she walked in, but he did spare a glance at the coffee cup she set on his desk.

"Colombian, black," she said as she sat in the chair across from him.

"Thank you."

She couldn't decipher the enigmatic gaze he slanted at her and instead chose to ignore it. "What do we have on the agenda today?"

"The two case studies I requested are back. We need to review them for accuracy, ensure the circumstances of the projects align with Royal Air's expectations and, if they're up to standard, incorporate them into the final bid document." He glanced down at his watch. "I have meetings at eight thirty, ten, one and four. You'll need to continue to review them while I'm away."

"Yes, sir."

He shot her another look. "You're doing that to annoy me."

Yes. It gave her a perverse pleasure to see something rattle that calm exterior and creep under his skin, especially something as innocuous as refusing to use his name. Only fair given that he'd left her tied up in knots for the past two weeks.

"What?"

He regarded her with a stare that at first amused her. But the longer he looked, the more she had to resist the urge to squirm as little tendrils of arousal wound their way over her skin. It wouldn't be so bad, she assured herself, if he wasn't so handsome, dark eyes set in that sharp, angular face that promised danger and charm.

"Are you happy here, Evolet?"

Surprised, she blinked and broke the seductive spell he'd woven with a single glance. "Happy?"

"Yes. Happy."

She tilted her head. "As happy as a temporary employee can be, I suppose."

"The staff speak very highly of you."

Pleasure warmed her before she squelched it. She liked Audrey, Julie, the people who had welcomed her with open arms.

But it shouldn't matter. Couldn't matter.

"You have a great team."

"Do you actually have an audition, or were you just deflecting Audrey's invitation?"

It took a moment for the full impact of his question to hit her. When it did, anger made her jaw clench and her fingers tighten on her tablet.

"Yes," she replied through gritted teeth. "I have an audition." She pulled out her phone and with a few taps forwarded her audition notice to his email. "I don't lie, Mr. Bradford."

His computer pinged, but he didn't even glance at it, keeping her pinned with that emerald gaze that saw far too much.

"You don't owe me any explanations, Evolet. However," he continued as she started to speak, "I am curious as to why you hold yourself back when the team here at Bradford Global is not only willing but wanting to socialize with you."

She felt her mask slip, knew he saw that there was more to her antisocial attitude than mere shyness or introversion.

"It's eight twenty, Mr. Bradford. You should head up to your meeting."

His fingers tapped on his desk once, twice. And then he stood without another word, gathered his laptop and walked out the door.

She silently cursed. They'd made it two weeks keeping things professional. He didn't ask about her music. She didn't ask how he spent his evenings. That she spent any time imagining him dining at luxurious restaurants with beautiful dates dripping in diamonds or hosting elegant parties in a penthouse suite annoyed her immensely.

Focus.

If she hadn't experienced the hottest kiss of her life with her temporary boss, she would be thoroughly enjoying her job.

Not only did she like the people, her office and the environment, but working on the bid for Royal Air was proving to be an enjoyable challenge. The bonus Bradford Global had added to her usual fee would allow her to take a couple months off after if she wanted. She could fill her days with music, creating content for the social media channels she maintained for her playing, and booking private events.

Her fingers drummed an impatient rhythm on the desk. It would be heaven at first. But, assuming she didn't get the position with St. John's, the Apprentice Symphony would be starting its summer break about the time her contract with Bradford Global was up. She didn't have anyone else in her life except Constanza and the occasional family outing with Constanza's son, Samuel. For so long, that had been enough.

When had she started wanting more?

Irritated, she stood up and walked down the hallway toward what was affectionately called the War Room, the massive open office space she'd passed on her first day that included the coffee bar exclusively for the use of Bradford Global's employees. A little coffee, a minute out on the outdoor balcony to take some deep breaths and center herself and then she'd get to work.

A smile crossed her face as she saw Julie at the bar. "Hi, Julie."

"Oh, hi, darling. How's it going?" Julie asked as she accepted a cup from the barista.

"Busy but good."

"I figured when I saw how late Damon's been staying."

Evolet frowned. "What?"

"The past two weeks, I don't think he's left his office before eight o'clock. I'm gone by five, but I review the security log every morning." She glanced down at her watch. "Speaking of time, I need to get back to my desk. Let me know if you need anything."

Evolet nodded absently as Julie walked off. Guilt niggled at her as she walked back to Damon's office, a latte in one hand and a biscotti in the other. The deadline was next week. Submitting on time was imperative. Submitting early was even better. She'd allowed her own preoccupation with their kiss to shadow her interactions with him, assume the worst when he appeared to be doing exactly what he'd said he would do and act in a respectful manner.

This was what came from letting emotions creep in, especially in business. She had let herself get distracted and missed the signs that her boss and the company she was working for needed a little more than she was giving. Time to mirror Damon's professionalism, stop acting like a moody teenager and do her job.

With her self-reproaching lecture over with, she sat down and began to work.

CHAPTER SEVEN

DAMON GLANCED DOWN at his watch and stifled a groan. His four o'clock meeting had started twenty minutes late and gone an hour longer than expected. Every time he'd spied Evolet throughout the day, she'd been working even harder than she had been the last two weeks. He had no doubt that a rough draft of the proposal, including the case studies, would be ready for his review. He wanted nothing more than to shove it aside, go home and relax on his balcony with a glass of bourbon and watch the sun set over the skyline.

Maybe next month.

Although the fact that he was wanting to leave before a project was completed unsettled him. For years Bradford Global had driven nearly his every action. He hadn't been able to, nor wanted, to relax if he had unfinished business. Given the continuing expansion and repeat business of satisfied clients, he almost always had something to do.

Perhaps it had been coming home to an empty apartment after he and Natalie had broken up. He didn't miss her. But walking into the empty penthouse, everything exactly as he'd left it, had begun to weigh on him.

Casual dates here and there suited him. Relationships were off the table. Maybe he should listen to Julie's advice and get a dog.

Evolet's face flashed in his mind. That was one entanglement he didn't need. Bad enough that he had kissed an employee like a starving man who'd just been granted his first meal in months. Worse was how she managed to do her job, do it well and not once look at him with the fire he'd glimpsed in her eyes in Central Park.

Never before had he been on the receiving end of an uninterested party. As arrogant as it sounded, women wanted to be with him, whether it was for sex, money, prestige or the occasional one who had professed to care about him. To have the one woman who had sparked his arousal for the first time in months—and to a degree he had never before experienced—treat him with cool professionalism grated on his usually steady nerves. It should have been impressive. Yet it almost seemed like she'd withdrawn into herself, become a milder, more placid version.

Once in a while, he caught a glimpse of the vivid spitfire he'd encountered at the gala, like her addressing him as "sir." From the tiny gleam of mischief in her eyes to the pertness in her voice, it had made him hard almost instantly.

Stop.

He needed to get a grip on himself. Not only was Evolet off-limits as his employee, but she had literally run away from him in the park. Whatever twist of fate had brought her to his company's doorsteps, he needed to focus on the positives of having someone with her experience and skill working on the Royal Air contract rather than this borderline obsession.

A rich scent teased his nose as he neared his office. Spices, meat, roasted vegetables. He hadn't eaten since lunch, and that had only been because Evolet had handed him a smoothie from the coffee bar in between meetings. Perhaps Julie had left him something, he thought with a fond smile. The woman had been a secretary for Bradford Global for over forty years, and she had treated all three CEOs like they were her children instead of executives over a multibillion-dollar company.

He opened the door to his office. And stopped.

Evolet was seated in one of the leather chairs, hair pulled up into a loose knot on top of her head, a few stray tendrils laying on her neck. He tightened his fingers into fists, a physical reminder to keep his hands to himself and not brush the hair off her neck before laying a kiss on her skin.

His eyes dropped down. Her legs were curled up underneath her, her bare feet peeking out from beneath the hem of her wine-colored dress. With a full skirt and sleeves down to her elbows, she should have looked matronly. Not sexy.

"What are you doing here?"

His frustration with the direction of his own thoughts made his voice snap out. Her head jerked up, her eyes widening at his tone.

"Um…working?"

He inhaled sharply and steadied himself as he walked to his desk. "You didn't have to stay late."

She shrugged. "Julie told me you'd been staying almost every night since I started. With the deadline next week, I wanted to make sure we would be ready in time."

He shot her an enigmatic smile that he hoped covered how oddly touched he was that she would be so invested in the work despite the temporary nature of her position. Then he spied two paper bags sitting on his desk. "What's this?"

"Dinner."

She set aside her laptop and sprang up. He watched, entranced, as she reached over with a soft smile and started pulling out containers.

"There's a Haitian restaurant on Beekman—Espwa. It's owned by a friend of Constanza's."

"Your adoptive mother."

She blinked up at him. "You remembered."

"I did. She's from Haiti?"

"Yes. Her father was Haitian. Her mother was from Puerto Rico. She came here after she lost her husband."

He watched, waited. She stared at him for a long moment before looking down at her food.

"My father died when I was three. I don't remember much, but he and my birth mother loved each other." Her lips turned down into a frown. "She didn't take his death well. I didn't have any other family, so I ended up in foster care when I was five. Bounced around for ten years until I landed with Constanza. She adopted me."

"I'm sorry."

"Nothing to be sorry about."

The casual shrug she gave him didn't distract him from the pain in her eyes, the slight bunching up of her shoulders, the nervous graze of her hand pushing a strand of hair out of her face.

"You lost both parents. I know what that's like."

Her head jerked up. His surprise at his own admission didn't stop him from holding her gaze. He wasn't sharing for himself. He was sharing to help her, an important distinction.

"Yes, I suppose you do."

"It hurts."

At last, she nodded.

"Very much. So does getting bounced around, never knowing where your next home will be."

"Does that have anything to do with your work for a temp agency?"

She speared him with an arched brow and a slight frown. "Is this an impromptu counseling session, or are we working?"

His lips curved up. "Do I make you nervous, Evolet?"

She held his gaze, as if to show him she could. But as they stared, he saw the change come over her, the rise and fall of her chest, the darkening of her eyes, the parting of her lips.

She was the first to look away, with a casual toss of her head as she stabbed her fork into one of the takeout containers.

"No."

Oh, he was a selfish bastard, he thought with a satisfied smirk. He enjoyed hearing the slight hitch in her breath, seeing the tinge of pink in her cheeks. The woman might've been cool and competent in her work, but she still felt the attraction between them, wanted him just as he wanted her.

"Daniel's a fantastic chef. I rarely make it down to this part of the city, but when I decided to stay, I thought you might be hungry because I was hungry and…" She trailed off, then took a deep breath before she surprised him with a chagrined smile that was simultaneously stimulating and endearing. "I'm babbling. I'm nervous and I'm babbling."

There you are.

Here was the woman he'd danced with in a glamorous ballroom, whom he'd followed into Central Park and kissed in the rain. Here was the woman who, for a couple minutes her first morning here, had verbally sparred with and aroused him with her spunky attitude.

"Why are you nervous?"

She shot him a look that told him he was an idiot. "I stayed past my usual quitting time without talking to you and took over your office. It might seem presumptuous or…"

"No, no," he said with a delighted smirk as the pink in her cheeks turned to a red similar to the shade of her dress. "Or what?"

"Like I'm trying to set something up. You know, to…seduce you," she finally choked out.

He threw back his head and laughed. "If that's what you were trying to do, telling me ruins the effect somewhat."

She bit down on her lower lip, but he saw the corners of her mouth twitch up as she looked away.

"Then fortunately that wasn't my plan. I figured you might

be hungry since you barely stopped to take a breath today. I hope you don't mind, but I ordered for you."

He ignored the slight reproach in her voice and inhaled as she pulled the lid off a large bowl.

"What is that?"

Unease furrowed her brow. "*Poulet aux noix*. It's spicy marinated chicken with bell peppers and cashews."

"It smells incredible."

Her face smoothed out into a relieved smile. "It tastes even better. I also ordered *makawoni au graten* and *pikliz*. Haitian macaroni and cheese and a pickled vegetable relish."

"I've never had any of this."

"Then you're in for a treat. Sometime I'll have to get you their hot chocolate. You've never had hot chocolate until you've had Haitian hot chocolate."

She set the food out on his desk and pulled up a chair on the other side.

"Did Julie get you your company card?" he asked as he forked up a bite of noodles dripping with cheese.

"My card? For what?"

"Purchases like this."

She frowned. "No, she's just ordered whatever I needed. I took care of dinner."

He paused with the fork in midair. "You bought dinner?"

"Yes."

"I can have Julie—"

She held up a hand. "If you say *repay me*, I will dump this chicken in your lap."

He arched a brow. "That could be considered assault."

"Pummeled by poultry?" Her smile carried a hint of steel. "The bonus you're giving me is more than enough to buy dinner. I know you've been working late, and I admire that you don't ask anything of your employees that you're not willing to do yourself. I was hungry. It was a reasonable assumption you were hungry. So I bought us dinner. My treat."

That same warmth that had appeared when she'd told him she wanted the company to succeed intensified and spread throughout his body.

"I can't remember the last time someone bought me dinner. Thank you."

Another genuine smile flashed across her face. God, he wanted to see that smile in the mornings when he came into the office, not the tiny little twerk of her lips before her mouth settled into a straight, unexpressive line.

"You're welcome. You've been nothing but respectful while I've been here, despite our…history. I'm grateful you encouraged me to keep working here."

Grateful. The word erased the warmth and nearly destroyed his appetite. He didn't want her to be grateful. He didn't want her to make him feel like even more of a cad for entertaining thoughts of her naked and spread across the bed in his penthouse, arching against him the way she had in the park but this time with her breasts bared to his lips, his tongue…

He steeled himself against his lust. They had at least an hour ahead of them, if not more. He could keep himself under control for that long. Tonight, he'd cool off in a long, icy shower.

And tomorrow…tomorrow he would set up a date with someone, anyone this weekend to help get his mind off the entrancing woman currently sitting barefoot in his office eating macaroni and cheese.

"You're welcome, Evolet."

CHAPTER EIGHT

EVOLET GLANCED AT the clock and suppressed a yawn. Nearly eight o'clock. She could easily stay until midnight reviewing and editing the proposal.

But, she acknowledged with a satisfied wiggle in the leather chair she had settled into, they'd gotten a ton of work done. Once dinner had been eaten, they'd attacked different parts of the proposal and settled into a steady pace of work. They'd exchanged ideas, argued over the merits of one particular client testimony and honed the proposal into something she saw as the best project she'd ever worked on.

She glanced up. At some point Damon had taken off his jacket and rolled up his shirtsleeves, leaving him in his tie, waistcoat and shirt. It was decidedly unfair, she thought as she looked away, that even his forearms were muscled. For the most part, she'd kept to her resolutions to stay professional. But as he'd relaxed, the aloof air had evaporated, replaced by an intelligent man with a quick wit who challenged her ideas, encouraged her.

Why, she thought morosely as she stood and moved to the window, *couldn't he have just been nice to look at?*

The substance behind his handsome face made him all the more intriguing and attractive.

With a quick shake of her head, she looked out over the city. The sun had just dipped out of sight, leaving the horizon a painter's dream of magenta, pale orange and violet. Over-head the sky had slipped into darkness, deep blue serving as a backdrop for the proud skyscrapers of New York City jutting up toward the heavens. She'd never seen the city from so high up, historic landmarks sharing space with new creations, all of them lit with millions of golden lights that gleamed warmly in the late spring evening.

"Beautiful, isn't it?"

She started. Her eyes focused on his reflection in the glass just a few feet behind her.

"I don't know if I'd ever get any work done with a view like this."

"You get used to it after a while."

"How? How could something this incredible become mun-dane?"

He shoved his hands into his pockets, his expression dark-ening as he glanced between her and the city.

"That's a good question."

Something heavy lay beneath his words. She almost asked but stopped herself, remembering how quickly he had shut down when she'd inquired about his mother at the gala. They'd achieved a working harmony she didn't want to risk by asking nosy questions that were none of her business.

"I didn't realize how late it was."

"I didn't, either." She moved back toward the chair where she'd left her shoes. "But we got quite a bit done."

"What about your practice?"

Surprised, she looked up at him. "My practice?"

"You bring your cello with you to work almost every day. And," he added with a ghost of a smile, "Audrey told me you often stop and play in the park on your way home."

Evolet paused, suddenly shy. "The audition you heard me talking about with Audrey is for the Orchestra of St. John's. It's Thursday. Even though the Apprentice Symphony—the group I played with for the fundraiser—practices on Tuesdays, I try to play every day, and that's especially true if I have an audition coming up. I usually hop off at Fifty-Ninth Street, play in the park when the weather's nice so I don't bother my neighbors and then go home."

"What do you when it's raining or cold?"

"I use the church community room the Apprentice Symphony practices in." She glanced once more at the darkening sky. "But if I did that tonight, I probably wouldn't get home until after ten. I've practiced enough I'm pretty sure I play in my sleep."

"Still, you didn't have to stay. I know your music is important to you."

The way he said it, with genuine inflection, twisted her stomach into knots.

"Thank you. I feel pretty confident about the audition and, worst case, there will be another one later."

He tilted his head. "You don't sound that enthused."

Her hand came up, grasping for an explanation. "Is it bad that I'm almost more excited for the audition itself than the orchestra? It's a good orchestra, and I would be disappointed if I didn't make it."

"But not devastated."

"No," she replied with a smile. "Failing an audition for the Emerald City Philharmonic, however, would be devastating. They were the first group I ever saw professionally in concert. Just getting a standard 'thanks for applying' email when I submitted my audition tape earlier this year was hard enough."

"That had to be hard."

"It was. But," she continued with determination, "I won't give up."

He returned her smile with one of his own that made her feel warm and feverish. "I've felt the same about contracts with other companies. I feel the same way about Royal Air as you do about Emerald City."

It wasn't just the physical attraction snapping between them, she realized, that electrified the air. It was a shared camaraderie, an understanding of the passions that drove them to achieve their goals.

Cold tendrils of fear stabbed through the warmth. Too much opening up. Too much vulnerability, especially with a man like Damon.

"It's getting late." Her smile morphed into a polite expression, one that hopefully clearly conveyed the personal confession portion of their evening was over. "We made a lot of progress tonight, and I want to be here on time tomorrow to wrap up the proposal."

"Would you like to practice before you go?"

She blinked. "Um, where?"

"Here. The office is soundproof."

"Ah, yes. Most CEOs I work with soundproof their office for the inevitable torturing of their employees."

It shouldn't have mattered so much to see humor flash in his eyes, see the ghost of a grin on his lips.

"When you deal with the kind of companies and money that I do on a regular basis, ensuring discretion and privacy is tantamount to keeping clients. Unless," he added with that same hint of potent masculinity he'd displayed when he'd all but dared her to work for him, "you don't want me to hear you play."

She scoffed. "You've already heard me play."

"In a crowded ballroom. Your solo was enchanting but only thirty seconds amid a slew of other performances. I would have thought playing for someone new might help you prepare for your audition. But if you're uncomfortable, I wouldn't want to push."

The hell you wouldn't.

Her chin came up. He shrugged, the grin turning into a full-blown, devilishly taunting smile. He was baiting her, and she knew it. But she couldn't let a challenge about her music pass by unheeded.

And unfortunately, he was right. Any type of practice in front of a new audience was good.

"I'll be right back."

Five minutes later she sat with her back to the city. As she tuned her cello, she could feel his eyes on her, hating the way her heart thudded against her ribs as a heated flush stole over her body. When she practiced with the Apprentice Symphony or performed at an audition, she was among other musicians, people who knew the craft as well and often better than she did. Her nerves in those circumstances were solely fixated on playing the right notes, achieving the right volume, harmonizing with her fellow musicians or accompanist.

But now, she felt naked, exposed to every sweep of Damon's gaze. She hadn't performed like this for anyone except Constanza in years. Even at her auditions, she always had an accompanist.

"You're stalling."

"How do you know?" she retorted.

He grinned. She shook her head, picked up her bow and began to play.

The bow sank into the strings, the vibration rippling through her body. Her eyes drifted shut as the music filled the room. Deep and somber, the notes blended together to tell a story of love and loss, of growing old and saying goodbye. She drifted into the music, her body swaying with the cello as she poured her own losses and grieving into the movements, each emotion made more potent by the glimpse of happiness she'd been given by the man sitting just a few feet away.

The music swelled into a crescendo, then drifted off into

sorrow. She sat for a moment, taking in a deep breath as her body relaxed.

At last, she opened her eyes.

And nearly swallowed her tongue.

Damon watched her. Never had one gaze conveyed so much. He leaned back in his chair, the same deceptively casual stance he'd been in when she'd first glimpsed him in the ballroom. Just like that night, his eyes burned with an intensity that ensnared her, tempting her to release herself from the restrictions she'd placed on her heart.

"You play beautifully."

Huskier than normal, his voice wound about her like a seductive spell.

"Thank you."

"Do you always play sad songs?"

The question caught her off guard and eased some of the sexual tension building between them.

"No. I play a variety. There're quite a few videos on my social media and a few on my website. Some are sad, some are happy, some are fun."

"Your solo at the gala was sad."

Her hand tightened on the cello's neck. "I was sad. So, I played something sad."

"Why were you sad, Evolet?"

If he hadn't said her name, she would have been able to resist. But the touch of the personal, the genuineness in his voice made her lips part.

"Constanza moved to an elder care facility across the river a couple years ago. She'd had a bad morning the day of the fundraiser. It's hard seeing her like that."

"Bad how?"

"Alzheimer's. She was diagnosed two years ago and is still in the early stages. But some days are worse than others." She looked out at the darkening sky. "That day she kept asking for Samuel and me. We were the only ones she could remember."

"Samuel?"

"Her son. The only biological child she had." She smiled wistfully. "But she fostered over one hundred children."

"And adopted you."

"Yes. She is my mother. The only one I've ever really had. I went to her home and played for her. The music usually calms her." She started to fiddle with one of the cello pegs. "And it did. Just hard to see her like that."

"You're doing it again."

Her head snapped up, her eyes narrowing. "Doing what?"

"Downplaying what happened. Like you did at the fundraiser when you told me how you got started with the cello."

"I don't share my personal life with strangers."

Silence descended. She realized they were in some sort of emotionally charged standoff as their gazes held, tension building between them as they each waited for the other to look away. His hand rose, one finger lying casually on his cheek as the others curled into a fist and eclipsed his mouth from her view.

"Play another for me."

She blinked but didn't waver. It almost sounded like a command, one she would have normally refused simply on the principle of saying no to an order. To establish that just as his private life was off-limits to her, so was her past to him.

But, she realized as she nodded and brought the bow up, she wanted to play for him. She wasn't capable of fully sharing herself with anyone else. She'd done so with Constanza, would always be grateful for it. But Constanza's diagnosis, moving out of the apartment they'd shared for nine years and into the facility, seeing the one human being she had counted on since she was a teenager become a shadow of her former self had cemented that she would never allow another person into her life. Too many times she'd gotten her hopes up. Too many times she'd been left alone.

Playing was the closest she came to a relationship. That Damon had heard her solo amid the chaos of the fundraiser, picked up on the emotions swirling beneath the notes meant something to her.

Instead of dissecting why it meant anything—or why she was driven to share with him at all—she dragged the bow across the strings once more and descended into a poignant, haunting song dripping with unrequited desire. She'd played the song before, a dozen times. But playing it for Damon in the intimacy of his office, the memory of his kiss burning on her lips, she could feel the fervor in the harmonious blending of the notes, lust and longing crashing together in a scorching spiral that promised a night of passion unlike any other.

She had never understood the story behind the song, couldn't envision the emotions that were supposed to bleed from the sheet music into her playing.

But she did now. She'd never made love before, had never been tempted by the few dates she'd gone on. Lackluster kisses and groping hands had never inspired enough interest to take someone to her bed. Some of the women at the agency had encouraged her to try a dating app. Given that she barely had enough time for her music, her work to pay the bills and visiting Constanza regularly, she hadn't seen the point in going on potentially disastrous first dates in search of a fleeting sensation.

Yet as she cradled the cello between her thighs and thought of Damon, thought of his hands on her skin, his lips on hers, his harsh breathing echoing her own as they'd kissed in the rain, she knew that with someone like him, making love could truly be this chaotic, this wonderful.

She opened her eyes as she neared the end. Whether he had her in his web or she had him, she couldn't have torn herself away from meeting his stare. As he watched, his eyes devouring every movement of her fingers, the slide of her bow, the tilt of her body, she discovered it was possible to have the second most sensual experience of her life without a man ever laying a finger on her.

The song ended. Her body throbbed, deep beats that left her feeling heavy and unfulfilled. He maintained the same position he'd been in when she had started playing, his mouth hidden by his hand, his gaze focused on her. She knew he had been just as affected as she. But the fact that he remained so calm on the surface clawed at her pride.

"Satisfied?"

"Very."

He stood in one fluid motion, the elegance of the movement contrasted by his sheer masculinity. He crossed to her, and her breath caught in her chest as he reached down and lifted her hand, bow still in hand, to his lips.

"Thank you, Evolet."

The simple words sliced through her, cutting through her defenses and jabbing straight at her heart. Before she could summon a reply, he turned from her.

"Music has never been a focus of mine. But I've always been impressed by musicians and the talent it takes to play."

Conversation. He was making casual conversation, she realized dully.

"Um…with practice, it's not too hard." She forced herself to stay calm, to not succumb to her own desire, nor her rising anger, as she stood. "I maintain that anyone who has an interest can become a musician."

"I flunked piano lessons at the age of seven. Spectacularly enough that my parents never bothered to book me another tutor again."

She heard the smile in his voice. The simple glimpse into his past cooled some of her irritation and stirred her sympathy.

The one happy memory she had of her father was of a deep, booming laugh and being tossed up toward the sun on a warm summer day. The memories she had of her mother mostly involved a pale figure draped across a couch or passed out on the floor with an empty bottle nearby.

To have primarily good thoughts of one's parents, even in loss, was a gift most took for granted.

"Let me show you."

He turned back to her, his expression unreadable. "Excuse me?"

She gestured toward the empty chair. "I'll give you a quick lesson before I go."

"No."

She arched a brow. "Ah. That bad, huh?"

"My mother was an eternal optimist. Even she believed I was a lost cause."

"I think you're scared."

It was fun to have both the upper hand in finally unsettling him as much as he did her and causing a flicker of irritation to make his eyes narrow.

"I am not scared. Just practical."

"Sounds like a synonym for a scaredy-cat to me." She shrugged and started to reach for her case. "No matter. You're probably right. You would have played terribly."

He stalked across the room. She bit back a smile as he sat, his shoulders tense, his hands resting awkwardly on his knees.

"Five minutes. Show me."

"Not sure how much I can actually teach you in five minutes, but okay."

She helped him hold the cello and the bow, adjusting for his significantly larger height.

"I thought you didn't let anyone else touch your cello."

"I don't let anyone else carry my cello," she corrected him as she grasped his hand around the bow. "There's a world of

difference between someone flinging it around like a duf-
fel bag and teaching someone how to handle it respectfully. I
give lessons in the park sometimes after I finish practicing."

"You teach?"

"Don't sound so surprised. I can be quite patient and charming when I wish."

He grumbled something under his breath.

"Come again?"

"Nothing. Now what do I do?"

"All right, make sure your thumb is in the center…good.
You're going to drag the bow across the strings and use your
elbow…"

She walked him through the steps. Each note he played
made her inwardly wince even as she pasted an encouraging
smile on her face. "Good."

"Liar."

She laughed. "A terrible one. Here…" She walked behind
him and laid her hand over his. The warmth of his bare skin
beneath her palm made her tense. "Lay the bow on the D
string. And then pull with your elbow…"

A rich sound filled the air for a second.

"See! You can do it."

He glanced over his shoulder, one eyebrow arched in amusement. "I get credit for that?"

"You do."

Suddenly she realized just how close her lips were to his.
One slight move and…

Stop! her rational mind screamed. *Don't be a fool!*

"Well," she said in what she hoped was a much cooler voice
as she stood and moved away, "it's late."

He stood, gently laying her cello inside the open case, his
back to her. She yanked her eyes away from his broad shoulders
and moved to the window, wrapping her arms around her middle as if she could protect herself from this ridiculous attraction.

"It is."

She saw him appear once more in the glass. Even if she hadn't seen him, she would have felt him, that warm, rich scent that reminded her of spiced whiskey teasing her as he moved so close, she could feel the heat of his body on her back.

"Miss Grey…"

She closed her eyes at his formal address. How could he have missed her ridiculous reaction to him? Was he going to tell her to leave? Fire her?

"Evolet."

He gripped her shoulders and spun her around. One arm wrapped around her waist and dragged her against him, his body like steel beneath his clothes. The other hand slid up her neck, dislodging the loose knot and sending her hair cascading past her shoulders.

"Evolet," he said again, her name sounding like both a prayer and a curse on his lips, "if you don't want this—"

She surged forward, wrapping her arms around his neck and kissing him. He froze for a moment before his fingers tightened in her hair and he groaned. He anchored her head, plundered her mouth. Her breasts swelled against his chest. She wanted, so badly, to have his hands on her bare skin, to see him without the barriers of clothing.

As if he'd read her mind, he swept her into his arms and carried her over to his desk. He sat her on the edge and moved between her thighs with a confidence that stole her breath. His lips returned to hers, sending spiraling shoots of heat through her veins. One hand moved to her back, and she dimly heard the hiss of her zipper, felt the cool air kiss her back.

"Dear God," he whispered. "You're not wearing a bra."

Insecurity flitted across her senses, leached away some of the heat.

"I didn't not wear one on purpose. My, um, breasts aren't that big, and the dress has a built-in—"

"You're babbling again," he said with a smile that managed to be both wicked and carefree. It surprised her so much that she stopped talking long enough for him to lower his head and capture a nipple in his mouth.

Sensation exploded, spread like vines twining over her skin, binding her to the point of pleasure as his tongue swirled over her, teeth lightly scraping. Seeing his dark head against her breast sparked a carnality that drove her to the edge of her control. She teetered on the edge, wanting so much more, scared to take even a drop of what was being offered. If he could arouse her like this, with just a look, a kiss, a touch, what would happen if she were to fully surrender? Sex with Damon wouldn't just be sex. He would demand everything: heart, mind, body and soul.

His hands tightened on her waist. Her head fell back, and he placed a soft kiss at the base of her neck where her pulse throbbed before trailing his lips down again. She let him push her gently down until she was stretched across his desk, her dress pulled down to her waist, her hair spreading out around her head.

With his hands and mouth working erotic magic on her skin, the ache she'd shoved away after their night together rising to the surface demanding relief, surrender suddenly didn't sound like a bad thing.

No, she thought as he kissed his way down her stomach, *it sounds like a very, very good thing.*

Damon stood and gazed down at her with a possessive need that thrilled her to her toes. She smiled up at him.

He blinked. She started to reach for him, only to let her hands drop down as she watched him stare at her with hunger blazing in his eyes before he clenched his hands into fists and took a deliberate step back.

The full weight of all the rejections she'd experienced over the years came rushing back, eradicating her desire in one rush that stole the heat from her body and left her cold, draped half-naked across her boss's desk.

Damon turned away with a harsh oath. She closed her eyes, willing herself not to cry. Not in front of him. She wouldn't give him the satisfaction of letting him see how much he had affected her. How much he had hurt her.

How could she have thought him different? She sat up, lifting her bodice, the fabric feeling coarse against her skin as she slipped her arms into the sleeves. He was just like all the others, building up her hopes and making her think that maybe, just maybe, she needed to let go for a bit, start to let herself feel.

She slid off his desk and picked up her cello case without a backward glance. She would walk out of here with her head held high and email her boss at New York Executives letting them know she and Damon had had a disagreement and ask to be reassigned. She had never asked them for anything in seven years. They wouldn't like it, but they would do it.

She started for the door, her heart thudding dully in her chest, one hand wrapped around her cello case like it was a lifeline.

"Evolet."

She almost didn't stop. But something in his voice, the harsh darkness coating her name, made her stop.

When she looked back, it was to see him perched on the edge of his desk, one hand in his pants pocket, the other pinching the bridge of his nose.

"I'm sorry."

"Don't be," she said breezily in what she hoped was a voice that sounded like an experienced woman of the world and not a foolish virgin. "I'm sure I—"

"It wasn't you," he cut her off.

When he looked up, she nearly took a step back at the restrained passion that glowed in his eyes, a bright green fire that jump-started her heart back into a rapid dance that made her feel dizzy.

"I want you, Evolet. I want you, and I nearly took you right here on this desk."

Why didn't you?

She cleared her throat. "I noticed."

His choked laugh sounded anything but amused. "I'm your boss, Evolet. Your boss. I've never kissed an employee, let alone started to make love to one."

"Technically I'm New York Executives' employee."

He waved her comment aside. "Don't make excuses for me or what happened here tonight. I owe you my profound apology for taking advantage of you like that."

Some of her earlier irritation started to return. "Funny, it seemed more like a joint effort to me."

"Whatever it was, it can't and won't happen again. I understand if you want to seek employment elsewhere."

Her mouth dropped open. "Are you firing me?"

"No. Just assuring you that if you choose to leave, I will make sure you have nothing but glowing references and the full amount for your contract with Bradford Global."

Her mind raced, his first words echoing in her mind.

I want you, Evolet. I want you, and I nearly took you…

An idea popped into her head. A completely mad, utterly ridiculous idea. But the more she examined it, the more it made sense. Not a decision to be made lightly nor in the heat of the moment.

But, she thought as she tilted her chin up, after a good night's sleep and a little more consideration, it might just be perfect.

"I didn't do anything here tonight I didn't want to. Now, if you'll excuse me, I need to get home and get some rest. I'll see you at eight tomorrow morning. Sir."

With that final petty but very satisfying snip, she walked out and gently closed the door behind her.

CHAPTER NINE

No matter how hard Damon focused on his computer screen, no matter how many times he reread the words, none of it stuck. His eyes kept darting to the clock, watching it tick closer and closer to eight.

What the hell had he been thinking last night? How could he have let himself lose control like that?

Too long without a lover had been one reason he'd conjured up at one in the morning when he'd lain awake staring at the ceiling. That damned song he'd encouraged her to play that had sounded like sex incarnate, another reason he'd grasped on to at four as he'd wandered into his kitchen and punched the power button on his coffee machine.

Or perhaps it was just that he couldn't get her out of his mind, which was what he'd finally settled on when he'd forced himself under an icy shower at five that morning. An experience that had been completely not worth the pain when he'd walked into his office and gotten hard just looking at his desk where Evolet had lain, golden hair spread across the surface, her body flushed a shade of pink that had looked all the more alluring against the contrast of her wine-colored dress yanked down to her waist.

When he'd pulled her dress down and uncovered her bare breasts, he'd nearly lost it then and there. The occasional shyness that cropped up, her embarrassment at appearing coquettish, had only added to her allure. The few times she let him see her—really see her—the contrasts of her personality intoxicated him. She could be calm and professional, analytical and perceptive. Their conversations last night—before he'd lost his mind—had stimulated him in a way no date had in a very long time. If ever.

But then she could be feisty, fire tempered by a compassionate nature he'd heard about from his employees and witnessed firsthand when she'd bought him dinner with her own money.

It shouldn't have mattered. But it did.

His computer dinged, and a notification signaled a new email. He clicked on it, his pulse ticking up. A calendar request for a meeting at eight o'clock from Evolet Grey.

She was probably going to quit. That or tell him she had filed charges against him for harassment. Nothing less than he deserved. Even if the emotional nuances of his attraction to Evolet weren't troubling enough, he had crossed a line.

The next nine minutes dragged on. Finally, the clock turned eight. His door opened not a second later, and Evolet walked in.

His chest tightened. Today she wore a black–and-white striped collared shirt and a pale yellow skirt with a black belt snug around her waist. Her hair was once more back in the severe bun. The memory of it spilling like silk over his wrists, caressing his skin as he'd kissed her, made his temper flare.

"Good morning, Evolet."

"Good morning. Is now a good time?"

With the resignation of a man heading to the gallows, he nodded. She crossed to the chair she'd occupied just hours before, curled up barefoot eating macaroni and cheese, and sat with the aplomb of a queen.

"I have two things to discuss with you—the first of which is the updated bid."

Business. He could handle business talk. He gestured for her to continue, and for eleven blissful minutes they reviewed the changes they'd made last night, discussed what work still needed to be done.

"Can we get the bid submitted before the thirteenth?" he asked.

"Yes. I would say at least a day before."

"Good."

Evolet cleared her throat. "Which brings me to the second matter I wanted to discuss with you."

Tension knotted his neck. "Yes?"

"Yes?"

Some of her bravado slipped. She breathed in deeply, her hands settling on her lap as she laced her fingers together. "I have a proposal for you."

"Interesting. Normally it's the man who does the proposing."

A blush stole over her cheeks. The sight of her skin turning pink tugged memories of the previous night to the forefront.

"Spit it out, Evolet," he growled.

"All right."

She looked him dead in the eye, and he suddenly had the feeling that the world was about to drop out from under him.

"I want you to be my first lover."

There. I said it.

Evolet's triumphant thought was swiftly followed by panic. *Oh, God. I asked him to have sex with me.*

She gripped her own hands tighter as she forced herself to sit and not run off like a scared little rabbit. The seconds ticked by, the tension ratcheting up with every passing moment.

And all Damon did was sit there, staring at her with an almost lazy air about him as if she hadn't just made the most indecent proposal of her life.

"Your first lover."

Finally, he spoke.

"Yes."

"As in…"

"I'm a virgin," she said impatiently.

"I see."

"After the contract is submitted. That takes precedent. Once the proposal is submitted, we can…" She waved a hand between them.

"Have sex."

"Yes." She smiled, pleased he was at least considering the possibility. "And then we go on our separate ways. I'll work at Bradford for the rest of my contract, and then we'll go on with our lives."

"Just like that?"

"Just like that."

Another long minute passed where she forced herself not to fidget. The more time passed, the more the weight of what she had just done settled on her shoulders, heavy and smothering. When she'd thought of it last night, she'd still been high on pleasure, desperate for him. Her solution had seemed like the perfect way to regain control, experience the thrills he had promised with his touch while adding an expiration date to their affair.

I want you, Evolet.

The raw yearning in his voice when he'd uttered those words had made her think that he would at least consider it.

But right now, sitting under his aloof, scrutinizing gaze, she felt like she had last night when she'd laid half-naked on top of his desk and he'd turned from her: Foolish. Ashamed. Rejected.

"Well, I guess that answers that." She stood and smoothed her hands across her skirt, the silky fabric calming some of her frayed nerves. "I'll make the same offer you made to me last night. If you're no longer comfortable with me serving in this role, I'll alert my boss and—"

"Why now?"

She blinked. "What?"

"Why, after twenty-five years of abstinence, are you looking to give up your virginity?"

"Because I've found someone I'm attracted to."

His brows drew together in a considering frown. "And you've never been attracted to anyone else before?"

"I have. But not like this." She shrugged, trying to appear nonchalant. "It's the twenty-first century. Women can ask men out, too."

He stood and circled around the desk, his face darkening into a thunderous expression. "There's a difference between asking a man out on a date and asking him to be the one to take your virginity."

The condescension in his tone sparked ire and embarrassment.

"Then forget I asked. I'll find someone else since you're not interested."

She started to turn away, but he moved quickly, coming up to her so fast she took several steps back until she bumped into the door.

"And how are you going to do that, Evolet? Post an ad online?"

"Not a bad idea," she fired back. "Do you think Click Here to Deflower a Virgin is too straightforward a title?"

One second they were standing nose to nose. The next he had placed his hands on either side of her head and leaned down until his mouth was so close she could feel his breath feathering across her lips.

"I didn't say no."

Warning whispered across the back of her neck as her skin prickled.

"So…is that a yes?"

"Where would this event take place?"

An image of the cramped apartment she'd lived in for the past ten years rose in her mind, her tiny bedroom barely big enough for a bed, her kitchen, living room and dining room all smooshed together in a space smaller than Damon's office.

"Um… I hadn't got that far."

"I'll pick the location, then."

Her heart sped up. "So that's a yes?"

"Are you comfortable continuing to work for me?"

"With you," she corrected. "Like I said last night, you're not my boss."

He made a noise that sounded almost like a growl. "Semantics."

"Not to me." She swallowed hard. "But I understand if the dynamic isn't one you're comfortable with. I could ask to be reassigned, or we could just not—"

He moved a fraction closer, cutting her off midsentence with his proximity.

"I'll respect your interpretation of our roles. But if at any point that changes, Evolet," he said, his voice turning harsh with emotion, "you tell me. Tell me, and I'll stop."

Touched, her hand came up before she could stop herself. Her palm settled on his cheek. He turned his head and pressed a heated kiss to her skin that made her gasp.

"Once the proposal is submitted, then."

Relief spiraled through her, followed by the intoxicating beat of anticipation mixed with desire. "Yes."

His gaze intensified. "Why me?"

"What?"

"Why me, Evolet?"

She started to make a joke, to pass it off as something not that important. But the way he looked at her, with something vulnerable flashing for a heartbeat, made her pause.

"Do you remember when we danced at the gala?"

"Vividly."

"You asked me to trust you." His eyes sharpened. "I did. It was the first time I trusted someone like that with my body in…ever. And you took care of me. I stumbled, and you caught me. We have something intense and sexy between us, which is a bonus. But…" She licked her lips. "I trust you. I want my first time to be with someone I trust."

Finally, he moved. He kissed her, fierce and hot, before he pulled back and walked back to his desk. She stood there, her back pressed against the door, her lips swollen to the touch.

"A kiss to seal the deal."

His eyes flicked up, lust burning so hot she could have sworn she would go up in flames on the spot. But then she blinked and the man disappeared, replaced by the distant CEO.

"We'll discuss details at a later date. But for now, we have work to do."

CHAPTER TEN

EVOLET CHECKED HER email for the dozenth time since eight a.m.

"We submitted it ten minutes ago." The dry humor in Damon's voice made her look up. Amused, he nodded to her computer. "It'll probably be Monday at the earliest before we hear if Bengtsson wants any revisions and probably another week or two before he makes any decisions."

She sank back into her chair with a huff. "Did I mention I'm impatient?"

His eyes darkened before he refocused on his own computer. "I noticed."

She shot him a teasing look, but nervousness had her biting back a witty reply. Today she'd awakened with uneasy energy snapping in her veins. Today was the day they submitted the final bid, a full twelve hours before Royal Air's deadline. Part of the tension vibrating inside her like a taut wire was from what would come next. They'd shared the occasional heated glance or accidental brush of physical contact that made her breath catch, but there had been no more discussions, no more flirtations, no more searing kisses. There hadn't been time. It had been a whirlwind of a week as they'd reviewed the proposal over and over again—fine-tuning, discussing, meeting with others in the company, then revising again. It had been a heartening experience to see the level of investment from everyone in the company.

She wanted the contract for Bradford Global, and not just because she was besotted with the company's CEO. She'd continued to witness the work Damon's business did, where manufacturing quality equipment was just as high a priority as keeping its employees healthy and happy.

Perhaps, if the company her father had worked for had had the same attitude toward investing in its employees, the course of her life might have been very different.

"Where did you go?"

His voice slid into her musings, gentle and deep. It was odd to have someone she'd known less than a month become so in tune with her and her emotions. Once their deal had been struck, she'd felt the shackles she'd placed on her emotions loosen and start to fall away. The wanting that had been stoked in her the night of the gala had flared to life. She'd let Damon see more of her, the real her, than she had let anyone see in years, including herself. She didn't analyze everything she was going to say before it was said. She'd let herself relax and laugh at jokes, engage with the other employees.

It had also helped her realize just how utterly exhausting it had been to keep up those barriers between herself and the rest of the world. Even Constanza had commented on her last visit how much happier she'd seemed.

And she was. Mostly.

The audition with the Orchestra of St. John's had resulted in a brief email over the weekend thanking her for her time, saying the orchestra had gone in a different direction but she was always welcome to audition at a later date. It had hurt more than she'd liked, shaken her confidence. She'd spent hours in the park practicing, listening for what she had done wrong, analyzing every note until she'd been irritated and exhausted.

The sad truth was that there was a bevy of talented musicians and only so many spots. She could either give up or she could keep going. She'd indulged in a pity evening, including an old musical, popcorn and a long soak in her tub, then gone back out Sunday and played again.

Monday had brought another test. Damon had taken one look at her face and known something was wrong. Letting down her barriers had certainly let in more joy. But it had also brought with it an uncomfortable vulnerability she hadn't experienced since her early years in foster care. She could handle more friendships, more outings with coworkers, finally letting herself experience a physical relationship with a man whose company she enjoyed and who she found incredibly attractive.

Yet sharing her body felt safer than opening her heart. That she wanted to share more of herself every time he asked was a major red flag. But God help her, she wanted to be with him, to experience sensual pleasure with someone she liked, someone she trusted, someone who could make her entire body ache with a single glance.

Which is why, she reminded herself as she tucked a loose tendril of hair behind her ear, *you came up with the arrangement.*

The terms were clear, finite. They would have sex. She would finish out her contract with Bradford Global. And then she would move on.

"I was thinking about how well you run your company," she finally said, finding a compromise on her thoughts. "I've never seen something run so smoothly or so strongly."

"Why did that make you sad?"

She tensed. "It didn't."

"Something did."

She looked up, ready to push back. The genuine interest and compassion in his eyes struck her, tugged at the strings she'd wrapped tightly around her heart. As a child, she'd rattled off her entire life story to the first two foster homes she'd stayed in. The families had been kind and considerate. One mom had listened to her and hugged her while she'd cried. Evolet had liked her a lot, had even started to envision staying with them and becoming a part of their family.

Only to have the system yank her out and place her in a new home three weeks before Christmas. She'd cried and begged to stay, but the family'd had the resources and training to care for a child with critical needs that many foster homes didn't. So Evolet had been transplanted to a home in a different school district.

Again and again, she'd gotten her hopes up, until finally one day she had woken up to the news that she was being transferred to yet another new house, another new school. Whether it had been the freezing cold hitting her in the face as she'd gotten off the bus or the sight of unfamiliar faces in a crowded school, she didn't know. All she knew was something had switched off inside her. Something only Constanza had managed to break through in the years since.

Until now.

Would it hurt anything? she wondered to herself.

Wasn't part of the reason she had propositioned Damon because there was something more than just attraction? Would sharing a small piece of herself be a bad thing?

"I was thinking about my father." She looked down at her teacup, fiddled with the string. "He worked as an electrician. Made good money, but if business was slow, things could get tight. The company he worked for cared more about getting things done than their employees."

She remembered his face the day he'd tossed her into the air, bright and vibrant. She also remembered it just a few months later, gray and wan, like someone had turned the light off behind his eyes.

"He worked an outside job in the cold. Got sick." She pulled the tea bag out, watched amber droplets fall and splash down into the cup. "Their equipment was old. He waited too long to go to the hospital because the company didn't provide health insurance. He didn't make it." She looked at him. "You make a difference, you know. The way you treat your people."

He watched her for a long moment, as if not sure what to make of what she'd just shared.

"Is that how you ended up in foster care?"

"I ended up in foster care because my biological mother preferred alcohol and pills over being a parent." She winced as the words came out, sharper and rawer than she had intended. "I was told she was a good mom before my father passed. I was only five when I went into care and don't have many memories before then."

He stood and moved to her, sitting down in the chair across from her. He leaned over, plucked the crumpled tea bag from her fingers and tossed it into the trash before sitting in front of her.

Why, she thought with sudden rising panic, *does this feel more intimate than kissing partially nude on his desk?*

"It's okay now," she said with a forced smile as she tried to discreetly scoot her chair back. "It's been years."

"Doesn't erase the pain."

She let out a breath. When she had shared pieces of herself with her foster families, they had always encouraged her to move on, to look to the future, to think about things that excited her. Never to grieve, to process what she had lost.

"No, it doesn't. Time lessens how much it hurts. And there are many days, weeks and even months where I don't even think of them. But then there are days like today where something hits and it hits hard." She sighed. "It's interesting, isn't it, how the smallest things can open the gates. Like seeing how nice someone treats their employees."

He reached out, slowly, then laid a hand on top of hers. This time the heat that spread was one of comfort, of support and understanding.

Silence descended. She was, she realized, not uncomfortable as they sat there. No, she was feeling…heard. Respected.

"I was told," he said quietly, "grief comes in waves. It starts off like a tsunami, and you think there's no possible way you can get out from under it. Then the waves get a little more manageable. Over time, they become ripples. But you'll still occasionally have that moment, that memory, that thought that knocks you off your feet. And that's okay."

She tilted her head. "I like that." She laid her fingers on top of his, the sight of their hands atop one another comforting. "I also heard that sometimes we hang on to grief because we're too frightened of who we are without it."

He stared at her, his face unreadable. She kept her hand on his, grateful when he didn't pull away. Had she gone too far? She saw so much of herself in Damon, the holding back to keep himself safe. But perhaps, after she had trusted him, he might feel the same way.

This time the silence that followed carried an edge. Damon held her gaze for what felt like forever before he gave her a small, opaque smile that made her feel cold. "Perhaps."

He squeezed her hand, stood and retreated back to his desk.

Dismissed, quickly and effectively. She might have been ready to unburden some of her darkest moments, to share with the man who was to become her lover. Clearly, he wasn't.

No reason for him to share, she reminded herself as she quietly excused herself and walked back to her office. *You're not his girlfriend.*

She knew a little about his past. A framed obituary in the lobby included a brief mention that a drunk driver had killed David and Helen Bradford when Damon had been in his senior year of college. Evolet hadn't been able to bring herself to do an online search to learn more. It had felt too much like an invasion of privacy if Damon didn't want to talk about it.

She closed the door to her office and sank down into her

chair. She picked up a pencil, twirled it absently in her fingers, set it back down. She'd taken a small risk, and while the moment of connection over loss had been affirming, Damon's lack of reciprocity had been a much-needed reminder as to what their arrangement was—as well as what it would never be.

Although perhaps after what had just happened, Damon would want to terminate their agreement. Just the thought twisted her stomach into knots.

Taking a deep breath, she focused on her computer and began to respond to the emails that had piled up in her inbox. Her fingers itched for her bow, to play a song or two and settle the somber restlessness inside her.

Later, she promised herself. Later she would play. And whatever came after that, she would deal with it.

Even if she dealt with it alone.

CHAPTER ELEVEN

DAMON KNOCKED ON the door to Evolet's office. At her soft "Enter," he twisted the knob and stepped inside, closing the door behind him.

She looked up from her computer, a small smile crossing her face. Relief filtered through him. He knew he'd been borderline rude with his response to her gentle prompt on his own sorrow. It hadn't been fair to prod her to share when he had no intention of doing so.

Although it went much deeper than simply not wanting to open up. Digging down into the depths of his grief, of ripping open a wound that had taken so long to repair to the point he could function was too much. Even just recalling memories of his parents sent pain lancing through him. While he appreciated the intention behind the hanging of the obituary in the lobby, an action taken in the weeks after his parents' deaths when there had been an interim CEO, he avoided looking at it every time he walked through.

"Is everything okay?"

He refocused on Evolet, who was watching him with guarded cautiousness. God, he felt like a cad. She'd trusted him with something incredibly precious—not just once with asking him to be her lover, but twice by sharing such an intimate part of her history.

"I don't talk about my parents."

She turned then to face him completely, folding her hands on the desk and fixing him with that golden gaze.

"I won't ever ask you to. I know what arrangement we have, Damon, and I—"

"You misunderstand," he said, trying to suppress the frustration in his voice. "It's cliché to say that it's not you, it's me, but it's true. Talking about them…" He paused, hardened his heart against the past straining to break free. "It hurts too much. I fell into a very dark place after they passed."

Memories of waking up, vivid nightmares of his parents' accident giving way to the crushing reality that they were gone, flashed through him. He had loved his parents, and they had loved him. But that love had come with a heavy price in the wake of loss.

A price he would never pay again.

Her face softened. "You must have loved them very much."

"I still do."

She stood and came around the desk. Before he could move, she took his hand just as he had taken hers in his office. Her fingers were so much smaller than his, pale and elegant against his skin.

"I understand."

Just like that, he was forgiven. Humbled, unsettled by her simple acceptance, he nodded at her computer. "Any word?"

The tension in the room bled out as she circled back around her desk and blew out a frustrated breath.

"No." She glanced at him, then laughed. "You've been checking, too, haven't you?"

He grinned. "I feel like a little kid at Christmas waiting for his present to arrive." He glanced down at his watch, then groaned. "And it's only ten o'clock."

Evolet sighed. "How am I going to survive the weekend?"

As soon as the words were out of her mouth, her head jerked up as her eyes darkened. His mind scrambled, thoughts of business scattering as possibilities opened before him, each idea more sensual and tantalizing until he was so hard it was almost painful.

The proposal had been submitted. Evolet would move to a different department on Monday. Nothing was stopping him now from fulfilling her request.

"Let's go."

Her eyes widened. "Go?"

"It's Friday." He walked closer until he was just on the other side of her desk. "The proposal is submitted. Bengtsson will take at least a week, possibly two, to review the proposals. On the off chance he jumps the gun, I have my phone on me."

"But you're the CEO. What if something comes up?"

"I told Julie I would be available off-site by phone. I also told her I was giving you the rest of the day off to thank you for your hard work."

She worried her lower lip with her teeth. "And our…arrangement… I know you didn't want me to be working for you…"

"As of Monday, you'll be reporting to my chief engineer, Nathaniel Pratt, and serving in a temporary role as executive assistant to three of his engineers. I've wanted to try out the concept of having assistants for our engineers for some time, and testing it out through the remainder of your contract is the perfect opportunity."

"Don't you still need an assistant?"

"Louise requested an extension of her maternity leave. She'll be gone for up to a year. One of the secretaries who works under Julie has been jumping at the chance to become an executive assistant, and this will give him a chance to get some experience." He arched an eyebrow. "Any other road-blocks you'd like to throw in my way?"

When she didn't answer, he held out his hand, his lips tilting up into a smile that challenged her to take a risk. "Let's play hooky, Evolet."

She stared at the outstretched hand. He heard the sharp inhale of her breath, watched as her breasts rose and fell beneath the silky white material of her shirt.

Unease skittered through him. Had she changed her mind?

Then she reached out, took his hand and gave him a smile that slipped past his desire and stirred something deep inside him. "Okay."

Fifteen minutes later they were pulling out of the parking garage, Damon behind the wheel of a vintage silver Aston Martin and Evolet's cello secured in the trunk.

"Did you have dreams of being a spy as a boy?" Evolet asked teasingly as he pulled out into the glorious mess of New York City traffic.

"What do you mean 'did'?"

He savored the burst of laughter, the uninhibited smile that made Evolet's eyes crinkle. The light turned green, and a cacophony of car horns blared behind them. As much as he appreciated having his own time, indulging in the seclusion of his office or traveling upstate to his family's estate in the Catskills, he took great joy in the city that had embraced his grandfather's company decades ago.

The simple pleasure of the moment, of leaving work early, had him letting down his guard. His fingers curled around the steering wheel as the car surged forward. The sensation of cool, smooth leather beneath his hands stirred a memory—the first time his father had let him drive the Aston Martin, punching up the volume of his favorite spy movie's iconic theme music.

"The car belonged to my father."

The words came out before he could stop them. He waited for the stab of pain, the curtain of depression to descend and blight out the brightness of the day.

Yet it didn't come. The sadness was there, yes. But mostly

he just felt the nostalgic warmth of one of the happiest times in his life.

"He had very good taste."

The simple reply, one that accepted the tiny bit he'd shared and didn't pry for more, helped him relax once more. Whether Evolet understood the significance of the simple admission or not, it felt surprisingly good to share something about his father. He hoped, too, it made up in some small part for his boorishness earlier.

"Where to?"

He felt her glance, sensed her confusion. Had she imagined he would just whisk her away to a hotel, have his way with her and then disappear?

No. He wanted nothing more than to slip that proper blouse off her shoulders, slide the skirt from her waist and finally make his most erotic fantasies come to life. But Evolet deserved more than just sex. If the woman wasn't working or practicing in the park, she was playing with the symphony or spending time with her adoptive mother.

She deserved a day without schedules, tasks and rushing to get to the next thing on her to-do list. She deserved a day just about her.

"Um…"

He reached over and grabbed her hand. She started, her body tensing a moment before she relaxed. When she twined her fingers through his, he felt the satisfaction of her acquiescence all the way to his bones.

"Where's somewhere in New York you've always wanted to go but never have?"

At the next stoplight he glanced over to see another smile spreading across her face, this one shy and sweet.

"The Empire State Building."

He guided the car down FDR Drive, the city gleaming under the morning sunlight to their left and the river shimmering to their right. They rode the elevator to the top of the Empire State Building.

When they walked out onto the observation deck, the sheer joy on Evolet's face made his chest fill with a happiness he hadn't experienced in a very long time. They slipped quarters into the coin-operated binoculars and circled the deck at least four times.

"That was incredible," Evolet gushed as they walked back out onto Thirty-Fourth Street and toward the private parking garage Damon had booked. "I can't wait to tell Constanza."

"Where does she live?"

Damon inwardly swore as Evolet's face dimmed.

"A memory care facility across the river. It's one of the best in the tristate area."

He frowned. "That sounds expensive."

Evolet shrugged. "Constanza's son, Samuel, is ten years older than me. He works as a welder and pays for over half. I contribute what I can."

His esteem for Evolet had already been high. Now, as she walked alongside him, her face tilted up to the sun, it skyrocketed. There were so many layers to this fascinating woman, each one more intriguing than the last.

He whisked her to a quiet French bistro off Union Square for a late lunch, where they dined on mushroom ravioli smothered in truffle fondue sauce and pan-seared salmon. They shared a dessert of poached pear topped with vanilla ice cream. After he grudgingly let her pay for the tip, he drove her to the Morgan Library and Museum, taking joy out of watching her mouth drop open at the sight of the three stories of walnut bookcases packed with manuscripts and the intricately painted arched ceiling.

As the sun slid across the sky, he drove back toward Billionaires' Row. The glass exterior of the One57 building that housed a hotel and condominiums, including Damon's own penthouse, glinted in the pinkening light of twilight.

"I'd like to take you one more place."

Evolet chuckled softly. Her eyes were closed, her lashes dark against her skin. "Just one more? I feel like I've lived more in one day than I have my entire life."

Her innocent words wrapped around him. When he'd taken Natalie out to dinner, the final bill had been more than what he'd spent so far today. Never had Natalie reacted with such unbridled excitement or joy. Nor had he enjoyed himself half as much.

"Come to my penthouse."

Her eyes shot open. He pulled the car off to the side of the road and turned so he was facing her.

"Your penthouse," Evolet echoed quietly.

"Yes." He gave in to the temptation that had been haunting him all day and reached out, cupping her face in his palm.

All around them, New York continued its frantic pace. Taxis and motorcycles battled for space with horns honking and tires screeching. A sidewalk musician wailed out a jazzy tune on a saxophone. Pedestrians streamed by, laughing, conversing and shouting as night descended.

But inside the car, only Evolet existed. Evolet and this moment.

"I'd like that."

Desire welled inside him, propelled him forward as he pulled her closer. Her lips parted, and their mouths met in a kiss that swept through him like wildfire.

As he pulled back into traffic and guided his car toward Billionaires' Row, he focused on the anticipation, the hot pulse of hunger.

And ignored the emotions whispering beneath the currents of his need.

CHAPTER TWELVE

EVOLET TURNED IN a circle, trying and failing to keep her mouth from dropping open. Three of the walls of Damon's living room were tinted glass with the kind of views of Midtown and Central Park some people would kill for. The room still had the old-library feel the Bradford Global office did. But here there was a touch of modern—soft gray leather furniture, black lamps and moody photographs of what she guessed was the Hudson River Valley upstate. On the other side of the glass, just off the kitchen that sported granite countertops and soft golden lighting underneath the custom black cabinets, was a balcony with artfully arranged plants and cozy outdoor furniture. If she craned her head enough, she could spot the pool at the far end.

"Pinch me."

"What?"

"This has to be a dream," she said breathlessly. "I can't believe real people live like this." She shot him a bashful smile over her shoulder before looking out over the park again. "Sorry. I live in a two-bedroom three-story walk-up in East Harlem. This is just…unreal."

Damon came up behind her, so close she could feel the heat from his body. "I'm glad you like it."

His voice seeped into her veins. She took a risk and leaned back, sighing as her back rested against his muscular chest.

Slowly, his arms twined about her waist, then turned her to face him before he lowered his lips to hers.

The kiss was no less powerful than the ones they'd already shared. But it was different, gentler, testing, even as his hands spread possessively across her back.

Nerves skittered across her skin. What if she disappointed him? What if they'd built up this attraction into something far more passionate than what the actual event would bring?

Sensing her sudden hesitancy, Damon pulled back but kept her tight in the circle of his arms.

"I want you, Evolet," he grated out. "But I won't take anything you're not ready to give. It's your choice." His breath rushed out. "It's always your choice."

That he would hold himself back, offer her a choice even as she saw the pulse pounding at the base of his throat, felt the restrained passion in hands that cradled hers like she was made of glass dissolved her resistance as if it had never existed.

"I'm ready."

Damon moved as soon as the words were uttered. He picked her up in his arms and carried her into his bedroom. She got a quick impression of dark navy walls and a massive bed before he set her on her feet. He reached over, flicked on a lamp and then moved his hands over her. Her blouse disappeared over her head, her bra unclipped in a matter of seconds.

"You've done that before," she said, amused.

"I have." His eyes feasted on her bare breasts. "But this…"

One hand came up, cupped the fullness of her breast. She moaned as his thumb whispered across her nipple.

"Evolet, you are so beautiful."

With that pronouncement lingering seductively in the air, he leaned down and captured her nipple in his mouth. Each flick of his tongue, each gentle suck sent her spiraling higher. He lavished the same attention on her other breast, driving her to distraction so that she didn't even register his fingers unbuttoning her skirt or sliding the material down until cool air kissed her naked legs.

Damon looked down, swore.

"What?" She glanced down, shyness threatening to overtake her as she realized she'd worn simple nude-colored panties instead of the red lacy lingerie she'd purchased after Damon had accepted her deal.

"Did I say beautiful?" He sank to his knees, captured her hips in an iron grip that made her knees weak. "Gorgeous." He kissed the sensitive skin above the fabric "Exquisite." Another kiss to her core, now throbbing with need. "Stunning."

He skimmed up her body so quickly she didn't have time to catch her breath. He scooped her up into his arms once more, then laid her on the bed as he raked her with a hungry gaze.

"Much as I like the panties," he said, his voice husky as he hooked his fingers into the material, "I want to see you naked."

And she wanted him to see her naked. Charged with confidence and desire, she lifted her hips, savored the parting of his lips and the lascivious gleam in his eyes.

Then she was bare. Shyness teased her, but she stayed still, watching him watch her. Each passing second increased the ache until she was filled with it, a pressure building in her chest as her body demanded satisfaction.

Finally, he moved, stripping off his clothes with decisive movements, tossing his dress shirt, pants and belt onto the floor. Was it odd to describe a man as beautiful? *Handsome* didn't do justice to his body, hard ridges and lean muscles honed by time and discipline. His erection jutted out proudly.

He sat on the edge of the bed and skimmed a finger over her skin. The touch was featherlight, but the trail of heat he left behind sank into her, made her bow off the bed as he drew patterns on her belly, her thighs.

Her legs bent, shifting restlessly.

"Damon…please…"

He moved over. His body settled on top of hers, a solid comforting weight that pressed her deeper into the embrace of the bed. The thrill of having his naked skin against hers nearly made her come undone as he kissed her again, slowly, romantically. As the golden light of the lamp caressed the angles and planes of his body, he made his way down hers with kisses, soft nips and gentle caresses that heated her blood and made her flush with need. When he placed his mouth on her most sensitive skin, she felt that blessed pleasure growing inside her, climbing higher and higher…

He stopped. She started to sit up, to protest, but he moved quickly, capturing her hands in his as he claimed her lips.

"I want to be inside you this first time." He kissed her cheek, the curve of her jaw, pressed the sweetest of kisses to her shoulder. "I want to feel you shatter around me."

Her thighs parted to cradle his weight. He groaned as her wet heat pressed against his hard length, and she smiled with sheer feminine satisfaction that she could bring this man just as close to the edge as he brought her.

"One moment," he ground out.

He rolled off of her and pulled a condom from the nightstand drawer. She watched as he rolled it onto his erection, her breath coming out in short pants as his fingers glided up and down. She reached for him, wanting to touch, but he caught her wrist and pinned it above her head as he lowered himself back down to her.

"I'm not going to have your first time involve me embarrassing myself."

"Do I drive you that wild?" she asked with a smile, her other hand skating down his back and slipping between their bodies to graze his him. He hissed, grabbed her questing hand and pinned it next to her head.

"Minx."

Her smile faded as she stared deep into his eyes.

"Damon…"

He watched her.

"Make love to me."

He released her hands and wrapped her in a strong embrace as he pressed against her. Her body welcomed him, pulled him deeper. There was a moment of pain, and she couldn't hold back her slight cry. He paused, soothed, kissed her eyelids, the tip of her nose as he held her tighter and whispered sweet nothings in her ear.

Slowly, her body relaxed, accepted him. He began to move with languid strokes that restoked the flames of desire. She rocked against him in an instinctive rhythm. Sighs turned to gasps. Dampness slicked their skin as they climbed higher, their bodies racing to the top. He braced himself on his elbows, lifted just enough to watch her face.

"Damon… Damon, I can't…"

"Let go. Let go for me, Evolet."

She let herself fly over the edge, felt sensation splinter then fracture into thousands of dazzling bursts of pleasure. She cried out again, this time in ecstasy, her legs coming up and wrapping around his waist as she pulled him to her.

He whispered her name, followed her a moment later. He shuddered, his arms clamped around her like a vice.

Slowly, so slowly, they drifted down, heartbeats slowing, breaths quieting as they lay tangled up in each other. Evolet's fingers drifted up and down his back—her lover's back—and she sighed in pleasured satisfaction. Damon brushed a soft kiss to her cheek.

Never had she felt so aware of her body, so sure of herself, so reckless in giving rather than protecting.

Reality tried to intrude, to remind her that he was her lover for just tonight, that to lie with him like this in the aftermath of their lovemaking was almost more of an intimacy than what they had just shared.

But she would not deny herself. Days, months, years later, when she looked back on her first time, she would relive the seduction, the foreplay, the incredible act of joining her body with his.

With the remnants of physical pleasure still flickering inside her, a pleasure made all the more potent by embracing the emotions she'd fought so hard to keep at bay, she closed her eyes and drifted off to sleep.

Damon looked up as Evolet padded into the kitchen, her hair rumpled and her eyes sleepy. The sight of her in one of his T-shirts with those beautiful legs bare sent a bolt of possessiveness through him.

Had it really been two days since he'd first taken her to bed? He hadn't planned on inviting her to stay the whole weekend. That first night they'd awoken in each other's arms around midnight. When she'd turned to him with a smile and a whispered thank-you, he'd suddenly wanted to extend the night just a little longer. He'd carried her into the bathroom, drawn a hot bath and cradled her in his arms as he'd washed away the remnants of her first time. His own tenderness had surprised him. He hadn't been prepared for how intense their first time together would be, the knowledge that not only had he been her first lover but her first choice, her only choice. It had humbled him, touched a part of him he hadn't known existed and made him want to gather her in his arms and care for her.

And then she'd turned to him, rising up like a siren with water sluicing down over her skin, beading on the tips of her breasts, as she'd arched her body and rubbed herself against him before taking him in hand and stroking him to the point of madness. He'd barely remembered to extract himself long enough to grab a condom out of the nightstand before sinking inside her once more.

Previous affairs had been mutually enjoyed, pleasant, sexy,

even invigorating. But never had a woman slipped past his defenses and stirred more than the faintest feelings of companionship.

They'd woken Saturday morning, ordered breakfast and eaten in bed. He'd had a swimming suit delivered so she could enjoy the heated pool he so rarely used. Although, he admitted to himself, it hadn't been just for her. Watching her body glide through the water had made him so hard he'd whisked her back inside and made love to her on the couch. Afternoon had turned into evening, and when she'd fallen asleep on him while they were watching a movie, he'd carried her back to his bed.

He'd never enjoyed time with a woman so much as he had enjoyed the past couple of days. And that put him on guard. This arrangement was supposed to be about a mutually pleasurable affair, introducing a woman he found interesting and intriguing to sex, not playing house.

Remember that, he ordered himself as he took a sip of coffee and inwardly swore as the scalding liquid burned his tongue.

"Good morning." He kept his tone casual, stayed with the barrier of the countertop between them.

Her smile punched him in the gut, sleepy and with a hint of bashfulness as she circled around the kitchen island, raised up on her toes and grazed his stubbled cheek with a kiss. "Good morning."

The husky thread in her voice had his muscles tightening. He forced the desire back and returned her smile.

"Did you sleep well?"

"Aside from getting woken up around midnight, yes," she teased as she checked him with her hip on the way to the coffee machine.

They'd turned to each other in the night, waking to find themselves wrapped around each other. He hadn't been gentle, but then neither had she. They'd devoured each other, bodies molded together as they caressed, demanded, took everything they could give each other.

It still wasn't enough, he thought as his eyes drifted down over her rear, her thighs, her bare feet.

Would it ever be enough?

The thought had him turning away from the intoxicating sight of her and back to the stove.

"I made breakfast. Eggs, bacon and pancakes if you're hungry."

As he flipped the last pancake, her arms wound around his waist. He tensed before forcing himself to relax. His own musings and hang-ups could take a break for just a little longer.

"Thank you," she whispered as she rested her cheek against his back.

He laid the spatula down and turned, wrapped his arms gently around her and breathed in the scent of her. "For?"

She gestured to the stove, her eyes suspiciously bright. "For breakfast. For...all of it."

She started to pull away, but he held tighter.

"What is it?"

Her throat worked as she swallowed hard, her gaze fixed on the plates of food.

"The last time someone made me breakfast was Constanza." Her small smile didn't reach her eyes. "That was the first thing she did that got through to me. It's not like I went hungry in my other foster homes," she added quickly, "but breakfast was usually Pop-Tarts, pre-made waffles, that kind of thing. But Constanza..." Her smile grew, her eyes crinkling at the corners as happiness chased away some of the sorrow. "My first morning I came down and she had made me Haitian patties and *mais moulin ak zepina*—pastries stuffed with spicy beef and cornmeal grits with spinach. It was one of the most delicious meals I'd ever eaten." She looked up at him then, and the mix of sadness with the beauty of nostalgia made his heart hammer in his chest.

"She looked at me and smoothed my hair back from my face and said, 'I made you breakfast, Evie.' And it was so simple, but she'd done it for me, just for me, and she remembered my name."

She suddenly shook her head and tried once more to pull away. His arms tightened around her.

"Sorry." She brushed the heel of her hand against her cheek to wipe away a wayward tear. "I guess sex and breakfast make me emotional."

"Don't do that."

Her head snapped up. "Do what?"

"Don't make excuses for how you feel." He captured her chin in his grip so she couldn't look away. "I can hear in your voice how much she means to you. Don't run from what you had with her—or what you still have even though it looks different than it used to."

"Thank you." She glanced down at her feet.

"What?"

"Just..." She sucked in a breath and then looked back up. "Doesn't that apply to you, too?"

He froze.

"Sorry—"

"You still have Constanza," he broke in. "You have someone. I don't."

She watched him for another long moment. Then, as if sensing she'd pushed enough, she simply said "Okay" and started to pull away.

Conscious of the tension that had descended between them, he tugged her back and dropped a light kiss on her forehead. "Let's eat on the balcony."

Minutes later, between the food and the warmth of the morning sun, the mood had shifted back to relaxed.

"I'll probably head home after breakfast."

She said it nonchalantly, not meeting his gaze as she speared a piece of egg with her fork.

He nodded even as his chest tightened. "I can drive you."

"No, thanks." She smiled slightly. "I like the subway."

"You *like* the subway?"

"Mmm-hmm. I'm sure part of it is finding my love of music in the tunnels, that nostalgia that pulls me back. But part of it…"

Her voice trailed off as she frowned. Before he could question himself, he rose and sat in one of the chairs across from her.

"Part of it?" he prompted.

The grin she shot him warmed his body. "You make it hard to keep myself all locked up when you're such a darn good listener."

"I like listening to you talk."

And he did. He liked her bravado, her honesty, her spunky fire.

"I'm really good at holding myself back. A skill you pick up pretty quickly when you get bounced from home to home. But on the subway…" She smiled. "Everyone's doing their own thing, but they also show all these pieces of themselves, little vignettes of their lives. It makes me feel connected."

"Do you want to feel connected?"

The frown returned. "I didn't used to." She shrugged. "Maybe I'm just getting older."

This time he laughed. "How old are you again?"

"Twenty-five."

He groaned. "God save me from women in their twenties who think they're old."

When she laughed again, tossing her head back with carefree abandon, the sound rippling across his skin, he took a chance and leaped.

"What would you think about extending our arrangement?"

She fell silent almost immediately, her eyes widening. "What?"

"I'd like to see you again."

"As in…?"

"Not a relationship per se. That's not what either of us is looking for. But I'd like to see you again, spend time with you…" His eyes drifted down to her legs, and he shot her a wicked smile. "Both in and out of bed."

She swallowed hard. "For how long?"

He paused. The part of him that was enjoying her didn't want to say. But it would be in both their interests to put an end date to whatever relationship they carried on. Something that kept things fun and light.

"Through the duration of your contract with Bradford Global." Just a little over a month. Enough to enjoy, but not long enough to get attached.

The seconds dragged out. Then, at last, she smiled.

"I'd like that."

Relief swept through him. It shouldn't have mattered, but it did.

"Good. Did you have anything on your schedule for today?"

"I need to practice later, but that's it."

"Perfect."

He plucked the fork from her fingers, picked her up around the waist and threw her over his shoulder, carrying her inside as she laughingly protested. The protests died on her lips as he laid her down on his bed, pulled the shirt over her head and lost himself in the pleasures of her body.

CHAPTER THIRTEEN

DAMON STARED AT his computer. He'd read the latest report from the manufacturing plant in Texas at least three times, and he still had no idea what was in it. In the last two weeks, his legendary focus had slipped. He still showed up to work early, accomplished his tasks, oversaw meetings and swiftly put out fires, from budgeting issues to a disagreement between two of his engineers.

But in the back of his mind, always, was Evolet.

It had been two weeks since she'd spent the weekend with him. During the day, they maintained a professional rapport. No stolen kisses, no frantic embraces behind closed doors. He was already straining his personal sense of ethics by indulging in an affair with someone on the Bradford Global payroll. Evolet understood. That she did, and respected his stance, just made him like her more.

And that was a problem. He didn't want to like her. He didn't want to reach for her when he woke up or think about her on the nights she spent at her apartment.

He was getting in too deep. Too deep, but he couldn't bring himself to end it. Not when they had such a short amount of time left.

Four more weeks. Four more weeks, and then she would move on. Their affair would end, and he could return to the life he'd led before she'd walked into his life.

The thought should have relieved him. Instead, it just made him feel depressed.

His phone vibrated, pulling his attention back from his morbid musings. He glanced at the email alert and then smiled as satisfaction returned him to the present. He walked down the hall at a brisk clip.

"There's an update from Royal Air," he said as he walked into Evolet's office.

She sat up straight, alert and ready. "And?"

"Bengtsson has selected two to move forward. Including," he said as pride filled his chest, "Bradford Global."

A smile broke across her face. She clapped her hands as a delighted laugh escaped her lips. "That's incredible!"

"Yes, but there's a catch. The CEO, Bryant Bengtsson, wants representatives from the final two to meet with him. A final interview of sorts before he makes his decision. He's invited two from each company." Damon looked up at her. "I want you to go with me."

Her eyes widened. "Me?"

"You know that proposal as well as I do, perhaps even better."

"And you want me to go with you to Sweden?"

"Not Sweden," he said with a smile. "We're flying to Bali."

Evolet looked down at the cobalt-blue waters of the Pacific. She'd never been to the West Coast, and now she was flying across it in a private jet.

She stole a glance at Damon. They'd both read and reread the proposal, privately and out loud. They'd talked through potential questions Bengtsson might throw at them, discussed risks and benefits.

Finally, she'd needed a break and had moved to the leather sofa that stretched along one wall of the plane.

Not just a break from work, but also from the turmoil still churning inside her.

The past two weeks with Damon had been some of the best of her life. More often than not, she spent the night at his penthouse, making love in his bed, the jet tub, the thick rug in front of the fireplace. She cooked him meals, replicating some of the Haitian dishes Constanza had taught her. They talked about music, books, movies, debated over which art pieces they'd liked best when they'd visited the Met and the places they wanted to travel. The more time they spent together, the more she shared about her upbringing with Constanza, her late-in-life musical training.

They talked about everything but Damon.

A soft sigh escaped her. It was his prerogative to keep his own secrets. He was a considerate, generous lover, thoughtful of her, yet still he held back. When she shared her own stories, like the first time she'd seen the Central Park Carousel, he'd held her in the circle of his arms, kissed her forehead and murmured quiet words that had wrapped around her in a comforting embrace. She hadn't anticipated letting herself become so vulnerable. She hadn't opened up to anyone except for Constanza in years. Yet it had happened naturally, her barriers coming down as she shared her body, and then the deepest parts of herself, with a man who listened, who cared and encouraged her.

And yet still he remained silent on his own past, his own desires beyond what he wanted for Bradford Global.

The more time she spent with him, the more vulnerable she allowed herself to be, the more acutely she felt his lack of confidence in her. In four weeks, she would be gone, both from Bradford Global and from Damon Bradford's life.

The longer she indulged in this affair, the harder it became to contemplate walking away.

Stop it, she ordered herself as she rubbed at her temple. He'd set boundaries, clear ones. If they were in an actual relationship, that would have been one thing, but they weren't. They were casual lovers.

She let her head drop back against the arm of the couch. The hum of the engine and the events of the past day made her eyelids heavy.

"There's a bedroom in the back of the plane."

She opened her eyes to see Damon crouched next to her. He reached out and smoothed a strand of hair back from her face, the simple gesture making her breath catch in her throat.

"That sounds nice."

He held out his hand and pulled her to her feet. "I'll walk you back."

She shook her head as she walked into the small room. A queen-sized bed covered in a silky emerald comforter took up most of the space, with a bathroom at the back and a closet off to the side. "This is amazing."

"I'm glad you like it." Damon paused. "Sit with me a moment."

Suddenly on guard, Evolet sat down with him on the edge of the bed. He didn't reach for her, didn't touch her, just speared her with a gaze that was simultaneously distant and wary.

"I told you before I don't talk about my parents. That it's too painful." At Evolet's nod, he continued. "What happened to them changed my life. The world I knew was gone in an instant. It showed me that things like love and happiness can be taken without warning. It's why I focused on Bradford Global. There are risks, but there's also control."

Evolet's fingers dug into the bedspread. She wanted to reach out, to smooth her hand over Damon's face and offer him comfort. But she wasn't sure where this confession was headed, what he needed from her.

"Continuing my family's legacy has given me purpose. It's filled my life."

But has it?

It was eerie to hear him say the same words she herself would have said just weeks ago, to notice the intensity running through his voice, as if he were trying to convince himself that what he said was truth.

"I'm glad you found something," she said carefully.

"Thank you." He breathed in. "I'm sharing this with you because I know we've become close the last couple of weeks. I want to continue our arrangement. But," he added gently, "I wanted to reiterate that anything beyond these weeks isn't an option. A relationship, love, none of that is in my future."

She willed herself not to cry. He was only repeating what she'd already known. But God, it hurt so much more after the past couple of weeks together.

"I understand." She said the words carefully, taking care to enunciate each one and keep her tone neutral. "Have I given you any reason to think I might ask or demand more after this is over?"

He blinked. "No."

"Okay." She reached over and laid a gentle hand on top of his. "I've been enjoying our time together, Damon."

He stared down at her hand.

"I have, too." He let out a quiet, derisive chuckle. "I like you. I don't want to hurt you or make you think that something more could happen. I'm not capable of it."

Evolet's heart cracked for the man before her, a man she had come to care very deeply for in such a short amount of time. She knew what it felt like that, to withdraw so deeply into oneself to keep pain at bay. But she had missed out on so much. She'd lived more in the past month than she had her entire life. She wanted that for Damon, too, this man who listened and cared and worked so hard.

Except he wasn't ready. She wouldn't push him, wouldn't cause him pain when he had reestablished the boundary between them.

So she offered him comfort the only way he would accept. She leaned forward, pressed a kiss to his cheek. He turned his head and captured her lips with his. The kiss catapulted from slow and tender into a desperate craving. With a groan he spun, pressing her down onto the bed. He yanked her shirt over her head, captured a nipple in his mouth as she arched over his arm.

He suddenly stopped as he cursed.

"What?" she asked breathlessly.

"Condom."

She paused. "I...um, I started the pill after you accepted my proposal. I didn't say anything because I figured you would want the extra protection and I was nervous about bringing it up—"

He cut off her words by wrapping one hand around her neck and hauling her against him for another kiss.

"You just might kill me yet," he growled against her mouth.

Their clothes ended up in a pile on the floor. He grabbed her hips and drove inside her.

She closed around him as if he'd been made for her. His head dropped to her shoulder. He slid out, then back in.

"God, Evolet." He moved inside her, each thrust driving her higher.

"Faster," she urged him in a throaty whisper.

"No." He lifted his head and smiled down at her. "I've never made love bare, and I intend to savor every moment."

His words hit her, the intimacy of what they were sharing made all the more potent by his admission. It made her wonder, made her hope that perhaps, with time, he might let his guard down even more.

He sank deeper inside her, moving with languid strokes of his hips, pressing his body fully against hers. His hands moved over her with a sensual mastery that stole her breath. The heat that seemed to always burn between them rose up and consumed them both as she cried out and he poured himself into her.

CHAPTER FOURTEEN

A THIN, hazy mist hung over the jungle's rich green foliage. The blue waters of the Bali Sea sparkled beneath the sun as waves pounded the beach below.

Evolet leaned against the balcony railing and sighed in pleasure. It was hard to believe that just a day ago she had been surrounded by concrete and steel, and now there was nothing but wilderness and ocean as far as she could see.

Perched on top of a cliff that sloped down to a private beach, the Bali Regency Resort combined elegance with the kind of relaxation one could only find at an exotic getaway. Stone villas were scattered among the trees, connected by weaving stone paths and drives. Pergolas beckoned guests to rest beneath shady trees, while wooden signs directed visitors to the spa, the oceanside restaurant and the departure points for tours of nearby temples and even a volcano. Their villa, a two-bedroom mini mansion situated on top of an ocean cliff, boasted a private pool among tall grasses and giant fuchsia-colored blooms, a private infinity pool outside the bedroom Damon had gestured for her to take and even a private cinema. It had been during her quick snooping through the villa that she'd discovered this balcony off of an upstairs library.

She heard the door behind her creak softly.

"This is incredible."

He came up behind her, hands settling on her waist. She

stiffened for the briefest of moments, then forced herself to relax and lean back against his chest. If she closed her eyes for a moment, she could almost imagine they were here for pleasure instead of just business.

"I'm glad you're enjoying it."

"I am. But," she added as she turned in the circle of his arms, "we have work to do."

He leaned down, brushed his lips across her neck. "Yes."

"Damon…" She put her hands on his chest, intending to push him away. When he kissed her neck, her fingers relaxed against the softness of his shirt. "What are you doing?"

"I'm restless." He straightened, a frown crossing his face. "I've never been restless before a meeting with a client."

"And taunting me helps you relax?"

A wicked smile flashed. "No. But it does help me think of other things."

He kissed her, the simple caress quickly turning heated as his tongue teased the seam of her lips and then slipped into her mouth. She returned every touch, savored the taste of him as her fingers wound in his hair.

"All right," he said as he pulled back. She was satisfied to hear his breathing was just as ragged as hers. "We've been asked to attend a dinner with Bengtsson, his wife and the other company at eight."

Panic suddenly seized her. "What kind of dinner?"

"The kind where you eat."

She smacked him on the shoulder. "Like fancy? I didn't bring any clothes like that, just a couple work outfits and some casual wear. I thought we'd be dealing with Bengtsson in a conference room."

He gently cupped her elbows and tugged her closer. "Is this important to you?"

"It is. I want to represent Bradford Global well. That means looking the part, too."

This time his smile warmed her in an entirely different way. "That's why I brought you with me."

"To wear fancy clothes?"

He laughed. "No. Because you care. And because you know that bid inside and out. Bengtsson is a good man, but he's crafty. He doesn't pull punches, and he enjoys trying to trip people up."

"Not giving me a lot of reason to feel confident here."

He squeezed her arms in a gesture of affection that unsettled her more than his kiss had. "Be yourself, Evolet. Be yourself and show Bengtsson an ounce of the knowledge and passion you have for this project, and I know we'll get it."

She blinked as the floor dropped out from under her. She knew how much the company meant to him. That he trusted her to this degree with what she had heard multiple people talking about as the biggest project Bradford Global had ever gone after thrilled and terrified her.

"Okay. No pressure. Where does one find clothes around here that would help me go up against a crafty CEO?"

Ten minutes later Evolet browsed through a boutique on the lower level of the resort's main building. Every now and then she glanced away from the jaw-dropping price tags and out at the sea. She saw the ocean on a regular basis living on the East Coast. But seeing it here, surrounded by so much natural beauty, was a different experience entirely.

She had just about given up when she spied a flash of green in the back corner. She grabbed the hanger and pulled the dress out, a smile spreading across her face.

It was perfect. Elegant, tasteful, with a hint of sexiness that would make her feel like she belonged among the elite guests at tonight's dinner.

And hopefully, she thought with a small smile, it would knock Damon's socks off.

* * *

Damon leaned against the stone wall that bordered the private terrace Bengtsson had booked for tonight's dinner and sipped a glass of champagne. Jazz played quietly from speakers hidden among the foliage. Crowley's chief operations and finance officers had been sent in the CEO's stead. While Damon believed in showing his personal investment in his clients and their contracts, Crowley was still a worthy opponent. Both of the executives were respected in the manufacturing community and very good at their jobs.

He took another sip of champagne and glanced toward the stone steps. Evolet had come back from her shopping with a bag in hand and a feminine smile on her face that had teased him. She'd told him to go on without her, promising that she would arrive before the dinner started.

Guilt whispered through him. Talking with her on the plane and reminding her that their affair could go no further than it already had had seemed like the logical thing to do. Every now and then he would catch Evolet looking at him, an emotion flickering in her eyes that both thrilled and terrified him. He suspected she was coming to feel more for him than what he could give in return.

Except she hadn't reacted the way he'd anticipated. There had been a flash of hurt, yes. But then she had handled it decorously, making him wonder if the hurt had been more because he'd brought it up when she hadn't done anything overt to make him doubt her.

That she had handled it so well had done the opposite of reassuring him. No, her sedate response had slipped under his skin, an uncomfortable sensation that prickled and taunted. He had tried to dissect it. But then he'd seen her standing at the balcony looking out over the ocean, blond hair streaming down her back, and cursed himself. He was getting exactly what he wanted. He was in Bali with a woman he found captivating, a woman whose company he enjoyed both in and out of bed.

He needed to accept that things were fine just the way they were and focus his attention on the matter at hand: securing the Royal Air contract.

"Ah, Edward!"

Damon turned to see a portly man wearing a Savile Row custom-tailored suit approach. Bryant Bengtsson's dress was always impeccable, his white beard trimmed and his elegant moustache styled. Yet his booming voice and perpetual broad grin set people at ease.

He returned Bengtsson's hearty handshake. "Thank you for inviting me."

"Nonsense. You and that intriguing executive assistant of yours put together quite the proposal."

"Thank you, sir."

Bengtsson glared at him. "Stop with that 'sir' nonsense. It's Bryant or Bengtsson."

"Understood."

"Good." Bengtsson tossed back another drink and winced. "This stuff's potent. Need to pause if I'm going to keep my wits about me tonight. Will your executive assistant be attending tonight as well?"

Damon glanced at him as he maintained a neutral expression. He respected Bengtsson, but the older man was razor sharp and looking out for the best interests of his own company. He had no doubt the man was playing things casually to give Damon an opportunity to either say something witty or plant his foot firmly in his mouth.

"Yes."

"I was surprised to learn it was a temporary assistant who helped you." When Damon merely continued to look at him, Bengtsson chortled. "I'd like to play poker with you sometime." He signaled for a refill on his drink from a passing waiter. "It's not like you to trust someone with something this big. Speaking of," he continued as he slipped briskly from teasing trickster to efficient business mogul, "I'd like for you and Crowley's operations officer to stay after dinner. Consider it a cocktail hour to discuss the final steps in the selection process."

"Of course."

A flash of green drew his gaze to the stairs. His breath caught.

Evolet descended the stairs, a vision in a strapless dark green dress. The bodice was molded perfectly to her chest, the full skirt flaring out from her waist and covered in big white flowers. Her hair was pulled back from her face to show off her exquisite features before falling in gentle waves onto her shoulders.

She saw him and smiled. The nervousness in her eyes, the slight hesitation in her step as she glanced at the other guests before squaring her shoulders and continuing down, all of it made his heart thud harder against his ribs.

Bengtsson clapped him once on the back.

"Dinner will be served in fifteen minutes. And Edward?"

Damon tore his eyes away from Evolet long enough to meet Bengtsson's suddenly somber gaze.

"I've always been impressed with what Bradford Global has accomplished under your leadership." His eyes flicked toward Evolet. "Just don't let business blind you to other important things."

With those parting words, Bengtsson moved over to his wife. Damon turned to watch Evolet glide closer. When she reached his side, he took her hand in his and raised her fingers to his lips.

"You look beautiful."

"Thank you."

Her breathy voice washed over him and made his chest

tighten. He plucked a champagne flute from a passing tray and handed it to her. They walked over to the stone wall that separated the private dining terrace from the plunge of the cliff down to the midnight waves of the ocean. Silver pinpoints of light dotted the sky.

"It's incredible," Evolet breathed.

"It is."

She glanced over at him, a shy smile tilting her lips up before she took a sip of champagne.

"No matter what happens, Damon, thank you. For all of this."

Another surprise, he reflected as they gazed out over the sea. Not receiving the Royal Air contract would be a harsh blow. But somewhere during the rush of the past three weeks, it had no longer become the focus of his life, no longer seemed a matter of life and death. And he had the woman at his side to thank for that.

Evolet rested her chin on her hands as she gazed out over the jungle below her. The warm water of the infinity pool lapped gently against her back. Somewhere in the foliage a bird let out a high-pitched squawk, followed by a series of chirps that made her smile.

During the day, the soaring trees draped in vines and steam rising from the greenery had appeared mystical, like something from a fairy tale. By night, with the trees draped in darkness and stars glistening overheard like a blanket of diamonds, the fairy tale had turned darker, more seductive.

She sighed, her eyes roaming over the landscape. Down below, lanterns flickered along the path that led to one of the resort's bars. A couple drifted down the stone walkway with their hands clasped tightly together. The man stopped, tugging his laughing companion back to him before he cupped the back of her head and kissed her.

Embarrassment heated Evolet's cheeks at observing the intimate moment. She pushed off the wall and floated on her back. Embarrassment and, she admitted with a wrinkle of her nose, longing.

Back in New York, there had been so many distractions to keep her from ruminating on the state of her relationship with Damon. But each night they spent together pulled at her, that thread she had used to tie her heart up unraveling at a rapid rate that both excited and frightened her. She had finally admitted to herself on the plane as she'd lain in his arms after they'd made love that she was falling—and falling hard. Perhaps it had been sparked that first night when he'd insisted on walking her through Central Park. Or maybe it had been seeing how well he treated his employees, how much he genuinely cared about their success as much as his company's.

Whatever had shifted her feelings, she needed to get them under control. A part of her hoped that something might change. But that hope needed to stay under lock and key. She would not force herself on Damon, wouldn't guilt him into something he didn't want.

Her chest rose and fell as she inhaled deeply. How many times had she indulged in hope as a child, thinking that perhaps she was arriving in what would be her last foster home? She had a sobering suspicion that she was repeating the same mistake now, ignoring the numerous warning signs that this affair was destined for only one place—heartbreak.

Perhaps when they got back to New York, she would spend a couple days in her own apartment. Since she and Damon had first made love, they'd been inseparable. She wouldn't be able to untangle herself from her emotions and prepare for the end of their affair if she didn't have a break.

It wasn't running away, she told herself. Not after what he'd told her on the plane. This was making a smart, informed decision of respecting his choices while protecting herself.

"You're thinking too hard."

She gasped and swallowed a mouthful of water. Sputtering, she stood up, whirled around and glared at him.

"Is your meeting with Bengtsson over?"

"Yes."

She frowned. "And?"

"And what?"

Her eyes narrowed. "Did Bengtsson say anything about the contract?"

"We'll know by Monday."

He walked toward the edge of the pool, each slow, methodical step kicking her heartbeat up a notch. It wasn't fair that he looked so damned handsome in tan slacks and a white linen shirt rolled up to his elbows. His eyes drifted down. Heat flared in his eyes as his body tensed. She looked down and saw the triangles of her bikini barely clinging to the globes of her breasts. Mortified, she sank down until the water came up to her neck.

He crouched down. "I've seen far more of you than that exquisite bikini covers."

She swallowed hard. "I'm aware."

His chuckle was a slow, sensual roll across her senses. He leaned down farther, and she found herself drifting toward him, her face upturned, her breathing unsteady. He stopped his mouth a breath away from hers, his lips curving up into a smile.

"Consider this payback for teasing me with that incredible dress tonight."

And then he pulled back. It took a moment for her brain to catch up to the fact that the bastard was taunting her. And damn it, he knew how much she wanted him to kiss her.

He chuckled again. Smug and self-assured. Her eyes narrowed. Impulse brought her hand up, her fingers fisting in the material of his shirt as she tugged. He tumbled into the infinity pool with a splash.

Evolet couldn't help herself—she laughed. She couldn't stop laughing as he stood, water dripping from the dark curls plastered to his forehead, his handsome face a dark glower. The laughter drifted away as she drank in the sight of his shirt clinging to his broad shoulders and the chiseled muscles of his stomach, the material translucent in the moonlight.

"It's not fair," she whispered.

"What?"

"You look like a damned underwear model."

"I have a personal trainer and a gym." He moved toward her, water rippling out from him as he drew near. "It helps me relax."

His arms circled her waist, his hands resting on her bare back. The feel of his skin against hers made her gasp and arch into him.

"You don't feel very relaxed right now."

He pressed his hips against hers, and her eyes widened, her body flooding with heat as she felt his growing hardness against her core.

"Damon…"

He stared down at her, his chest rising and falling, his breathing harsh. "I want you, Evolet."

Oh, yes, she was definitely in trouble. Her body grew heavy even as desire shimmered through her veins, made her breasts feel full and an ache start to hum deep inside her. But his erotic words didn't just inspire lust. No, they took those dratted feelings and fanned the flames into something far brighter and more dangerous.

Empowered and touched, she threaded her fingers through his hair and pulled his lips down to hers. Their mouths met, and she could swear the air rippled with the strength of the passion between them. He molded her body to his as he returned her kiss. He started off slowly, a firm press of his mouth against hers. Then a slow descent into something deeper as his tongue teased the seam of her lips until she laughed and opened for him.

The second their tongues met, the teasing disappeared. He growled and hauled her against him. She wrapped her legs around his waist, moaning as her back bowed, her breasts pressing against the wet material of his shirt.

Wildness seized her, and she reached back to undo her top. She wanted, *needed* to feel his chest against hers. But he reached up, caught her hand in his.

"Not yet. I like this, seeing you just barely covered." He nipped her earlobe with his teeth. "Knowing what's underneath." One hand tightened possessively on her rear. "Knowing I'm the only one who's seen you bare skinned, the only one who's been inside your glorious body."

The evocativeness of his words made her gasp right before he kissed her again. This time he plundered, claimed, making love to her mouth as sensation built, tearing her in a dozen different directions as the ache between her thighs grew.

He scooped her up in his arms and moved to the edge of the pool. He set her on the edge, then kneeled in the water between her legs and settled his hands on her thighs. Shyness overtook her as his intent became clear.

He looked at her, then paused, rising up out of the water to cup her face with his hand. "We can stop."

She had been on the verge of asking him to pause, to let her catch her breath, to mentally prepare for placing herself in such a vulnerable position. His words banished her hesitation. She leaned forward and placed the softest of kisses on his mouth.

"Please don't," she whispered against his lips.

He returned her kiss, so light it could have been the whisper of butterfly wings on her flesh. He trailed his mouth down over her jawline, her neck, his tongue a molten flash of heat against her sensitive skin, then down over the exposed swells of her breasts. When his mouth closed over one nipple through the thin material, she cried out. He repeated the same heated caress on her other breast before kissing his way down her stomach and settling once more between her thighs.

He slowly pulled the wet material of her bikini bottoms to the side. Cool air kissed her thighs. His hands slid under her legs, pulling her closer to the edge of the pool. Closer to him.

And then his mouth was on her, kissing, licking, sucking, doing incredibly wicked things to her most sensitive skin. She could feel the sensation building, pulsing between her legs until she reached a fever pitch, as if her body were stretched so tight she might burst if something didn't happen, if he didn't do something to relieve ache that threatened to pull her under.

"Damon," she whimpered. "Damon, please."

One long caress with his tongue, one open-mouthed kiss to her most sensitive skin, and she came apart. Her body thrashed as she bowed up into the relentless heat of his mouth, her fingers grasping at his hair, his shoulders, anything to grab onto to steady her through the storm. She cried out his name, or at least she thought she did as her pleasure hit its pinnacle.

And then she slowly slid back onto the deck, her legs still draped wantonly over his shoulders. Ten minutes ago she would have been embarrassed. Now she was too sated, too limp to care.

"We should do that more."

He chuckled as he hauled himself up out of the pool and laid on the deck next to her. Before she could make another joke, something to help her heart stay strong against the tenderness settling over her like a warm blanket, he reached down and smoothed a strand of hair out of her face.

Her breath caught as tears pricked her eyes. The way he looked at her, with such gentleness, pulled that tenderness up from the heaviness of satisfied passion and brought it far too close to the surface.

Before she could say anything, he picked her up in his arms

once more and carried her inside the villa. He carried her to his room and into his shower. He undressed her, then himself, tossing their soaking wet clothes into a pile on the floor. Each caress, each stroke of his hand, stoked her desire once more so that she was wet and panting when he slid inside her. He made love to her slowly against the wall of the shower, swallowed her cries with a kiss that burned itself into her heart.

As she drifted off that night, secure in the circle of his arms, an exciting and terrifying thought drifted through her mind.

If she wasn't in love with Edward Charles Damon Bradford, she was damned close.

CHAPTER FIFTEEN

DAMON STOOD AT the window of his office. The sun rose over New York City, casting a rosy golden glow on buildings that had stood for over a century, on new construction, on early morning commuters and joggers and tourists walking the maze of sidewalks, subway tunnels and avenues.

The city that never slept. He'd never been in his office early enough to see the sun rise, and now, seeing its beauty first-hand, he couldn't fathom why.

Even though he had arrived at a quarter till five in the morning, which would have put Bryant Bengtsson at just before five in the afternoon in Bali, to take the most important call of his career so far, he'd carved out an additional hour to watch the sun rise.

Because of Evolet. Because she had stood at the window and talked about how beautiful the sunrise must be on the city.

Like so many things, Evolet had made him see the city differently. He'd always prided himself on how he ran his company, the relationships he maintained with his employees. Yet work had ruled his life. She had made him stop so many times over the last few weeks, savor, relax, enjoy, like he never had.

And now…he cast a glance back at his desk, at the printout of the initial contract Bengtsson had sent over.

The contract naming Bradford Global as manufacturer of Royal Air's new fleet.

It meant something that his first reaction hadn't been pride in his company or satisfaction in the achievement of his employees. No, it had been excitement at the prospect of sharing with Evolet what their hard work had achieved.

Unsettled, he crossed the room to pick up the contract. Never had he wanted to share something so important with another person since his parents had passed. The most important thing in his life had been Bradford Global.

His rational side urged him to terminate their arrangement. She had become too significant far too quickly. His walls were coming down. He found himself anticipating not only their nights spent in his bed but what she would think about this decision, what witty remark she would have for him following a contentious meeting. He didn't just want sex.

He wanted her.

But the pleasure he found, both in bed and in her company, was coming at a price. They'd departed Bali and, with the time change, arrived in New York on Sunday morning. Evolet had been oddly quiet on the flight, opting to go back to her apartment when they'd landed and insisting she just wanted some time to decompress. He'd disliked how much he'd wanted her to stay, so he'd let her go. When he'd awoken in the night tangled in his sheets with sweat cooling on his skin and the imagined screams of his parents in their final moments echoing in his ears, he'd been grateful she hadn't been there to see his past rising up to claim him once more.

This was what happened when he let go of his control, when he entertained thoughts of his past and gave in to the craving for the woman who had become important to him. It had been years since he'd had a nightmare about the night his life had changed. He was perched on the edge of a very slippery slope.

He needed to step back.

A crackling sound drew his attention downward. The contract, now wrinkled, was clutched in his fingers. Slowly, he set it down, smoothed it out. He'd print off a new copy before anyone arrived.

With a heavy sigh, he sat in his chair and spun around again to watch the city come to life under the early morning light. The reasonable course of action was to end things with her. She'd told him that night on his balcony that one day she might want something more, a husband and a family of her own. He had opened up to her more than he had to anyone else since he'd lost his parents. But that didn't mean he was anywhere close to wanting a relationship. Evolet deserved to be with someone who could let himself feel without reservation, who could love her.

Except that every time he even contemplated the possibility of another man touching Evolet, to hear her whispered murmurings and have *his* name on her lips, Damon wanted to hurl his desk chair out the window.

No more.

It would hurt, yes, far more than he had expected when he'd first agreed to this insane arrangement. But it was for the best. He couldn't love and lose another person. He wasn't capable.

A weight pressed on his chest. He wanted to be capable. He wanted to be strong enough. For himself. For her. But what if he failed? What if he spiraled downward, back into that ugly hole he'd barely crawled out of the first time? A pit filled with anger and hate?

No. It wasn't worth the risk. Before Evolet, it had been about protecting his own heart.

But now…now it was about protecting her. About setting her free.

He had arranged a surprise for her for this weekend, either a conciliation getaway if they didn't receive the contract or a celebration if they did. One more weekend, and then they would go their separate ways.

It would be enough. It had to be enough.

Dimly, he heard the sound of heels clicking on the tile. He frowned and turned his head toward the door. Julie must be exceptionally early today. A surprise, given that he had seen her on several occasions before her morning coffee. The cheery side of her personality was decidedly enhanced by several shots of espresso.

A tentative knock sounded on the doorframe. He stood. "It's open."

The door opened, and his heart hammered into his chest. Evolet stood there in a voluminous red skirt and a navy shirt that hugged her breasts. A braid fell over one shoulder, tendrils curling to frame her face.

"Hi."

The simple greeting shot through him, not just with the sexual heat he'd come to expect around her but something deeper.

Longing. Longing to go to her, pick her up and swing her around the waist as he kissed her and told her the good news. He released a breath he hadn't even realized he'd been holding since his limo had dropped her off at her apartment and he'd watched her disappear inside the building, wondering if she was going to end their affair early.

Because, selfish bastard that he was, he wanted just a little more time.

He laid his hands on the desk, pressed his palms firmly against the cool surface. "Good morning."

She smiled shyly.

"I know it's early, I just..." Her eyes dropped down, then widened as she saw the crumpled contract on his desk. "Is that..." At his nod, she rushed into his office, around his desk and flung her arms around his neck.

"Oh, Damon, congratulations!" She kissed him, her enthusiasm teasing a smile from him. "I'm so happy for you. You must be so proud."

"I am."

She pulled back, her expression turning to one of confusion. "What's wrong?"

"Nothing." He dropped a quick kiss onto her forehead, then gently unwound her arms from his neck. "It's early, and it still hasn't fully settled in."

"Oh." Her cheeks turned pink. "I'm sorry, I shouldn't have…" She motioned to his mouth. "Kissed you. I know you said nothing in the office."

"It's all right." He leaned down, letting his smile widen. "We can celebrate properly this weekend. I'd like to take you somewhere."

She returned his smile with a cautious one of her own. "We just got back from Bali."

"This is much closer. Just us."

"I'd like that." She stared up at him, her eyes large and gold. "Are you sure you're all right?"

"Yes." To reassure her, he cast a quick glance at the door, then leaned down and pressed a lingering kiss to her lips. "See me again in a couple hours after I've had some coffee and recovered a bit more from jet lag. You won't be able to stop me from talking about it."

She returned his smile with a tentative one of her own. He didn't like it, didn't like her lack of a feisty comeback or a prim remark. She was worried about him. Worried because of how he was acting.

But he couldn't play nice. He had to prepare for the end, to handle this as he should have been handling it all along.

As she walked out, her skirt swinging back and forth like a bell, he told himself that it was for the best.

Now if only he could believe it.

Evolet forced herself to lean back into the seat of the limo. A red rose and a sparkling glass of champagne had awaited her, along with a friendly driver who had told her "Mr. Bradford" would meet her at the airport.

Her fingers drummed a nervous rhythm on the shining wood of the console. Was she analyzing his absence too much? Did it mean something, anything?

She sighed and took a fortifying sip of champagne. Riding the emotional roller coaster of the past week had once again reminded her of the ups and downs of her time in foster care. Getting comfortable, adjusted, making friends, only to be yanked away and shoved into another stranger's house, one who might be nice or one who tolerated her presence for the monthly check.

She glanced down at the little yellow suitcase resting at her feet. She'd packed, unpacked, then repacked at least a half a dozen times.

What, she had mused more than once, did one pack for a celebration weekend away with one's lover-not-boyfriend?

It had taken a glass of wine to summon enough courage to pack the lingerie she'd picked up with her bonus check at a pricey boutique in the Upper West Side.

Just a week ago, she would have packed it without a second thought. But she'd spent the past four nights alone. On Tuesdays, traveling from the church in Harlem where she practiced with the Apprentice Symphony back down to Midtown didn't make sense. But Monday, Wednesday and Thursday, Damon had had late meetings, dinner with his administrative team and other excuses he'd delivered with a coolness that reminded her of how he'd been toward the end of their dance at the gala fundraiser.

A stark difference from the weeks before when it had seemed like Damon hadn't wanted to be apart from her. Dinners, trips to museums and parks, waking up to find him pressed against her. Even though he hadn't been able to say the words, the way he'd treated her had made her wonder if there was something more. That perhaps he was starting to feel something for her.

But things between them had changed drastically. Gone was the warm camaraderie, the relaxed pleasure they'd found in each other's company. Had she made Damon feel suffocated, allowed too much of her own emotions to show through? Is that what had prompted the conversation on the airplane? Or was he simply tiring of her?

Stop it.

She'd played these mind games with herself before, always wondering what she could have done differently to make a foster family care more, make them consider adopting her. In reality, there had been nothing she could've done.

Just as there was nothing she could do right now, except enjoy what time she had left with Damon. Whether or not he felt anything for her was irrelevant as long as he held on to his belief that he was incapable of love or a relationship.

A rational conclusion. Too bad her heart preferred to cling to irrational hope.

She traced a finger over the velvety rose petals. Not spending the evenings with him had been a good wake-up, though, that she had spent far too much time with him. She'd used the nights to return to a schedule similar to the one of her former life. Her life before Damon. If it suddenly felt a little emptier, a little lonelier than it had before, well, she'd adjust. She'd keep going, just like she always did.

Satisfaction slipped in and eclipsed some of her moodiness. She'd become invested in seeing Bradford Global succeed, more so than any organization she'd worked for. Being an executive assistant would never replace her own passions and goals. But it had been the first time in a long time that she'd let herself care about anything other than her music and Constanza.

Still, she had tried to focus on the positives of the nights to herself. Monday and Wednesday had been spent in the park practicing and taking photos and videos for her social media accounts. Tuesday had been her weekly session with the Apprentice Symphony. This time, when her section leader had invited her to join the others for a drink, she'd said yes. And, she reflected with a small smile, she'd had a great time.

By Thursday, she hadn't spoken with Damon privately since that brief moment in his office at the beginning of the week. She'd barely even seen him at work aside from passing him in the hall or glimpsing him in a meeting in one of the glass-enclosed conference rooms.

When her phone had pinged at six o'clock Thursday night, her heart had started to pound frantically against her ribs when she'd seen his name on her screen. His text had been short, telling her a limo would pick her up the following evening and take her to the airport. It had taken her twelve minutes to come up with her brilliant reply—See you then—before she'd run around the apartment like a maniac.

All to pack one small suitcase that hopefully made it look like she'd artlessly tossed a few things together and waltzed out the door.

The limo turned into a small heliport next to the river. Her breath escaped in a whoosh. She had no idea what to expect. If Damon was as cool and distant as he had been Monday, would she be able to enjoy the weekend? If he greeted her with the same chaste kiss he'd bestowed upon her in his office, would it be better to tell him she changed her mind and have the limo take her home?

She'd taken the tags off the lingerie, she thought with a grimace as the limo stopped next to a sleek black helicopter. Oh, well. If she went home, she could slip into the scarlet teddy, pour herself a glass of wine and watch spy movies in luxurious silk.

Damon walked around the helicopter, his face turned up

toward the rotor blades, his body silhouetted against the back-drop of dusk in New York City. She stared at him from be-hind the tinted window, drinking in every detail. The sharp jut of his chin, the broadness of his shoulders, the wind ruf-fling his thick hair.

Steeling herself for whatever was to come, she lifted her chin and started to open the door, only to find her hand brush-ing air as the limo driver opened it for her.

"Welcome to the Harbor Heliport, ma'am."

"Thank you. And thank you for the ride, too, Adam."

She turned and nearly melted at the smile Damon shot at her as he loped across the tarmac to her side.

"Hi." He took her hand in his and brushed a kiss across her knuckles that made her breath catch.

"Hi," she replied.

His grip tightened on hers as he nodded toward the heli-copter. "Are you ready?"

She breathed in deeply. She would enjoy the weekend, enjoy her time with Damon, however much she had left. No regrets.

She looked at him, smiled and squeezed his hand. "I'm ready."

The helicopter ride was a wondrous experience. It was in-credibly sexy watching Damon manage the controls, forearms flexing as he expertly flew first over the city and did a quick circle around the Statue of Liberty before turning the heli-copter north. As the city gave way to suburbs and then long, beautiful stretches of ocean to the right and the coastline to the left, he played both the role of pilot and tour guide. An hour flew by in the blink of an eye.

And then the house appeared. The sun clung to the pine trees and gave enough light to show the Bradford Estate at its finest. Golden-brown cedar shingles stood out against white trim. Evolet counted at least four porches, five balconies and one stunning staircase off the back that descended onto a green lawn. Beyond the retaining wall, a sandy beach beckoned along the banks of the Hudson River.

Once he'd landed and secured the helicopter, he grasped her hand in his and escorted her inside. The interior was equally incredible. Unlike his company's headquarters, cozy with its dark colors and plush leather furniture, here the chairs were cream trimmed in blue, the walls a mix of white wood and red brick and the art vivid paintings and photographs of the ocean and nearby town.

Eventually they ended upstairs in the primary bedroom, complete with a white four-poster king-sized bed piled high with fluffy pillows and a veranda that overlooked the river. She moved to the balcony doors and gazed out over the rolling, tree-covered slopes of the Catskill Mountains.

"This is beautiful, Damon." She glanced over her shoulder at him and smiled. "Thank you."

He moved behind her, his arms circling around her waist. She sighed and leaned into his embrace. Her hands settled over his. He stiffened, the movement so quick she wondered if she'd imagined it.

Before she could analyze it, he turned her around and pressed his lips to hers. She circled her arms around his neck, moaning into his mouth as his hands moved over her body with a lover's intimate knowledge. They stripped each other of clothing, their movements almost frantic, as if they both needed the comfort of each other's touch. He laid her down, then covered her body with his own. She slipped her fingers into his hair and tried to tug him down for another kiss, but he evaded her, trailing his lips down her neck and over her breasts, stopping to suck first one nipple and then the other into his mouth. By the time he reached her most intimate skin, she was trembling, begging. He teased her with gentle kisses and little nips of his teeth before placing his mouth over her. She arched into him, cried out as she shuddered with her release.

When he slipped inside her, she wrapped her arms around him, savored every stroke as they moved together, climbing higher until she called out his name and crested. He followed a moment later, his groan of satisfaction reverberating throughout her body.

Yet as they lay together, she couldn't help but notice that he didn't press a kiss to her forehead, didn't let his hand drift down to rest possessively on her stomach. Even though he relaxed right next to her, she felt the distance between them widen a fraction more.

CHAPTER SIXTEEN

THE PLATES GLEAMED on top of silver chargers. A lone red rose stood proud in a glass bud vase, the petals unfurled so perfectly it could have been captured in a photograph. A light wind blew in off the river and made the flames of the votive candles flicker. The scent of clams steamed in butter, white wine and garlic wafted from one of the silver-covered platters on the side table.

It was perfect.

So why, Damon mused as he shoved his hands into his pockets and stood at the edge of the balcony, *do I feel hollow?*

They'd spent most of Saturday in the house, curled up in front of a roaring fire as a morning spring rain had chilled the air outside. They'd made love on the rug before lunch, then again in the lavish bed after. She was like a drug in his system. If she wasn't in the room, he was wondering where she was. If she was by his side, he was contemplating how soon would be too soon to take her into his arms again.

Then there had been the library. The rain had continued through the afternoon. He'd shown her the library, an enchanting room with gleaming pine bookshelves that stretched up nearly twenty feet, plump cream-colored chairs and couches that encouraged one to sink into their depths and read. Evolet had picked a mystery, he a science-fiction epic, and they had sunk down onto the couch, reading with her legs draped across his knees as the rain pattered softly on the windows.

There had been no heat, no foreplay, no sex. They'd simply existed together in mutual contentment. She'd practiced her cello after dinner before the fire. Had she noticed the difference in her own playing, he wondered, or was he imagining it himself? The newfound sensualness of how she held the cello between her thighs, the confidence in her hands as she drew the bow across the strings? Every move had been amplified, every note ringing with passion instead of the sadness he'd heard the night of the fundraiser, the bitterness of regret and loss when she'd played for him in his office.

Part of him wanted to end things now. He'd thought this weekend would be enough—one last fling before ending it.

Just one more night.

He refocused on the moment at hand. His grandfather had picked an incredible spot to build his retreat. The river sparkled like a jewel as the sun slowly sank behind the mountains to the west. Red oak and sugar maple trees jutted proudly from the slopes and rises of the Catskills. Bursting with green leaves, they would turn in the autumn to burgundy, orange and amber, a rich display that set the hills on fire.

He wanted to ask Evolet to come back with him, to lie with him under a blanket on the balcony and gaze out over the river, then turn to each other as darkness settled and the air turned cool.

His fingers curled into fists. He'd known from the moment she'd stepped out of the limo and onto the tarmac at the helipad that he was risking far too much by indulging in this weekend with her. But God help him, he'd been too weak to resist.

The same weakness that whispered to him that this could continue beyond tomorrow. That they could continue this affair and he could bring her back with him in the fall.

No.

He was fortunate he hadn't a repeat of the nightmare he'd experienced when they'd returned from Bali, although he attributed that to reclaiming the reigns he normally held tightly on his control. Another example of how opening himself up would only lead to trouble.

He had never been vulnerable to another human being after his parents had died. He'd wrapped himself up in work, used it to help him focus and eventually move on from their deaths. Each success of Bradford Global had brought respite, had healed him as he worked to preserve his family's legacy, to honor his father's memory and the trust his father had placed in his son. Numbers, contracts, output—these were tangible results, ones achieved with the right initiative, hard work. Measurable results that kept him grounded.

Emotion offered no such stability. The slightest indulgence of feelings opened the door to the utter loss, the bone-deep grieving that had threatened to render him catatonic in the days after the accident.

Emotion could be incredible, a high unlike any other.

It could also spell doom, pulling one into a pit so deep it would be almost impossible to climb out of. He'd barely clawed himself out of depression before. He couldn't risk being on the brink of such loss again.

More importantly than that, Evolet deserved better than what he could give. In the weeks they'd been together, she'd blossomed. How long could she keep growing, keep rising above her own pains and insecurities if all he did was drag her back down into the dark?

A sailboat rounded the bend, white fabric billowing under the spring breeze as it sailed between the two falls of mountains that sloped down to the river. Damon watched the boat, remembered the look of sheer pleasure on Evolet's face as he'd taken her out on the speedboat this afternoon, watched her hair whip in the breeze as she'd taken the wheel and laughed.

Yes, it was best to follow the original plan and end things tomorrow on their way back to New York City. He would have memories of this weekend, of their mind-blowing affair and the incredible gift she had given him to warm him in the coming months and years.

The rational pep talk did little to soothe the tempest churning inside his chest.

He knew the moment she stepped onto the balcony even though she hadn't made a sound. He breathed in deeply, steadied himself and turned.

And felt like fate punched him in the gut.

She stood framed in the doorway, her hair tumbling over bare shoulders in loose waves. Vivid red clung to her torso, strips of material wrapped around her arms like a lover's hands, while the skirt flared out and down to her knees. Her feet were bare, an erotic contrast to the romantic sweetness of her dress.

"Hi."

After the many times they'd made love, after they'd tasted each other, she could still sound breathless like she was seeing him for the first time. Her eyes sparkled like the tiny diamonds at her ears, the only jewelry she wore.

"Good evening."

He stepped forward, took her hand and escorted her to her seat. Everything he did—filling her bowl with clams and placing a thick slice of crispy baguette on her plate, pouring a glass of sparkling white wine—brought a charmed smile or a soft flare of excitement to her eyes.

It was, he realized as the sun continued its descent and set her golden hair aglow with rays of red and orange, one of the things he enjoyed most about her. How much she delighted in the little things, from the spinning of the carousel in Central Park to him cooking her breakfast. As much as he had tried to stay grounded as Bradford Global had grown by leaps and bounds, he had grown used to the luxury, the opulence afforded one with millions of dollars at his fingertips.

Dessert was a decadent chocolate mousse topped with fresh whipped cream. Afterward, they reclined in their chairs and watched the stars appear in the velvet darkness.

"The perfect weekend," Evolet said on a soft sigh.

"It is." Damon leaned forward and clinked his glass to hers. If he could just focus on what they had enjoyed, on the time they'd spent together and not the inevitable end, he would get through this evening without making a fool of himself.

"Damon…"

The hint of melancholy in her voice pulled at him. She stared out over the river, her profile lit with the silver wash of moonlight. Slowly, she turned to look at him.

"Make love to me."

Did he imagine the slight catch in her voice? The emotion in her eyes? It called to him, seduced him.

Then he pushed it away.

Of course she feels something, he told himself as he rose.

He was her first lover. She confided in him, yes, pushed him to share more of himself with her. But she hadn't said a word about how she felt about him, about continuing their affair beyond her contract time at Bradford Global. Perhaps he was more conflicted than she.

The thought should have brought him comfort. Instead, it just left him empty.

He moved to her and swept her into his arms, cradling her body close. He carried her inside. They undressed each other with gentle, languorous movements, savoring each other's bodies until they lay naked on the bed. When he pressed his body into hers, felt the arch of her hips against his as he claimed her with slow strokes, he almost asked her to stay. When her nails dug into his back and she cried out his name as she came apart in his arms, he almost told her he felt something, more than anything he'd ever felt for a woman.

And as she lay in his embrace, her breathing deep and even,

he kissed her brow and acknowledged that Evolet Grey had, for better or worse, changed his life.

Evolet had always pictured hell as being a place of fire and brimstone, wails of grief and gnashing of demon teeth.

She'd never pictured it as the black concrete of a helipad rushing up to meet the landing skids of a helicopter. But as Damon expertly maneuvered the helicopter down, as she felt the slight bump signaling that they had landed, her heart shuddered.

When she'd woken this morning, it had been to an empty bed. And when she'd walked down the stairs, Damon had been wearing a crisp white dress shirt and navy pants, a black belt notched at his lean waist and an expensive watch glinting in the light as he'd sipped a cup of coffee and scrolled through emails on his tablet.

He'd looked up at her, smiled. But it had been a dull smile, one she imagined he reserved for placating annoying business partners or one-night stands who overstayed their welcome.

And then, as she'd poured herself a cup, he'd said it.

I've enjoyed our time together, Evolet. But it's time for us to go our separate ways.

The roaring in her ears had drowned out most of what he'd said, although she'd caught something about how he'd wanted to tell her here, in private, in case there was anything they needed to discuss.

She'd said no, plastered a smile on her face and excused herself to go pack. She'd discovered that crying her heart out in the shower had its benefits, like the stream of the water covering up her sobs. She had suspected this might be coming sooner rather than later. All through the weekend there had been a distance to him, as if he'd been trying to make the time into what she had originally proposed: a quick fling.

She just hadn't expected him to end it like this, before they'd even headed back to the city.

The quick bout of tears helped her steady herself before she'd gone back down. He'd looked at her then, his eyes running over her as if searching for signs that she was about to break. She'd merely lifted her chin up and asked if he was ready.

Falling in love with him had been her own choice. One day, hopefully sometime soon, she would be grateful for all he'd shown her, for helping her realize she could still love even if she knew pain would follow.

But not today. Today was for mourning.

The flight back to New York had been stilted. The camaraderie and fun conversation that had filled their journey to the river valley was nonexistent on the ride back. She'd kept herself distracted with a book, her eyes only occasionally flickering to his hands as he'd maneuvered the controls or to his handsome profile while he'd gazed out over the scenery below them.

And now, she thought as the helicopter blades slowed above them and several helipad employees rushed forward, it was over. Three days gone in the blink of an eye.

Her one meager suitcase was moved to the trunk of another limo parked at the edge of the helipad. She removed her cello case herself and carefully set it inside.

She turned to see Damon walking around the helicopter, talking to one of the employees as he gestured toward the tail of the helicopter. It was still morning, the sun gathering force from the encroaching summer season and shining its full heat down on the city. A bead of sweat trickled down the back of her.

He turned and smiled at her, a flash of white against his tan skin. Hope bubbled in her chest as he walked over to her.

"So…" He glanced at the limo. "You're ready?"

The hope burst, leaving her adrift.

"I am."

They stood no more than a couple feet apart. Yet she felt an ocean separating them, deep and dark and churning with secrets that would never be revealed.

Why, she suddenly thought. *Why can't we just talk about this? What if he feels something, too, and is just doing what I did, shoving the emotions away to keep the pain at bay?*

But the thought was banished as soon as she looked up. He was cold, the same unapproachable mask he'd wielded in the meeting she'd walked into all those weeks ago. In that moment she knew that if she were to give voice to her heart, he'd reject her.

He held out his hand. Hurt sliced through her, so sharp she had to bite back a gasp. How had the incredible passion, the beautiful moments they'd shared come down to this? A handshake when just last night he'd kissed the pulse beating at her throat, the slopes of her breasts, her lips as he'd joined his body with hers?

But this was how it had always been fated to end, she reminded herself. She'd proposed it. Damon had agreed to it. She had no reason to be upset.

She squared her shoulders, mentally prepared herself, and clasped his hand in one quick, businesslike shake.

"Thank you, Mr. Bradford." She inclined her head. "Have a good week."

With those mundane parting words hanging in the air, she turned and walked away from Damon Bradford.

The only man she'd ever loved.

CHAPTER SEVENTEEN

EVOLET LEANED AGAINST the cool wall of the subway platform, her eyes drifting up to the marquee with the arrival times. A train rushed by, a blur of light and faces, before it disappeared back into the dark.

A sigh escaped her. It had been three weeks since Damon had ended their affair. One week since she'd walked out the doors of Bradford Global for the last time. She'd technically had one week left on her contract, but the Monday after their final weekend, she'd arrived at work to find that Damon had taken himself on a tour of Bradford Global's manufacturing facilities. She'd managed to power through the following two weeks, wrapping up the mundane list of tasks and busy work he had left with speedy efficiency. By the end of the first week, she'd knocked out everything. By the end of the second week, after seeking out work from several departments and spending most of her afternoons twiddling her thumbs, she'd reached out to her agency, who had arranged for her contract to end early due to "assigned work being completed." Her agency had also approved a two-week sabbatical. Time for her to breathe, to relax.

To heal.

Walking out on her last day had been painful. But it had been necessary.

She'd filled the last week with practice sessions in the park, visits to Constanza and far too many lattes at a roastery at the southern edge of East Harlem. Not to mention the two glasses of wine she'd imbibed last night as she'd sat on the fire escape of her apartment and soaked in the symphony of her neighborhood—the raucous honks of taxis and shrill shriek of sirens, the lilting phrases of Spanish, Creole and French drifting up from the sidewalks.

Escapism. Yet the nutty, caramelized scent of Italian roasted espresso, the sound of birds chirping in the background as she'd wrung heartbreak from her cello in Central Park, the dark taste of the merlot she'd sipped as she'd gazed up at the moon had all given her what she needed to survive having a broken heart.

The first day, every time her phone had pinged she'd forced herself to wait one minute, two, three before she'd picked it up with a tremor she wished she could deny but didn't. And every text, every notification had all had one thing in common.

None of them had been from Damon.

By day two, she'd cried more than enough tears. By day three, she'd accepted that he wasn't going to contact her.

It had been so tempting to shut down again. And for a couple days she had. But then Tuesday had rolled around. She'd forced herself to say yes again to pizza after practice with the Apprentice Symphony. She'd even invited another cellist, Ashley, to join her in the park that weekend, where they'd practiced and filmed videos for their social media. She had booked several independent performances through her website and, hopefully, would land an audition or two in the coming weeks.

Slowly, day by day, she was coming to accept that her affair with Damon had brought about some very good changes. Good change didn't mean the pain was gone. Her chest still ached. When she closed her eyes at night, Damon's face rose in her mind. But each day was getting a little better. And, most importantly, she wasn't going to allow herself to crawl into a hole of regret. Her time with Damon had been incredible. To focus on the aftermath instead of the miracles of pleasure that had occurred would only be hurting herself.

A mechanical voice broke through her thoughts as it announced the train that would take her to her new assignment for a fancy law firm in downtown Brooklyn was just four minutes away. Another subway barreled down the tracks in the center of the station, the wheels groaning as the cars carried hordes of Monday-morning commuters squished inside like sardines. Wind kicked up in her face, and she glanced away from the tracks.

Just in time to see Audrey Clark from Bradford Global rush through the turnstile.

"Evolet!"

Her resolve splintered and nearly collapsed as Audrey rushed forward, curls bouncing and tumbling over her shoulders in time to her energetic steps. She enveloped Evolet in a hug.

"What are you doing here?" Audrey asked with a laugh as she stepped back.

"I live just a couple blocks from here."

"I didn't know that. Some of the cafés and restaurants up here are so much fun. And that garden shop under the bridge was such a surprise!"

Evolet listened to Audrey chatter, soaking up the sound of a familiar voice, the relaxed nature of inane conversation with someone whose company she enjoyed.

"I'm glad you like it up here. Were you up here just for fun?"

Audrey's smile widened. "I was on Saturday night. Then I met someone, and Saturday turned into Sunday and Sunday turned into...well, now." She grasped her hands together and sighed. "She made me breakfast. I've never stayed the night with someone and had them make me breakfast the next day. I think it means something."

The rest of Evolet's resolve crumpled into a shattered mess in her chest, jagged shards that cut deep. Would she ever be able to eat pancakes again without thinking of green eyes and hot hands roaming over her body with the assured confidence of a lover who knew her body as intimately as she knew her own?

"Hey." Audrey laid a hand on Evolet's shoulder, her brow creased with worry. "Are you okay?"

"Yeah." She forced a smile as she scrambled to come up with something before opting for as close to the truth as possible. "I was just remembering when someone made me breakfast after...well, you know."

"Sex," Audrey said with another laugh as Evolet blushed. "I do know."

"I think it means something, too."

"I hope so. I really like her. We have another date tomorrow night. But," Audrey added with a probing gaze, "I'm guessing the one who made you breakfast didn't do the smart thing and hold on to you."

"No, he didn't, but that's in the past." She squeezed Audrey's hand, her smile this time genuine. "Today is about you and someone who made you breakfast and who might turn out to be very special."

Audrey returned the squeeze. "I miss you, Evolet. We should get coffee. And by that I mean actually get coffee, not say we will and then never do."

She laughed. "I'd like that."

"Have you ever thought about quitting the agency and coming to work for us full-time?"

"I liked it a lot, but no. I need something with flexibility that will let me perform with my orchestra and go to my auditions."

"I bet Damon would be flexible with you," Audrey said, nearly making Evolet choke on a pained laugh. "He seemed to really like your work. You made a big impact on us getting the Royal Air contract."

Evolet's phone pinged, and she grabbed it, thankful to have

a reason to look away before her emotions became visible in her eyes and betrayed her.

"Oh! Which reminds me…"

The sound of Audrey's voice faded as Evolet read the subject line of an email, then reread it again. Cautious hope bloomed in her chest, followed by a swift, all-encompassing joy.

"Evolet? Evolet, is everything okay?"

She looked up, her lips parted in shock. "I have an audition with the Emerald City Philharmonic. Today."

Audrey squealed and threw her arms around her. "Evolet, that's fantastic!"

"Thank you. I…" She was certain if she looked away, if she blinked, the email would disappear. "I can't believe it. I sent in my audition video months ago and never heard, but someone canceled and I… I have an audition!" she finished gleefully as she returned Audrey's hug, suddenly and fervently grateful that she wasn't alone, that she had someone to share this moment with her.

I wish Damon were here.

She squelched that thought. He wasn't here. But Audrey was, and she would tell Constanza as soon as she got out of the station. She needed to call Miranda, too, have her find someone else to cover the first day at the law firm. She hated to do it, but this audition was too important to risk.

She glanced at her watch. It was still early. Perhaps if she went down to the firm in person, spoke with them directly and explained the situation, she could smooth any ruffled feathers while Miranda found a replacement.

"Well, that answers my question about the party."

"Party?" Evolet looked up then. "What party?"

"The party Damon's hosting tonight for everyone at Bradford Global. To celebrate the Royal Air contract."

Pain lanced through her, sharp and hot. She'd known—of course she'd known—that things were over. But it still hurt to not be invited, not after the credit Damon had given her. Just one more time she had started to feel like a part of things, to let down her guard and let herself care, only to have it taken away.

"Surely Damon invited you."

"It doesn't matter," Evolet replied breezily. "The audition's at six and—"

Her phone rang as her train pulled into the station. She glanced down at the screen and frowned. Why would Samuel be calling her on a Monday? Fear bubbled in her stomach.

"Samuel?"

His sob made her go cold.

"Samuel? What is it? Where is she?"

"Hospital," he gasped out. "Evolet, she fell and they couldn't—"

"Which hospital?" she demanded as she turned and ran for the stairs. Audrey called out to her, but she couldn't think, couldn't stop to explain. As she ran up the stairs and into the light, frantically searching for a taxi, her heart pounded so hard she could barely breathe. She couldn't lose her, couldn't lose someone else, so soon.

Please, Constanza, just hold on. I'm coming.

The harsh scent of antiseptic mixed with burnt coffee and wilting flowers. A bland voice paged a doctor over the intercom as someone wept uncontrollably. Damon hadn't been in a hospital since that night twelve years ago, but the smells and sounds didn't change.

He stalked down the hall to the nurse's station. Fear tangled with indecision, which set him further on edge. He never questioned himself, didn't hesitate. If he made a mistake, he would examine it, find the flaws, note the successes and never repeat it again.

But now, as the cool-faced nurse looked up Constanza George's room number, he had never felt so conflicted. When

Audrey had called him spouting off about Evolet, his first reaction had been instant longing, a need spreading like lightning through his body at the mere mention of her name. It had shifted from heat to ice instantly as Audrey had told him about what she'd overheard at 116th Street station.

I should have been there.

The thought pulsed through him, digging its insidious claws into his heart a little deeper each time. How many times had he pulled his phone out, started typing out a text message inviting her to the party, asking if she'd had any auditions, checking on Constanza…?

Anything and everything that would give him just one more chance to talk with her.

He'd screwed up at the heliport. He'd known as soon as he'd held out his hand. For God's sake, he'd taken her virginity, and he'd ended the most sensual, erotic, emotional affair of his life by shaking her damned hand?

It had been the act of a coward. He'd seen the indecision on her face, the faint hint of an emotion so deep and raw in her tawny gold eyes it had both thrilled and paralyzed him. Thrilled him because no one had ever looked at him like that. Paralyzed him because he had realized that she felt something for him, something more than just simple affection. He'd wanted it, wanted it so badly he had nearly asked her to go back with him to his penthouse, for them to find a way to make this work.

The possibility of what they could have—and lose—had scared him. So he'd made a decision in the heat of the moment.

The wrong one. One he'd been regretting since the emotion had winked out of her eyes and she'd coolly shaken his hand, turned and walked away without a backward glance. Taking a tour of the manufacturing facilities the following two weeks had been a logical step, and one that had thankfully given them space.

Coming back and learning that she had left a week early had cemented his conclusion. He'd screwed up. Bad.

But had he fixed his mistake? No, he'd just done what he'd done the first time he'd experienced such a devastating loss. He'd thrown himself into work the past week, sometimes staying the night at his office. More than once he'd woken up and reached for her, his fingers brushing empty space.

If he hadn't been a coward, she would have called him this morning when her world had started to fall apart. He could have been there for her so she didn't have to face the potential of loss alone again.

God, could he have been any more an idiot to let her walk away?

"Are you family?" the nurse asked, breaking through his mental self-flagellation.

"No, but—"

"Only family," she intoned, dismissing him as she looked at something on her computer.

"I'm not officially family, but—"

"Official is all we deal with around here," she replied with an arched eyebrow.

He fought back the sudden insane urge to laugh. All the times he had wanted to be treated like just a regular guy on the streets instead of a billionaire. Now, of all the times for his wish to be granted, it had to be when he needed to be by Evolet's side. And Constanza's. He'd never met Evolet's adoptive mother. The thought of never meeting the woman who'd rescued Evolet from her life of solitude, who had introduced her to music and family made his stomach twist so tightly it nearly made him sick.

"Look… Katelyn," he said as he glanced down at the nurse's name tag, "I need to see Constanza. She's very important to someone I…"

His voice trailed off. How could he describe how he felt

about Evolet? How much she meant to him? How he needed to be with her if she lost the one person she had in the world who hadn't let her down?

"I don't know what happened today, but I need to see her in case…" His voice faltered as he remembered running through the hospital, past the crying and the muffled conversations and the steady beat of monitors, only to be confronted with a wall of silence in the room his mother had been taken to. Silence except for the dull thudding of his heartbeat as he'd stared at her bruised and broken body on the hospital bed.

The nurse's expression relaxed a fraction.

"Sir, I'm sorry. Truly," she added with a gentle pat on the back of his hand. "I can talk to her kids and ask, but—"

"Damon?"

Evolet's voice rolled over him, soft and roughened from crying. She stood in the middle of the hallway, blond curls falling out of her ponytail, her eyes rimmed in red and her face pale. Her arms were wrapped around her waist, as if she were comforting herself from whatever she'd just come from.

His heart catapulted into his throat. "Constanza?"

Evolet let out a shuddering breath. "She's going to be okay. She fell and hit her head. She's a little disoriented, but so far all of the tests are coming back okay."

She spoke as if she were far away. Which she was, he realized with a spurt of panic as she didn't move, didn't flinch as a doctor rushed by and brushed her shoulder. She just stared at a point over his shoulder, her eyes blank. Only six feet away, but she might as well have been on the other side of the world.

"How are you?"

Her eyes shifted to him then. He waited to see something, a flicker of emotion, a flare of feeling.

"I'm here."

To hell with being careful.

He moved forward and pulled her into his arms, enfolding

her in a tight embrace. His breath rushed out as her familiar scent washed over him, clean and sweet. Three weeks since he'd woken up to her in his bed, since he'd drawn her into his arms and kissed her like it was the last time he ever would.

It felt like a lifetime.

"Thank you for coming, Damon."

She didn't relax into his arms, didn't rest her head on his shoulder. She stayed stiff as a board for one long, drawn-out moment before planting a hand on his chest and gently but firmly pushing him away.

Don't! he wanted to shout. *Don't push me away.*

But he had no right to ask that of her. Especially right now, when tucking herself safely behind that wall of ice was probably the only thing keeping her on her feet.

"Don't worry about costs, Evolet, I'll—"

"No!"

He blinked at her vehement denial. Color rushed back into her cheeks, burning a hot pink as her eyes suddenly glittered with what he recognized as anger.

"This isn't your problem, Damon. It's mine and Samuel's."

"Don't be a fool," he replied, keeping his voice even. "I can make sure she receives the best of care and—"

"I'm her daughter," Evolet retorted. "It's my responsibility."

He paused, tried another tactic. "Audrey said right before Samuel called you got an audition with the Philharmonic. Are you going to give up on that, too?"

"It was for tonight. I can't leave her."

"Call the orchestra and tell them what happened."

"It's not like taking sick leave at work. There's one semifinal audition date, and today is it."

He didn't miss the slight crack in her voice, watch as she pulled herself back together and tried to yank the emotionless mask back in place.

"So what? You're going to bury yourself in medical debt and

spend your best years working to pay it off instead of going after your dream? You think that's what Constanza wants for you?"

"You don't know her." Evolet's whisper came fiercely, adamantly. "And you don't know me, Damon. Don't act like you know what's important to me."

His hold on his temper began to slip. "If you need to use me as a punching bag, fine. But," he added as he closed the distance between them once more, stopping so his body was just a breath away from hers, "don't you stand there and say I don't know you. I know you better than anyone."

Her chin came up, eyes blazing. "We had sex. That's it. Over and done."

Perhaps this was the punishment he deserved after his casual liaisons, the coldness he'd wielded like a weapon to keep previous lovers at bay. The savage decisiveness he'd used when ending his affair with Evolet. Had his past partners experienced the powerless pressure of shock, the swift anger that raced up the spine, only to peter out into a desperate hopelessness that left one empty?

"Is that all we were, Evolet?" He leaned down, knowing he should leave, that now was not the time or place to be having this discussion. "You asked me to be your first lover."

"Lovers implies love. We didn't love each other. We had an agreement. We had fun. We had sex. Now it's over."

But I do love you.

The realization hit him hard. He was in love with Evolet. It stunned him into silence. He couldn't say it now, not in the midst of so much fear and pain, not when she was so angry and might not believe him. Not when she had every reason to doubt him with how he'd kept her at arm's length even as he'd greedily taken everything she'd offered.

Had she been in love with him? He was certain she had at least cared for him. But she had told what had happened the times she had loved and lost. She'd shut down, withdrawn so deeply into herself it had been years until she'd finally opened her heart again. Would there ever come a time when she would believe him? Or had he lost his chance?

"Go away, Damon," she said suddenly, weariness creeping into her voice as her shoulders slumped. "You shouldn't even be here. You have your party tonight."

He hadn't just made one mistake or two. No, he had to have made at least a dozen where Evolet was concerned. She had been a crucial part of landing the Royal Air contract. Her passionate defense of Bradford Global and the work they did had meant something to Bryant Bengtsson. He'd almost invited her to the party half a dozen times over the past week, each time coming up with excuses that in retrospect were ungrateful and cowardly. Chief among them had been that he knew if he invited her, it was admitting that he wanted more from her than just a brief affair. He hadn't wanted to make himself vulnerable, hadn't wanted to risk showing his hand.

"Evolet—"

"Please." Her plea cut him so deeply he wondered if he'd ever heal. "Please, Damon. Just go, and don't think of me again."

He wanted nothing more than to go to her again, to draw her into his arms and stroke her hair, her back until she melted against him and laid her cheek over his heart as she sighed. He wanted to carry her to his bed and curl up with her under the covers and hold her through the night.

He wanted everything she couldn't give him right now. His very presence hurt her.

Love, he realized, didn't always mean getting to be with the one you wanted. Sometimes it meant walking away.

So he did, without another word or a backward glance at the woman he had loved and lost.

CHAPTER EIGHTEEN

EVOLET LEANED HER forehead against the cool glass of the hospital window. The morning sun that had taunted her when she'd burst out of the subway this morning, bright and warm as she'd gone cold with fear, was now buried behind dark gray clouds that eclipsed the tops of New York's skyline. Lightning forked across the sky, a brief flash of brilliance, followed by a very angry grumble of thunder.

It was almost as if she'd summoned the weather with her own foul mood. Once the last of the tests had come back negative and Constanza had eaten an early dinner before settling into the comforts of her pillows for a game show, the lingering fear that something else would end up being wrong had slowly ebbed away.

Unfortunately, it had left room for other emotions to creep in. Ugly emotions she couldn't seem to control. One minute she was furious at Damon for daring to question her, push her during one of the worst days of her life. The next she was livid with herself for losing control.

Beneath it all, heartbreak pounded so fiercely she could barely keep her tears at bay. When she'd seen Damon standing there, looking so handsome and commanding, she had wanted to run to him, to throw her arms around his neck and seek comfort and strength. She'd had to wrap her arms around her waist to keep herself from doing just that.

The more they'd talked, the angrier she'd become. As if breaking up with her hadn't been enough, he'd made his stance perfectly clear at the helipad when he'd held his hand out and shaken hers like they were nothing more than business associates. By not inviting her to be a part of the celebrations for the Royal Air contract. By not contacting her at all for nearly a month.

By doing what he always did and never letting her into his life.

And she'd accepted it. Yes, it had hurt, but she had respected his decision and stayed away, begun the slow and laborious process of rebuilding her life.

A process he had disrupted by reappearing at one of her most vulnerable points. Why had he bothered coming all the way uptown to the hospital? He'd reopened the wounds she'd worked so hard to close, kindled hopes that his presence meant something more than just concern. His offer to pay for Constanza's medical bills had infuriated her. She didn't want him to have any kind of presence in her life, any kind of impact. She wanted—*needed*—a clean break if she was going to survive this.

She closed her eyes as a particularly loud boom of thunder rattled the window. The stitches she'd spent so much time working on had been strained under the pain of his reappearance. They'd been ripped asunder by the words she'd hurled at him in anger.

Words she now deeply regretted. No matter how hurt she had been by his decisions, no matter how sad she had been by knowing he would never feel the same way about her as she felt about him, she had been deliberately cruel to the man she loved.

Lovers implies love. We didn't love each other.

"I can hear you thinking from here."

Evolet looked over her shoulder to see Constanza watching

with an alertness she hadn't seen in a long time. She moved to the bedside and reached for a pillow.

"Fluff that pillow and I'll never make my hot chocolate for you again."

A small smile pulled at Evolet's lips. "Now that is a dire threat."

"Everyone keeps coming in to check my water, check the volume on the TV, fluff my pillows." Constanza huffed. "You can only fluff a pillow so many times. They're keeping an eye on me."

"It is a hospital, Constanza. And you did have a nasty fall."

Constanza's eyes softened.

"I fell. But I'm here." She reached over and grasped Evolet's hand. "I'm not going anywhere. Not yet."

A lump formed in Evolet's throat. "I was scared."

"I was, too." Her silver head dipped, her voice lowering. "I know sometimes I slip away. I know it happens more than I'd like. Every time I come back and realize I've forgotten for a while, it feels like I've lost another piece of myself." She looked up then and smiled, tears gathering in her eyes. "But then I see Samuel or I see you, and I take joy in those moments."

Evolet slowly sank down into a chair. She leaned forward and smoothed a curl back from Constanza's wrinkled face.

"How do you do it?" she asked. "How do you stay so strong?"

"I don't always. There are days when it's hard to get out of bed, moments when I come back from wherever I drift off to and I feel angry or confused or sad. But there's no guarantee that life will be perfect, child." Constanza cupped Evolet's cheek, her skin cool and dry, a balm against the heat of sorrow and anger. "In fact, it would be quite boring. I've told you of my life before I came here. So much loss, but so much joy, too. I am more resilient, and happier, because of the hardships I faced."

Half an hour later, after Constanza had fallen asleep, Evolet slipped downstairs and out into the night air, her adoptive mother's words of wisdom whirling inside her head. The thunderstorm still grumbled in the distance, but the rain had abated to a light mist that added a mystical air to the shops and restaurants that lined Madison Avenue. Golden light spilled out the windows of a bakery. A florist carried buckets overflowing with tulips and roses inside as he prepared to close for the night.

She sat on a bench under a blue awning. In the building behind her, babies were being born. People said their final goodbye to loved ones. Hope was given, and hope was taken away. In front of her, she watched people walk by, many clutching umbrellas, some sporting raincoats and a few braving the elements, dashing to and from jobs, dates, nights out with friends.

The world moved on. She needed to, too.

Even after she'd let Constanza into her heart, she'd kept it closed to everyone else. She'd told herself the temporary nature of her work gave her the flexibility to pursue her music career. That it had let her keep herself distant had been an added bonus. It had also served as an excuse to keep the members of the Apprentice Symphony at arm's length. She'd made progress over the past months, yes. But those had been baby steps, easing in without taking any true risks.

The one thing she had told herself she did without inhibition had been her music. But even that had been a lie. She had acquired the skills needed to play, yet she'd held herself back, hidden the passion she'd felt in the subway tunnels behind what she thought professional orchestras would want to hear.

She stood and moved to the edge of the awning. She watched the florist pick up another bucket, this one teeming with scarlet roses. A couple petals fell onto the sidewalk, bloodred against the rain-splattered gray concrete.

She'd hidden her passion for Damon, too. Oh, she'd loved

him, had let herself feel more than she'd ever thought she would. But she hadn't told him. She'd kept it tucked safely away, a secret only she knew.

One step took her out into the rain. Soft drops felt cool on her exposed skin.

She hadn't even given him a chance. She'd waited for him to make a move, waited to see some confirmation that he might be feeling more. She had wanted all the joy, the pleasure that came from loving someone and none of the pain.

Perhaps, if she'd told Damon how she truly felt, he would've told her he didn't feel the same. Just the possibility of it left her shaken. But it would have been like the other moments she'd shared with Damon: her childhood, her music, the impact Constanza had had on her life. As she'd unburdened herself, the wounds she'd thought carved forever into her heart had begun to heal, enabling her to take those tiny steps that had already enriched her life so much. Whether Damon would have welcomed or returned her feelings was only part of it.

Still, she'd never given him the chance to tell her. And perhaps, in light of his coming down to the hospital today, there was a chance. A foundation, however small, they could build on to create something more. It might be a summer, a year, maybe longer. But she knew, with every fiber of her being, that she wanted to try.

She stepped back under the awning and pulled her phone out of her pocket. She would give him, and herself, a few days before she did anything rash like she'd done tonight.

She punched a number into her phone. There was one thing, though, that couldn't wait.

A male voice answered. She swallowed hard.

"Hi. This is Evolet Grey. I'm calling about my audition."

Damon stood in the middle of an empty warehouse-like building in Queens. Floors gleamed underfoot. Massive fan blades swirled in lazy circles. Newly installed lights lit up the space, including the upgraded bathrooms and employee breakrooms installed in the back. Offices had been added, including one for the plant foreman at the top of a flight of stairs with a bank of windows that would overlook the manufacturing of parts for Royal Air's luxury jets.

His tour had included designating a primary manufacturing site from one of Bradford Global's numerous properties. Come next Monday, it would be filled with contractors installing equipment, a team from human resources ready to oversee the massive hiring that needed to happen to stay on schedule, and cameras from the public relations department to document everything.

It was Bradford Global's biggest triumph in the history of the company. And Damon still felt empty. Gone was the pride that had previously filled his chest. The bone-deep satisfaction he usually experienced as he completed a tour of a facility before it started a project was absent.

All he could think about, standing inside the cavernous building, was that there was no one to share it with.

He walked across the floor, footsteps echoing off the soaring ceiling. For so long Bradford Global had been his family, his purpose. He controlled the outcomes, the successes and losses with what he invested in the company and in the people who worked for him. Any time he had felt that emotional tug, the subtle urge to get involved beyond the surface with someone, all he had to do was think back to the depths he'd sunk to in the weeks after his parents' deaths. The nights he'd drunk himself into a stupor, waking up on the floor of his bathroom while pain screamed through his head. The days he'd spent in the courthouse pews at the trial for his parents' killer, barely keeping his rage in check as he'd watched a scrawny kid with floppy hair sit behind the desk with his head bowed.

The grieving that had followed. The slow, painful journey

to reigning himself back under control. The welcome relief of focusing on work, on throwing himself into working for his family's company and carrying on his father's legacy. The small allowances he'd made for himself to experience gratification with each achievement as Bradford Global had climbed higher and higher.

Alone had been safe. Alone had been his choice.

Now it was just lonely. Without someone to share with, without *Evolet*, he felt hollow. His fascination with her might have started with physical attraction. But it had so quickly bloomed into something more. Something he now knew, and accepted, as love.

He was thirty-three years old, and he was in love for the first time.

Slowly, he turned in a circle, imagining what it would be like to bring her here. She would pepper him with questions, want to know the how and the why and the when. He would soak up every moment, proud and happy knowing he had someone in his life who cared about the company, its people, its mission.

He'd hurt her. More than once. But he loved her. They had brought out the best in each other. He hadn't overcome everything he had in his life to give up now.

With determination twining through his veins, he pulled out his phone.

"Julie? I need you to do something for me."

CHAPTER NINETEEN

THE LANTERNS LINING the sidewalk cast a golden glow over trees flush with green leaves. Warmth lingered in the air, a pleasant heat that promised long nights, relaxation and the freedom that came with the onset of summer. People walked along Center Drive as it sloped up toward the bridge that overlooked the Central Park Carousel.

Evolet clutched the handle of her cello case tighter. It had been just shy of a week since Damon had done exactly as she'd asked and walked out of the hospital. A week that she hadn't heard from him. Not that she could blame him, she reminded herself sternly as she walked at a brisk pace past a playground. He'd done exactly as she'd asked. It was up to her to offer the olive branch.

Wednesday, she told herself firmly.

Her make-up audition was Tuesday. And then she would contact him.

Butterflies fluttered in her chest. She'd been torn on whether she should contact him sooner. But she had finally decided to wait until after the audition. She wanted to tell him that not only had he been right to challenge her but that she'd done it. Even if he told her he couldn't return her love, even if things were truly over, she wanted him to know the difference he'd made in her life.

Waiting had turned out to be a wise choice. The week had

flown by. If she wasn't in Constanza's room playing, she was in the park or the Apprentice Symphony's practice room. She'd swallowed her nerves and reached out to Ashley and some of the other musicians, who had responded as if they'd been best friends for years and came to listen and critique her playing. More than once she'd turned away so they didn't see just how deeply moved she was by their support and burgeoning friendship.

She'd practiced the pieces on the audition list until concertos infiltrated her dreams. She hummed the melodies on the subway, the sidewalk, even in the grocery store until she'd seen a woman slowly sidle away from her in the produce aisle. No sooner had she decided that morning to take the day off than her phone had pinged with an email request from her website. A man named Charles was proposing at the Central Park Carousel and wanted her to play.

Her chest had tightened. Vivid memories had washed over her, standing so closely she'd felt the heat emanating from his body, soaked in his handsome profile lit up by the lanterns and carousel lights. Remembered how quickly her heart had pounded as an attraction she had never experienced nor expected had settled over her skin until her limbs had been heavy with the weight of her need.

She'd nearly ignored the email. But, she had decided after a few minutes of staring morosely into her tea, it was exactly the distraction she needed. The carousel had long been a source of enjoyment for her. Regardless of how things turned out with Damon, their walk that night had been an incredible moment in her life. One day, if she was fortunate enough to have a family of her own, she would take them to ride the carousel.

She wouldn't let the bleak moments take away her joy. Not anymore.

The carousel came into view. The lights were on, but the speakers that normally played the majestic music that accompanied the rise and fall of the horses were silent. No crowds of kids waiting excitedly outside the ticket booth, no parents armed with cameras.

Because of a barrier, she realized as she drew closer. Crowd-control barriers had been erected at the three sidewalk inter-sections that led to the carousel, with a security guard standing near each one. Signs hanging from the silver steel proclaimed: *Carousel closed for private event. Unlimited free rides to the public beginning at eight p.m.*

Her eyebrows shot up. The mysterious Charles had paid tri-ple her normal fee, another incentive for her to accept the job, including a brief *Sorry for the late notice* note on his booking. Money was obviously no concern if he had rented the entire carousel for an hour and paid for the public to ride as much as they wanted the rest of the night.

She gave her name to one of the guards, who waved her through. She walked up to the carousel, her heels clicking against the pavement.

"Hello?"

"In here."

A muffled voice sounded from inside the carousel hall. She glanced around, taking some comfort in the presence of the security guards nearby, as she walked through the archway.

Her breath hitched as she drew closer to the carousel. She'd never gotten this close, always holding out for…something. Just another thing she had denied herself.

A chestnut-colored horse caught her eye. A bright orange saddle trimmed in reds and blues rested on its back. Its head was thrown back, the black mane shaped into wild spirals as if it were blowing in some imaginary breeze. She moved closer and laid a hand on the muzzle.

Tonight, she decided as she smiled. Tonight she would ride.

"Beautiful, isn't it?"

The tones of his voice, deep and smoky, rolled over her. She waited one moment, then two. Maybe she had just imagined it, manipulated someone else's voice in her head to sound like his.

Then she saw his reflection in the shiny wood that made up the horse's neck.

Slowly, she turned. He stood just a couple feet behind her, hands tucked casually into his pockets, his handsome face smooth and serene.

"What are you doing here?"

"Waiting for you."

"But where is…" Her mind fumbled, then latched on to a distant memory as they'd verbally sparred in his office. Her eyes narrowed. "Edward *Charles* Damon Bradford."

One corner of his mouth curved up as mischief glinted in his eyes. "I took a risk using Charles, but I didn't think you would remember."

"You could have called. Or texted." She glanced out the arch at the barricades and security guards. "You didn't have to go to all this trouble just to get me to talk to you."

His face sobered as his gaze sharpened. "The last time I saw you, you told me you didn't love me and to go away."

Heat flooded her face. She wanted to look down, away, anywhere but at the pain in his green eyes. But she didn't. She'd caused that pain, and she needed to take responsibility. "I did exactly what you accused me of. I used you as a punching bag that day. I'm sorry, Damon."

"I deserved it. And," he said as he took a slow but deliberate step closer, "I owe you an apology."

"For what?"

"The heliport. The way I let things end. Not opening up to you." His eyes rested on her face with sorrowful intensity. "Not letting you in because of my own pride and fear."

Her throat tightened as she remembered the coolness in his eyes, the efficiency of his handshake just hours after he'd seduced her with slow, drugging kisses.

"I set the terms of our arrangement, Damon. Yes, it hurt," she admitted, "but it was over. I knew not to expect more. If I did, that was on me."

"Don't do that," he whispered as he reached out and grabbed the cello case handle. His fingers brushed hers. The fleeting contact sizzled across her skin, and her lips parted on a sharp inhale. She let him take the case from her, set it down behind him.

When he took her hands in his, she swallowed hard.

"Damon..."

"Five minutes, Evolet. Just five minutes to say what I need to. After that, if you still want me to go, I will."

She let him lead her to a chariot painted blue and trimmed in gold. He sat next to her and continued to hold her hands in his, his fingers stroking gently over her knuckles.

"I loved my parents."

He paused, his focus riveted on their hands. She waited, giving him time.

"It was easier for so long to just not talk about my parents. If I didn't talk about them, it wouldn't hurt. Sometimes I could even pretend they were just away on an extended vacation.

"I'm starting to realize how much of a disservice I'm doing to their memories, to what they did for me. There were sad ones, but there were good ones. So many good ones I'd just... banished." His voice faded as he turned to look at her. "It hurts to remember. But I think I'd rather hurt and remember than keep living without thinking of them from time to time." He leaned forward, forearms resting on his knees, hands clenched together. "My mom would make me breakfast every morning before she went to the hospital. She worked as a nurse delivering babies. Most days were happy, but sometimes she would come home sad. She felt every joy, every loss like it was her own, and her patients loved her for it. Even after Bradford Global grew, she kept her job."

His fingers tightened around hers.

"My dad…my earliest memory is walking through one of our factories with him holding my hand. He took me everywhere, told me if I wanted to be a part of Bradford Global I could but I'd have to earn it. He told me…a week before he died…that I had surpassed all of his expectations. That he was proud of me."

He grated the last words out before he bowed his head. She didn't offer empty words of comfort or push him for more. She just wrapped her arms around his neck and held him close. He buried his face in her hair and breathed in.

"They were driving home from a date. Married twenty-three years and they still went on a date every week like they were teenagers. It wasn't even nine o'clock at night, and some drunk college bastard was driving eighty miles an hour through their neighborhood."

Evolet's hold on him tightened.

"I loved them. I loved them, and then they were gone. It was just the three of us for so long. I had friends, of course, girlfriends in high school and college. But my parents… I loved them deeply. When I lost them, I lost myself for a long time. At first I could barely get out of bed. Getting out of bed meant having to face an empty house, walk past their rooms and know they were never coming back. I had nightmares. I drank too much. I couldn't control my grief.

"And then I got angry. I'd never felt so much anger.

"I attended the trial for the driver who killed them. When the judge announced he would get the maximum sentence for what he'd been charged with, fifteen years in prison, I almost smiled. I felt…happy. Happy that he was being punished. A pale comparison to the price my parents had paid, but at least some justice had been done."

She gently lifted one hand to his cheek. He turned his head into her caress, pressed a kiss to her palm.

"And then I saw the same skinny kid turn to look at his parents and burst into tears. I watched as his father held him, his mother kissed him. They walked up to me as their son was taken away in shackles and told me they were sorry for what their boy did. The woman handed me a sympathy card. Her hands were shaking."

Evolet's heart broke for all the losses suffered. But most of all for the man just out of boyhood who had lost the people he loved the most.

"I sat in the courthouse long after they'd left, holding the card, and grieved. My parents lost their lives. Two other parents had theirs forever changed. And while that boy will have some time when he gets out, he lost so much because of one selfish, stupid decision."

He looked up at her then, his eyes fierce. "I lost myself in my emotions during those months. One moment I was filled with hate and rage, the next I felt like I was drowning."

With her heart in her throat, she slowly slipped her arms around his waist. He let his head drop, rested his forehead against hers as he pulled her closer until she held tight against him, their breaths mingling in the summer air.

"After I walked out of the courthouse, I swore I would never let myself feel like that again. I twisted it in my head that loving someone as deeply as I loved my parents was opening the door to how I felt in those months after I lost them. And once I saw how that boy's parents were affected, saw him cry and turn to his mother for comfort, I felt the hate drain out of me. It left me feeling empty."

He pulled back, caught her chin in his hand.

"Empty was easy. Empty meant not opening myself to get lost again, to be so hurt. And for a long time that worked. Until you, Evolet."

A tremble passed through her as she realized the emotion in his eyes had changed from sorrow to something bright. Something that made hope bloom in her chest. Once she would have squashed it, pulled back rather than risk getting hurt.

But not anymore.

"It took me too long to figure out what I felt for you." He stood, bringing her with him, her body molding to his. "Some part of me knew that day at the heliport, told me I was an idiot for letting you walk away. I was too damned scared to admit that I had fallen in love with you, Evolet."

She surged forward, throwing her arms around his neck and kissing him with a wild abandon that just weeks ago she wouldn't have let herself surrender to. Damon groaned and held her so tightly it was a wonder they didn't melt into each other.

"Damon," she whispered between kisses, "I lied." He started to jerk back, but her fingers slipped into his hair and kept him close. "I love you, too."

He laughed, uninhibited and deep and joyful. "I missed you."

The simple words brought tears to her eyes. "I missed you. I was going to call you on Wednesday after my audition—"

"Your audition?" A smile spread across his face. "You called them."

"You were right." She brushed at her eyes. "I knew I was in love you, but I alternated between hoping you would say something first or telling myself it would never go beyond our arrangement, so why bother. It made me realize how long I've been holding pieces of myself back, even from my music. So I called, and I audition on Tuesday. I wanted to wait until I went, until I did it, so I could tell you that I love you and that you were right and that even if I didn't get it I tried and—"

He cut off her babbling with another kiss that thrilled her all the way to her toes. "I'm proud of you, Evolet."

She did cry then, happy tears that slid down her cheeks as he stood and swept her up into his arms.

"Which horse do you want to ride?"

She pointed to the horse that had first caught her eye. He carried her over and set her on its back.

"Aren't you going to join me?"

"Yes. I'm looking forward to being your first. Again," he added with a wicked grin that sent a bolt of electricity careening through her. "But first things first. When I booked your services, I asked for you to be present for a proposal."

Blood roared in her ears as he reached into his back pocket and pulled out a small black box. Her breath caught as he flipped the lid to reveal a silver band with a glittering amber-colored jewel.

"When I saw this stone, citrine, it reminded me of your eyes."

Her tears began to fall harder. "Damon…"

"Marry me, Evolet. I don't want to go another day without you in my life."

She framed his face in her hands and poured every ounce of love she felt into her kiss. "Yes, Damon. Yes."

He slipped the ring onto her finger, a perfect fit.

"One moment."

He jogged over to the wall, pressed a button and then came back over as the carousel sprung to life. Music filtered out as the horse rose up. Damon placed his foot in the stirrup and swung himself up behind her, pulling her snug against his chest.

"I think it's one rider per horse," she teased.

"Are you complaining?"

She felt him grow hard against her back and pressed against him, savored his groan. "Not if you're going to take me somewhere after to seduce me."

"Didn't I mention that was part of you agreeing to marry me?"

She laughed and leaned back into his embrace. The carousel spun, horses rising and falling, music playing, the jewel of her ring glimmering beneath the lights.

"Damon."

"Yes?"

"I love you."

He pressed a tender kiss to her cheek.

"And I love you, Evolet." She felt his smile. "We're going to have a wonderful life together."

EPILOGUE

Seven years later

CHARLES BRADFORD LOOKED up at his father, a crease between his barely there eyebrows, as a horrific screeching filled the air.

"I agree, son," Damon said with a wince. "Your sister needs more practice."

Footsteps sounded on the stairs. Evolet walked down, a forced smile on her face as she glanced over her shoulder. Seven years of being married hadn't stopped Damon's breath from catching when he saw his wife. Her hair fell shorter these days, easier to manage as a mom of two and a professional cellist with the Emerald City Philharmonic.

"Yes, honey. It does sound a little better." She shot Damon a hot look as he chuckled. "She's holding the bow better than she did last week."

"Too bad she's not playing better than she did last week," he said with an affectionate glance up at the ceiling. Rashael Bradford was proving to be a very determined, though not talented, cello player.

Evolet started to protest, then sank down into a chair next to Charlie's highchair with a grin and kissed his chubby cheek. "Not even the slightest."

Charlie babbled at his mother before resuming his destruction of the eggs on his plate. Wisps of blond hair had finally started to cover his bald head. Between his gummy smiles and big green eyes, Damon was besotted with his son.

As besotted as he'd been when he'd held his daughter in his arms for the first time four years ago and realized he could fall in love more than once in a lifetime.

"Don't take it too hard, darling." Damon moved to his wife, tilted her chin up and kissed her. "Not everyone can be a child prodigy."

She smiled against his mouth. His body stirred.

"When does Charlie go down for his nap?"

Evolet glanced at the clock and groaned. "Not until eleven."

"And where will Rashael be at eleven a.m.?"

"With Samuel, Sarah and Constanza at the park."

Damon's wedding gift to Evolet had been converting part of his penthouse into a small apartment for Constanza. Having Constanza join them in the mornings for breakfast, relaxing on the terrace or, most importantly, spending time with her grandchildren had not only made Evolet and Constanza happy, it had also given Damon another taste of having a maternal figure in his life. Getting to know Constanza's son, Samuel, and, as of five years ago, his new wife, Sarah, had added more faces around the table for Sunday dinners and holidays.

It wasn't always easy. He and Evolet had both noticed Constanza struggling a little more with losing track of time or fumbling with names. The disease had progressed and would continue to do so. But he also knew that he and Evolet would be there for Constanza to help her navigate the changes in her life.

Just as they would be there for each other, for the good times and the bad.

Damon rubbed his hands up and down Evolet's arms. "So, what I'm hearing is we have an empty penthouse, a sunny day and a beautiful pool."

"Why Mr. Bradford, are you proposing playing hooky from work?"

"I think I'm overdue for some time off."

The Royal Air contract had been the beginning of a massive expansion of Bradford Global. When they had delivered the planes not only on time but under budget, business had skyrocketed with requests coming in from around the world. New plants were going up every year. Offices had expanded.

And Damon had hired more administrators to share duties with. Bradford Global still held an important place in his life and always would.

But, he thought as Evolet's arms twined around his neck, *not the most important.*

He was leaning down to kiss his wife again when another blast of music echoed down the stairs.

"Any chance we could get her to switch over to the drums?"

"I'm not sure which would be worse. She still insists she's ready to play in the concert at her preschool tomorrow." Her nose scrunched as Rashael's cello let out another indignant squawk from above. "What do I do?"

"Let her. She'll have fun. Next week she'll be on to something else."

She smiled, then reached up and framed his face with her hands. "Have I told you lately that I love you very much?"

"I believe you said something about it this morning when you woke me up."

"Uh, I believe it was you who woke me up when you slipped my nightgown off," Evolet replied as her hands slipped down over his neck, her fingertips grazing his skin. "Not that I minded—"

"Mommy!"

Rashael hopped down the stairs, her round face framed by dark waves of hair, her golden-brown eyes round with excitement. "I'm ready for the concert!"

Evolet grazed Damon's lips with her own once more before moving over to the stairs to sweep their daughter into her
arms. "I can't wait to see you play, baby."

"And we get to go to the carousel afterward, right?"

"Absolutely."

Damon leaned against the kitchen counter, his eyes flickering between his wife, his daughter and his son. Evolet looked
up at him, love shining in her eyes.

"What are you thinking?" she asked softly.

"That I was right."

"Oh?"

"Yeah." He pulled her into his arms against the backdrop
of Rashael's delighted squeal. "We have a wonderful life."

* * * * *

COMING SOON!

We really hope you enjoyed reading this book. If you're looking for more romance be sure to head to the shops when new books are available on

Thursday 9th November

To see which titles are coming soon, please visit

millsandboon.co.uk/nextmonth

MILLS & BOON

MILLS & BOON®

Coming next month

A BILLION-DOLLAR HEIR FOR CHRISTMAS
Caitlin Crews

'What exactly are you trying to say to me?'

Tiago sighed, as if Lillie was being dense. And he hated himself for that, too, when she stiffened. 'This cannot be an affair, Lillie. No matter what happened between us in Spain. Do you not understand? I will have to marry you.'

Her eyes went wide. Her face paled, and not, his ego could not help but note, in the transformative joy a man in his position might have expected to see after a proposal. 'Marry me? Marry *you*? Are you mad? On the strength of one night?'

'On the strength of your pregnancy. Because the Villela heir must be legitimate.' He looked at her as if he had never seen her before and would never see her again, or maybe it was simply that he did not wish to say the thing he knew he must. But that was life, was it not? Forever forcing himself to do what was necessary, what was right. Never what he wanted. So he took a deep breath. 'We will marry. Quickly. And once that happens, I will never touch you again.'

Continue reading
A BILLION-DOLLAR HEIR FOR CHRISTMAS
Caitlin Crews

Available next month
www.millsandboon.co.uk

OUT NOW!

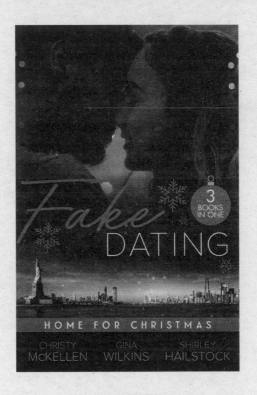

Available at
millsandboon.co.uk

MILLS & BOON

OUT NOW!

Available at
millsandboon.co.uk

MILLS & BOON

LET'S TALK

Romance

For exclusive extracts, competitions and special offers, find us online:

f MillsandBoon

𝕏 @MillsandBoon

⌾ @MillsandBoonUK

♪ @MillsandBoonUK

Get in touch on 01413 063 232

MILLS & BOON

THE HEART OF ROMANCE

A ROMANCE FOR EVERY READER

MODERN
Prepare to be swept off your feet by sophisticated, sexy and seductive heroes, in some of the world's most glamourous and romantic locations, where power and passion collide.

HISTORICAL
Escape with historical heroes from time gone by. Whether your passion is for wicked Regency Rakes, muscled Vikings or rugged Highlanders, awaken the romance of the past.

MEDICAL
Set your pulse racing with dedicated, delectable doctors in the high-pressure world of medicine, where emotions run high and passion, comfort and love are the best medicine.

True Love
Celebrate true love with tender stories of heartfelt romance, from the rush of falling in love to the joy a new baby can bring, and a focus on the emotional heart of a relationship.

Desire
Indulge in secrets and scandal, intense drama and sizzling hot action with heroes who have it all: wealth, status, good looks…everything but the right woman.

HEROES
The excitement of a gripping thriller, with intense romance at its heart. Resourceful, true-to-life women and strong, fearless men face danger and desire - a killer combination!

To see which titles are coming soon, please visit

millsandboon.co.uk/nextmonth